UNBRIDLED PASSION

"Please," she whimpered, making a futile attempt to cover herself. "Please don't do this."

But the captain wasn't listening.

Warm, moist lips found hers and Jennifer closed her eyes, the sensation it sparked taking her breath away. He kissed her with the kind of tenderness she had expected from a man who loved her, and for a moment, she was confused. He didn't care about her, so how could he pretend he did? But what puzzled her more than anything was the strange warmth his kiss aroused from deep within her, and unknowingly, she relaxed, enjoying the way his mouth moved hungrily over hers. . . .

THE PIRATE'S LADY

Kay McMahon

ZEBRA BOOKS
KENSINGTON PUBLISHING CORP.

ZEBRA BOOKS

are published by

Kensington Publishing Corp.
475 Park Avenue South
New York, NY 10016

First printing: July 1987

Printed in the United States of America

For Ginny

Chapter One

March, 1741
Somewhere in the Atlantic Ocean

Black, turbulent clouds hugged the horizon, choking out the last bright, golden rays of sunshine. The air, thick with moisture and the promise of a raging tempest, hung breathless and still as if anticipating the oncoming storm. In the distance, thunder rumbled with increasing volume, while lightning flashed about the sky. The blue waters of the ocean calmed and the huge ship, its sails limp and useless, drifted aimlessly across the endless plane. Yet, as the captain of the vessel stood near the helm, his eyes were not affixed to the crew who raced about the decks preparing to do battle with the thundersquall, but rather were concentrated on the frigate silhouetted against the blackening sky. Since early morning, he had watched it, raced with it, planned his strategy, wondering now if it had all been worth the effort since both his merchant ship and the pirate vessel that pursued him were at God's mercy.

"Captain?" a sweet and gentle voice called up to him, and he shifted his attention to the one who spoke, his worried frown melting into a warm smile.

"Miss Grey." He acknowledged her presence with a polite nod of his head.

"May I join you for a moment?" she asked, blue-green eyes framed in thick, dark lashes dissolving his tough exterior. "I know passengers are not allowed—"

"It's quite all right, Miss Grey," he smiled, breaking his own rule. Who could resist such a beautiful young woman as this? He left his position beside the helmsman and crossed to the steps, where he held out a hand to assist her up to the bridge.

It was never Captain Lucus's custom to inquire about any of the passengers sailing on his ship. But the moment he had seen Jennifer Grey ascending the gangplank of the *Sea Lady* at the dock in Chesapeake Bay he had noticed a sadness in the way she walked, and that she did not smile, so he had asked his first mate about the lady. He hadn't learned a great deal other than that she was on her way to England to marry a gentleman, and that her father had died a few short weeks before. As he thought about it now, he decided that information must have been the reason he had so easily taken on the responsibility of caring for this young lady while she was on his ship. He had never married in his fifty-two years, and many times he'd wished he had. He would have been proud to have had a daughter like Jennifer Grey.

"It worries you, doesn't it, Captain?" she quietly asked, staring toward the horizon and the spot Lucas had studied for more than an hour. "I've been watching you."

He took the opportunity to enjoy her loveliness while her gaze was elsewhere, thinking how much her hair reminded him of the color of sunlight, the shimmering pale yellow of early morning and the deep, rich tones of golden sunsets. Her features were delicate: high cheekbones, thin nose, softly arched brows; and her flawless complexion tempted him to touch her cheek with the

8

backs of his fingers. She had a fragile beauty, yet her mien hinted at a strong character hidden deep within her, one, he was sure, that would surface if tested. He envied the man who awaited her in England, the man who would make her his bride. He forced himself to look away.

"Storms at sea are something a captain must always be concerned about, Miss Grey."

A vague smile parted her lips, and she lifted her chin to look at him. "I didn't mean the storm, Captain. I meant the ship that has been following us for some time now. It concerns you more than the storm."

Arnold Lucus's snowy white brows came together in a woeful frown. He blinked and couldn't bring himself to look at her.

"Are they pirates, sir?" Jennifer pressed, her own expression one of apprehension.

Lucus felt the need to lie. "Don't honestly know, miss. They keep their distance and are out of range of my spyglass." He rested his hands on the rail, silently praying that the storm would take the ships in different directions. The frigate flew no colors that he could see, but the cannons protruding from her sides bore evidence that this was no mere merchant ship. "'Tis best you go below decks, Miss Grey. Won't be long before—"

"But you think they are," she interrupted with firm conviction, her words laced with worry. Shocked by her own straightforwardness, she quickly lowered her head in an apologetic manner when Lucus turned startled eyes upon her. "I'm sorry, Captain. 'Twas rude of me to speak out of turn."

The *Sea Lady*, its crew and passengers, had left the Colonies in America more than three weeks ago. They had encountered two storms. Both had blown them off course, and considerable damage had been done to their sails and one of the masts, all of which had delayed them. Yet, through it all, Jennifer Grey never spoke what

9

was on her mind as the other passengers had, and hearing the fear in her voice, seeing it in her eyes, because of something that hadn't yet happened truly surprised him. Of course, none of their previous misfortunes had had anything to do with pirates.

"'Tis not rude to want to know the truth, Miss Grey," he smiled comfortingly, taking her elbow and leading her toward the steps. "And 'tis not as bad as it seems. Aye, I do suspect it is a pirate ship, but they must deal with this storm as we must. God willing, He will set us apart, and they will present no further threat." They paused at the top of the ladder and he took both of her tiny hands in his rough and callused ones. "And I swear to you that should our luck run out, I will see that no harm comes to you. I will protect you with my life."

Tears sparkled in the blue-green eyes staring back at him, and a moment later, Jennifer stretched up on her toes to place a kiss on his weathered cheek.

"Thank you," she whispered, then turned and descended the steps.

Arnold Lucus watched the trim figure in the soft lavender gown with lace trim in its full skirts, watched until the young woman had disappeared into the passageway leading below decks. He had meant what he'd said, that he would lay down his life for her, and he hoped that was what she'd needed to hear. His tired brown eyes drifted back to look in the direction of the frigate in the distance. What he wouldn't tell her was that, should the pirates attack and board the *Sea Lady* and escape be impossible, he would put his pistol to her head and pull the trigger. In such straits, death was the better choice.

A sudden gust of wind billowed the sails, stretching them full and taut, and Lucus glanced up at the sky overhead. Black, swirling clouds churned the heavens, and he knew that this would be the fiercest of storms. He prayed—only briefly—that God would guide him, and

10

spare his ship and crew and the passengers who had put their trust in him; then he turned and shouted orders to his men.

The small cabin—it had been her world of late—seemed to close in on Jennifer as she stood staring out at the turbulent waters of the sea, wondering if, perhaps, this time her prayers would go unheard. As each new wave crashed against the side of the ship, its thunderous violence resounded within the tiny confines of her quarters and the fragile glass in the porthole rattled. It had become more and more difficult for her to remain on her feet without hanging onto something, for the ship rolled and pitched fore and aft, as well as port to starboard. But she vowed she would stay erect because she had already learned that if she watched the convulsive movements of the water her stomach didn't churn as badly. Yet, what frightened her more than the unnatural rocking of the ship was the eerie shade of blackish green where once had been a bright blue sky. No longer could she distinguish the horizon, and it seemed God had forsaken the tiny vessel fighting to stay afloat in the savage violence of the storm.

A quarter of an hour passed, but the storm raged with more force and magnitude than when it had begun. Several times, Jennifer lost her grip on the frame of the porthole because a huge wall of water slammed against the side of the ship and the jolt knocked her to the floor. What finally made her decide to stay put rather than struggle to her feet again was the pain that shot up her leg. She didn't have to have a doctor examine her ankle. She knew she had twisted it and that standing on it would be too much to bear. Half-dragging herself, half-crawling, she inched her way across the floor to her bunk, thinking she preferred being sick to breaking something. Then

11

she forgot her own misery when she spotted Kinsey, the ship's cat, crouched in the far corner.

"What are you doing here, Kinsey?" she cooed, pulling herself up on the thin mattress. Huge, fearful gold eyes stared back at her, and Jennifer could see that the tiger-striped cat was trembling. He howled when a clap of thunder reverberated in the small cabin. "Don't be afraid, Kinsey." She smiled. "I'll protect you." Scooting closer, she gently took him in her arms, braced herself back against the wall, and tenderly stroked the cat's head. "It's just noise," she assured him. "We'll be all right."

But the words did little to calm the frightened feline and they sounded ludicrous in her own ears, for the tempest that so viciously attacked the ship seemed to mock her very pledge. A frown furrowed the smooth line of her brow as she listened to the wind continue its onslaught, its howls blending with the terrified cries of the other passengers. She had been warned of the hardships one must endure when crossing the ocean, but somehow she had never expected anything quite like this. Suddenly, a bright, searing flash of lightning flooded the cabin, followed by the explosion of thunder; and both she and Kinsey jumped when there was a loud crash overhead, preceded by the splintering and ripping of wood. Jennifer knew one of the ship's masts had broken in two. She closed her eyes, frantically hung onto the cat when he tried to wrench free of her, and uttered a prayer that God would spare them. But no sooner had the words formed in her thoughts than the huge vessel lurched violently to starboard, throwing Jennifer and her companion out of the bunk and onto the deck. She struggled to regain her balance and push herself up onto her knees, but the ship suddenly jerked upward, tossing her back against the wall, before it careened oddly to one side and appeared to be almost dead in the water for a full minute. Instinct warned her that something was amiss even before the ship plunged downward, hurling her across the cabin. Thunder roared again, drowning out Jennifer's cry of pain when her shoulder struck something hard and immobile, and, in the next instant, water burst into the tiny cabin through the shattered pane of the porthole.

"Abandon ship!" someone shouted, and Jennifer forgot her injuries.

Scrambling to her feet, she threw herself at the cabin door and fought to pull it open. But the pressure of the water quickly filling the room made that impossible.

"God, no!" she screamed, pounding her fists against the solid barrier. "Please . . . I don't want to die!"

Suddenly the ship rocked again, more violently than it had in the last hour, but Jennifer's descent to the floor was cushioned by the swirling water that was now more than knee-deep. Lightning flashed overhead and it took her a full minute to realize that the blinding glare of light hadn't come through the portholes, but through a gap in the ceiling just above her, and that what she'd thought was thunder was actually the sound of the *Sea Lady* breaking apart. Knowing the opening above was her only chance of escape, Jennifer frantically hauled herself up on the small table that was anchored securely to the wooden planks of the deck, and was about to pull herself up and out of the cabin when she heard Kinsey's terrified howling. Spotting the poor, wretched animal splashing about in an effort to stay afloat, she dropped to her knees, grabbed the cat by the back of his neck, and lifted him to safety ahead of her.

Kinsey had disappeared by the time Jennifer was able to pull herself through the opening and onto what was left of the main deck. And concern for his welfare vanished just as quickly as he had, once she saw the destruction that surrounded her and heard the woeful

13

cries of the others aboard the sinking, broken ship. The storm relentlessly continued its assault against the defenseless vessel, and those on deck clung desperately to anything that would stop them from being washed overboard. For a fleeting moment Jennifer wondered why they did so. The *Sea Lady* was going down.

At the far end of the ship, amidst debris, a group of men were fighting to free the longboat from its mooring lines so they might set it adrift, and it was in this direction Jennifer decided to go. The way was slippery, and she fell several times, blinded by the pouring rain and knocked off balance by the waves crashing against the ship. She had traveled nearly half the distance when lightning cut through the blackened sky, kinked earthward and struck the top of the one remaining mast, searing down the side of it and splitting it in two. The sound it made was deafening, and Jennifer looked up in time to see the monstrous wooden spear hurling toward her. Left with no alternative, as it was evident she would be unable to escape its crushing blow, Jennifer turned and dived into the angry sea.

The scream of a hawk silhouetted against the bright, blue sky pierced the quiet, sun-drenched afternoon as the majestic bird of prey swooped down upon a rodent scurrying out of harm's way. A soft breeze rustled the treetops, and the fragrance of wild flowers filled the air. The deserted stretch of white, sandy beach bore little evidence of the fierce and violent storm that had passed over only a short time before, and though seemingly peaceful, the solitude of the island struck fear into the beautiful young woman standing on the shoreline.

Jennifer had no idea how long she had drifted in the churning waters of the sea or in what direction she had come, only that it seemed God had reached out a hand

14

to her when she'd come upon a broken section of the hull belonging to the *Sea Lady*. It had taken all the strength she'd had left to pull herself up on it and then hang on while the winds and the churning waters carried her away. She had managed to look back only once, and what she'd seen would live forever in her mind. The huge merchant ship, her captain at the helm and her crew fighting for their lives, was sitting oddly in the water, her leeward side sinking rapidly. Then, unexplainably, as if the vessel were nothing more than a twig floating upon a narrow river, the *Sea Lady* lurched upward, rolled onto her side and vanished beneath the green, turbulent surface of the sea. A scream lodged in Jennifer's throat, and for a moment, she thought to abandon her makeshift raft and swim back to where the ship had gone down, foolishly supposing she could be of some help. But the storm's fury hadn't lessened, and as if it were warning her not to try, thunder boomed loudly overhead and a huge wall of water lifted her up and swept her farther away.

What seemed to be a lifetime elapsed before the winds calmed and golden sunlight broke through the dark clouds that enshrouded her, and if Jennifer hadn't been clinging to a piece of the wreckage from the *Sea Lady*, she might have believed the whole experience had been nothing more than a terrible nightmare. But it wasn't. And now she had a different kind of challenge to face. She had been spared the fate of the others aboard the merchant ship, but she couldn't truly understand why. Was it merely to prolong her death? What sense was there in floating about the ocean with no food or drink, no hope of being rescued? Then she saw it. Against the horizon, a black line appeared, faint and indistinct. An hour passed before she could distinguish the markings of land. Overcome with joy, she stretched out on her stomach and began to paddle toward the shore. But the

15

closer she came, the more she realized that this wasn't the coastline of England or France or even of Spain. This was nothing more than an island, a small body of land in the middle of the Atlantic Ocean. Coming up on her knees, Jennifer could only stare at it, tears filling her eyes. She was alive . . . but alone. Her final days would be spent in solitude.

Drifting into shore, the raft had jerked to a stop, its underside dragging in the sand, and Jennifer had reluctantly stepped into the water, surprised by the warmth of it as it raced across the beach and chased back into the clear, blue depths surrounding her. But it did little to cheer her or soothe her worried state, for she was the pampered daughter of a tobacco planter in the Colonies. She had no knowledge of how to survive on her own.

The hawk screamed again, and Jennifer lifted her eyes to watch it glide effortlessly through the air. It circled several times, and she soon realized that it must have spotted something on the ground. In the next instant, the fierce bird dove earthward, and she turned her head away, cringing when it reached out sharp talons and plucked a tiny mouse from the underbrush. The brutality of the attack made her retch, but at the same time it clearly told her that if she didn't want to starve to death after all she had been through, she'd have to behave in much the same manner. And unless she could figure out a way to catch a fish or two, she'd have to resort to seeking the same kind of meal the hawk had just devoured. Bile rose in her throat. She didn't know how at this moment, but she vowed she'd never eat anything she hadn't caught in the ocean. Sneaking one last peek at the bird to find him tearing apart his prey as if he weren't even aware that he shared the island with someone, Jennifer squeezed her eyes shut, took a deep breath, and lifted her heavy, water-soaked skirts in both hands. Right

16

now, she wasn't interested in food. All she wanted was to be dry again.

Since there wasn't much of a chance that anyone would see her, she seated herself on a large, flat rock a good distance from the edge of the water that steadily lapped at the sandy beach with a hypnotizing effect, and kicked off her shoes. Next she removed her garters and hose, which she hung on the limb of a nearby bush. Rising, she shimmied out of her petticoats and draped the cumbersome garments on the branch of a tree. But when it came to unfastening the buttons on the front of her dress, she paused, unsure, until she had surveyed the long stretch of beach to her left, then to her right, and finally the watery horizon ahead of her just to make certain she was truly alone.

The damp chill that had rattled her teeth quickly left her once she had shed all of her clothes except for her camisole, and that dried quickly beneath the bright, warm rays of the sun. Lifting the thick mass of hair off her neck, she twisted it into a long cord, squeezing what water she could from it, then shook her head and let the golden strands fall in wild disarray about her shoulders to dry. Suddenly, exhaustion seeped into her bones, and since there was nothing else to do, she lay back on the rock and closed her eyes. There was plenty of time to decide what course of action she should take next. She'd sleep first, then contemplate seeking food and building some kind of shelter.

The sound of the surf rolling into shore lulled Jennifer to sleep, but her dreams were not peaceful. In them, the bright, clear sky changed to an ominous, black abyss filled with swirling clouds and glaring flashes of light. Thunder resounded in her ears, and the vision of the *Sea Lady* flared up to grip her heart with icy fingers. Captain Lucus's face loomed before her, then vanished. She saw each member of the crew, the passengers; and

17

relived the sight of the huge mast spiraling toward her. But it was Kinsey's terrified howling that brought Jennifer out of her nightmare, and she bolted upright on the rock, hugging her arms to her and fighting to control the violent trembling of her tiny body, to rid her mind of the horrified yowling of the cat. When the howls continued, she clamped her hands over her ears and closed her eyes. She could finally breathe a little easier when that seemed to help. A long while passed before she had the courage to take her hands away and open her eyes. But to her dismay, she could still hear the tiger-striped tom's mournful wails, and she wondered if she would ever be free of them. Then, suddenly, she realized that they weren't a part of the dream, for she was wide awake and thinking rationally. Scrambling to her feet, she stretched up on tiptoe, scanning the choppy surface of the sea for any sign of the cat.

"Kinsey!" she screamed. "Kinsey, where are you?"

Silence followed and for a moment, Jennifer thought that perhaps she had imagined the howling after all. Then the frightened cries of the animal came again, drawing her attention to a small piece of wood bobbing in the water several hundred feet out to sea. Darting off her perch, she raced across the beach and into the water, diving once it was knee-deep. The cat had gotten this far, and she wasn't about to let him drown now.

"Oh, Kinsey," she half-laughed, half-cried once she'd reached him and latched onto the end of the wood. Pulling it and the animal toward shore, she said soberly, "I think you've just about used up your nine lives. We'll have to take special care of you from now on."

Crouched low against the board, every claw bared and digging into it, Kinsey howled in return, making Jennifer laugh for the first time in a long while. He was the most pathetic sight she had ever seen, and even though she knew a cat was quite capable of taking care of itself,

18

adopting the attitude that he was her responsibility gave her something to strive for. And given the rather dim outlook on how she'd spend the rest of her life, playing surrogate mother to a four-legged, furry, ill-tempered cat was probably the only hope she had of keeping her sanity.

Upon reaching the shore, Jennifer gently took Kinsey in her arms, cooing softly to him as she walked with him to where she had hung her clothes. Wrapping him in her dry petticoats, she sat down and held him tightly while she briskly rubbed the moisture from his fur. Before very long, the huge tomcat began to purr his appreciation.

"Feel better?" Jennifer smiled, wincing when his sharp claws slowly curled around and penetrated the fabric covering her legs. She quickly set him from her. "I would think you could show me in a less painful manner, Mr. Kinsey," she scolded playfully, watching the animal stretch, then shake his entire body, starting with his head and working to the tip of his striped, yellow tail.

Suddenly, the chirping of birds in the trees behind her shattered their light-hearted mood, for the instant Kinsey heard them, his ears came up, his eyes focused intently on the direction of the noise and every muscle in his sleek, lanky body tightened. Jennifer remained perfectly still so as not to frighten the birds away. The cat was hungry, and she wasn't about to ruin his chance for a delicious supper. Crouched low, he took a step forward so slowly that Jennifer could hardly see him move. Then he paused, waited, and moved again. Over and over he repeated the process until he had finally reached the covering of the underbrush. A moment later, he disappeared into the thick foliage, and Jennifer silently wished him good luck on his hunt.

Judging by how low the sun hugged the western horizon, Jennifer guessed that it wouldn't be very long before night was upon her, and since she had no idea how cold it would get on the island or what animals roamed about in the dark, she decided to gather firewood. In the morning, she'd figure out a way to make some sort of trap in which to catch fish.

Bright, golden sunlight raced across the beach, bringing life back into the sleeping creatures on the island, and boldly intruded upon Jennifer's dreams. She stirred, stretched, then came fully awake once she remembered where she was and how she had gotten there. The past evening had been a productive one for her. She had gathered sticks and other debris for her campfire, and had been fortunate enough to find a small piece of flint with which to spark a flame. Once she'd had a roaring blaze started, she'd torn off some of the large leaves from a palm tree, intending to use them to line the hole she had dug in the sand, where she would sleep. By then, her stomach ached from lack of food, so she had ventured a short ways into the thicket in search of berries or nuts to eat. Her exploration had rewarded her with enough of the treasured delicacies to satisfy her hunger, and by the time she had settled down next to the fire, she'd been too tired to think or even relive her nightmare.

She hadn't seen Kinsey since the moment he'd disappeared into the dense undergrowth, and now with the coming of dawn, she feared her only companion on this lonely isle had chosen not to stay with her. It was a depressing thought, but one she quickly pushed aside, knowing that she mustn't let anything disturb her overmuch. To survive, she had to be strong—both in body and in mind.

The fire had died in glowing embers, and Jennifer quickly added several more pieces of wood. It had been very difficult for her to get it started in the first place, and if the fishing went well for her, she needed the blaze to cook her breakfast. The idea of eating raw fish turned her stomach.

She had donned only her torn and wrinkled lavender dress to sleep in, certain the numerous petticoats would be too bulky for her to rest comfortably, and now as she stood staring down at them, she decided they'd only get in her way while she worked. As for wearing shoes—well, she'd be forever having to stop and pour the sand from them. Besides, the warmth of the tiny particles beneath her feet felt good. She giggled impishly. She'd only been here one day, and she was already abandoning the manners of a lady.

The next hour found her stripping thin pieces of bark off a tree and weaving them into a rather odd-looking basket, wide on one end, narrow on the other. When she had finished, she stared at it for a long while, wondering how she would be able to keep a fish trapped inside long enough for her to lift the basket from the water. A lid wouldn't do it for the simple reason that there was no way to close it the moment the fish swam inside. Jennifer sat down on a rock to think about an alternate method, feeling hopelessly inadequate. What she needed was a net, a big one with weights on each corner. That way she could stand knee deep in the water and wait until a school of fish swam near, then toss the net out over them and possibly snare a couple of them as she pulled the net back to her. But what could she use that was flexible enough? The smooth, flawless line of her brow puckered thoughtfully. It would take her a week to strip enough bark, and even then it would be too stiff to tangle itself around a slippery fish. Frustrated, she stood and headed back toward camp, coming to a sudden stop once she spotted the mound of white cotton petticoats.

"Necessity has far greater importance than fashion," she announced, dropping the basket.

It took Jennifer the rest of the morning to tear the

fabric into long, thin strips, crisscross them, tie them together and fasten rocks at each corner. And the afternoon had elapsed before she had caught a single fish. But as night closed in around her, and she sat eating the rewards of her day's work, it all seemed worth the effort. Feeling quite content, she leaned back against a rock, quietly munching on the berries she had picked for dessert, studying the bright flames of the fire, thinking that in the morning she would try a different place to fish. If she was successful early enough, then she planned to follow the narrow stream of water she had found while looking for berries. If her luck held, she might be fortunate enough to discover a pond where she could bathe or at least be guaranteed fresh drinking water.

A rustling noise in the bushes to her left brought Jennifer to her knees in a flash. Her eyes trained on the spot, she inched her way closer to the fire and to one of the pieces of wood lying next to it. Gripping it in one hand, she raised it above her head, ready to strike the instant the creature made himself seen. Several minutes ticked away, during which time Jennifer scarcely breathed, for she was imagining that some horrible animal with long, sharp teeth was about to attack her. Thinking that perhaps she would have a better chance to fight off the creature if she were on her feet, she was about to rise when her attention was quickly brought around to a spot in the bushes where the leaves jiggled out of the way to permit a huge, striped tomcat to step into the light of the campfire.

"Oh, Kinsey," she moaned, lowering her weapon. "You'll never know how close you were to having your brains bashed in." Dropping to her knees, she tossed down the stick and gathered the furry cat in her arms. "Where have you been? I thought I'd never see you again."

Purring loudly, the cat eagerly accepted the attention he received, burrowing his broad head in the crook of Jennifer's arm.

"I wish I had a bell to tie around your neck," she told him, curling her legs beneath her and leaning back against the rock once more. "Then you wouldn't be able to sneak up on me. Remember, you only have one life left, and I prefer not to be the one to use it up." Hugging him happily to her, she buried her face in his fuzzy neck and shook her head, enjoying the scent of him and his companionship. "If you had come a little sooner," she added, settling comfortably in the warm sand, her back against the rock while Kinsey curled up on her lap and closed his eyes, "you could have shared my fish. But I suppose you've had your fill of something else or you wouldn't be here now." Gently stroking his head, she smiled down at him and sighed before turning her attention back to the fire and the flames dancing brightly in the dying sunlight.

During her first day on the island her mind had been too preoccupied with finding enough to eat for her to give considerable thought to her plight. But now that her stomach was full and she sat contentedly before the fire feeling reasonably safe and sure that, at least, she wouldn't starve to death, her thoughts wandered back to the beginning of her fateful journey and to the reason she had boarded the *Sea Lady*.

Her father, George Grey, was well born. He had had property as well as social standing in England, and although her family had left her homeland when Jennifer was a very young girl, she could still remember the huge mansion where she had been born. She had never understood why her father had sold everything and moved to the Colonies. That tragic voyage had taken the life of Jennifer's mother. Because Katherine had always been sickly, the long trip across the ocean had been too

23

much for her, and she had died of a fever long before their ship had reached the docks near Jamestown, Virginia, a place she was to call home. Nor had Jennifer's father ever forgiven himself for his wife's death. Something else Jennifer couldn't understand was why her father continued to honor the engagement between her and the son of his best friend when an ocean separated them and Jennifer had no intention of ever returning to England. She had made America her home. England was nothing more than a memory.

Tears gathered in her eyes as she recalled the final conversation she had had with her father. It had occurred the day he had died, and two weeks before she had booked passage on a ship sailing for a distant continent. Until that moment when George Grey had told his daughter the truth about his past, Jennifer had planned to risk going against her father's wish that she wed Charles Wadsworth! It wasn't that she had fallen in love with someone else that set her mind against marrying Charles, but that she would have to live in London to do it. The plantation where she had spent most of her life was her home, and she had no desire to leave it.

"Oh, Papa," she whispered, gazing out through her tears at the golden sunset sparkling on the clear, blue waters, "why didn't you tell me sooner? We could have saved all our money and bought our own plantation. Your friend Charles would have understood. He helped you once because he cared about you. I'm sure he would have done so again."

Overcome with grief as well as feeling the hopelessness of her situation, Jennifer hugged the huge, yellow cat tightly to her and wept forlornly.

A week had passed since Jennifer's arrival at the island, but it was something to which she gave little importance. With the dawning of each new day came the task of making her life more bearable on this lonely piece of land, a challenge that kept her busy well into the twilight hours. And it was also a way to help her pass the time while she waited for a ship to appear on the horizon, the one she was sure would be coming. Maybe it was foolish of her to think she would ever be rescued, but that hope saved her sanity whenever her solitude began to close in and threaten to overwhelm her.

She had decided to make her crude lodgings near the shore where she could keep a watchful eye out for a passing ship, and she made sure that the pile of wood near her campfire was always sufficient to start a roaring blaze since she realized that would probably be the only way to catch someone's attention. She had constructed a hut out of bamboo poles and palm leaves, complete with a window and a door, and although it was a little lopsided and lacked the amenities with which a lady of gentle upbringing was expected to live, the simple dwelling served its purpose and made Jennifer quite proud of her accomplishment, despite the fact that it was comical to look at. Maybe this wasn't the same as living on a tobacco plantation in the Colonies, but with each day that passed, she managed to add a few more luxuries—such as the hot bath she took every morning in the mineral spring she'd discovered on one of her treks into the woods to seek berries, or the wooden utensils she had carved with the use of a flat, sharp-edged stone. She had even managed to make herself a hammock, and therefore no longer had to sleep on the ground. Fishing was good every day, and on occasion she would trap a turtle in her net or find oysters washed ashore. All in all, her existence on Grey's Island, as she proudly called it, wasn't that terribly barbaric. The only thing that worried her, however, was that she hadn't found anything so far from which to make clothes. All she had was the one camisole and her lavender dress, and

25

they were already showing signs of wear.

Even Kinsey had adapted to life on the island, spending his nights searching for food, his days sleeping in the hut, and always welcoming Jennifer's affections or trying to steal a bite of whatever she was eating, as he was doing now.

"Don't you ever get full?" She laughed, jerking her fingers away when his sharp teeth came too close. "I swear you'll weigh more than I do if you keep this up." Having had her fill, Jennifer set the bowl of fish on the ground next to him, patted his wide head and stood. "I think I'll go exploring today," she announced. "Want to come with me?" She laughed again when the cat ignored her to gobble up the rest of her meal. "All right. Then anything I find, I won't share with you," she taunted, before turning away with her tiny nose raised in the air as if offended by the tom's disinterest.

If she hadn't actually lived through the violent rainstorm a week ago, Jennifer wouldn't have believed such turbulent weather was possible. The sky had remained clear and devoid of clouds during her entire stay on the island, with only a gentle breeze tugging at her skirts or lifting a strand of golden hair from her shoulder. Everything was peaceful, and it felt good to walk along the warm, sandy beach without any shoes. There were even moments when she thought living here would be better than in a stuffy old house in London with a man she couldn't even remember.

The stretch of shoreline where she had made her home spread out a good distance in both directions with little change in the scenery, and since she had no particular destination in mind, she headed away from the sun. She strolled idly along the beach, picking berries and watching a pair of hawks circle overhead, until she was struck by a playful mood, and she began to chase the receding water out to sea and then dash back to shore before it could catch her. She had walked for nearly an hour when she glanced up and saw a cluster of huge rocks breaking the smooth plane of the shoreline and spilling out into the sea. The surf crashed angrily against them as if objecting to their presence. But what truly piqued her interest was the flash of color she saw among the rocks. She looked up at the hillside thick with green foliage, then out across the whitecapped waters, suddenly filled with hope that she wasn't the only one who had survived the storm. Breaking into a run, she raced down the beach and into the foamy-surfaced current swirling around the large boulders, stumbling to a stop once she reached the blue piece of cloth caught on a jagged rock. Yanking it free, she studied it for several moments, a frown knotting her brow. If this had washed ashore, then perhaps there was more. Her heart pounding excitedly in her chest, Jennifer dropped the piece of material, and began to climb over and around the numerous rocks in her way, thinking that just on the other side, she would find a hut similar to her own with a campfire burning brightly and maybe even a yellow cat devouring the remains of someone's supper. She staggered to a stop high atop the tallest rock and slithered to her knees when the scene before her produced nothing more than a continuance of deserted beach.

"You didn't really think to find someone, did you?" she muttered, willing herself not to burst into tears. Heaving a disgusted sigh, she started to rise when a movement in the waters below her caught her eye, and she craned her neck to see what it was. A smile broke the downward slant of her mouth once she spotted a somewhat battered wooden trunk bobbing in the foam, and she hurriedly slid from her perch, climbed down the remaining assemblage of rocks, and jumped to the sandy ground, ready to scamper into the water to retrieve her treasure. But once she had a clear view of the area, she let

27

out a joyful cry upon discovering that not only the trunk, but several wooden crates and barrels were caught among the rocks. Surely there would be something of use in one of them, some item to ease her stay on the island. Uttering a prayer of thanks, she hiked up her wet skirts and stepped into the water.

Sharp-edged rocks, twigs, and other debris lay in her path, making her travel slow and difficult. Twice she stumbled and nearly fell, and she cursed her lack of foresight in not wearing shoes. But she was determined to have the trunk and its contents no matter how much the stones bruised her bare feet or the current threatened to knock her down; and she had just about reached it when something floated out from the dark cavity between the huge rocks beside her and struck her leg. Glancing down at it, a terrified scream lodged in her throat and she stumbled back, her eyes affixed to the broken, half-eaten remains of a man. The trunk and whatever it held quickly forgotten, Jennifer staggered backward out of the water, turned, and raced across the beach and into the protective covering of trees, tears blinding her and no thought in mind of where she fled. A thorny branch snagged her skirts, and with no consideration as to damage, she tore it free. It didn't matter. All she wanted was to get as far away as possible.

The gruesome sight burned its image in her brain, and made the bile rise in her throat. Knowing she was about to retch, she fell to her knees, losing the meal she had eaten only a short time before and giving way to emotion. This whole, incredible journey had been too much for her to bear. She struggled to her feet in near hysteria, only to fall a second time. Too weak to move, she buried her face in the crook of her arm and wept hard and long until exhaustion finally calmed her and she tumbled into a weary slumber.

*   *   *

Voices intruded upon Jennifer's troubled mind, stirring her from sleep and confusing her. Was this, too, all a part of her nightmare? she wondered, listening to the laughter, excited yells, and light-hearted bantering of a group of men somewhere close by. Then explosions—gunfire—shattered the stillness, assuring her that it wasn't, and she covered her head with her arms, fearing her life was about to end.

"Looky 'ere, Cap'n," someone shouted in a gravelly voice, and Jennifer slowly lowered her arms. "I found somethin' yer whore might like."

Without moving, Jennifer quickly surveyed her hiding place to make sure no one would see her when she sat up unless she wanted them to. Then she bit her lip to stifle a gasp. Not ten feet from her sat a broad-shouldered figure of a man, his back to her. Quickly, she crouched down amid the bushes intending to observe the stranger and the scene before her.

To all appearances, these men were pirates, for not a one of them wore the uniform of the British Navy. Each had a pistol or two stuck in his belt and several carried knives or long-bladed swords, something the crew of the *Sea Lady* hadn't done. They had collected the barrels and crates, as well as the trunk she'd found earlier, and had carted them to shore, there to rip them apart and ransack the contents, scattering what they thought was useless about the beach. Suddenly, a fight broke out between two of the men over a dark, leather pouch one of them had found, and as Jennifer shrank back further into the protective cover of underbrush, the man sitting near her suddenly stood up, pulled out his pistol, and fired a round into the air.

"You know the rules, mates," he warned in a deep, clear voice that bore evidence of good breeding. "Gold is divided among us. Anything else belongs to the man who found it."

Jennifer didn't notice if those who argued over right of

possession complied with the statement or not. She was simply too caught up in the hypnotizing effect of the tall, muscular stranger to care. Even though she couldn't see his face or much of his profile, she deemed him the most alluring man she had ever seen . . . and probably the tallest. His wide shoulders, covered by a white silk shirt with billowing sleeves, narrowed to slender hips. Dark cotton breeches hugged them and his well-formed thighs, and the knee-high boots he wore fit perfectly over the sinewy shape of his calves. Jennifer was surprised at how neat and clean the man appeared. He certainly wasn't her image of a pirate. She held her breath when he turned slightly and sat down on the rock again. His tousled, raven black hair caught a stream of sunlight that stole in through the dense canopy of leaves overhead and shimmered to an almost purplish hue as he reached out a muscular arm and laid his weapon on the ground beside him. Only then could she force her attention back to the others on the beach, and set her mind on a way of leaving that place without anyone seeing her. There were too many of them for her to hope to fight them off should one spot her.

Two men were rummaging through the trunk, a third standing off to one side watching them. He didn't appear to have any interest in what they found until one of them lifted a book from inside. Taking it from him, the man briefly scanned its pages, then snapped it shut and turned in Jennifer's direction.

"Don't imagine it's much good, Cap'n," he called out to the dark-haired stranger sitting near her, "but maybe you'd like to take a look at it."

"What is it?" came the reply, and Jennifer felt her pulse quicken at the deep timbre of his voice.

"The ship's log," the other informed him.

A huge hand was raised and long, brown fingers motioned for the man to toss it over. Jennifer's eyes widened as she watched the leather-bound book sail through the air, out of the captain's reach, and land with a thud only a yard or two away from her; and her breath seemed to leave her when the dashing pirate rolled onto one hip and leaned back to grab for the book, presenting her with a full view of his face. He was recklessly handsome, with exquisite dark brows and sinfully thick lashes framing his brown eyes. Wide cheekbones, a square jaw that was in need of a shave, and the gold earring in one lobe gave him a masterful air that Jennifer doubted any man would test knowingly. His mouth was set in a hard line, its only visible imperfection a thin scar starting in the center of his lower lip and running almost to his chin. It in no way detracted from his handsomeness but rather enhanced it, and Jennifer blushed when she realized she was wondering what it would be like to be kissed by those full, sensuous lips. What she didn't notice, however, was that his gaze shifted to the left of him when something caught his attention, nor did she spy the subtle way he studied the lavender and lace piece of cloth hanging on a branch. He stood up suddenly, and Jennifer ducked further behind the shrubs, watching him brush the sand from his clothes and pick up his pistol, as well as the book, as if he intended to leave. She was filled with mixed thoughts of calling out to him. Had he been alone, she might have done just that. But those with him didn't strike her as understanding or sympathetic. No, she decided, it was probably better to take her chances on her own than to place herself in the hands of the likes of these men. She had heard too many rumors about what pirates did to helpless women.

His stride was long and sure as he walked away from her to return to his men, and she watched with mild admiration. It wasn't until the group headed down the beach that she realized there was no ship anchored offshore. Where had they come from? And where were they going now? Had they made camp somewhere close by, just as she had? Suddenly, Jennifer realized the danger she was in. As soon as they were out of sight, she would return to her hut, gather her meager belongings, and find someplace else to live . . . perhaps on the other side of the island.

Chapter Two

Captain Chad LaShelle sat brooding at a far table in the pub, his dark brows drawn tightly together as he glared into his mug of ale and ignored the merriment of his men. Supplies were low on the island, and the merchant ship he and his crew had followed was to have corrected the problem. Usually a ship sailing from the Colonies to England meant a cargo hold full of tobacco and cotton, and the promise of gold and jewelry that could be taken from its passengers, some of which could be sold in Spain for a considerable profit. But the storm at sea had destroyed their chances of capturing such a treasure and had left them only the slim pickings of a few crates and boxes. Yet, this wasn't what truly upset the captain. Something far more valuable had gone down with the ship, something he would have given his entire wealth to have. Twisting sideways on the bench, he rested his foot on the seat and draped an arm over his bent knee, a mug dangling from one hand while he opened the ship's log with the other. The name Jennifer Grey practically leaped from the page.

"So, Captain."

His thoughts interrupted, Chad looked up to find his friend and first mate, Jason Bingham, sitting down across the table from him.

"Are you going to tell me what it is that's intensified your usually black mood?" Bingham asked. "Or do I have to guess?" Green eyes glanced down at the open book. "I assume it has something to do with that."

Without comment, Chad lifted the mug of ale to his lips and took a long drink of the warm, dark beer.

"All right," Jason conceded with a sigh, setting down his own mug of ale on the table top and leaning forward on his elbows. "I'm to guess." He pointed at the book. "May I?"

Jason took the captain's continued silence, as well as his seemingly disinterested frame of mind, to mean consent and reached out to slide the tome his way, a puzzled frown wrinkling his brow once he had examined the page revealed to him. It was a list of passengers, those who had been on board the *Sea Lady,* and it was the first time for as long as he could remember that such information was of any interest to his captain.

"Did you know one of these people?" he asked without looking up. "Is that what's bothering you? A relative, perhaps?" Jason silently answered his own question with a shake of his head. The only family Chad LaShelle had lived in England, and their names weren't on the list. He began to thumb through the rest of the book, his light brown brows lifting in surprise to find that the captain of the merchant ship had kept a diary. "Did you see this?" he asked, his attention still focused on what he'd read. "Seems the captain took a special liking to a certain young woman on board. Pretty name, Jennifer Grey."

Envisioning a beautiful brunette with green eyes, he smiled up at his captain, ready to voice his description of the imaginary woman he thought would fit such a name, but he changed his mind once he saw the hard set of Chad's mouth and the way the muscle in his cheek flexed.

He glanced down at the book again, then up at his captain.

"Who was she?" he asked simply, quietly.

Chad's nostrils flared as he sucked in an angry breath, his gaze fixed on something across the room, though Jason doubted he truly saw it. The muscle tightened in his cheek again as he ground his teeth, and several minutes passed before Chad decided to finish off his ale in one long gulp. That done, he slammed the empty mug on the table and leaned back, his broad shoulders cradled in the corner where the two walls joined together. An old hatred darkened his eyes and gave his friend cause to suspect that the past had flared up to haunt him again. When Chad absently traced the scar on his chin with one thumb, Jason was sure of it. The two men had known each other for more than ten years, and every time something enraged Chad LaShelle, he did exactly what he was doing now.

"She's connected in some way to your father, isn't she?" he dared ask, inwardly cringing when Chad set a murderous glare upon him. Any other man would have made a hasty exit, but Jason didn't frighten easily. He silently credited his courage to the fact that in all the time they'd spent together, Chad had raised a fist to him in anger only once. And that had been many years ago.

"What difference does it make?" he growled. "She's dead."

"It makes a difference to you or you wouldn't be looking at me like you're about to tear my heart out," Jason observed. He closed the book and slid it back across the table. "Want to talk about it?"

"No," Chad snarled and turned his head away, running his thumb over the scar again. "Talking about it doesn't do any good."

"How do you know? You never tried," Jason pointed

35

out, lifting his mug to his lips and taking a drink. Their discussions always started out this way, and he knew that with enough prodding on his part, Chad would give in and reveal one more tiny aspect of his troubled personality. He smiled into his mug and took another sip of ale. If asked, he probably couldn't name the reason why he liked this ill-tempered, secretive man, but he did. "I don't think I have to tell you that anything you say to me will never go any further than this table. I'm your friend, and that's what friends are for . . . to ease each other's hurt."

Chad snorted derisively and waved at the barmaid to bring him another mug of ale. "Who says I'm hurting . . . friend?" he seethed.

"Do you think I'm blind? Or just stupid?" Jason rallied. "I'm the first to admit that it's difficult to distinguish your good moods from your bad, except, of course, when you're truly angry you don't say anything at all."

"All right." Chad yielded with a touch of sarcasm, taking the full mug of ale from the barmaid. "Then I'm angry."

"Oh, I'll agree with that," Jason countered. "You're upset because this Jennifer Grey got herself killed without asking your permission. But you're hurting because there's something about her that reminds you of your father."

Dark, piercing eyes flashed a warning. "Let it lie, Jason," Chad hissed through clenched teeth. "It doesn't concern you."

Bingham ignored Chad's advice. "Would you like to know how I know? Well, I'll tell you. Every time you think about your father or something that happened when you were a child, you run your thumb over that scar on your chin. Gives you away without fail."

Dropping his feet to the floor, Chad leaned forward and asked in a low voice, "How would you like one to match it?"

Without blinking, Jason stared at his companion for several seconds before picking up his ale and taking a leisurely drink of it. "If you really wanted to split my lip, you wouldn't have wasted time asking." He smiled lazily. "So why don't you just tell me why her death bothers you and get me off your back?"

Chad's nostrils flared again, and he glowered at Jason for a long while before answering. "Her death means nothing to me. But alive, she could have played an important part in my getting even."

"Even?" Jason echoed, watching his friend collapse back against the wall again. "With whom? For what? What the hell are you talking about?"

The corner of Chad's mouth twitched, and for a moment, Jason thought the man was going to smile. But more surprising than that, he sensed he was about to learn what it was that drove this man so relentlessly. He settled in closer so as not to miss a single word; then, to his dismay and great irritation, Chad's attention was abruptly drawn away by the high-pitched, honey-coated greeting of Modesty, the island whore who claimed Chad as her man.

"'Ello, gov'na," she purred, whirling around the end of the table to deposit herself on Chad's lap. "Danny told me ye found somethin' I'd like. Is it a bobble for me neck?"

"How about a cork for your mouth, Modesty?" Jason sneered. "Can't you see the two of us are talking?"

"Talkin', is it?" She smiled alluringly at Chad, and wrapped her arms around his neck, giving him an unrestricted view of her ample bosom as her low-cut blouse drooped down. "Weren't talkin' I 'ad in mind."

"You never do, Modesty." Jason frowned. "I doubt you could hold a conversation that consisted of more than two sentences."

37

Her dark red hair shimmered in the diffuse sunlight coming in through the grimy windows of the tavern as she turned her head to glare at him. "Ye're just jealous, Jason Bingham, 'cause it ain't ye I'm interested in."

Jason rolled his eyes, and for a moment it appeared that he was going to be sick. Half-muttering to himself, he glanced upward and said, "Thank you, God, for letting me know you're still there."

Outraged by the insult, Modesty jumped to her feet. "Ye bloody bastard," she shrieked, grabbing Chad's mug so she could toss the contents in Bingham's face. But a strong, powerful hand caught her wrist as Chad came to his feet and pulled her away from the table before any damage could be done.

"Chad, wait!" Jason shouted when the couple started across the room on their way to the stairs. He knew that if his captain mounted them it would be some time before he would have the chance to speak with him again. "Just tell me how the girl could have helped."

With his arm draped around Modesty's neck, Chad paused, then turned his dark head to look back at his friend. "There was a time—before you and I met—when I was supposed to marry Jennifer Grey. Then my father suddenly decided I wasn't good enough for her, so my half-brother took my place," he announced coldly, bitterly, his rugged features twisted with hatred; and for the first time in all the years Jason had known this man, the look Chad gave him chilled him to the bone.

"Come back to bed, lovey," Modesty invited, her darkly painted red lips pursing into an unflattering pout when the captain ignored her to stare out the window. She sat up, letting the thin sheet fall to her lap. "I can make ye forget yer troubles."

Her eyes roamed freely over the muscular curves of

38

wide, bare shoulders, and her pulse quickened again. She had bedded many a man, but none as handsome and titillating as Captain Chad LaShelle, and if Modesty Copeland was capable of love, then this tall, mysterious, perfect specimen of a man deserved all she could give. She had lived her entire life in London until two years ago when the wife of a prominent member of Parliament, having caught her husband in bed with Modesty, had used her influence to have the young woman sent to debtor's prison. It had been Chad's men who had freed Modesty and brought her to this island. In fact, most of the people who lived here came from debtor's prison, though a few had been bound for the gallows. Hidden away on this small piece of land somewhere in the Atlantic, they had formed their own little society of misfits—outcasts doomed to a bleak existence by the high and mighty of London. And all of this was possible because of one man—Captain Chad LaShelle, himself sent into exile by an unforgiving father.

No one knew the whole story of Chad's past, only that he was the illegitimate son of a very wealthy, influential lord, and that after a bitter argument with his father, Chad had left London to start a new life. Without the necessary coins it took to support himself, Chad had taken to stealing, and before he'd reached the age of twenty, he'd become the most feared pirate to sail the Atlantic Ocean since the death of Edward Teach some three decades ago. Everyone on the island considered Chad their leader, never questioning his decisions, knowing that if they did, they would be sent back to live out their lives rotting in prison. Only Jason Bingham ever had the courage to stand up to Chad LaShelle, but no one had ever made LaShelle laugh . . . not even Modesty.

"What ye thinkin' about, love?" she asked, sliding off the bed and reaching for her flimsy wrapper. Pulling its sash tightly around her waist, she sauntered up behind him, slipped her arms around him, and rubbed her breasts against his back. "Thinkin' o' me, are ye, lovey?" Her hands slid to the buttons of his breeches. "An' all the things I can do to please ye?"

She stumbled back a step or two when he turned and firmly set her from him, then gaped in wide-eyed surprise while he picked up his shirt and jammed his arms into it, silently declining her bold suggestion that they spend the rest of the day in bed. Tears glistened in her eyes as she watched him sit down on the mattress, pull on his stockings and boots, then head for the door as he buttoned up his shirt. This wasn't the first time he had left her in this manner, and she doubted it would be the last. The only thing that eased the hurt of his sudden dismissal of her was the knowledge that his abrupt departure had nothing to do with her. He'd be back. She was sure of it. Of all the women on the island, she was the only one Chad lay with. Taking comfort in that fact, she raised her nose in the air and got back into bed. Whether sharing the space or not, she didn't intend to do anything more physical than lie there for the rest of the afternoon . . . unless, of course, Chad had something else in mind.

He had almost forgotten about the scrap of lavender and lace cloth, the delicate footprints he had seen in the sand near where his men had found the debris washed ashore from the *Sea Lady*. Having learned that his half brother's fiancée was one of the passengers had distracted him. But it didn't now. Leaving instructions with his first mate that no one was to follow him since he wanted to be alone for a while, Chad headed for the livery stable and the black stallion he prized so much. Not bothering with a saddle, he took the reins in one hand, grabbed a fistful of thick, rich mane, and swung himself up on the wide back of the steed, guiding the animal away from the village and in the opposite direction from the beach. Although no one had ever gone against his orders, he still didn't trust a single soul.

Once he was out of sight of the tiny hamlet, he changed course and guided the animal across a rocky ledge so it would be difficult to track him. He wanted to be the first to reach the place where he suspected he would find a young woman since it was his rule that anything other than gold belonged to the man who found it. He had grown tired of Modesty and welcomed the prospect of someone new. What puzzled him was how she had gotten on the island. The *Sea Lady* had gone down miles out to sea, making the possibility of her being one of the passengers highly unlikely.

Through the dense growth of trees atop the ridge overlooking the shoreline, he traveled for nearly an hour before he reined his stallion down a steep incline and onto the sandy beach. Dismounting, he guided the animal toward the place where his men had rummaged through the crates and boxes they had found, carefully studying the area for tiny footprints that obviously didn't belong to his crew. His suntanned brow wrinkled in confusion when he couldn't find them, and he wondered if, perchance, his mind had played tricks on him. Then he spotted the piece of cloth entangled about the lower branch of a bush and realized that whoever he was trailing was not an ordinary woman, for this one had obviously taken the time to hide her tracks. A vague smile lifted one corner of his mouth. What she hadn't realized, however, was that she had left behind an even larger clue to her whereabouts. All he had to do was follow the brush marks in the sand, for she had swept a tree branch over the footprints she'd left in the soft earth. Feeling the excitement of a chase, Chad tossed the reins over his horse's neck, pulled himself up on the animal's back, and carefully guided his steed around the rocks lying in the way. Once they were clear of them, he kicked the stallion's sides and bolted off down the beach.

Jennifer had to settle for a cold supper of nuts and berries as there hadn't been time for her to fish nor did she want to run the risk of starting a fire. Once she had gotten back to camp, she had hurriedly gathered all she could carry, including Kinsey, and had set out down the beach in search of a place to spend the night. Not knowing how large the island was, she thought the short trip she had made wasn't enough. She'd get up early the next day and start again. Maybe by noon she'd pick a new spot to live. Her only regret was that she hadn't been able to dismantle the hut and bring it with her. Now she'd have to build another.

With Kinsey curled up in her lap asleep, Jennifer leaned back against a rock and stared out at the fiery sunset, sadly wondering if she would ever again view such splendor while sitting in the company of others. Her throat tightened as she recalled the countless times she and her father had enjoyed such scenery from the front porch swing of the manor house. No matter how busy his day had been, George Grey had always set aside a moment or two to be with his daughter, and Jennifer treasured the memory of those moments. What she couldn't accept—even though she had heard it from his own lips—was that her father was a murderer. He had killed a man in a duel, and because of it, he and his wife and young daughter had had to flee England. It had been his good friend and neighbor, Sir Charles Wadsworth, who had helped him, given him the money he'd needed to buy a plantation in the Colonies; and he and Wadsworth had made a gentleman's agreement that Grey had been determined to honor at his dying breath. Now, through a twist of fate, Jennifer would not carry it through, for she doubted she would ever live to see the streets of London or marry the son of her father's best friend.

She jumped when Kinsey awakened suddenly, his ears alert and his round gold eyes staring past her into the trees. Holding her breath, she listened for whatever sound had brought the cat out of a deep sleep, but the breaking surf rolling inland and splashing over the sandy beach was all she could hear.

"What is it, Kinsey?" she sighed, rubbing his head. "A mouse? Is it your supper you hear?"

Distracted, the huge tom arched his back, fondly accepting the gentle attention he received, before stretching out of her lap and onto the sand. As he headed into the thick undergrowth, she added, "Please be back by sunup or I'll have to leave without you." The swish of a long, striped tail was the only answer she received before the cat disappeared into the dense covering of foliage, and Jennifer laughed at the aristocratic manner in which she had been dismissed.

One of the new delicacies she had found on the island was the fruit of the coconut palm, and although breaking it open had proved to be quite a task, the delicious milk inside made it worth the effort and came as a welcome alternative to water. Settling comfortably against the rock once more, she sifted through the articles she had brought with her, frowning when she discovered this was the last coconut she had. Stretching her legs out in front of her, she placed the hard shell between her knees and, holding the sharp point of a rock against one end of the coconut, beat the other end with a second rock. It was tedious work, and it took her nearly ten minutes to puncture a tiny hole in the top of the shell, but her success brought a smile to her lips as she anticipated what she was about to enjoy. Then, just as she lifted the coconut to her lips, the thunderous pounding of giant hooves on hard-packed sand exploded all around her, and Jennifer bolted to her feet.

43

Fear paralyzed her once she saw the huge black stallion racing down the beach toward her, its sleek, well-muscled body stretching out in long, sure strides, its nostrils flared, its mane snapping in the wind, and its tail held high. For a moment she thought the beast intended to crush her beneath its powerful hooves. Then its rider jerked back on the reins, and the animal reacted within a split second to the command, nearly burying his hindquarters in the sand as he came to a climactic halt, rearing up and wildly clawing the air only a few short yards from her. Yet her attention no longer centered on the majestic black stallion who pranced sideways, impatient to be set free again, but on the man who held the reins and sat astride the animal as if he had been born to ride.

A chill permeated her thinly clad body, and she trembled. She knew this man. He was the one she had watched while those with him, the men she had labeled as pirates, had torn apart the wreckage of the *Sea Lady*. She stumbled back a step. And he was the one they called their captain. Her gaze darted past him to see if the others were close behind. He was alone, but Jennifer took little comfort from this knowledge. Even though they would have outnumbered her ten to one, she sensed the odds would be more in her favor were she fighting off the lot of them instead of dealing single-handedly with this pirate captain, for she doubted he had gained the right of command easily.

She jumped back when he swung a long leg over the horse's neck and effortlessly slid to the ground. He didn't have to voice his reason for coming. She could see it in his dark eyes. He wasn't here for idle chatter or to inquire about her health. He wanted her, and Jennifer knew that no amount of pleading on her part would change his mind. Her lip quivered, and she bit it in an effort to still the tears that threatened to race down her cheeks. She had to remain calm and level-headed if she was to outsmart him. Remembering the coconut she still held in one hand, Jennifer waited until his eyes moved away from her to inspect their surroundings before she brought it up and hurled it at him with all the strength she could muster. It sailed through the air, zeroing in on her target, but to her horror and disbelief, the pirate captain glanced up in time and agilely ducked to one side, out of range. The stallion wasn't as lucky. The hard-shelled fruit struck him in the flank, and before his owner could grab the reins, the animal reared up on his hind legs, spun around, and raced off down the beach. The rage she saw burning in the man's eyes when he turned back to glower at her set her feet in motion, and Jennifer did a quick about-face and dashed off with her tattered skirts held high.

She didn't bother glancing over her shoulder to see if he chased after her. She could feel every inch of him closing the distance between them. The soft sand beneath her slowed her pace, and her breath grew labored in the short span of time it took her to run only a dozen yards or so. She quickly realized it would be a matter of seconds before he caught up to her. If she stood any chance of eluding him, she would have to do it by slowing him down. With this thought in mind, she changed direction and scampered into the serried growth of trees to her right, ducking the low-hanging branches and deftly jumping the rocks and tree roots lying in her path. Her side began to ache, but she vowed not to give up. Her very life depended on her getting away.

Suddenly, from out of nowhere, an arm seized her around the waist and pulled her off balance. She screamed when she was lifted and twirled, then fell. She winced, expecting to hit the hard ground with her hip and shoulder, but instead, the blow was cushioned by the muscular frame of the man who held her. Knowing that

45

once he pinned her down all hope of escaping would be gone, she jabbed her elbow into his ribs as hard as she could and rolled from on top of him when he let go, aptly leaping to her feet and racing off once more.

Confused now, Jennifer wasn't aware that she was heading back toward the beach until the way opened up before her. She stumbled to a halt, not knowing which way to run. A twig snapped behind her, and she spun around to find the dark-haired pirate closing in on her. In a panic, she decided to confront him and quickly bent to scoop up a good-size tree branch broken off by the storm. With that held in both hands, she began to back away from him, her blue-green eyes glistening with tears, her chest heaving.

Chad hadn't expected to find someone quite as tempting as this half-wild creature who stood braced and ready to attack him. At best, he'd thought to come upon a skinny, bedraggled woman half out of her mind, with thinning hair and sagging breasts. This comely wench was far from that. His gaze dropped to the firm swell of her bosom, the tiny waist, well-rounded hips, the long length of thigh showing tan and lean beneath the rip in her skirt. His blood warmed, and he decided any pain he might endure while trying to subdue her would be well worth it. He studied her face again. Perfectly arched brows accentuated the beautiful shade of her eyes, and her thin, straight nose was pink from the hours she had spent in the sun. Her lips were full, her chin delicate, and he longed to run his fingers through the thick, golden hair falling about her shoulders. She was probably the most enticing woman he had ever seen, the kind men fought over, and he smiled to himself. There was no one here to challenge him. She was his for the taking. And take her, he would. His hands moved to the buttons on his shirt.

Jennifer's heart lurched in her chest as she watched

46

him unfasten the front of the white linen fabric, then pull the garment free of his breeches and toss it carelessly aside. Next came his boots, then his stockings. She could hardly believe her eyes. He was disrobing right there in front of her! She blinked and a tear raced for her chin. How could a man, any man, force himself on a woman? And why her? What had she done to provoke such treatment? She hadn't teased him, played with him the way she had seen some women do—and those fine ladies called it flirting. But most assuredly, their victims never— A sob lodged in her throat when she thought of what he intended to do to her, and she hurriedly backed away when he started to advance, her weapon held to one side, ready to be swung.

Wanting desperately to keep a safe distance between them, Jennifer failed to realize that with each step she took, she got closer to the water's edge until a sudden swell of surf rolled in and caught her across the backs of her calves. It knocked her off balance, and she stumbled forward. But her eyes never left the man who stalked her, and when he lunged, Jennifer brought the club around with the force of her body behind it, striking him across the left shoulder. He winced in pain, but didn't utter a sound, and her own hands ached from the blow she had given him for it seemed the piece of wood had struck the trunk of a sturdy oak tree. She realized her fate when he calmly took the weapon from her and flung it away; nothing was going to stop him from having what he wanted. Maybe God had spared her from meeting her death in the watery clutches of the sea, but she decided she would rather be dead than at the mercy of this man. Spinning around, she raced into the foamy surface of the ocean.

The water, cool against her fevered flesh, revitalized her spirits. Perhaps she wouldn't let herself drown, after all. Perhaps she could outswim him. But just as the water

47

became deep enough for her to dive, she stole a glance over her shoulder to find him hurling through the air. There wasn't enough time for her to scream, and the current was too strong for her to get out of the way. She was trapped, and as his arms came around her and pulled her into the water with him, she prayed for the strength to fight him off.

The weight of their bodies carried them to the sandy bottom, and although Jennifer should have been more concerned about the water swirling around her, she discovered, instead, that she was struggling to break his hold on her. She couldn't. His strength was simply too much for her. One arm was clamped securely around her waist, and just as she thought he was about to let go of her, he twisted her around and crushed her against his chest, his mouth coming down hard against hers as he lifted them both from the water.

Being on her feet now gave Jennifer more leverage, even though he still held her tightly against him, one huge hand locked in the hair at the base of her skull, the other pressing her hips to his. If she timed it just right, she'd use the force of the surf rushing toward shore to catch him off balance. Then she'd work her arms in between them and shove with all her might. God willing, it would be enough to set her free. Concentrating on the sounds of the waves breaking around them and the current drawing them deeper into the ocean as a new whitecap formed, she wedged her hands up against his chest and waited, pretending that she had surrendered to him. The strategy worked, doubly well, for the moment her captor lessened his grip, they were hit full force by the crest of a wave, and Jennifer straightened her arms, flinging him from her to dive into and ride with the surf, crashing onto the beach.

Once she felt the sand beneath her, she staggered to her feet, intending to flee into the woods and hopefully lose herself among the trees and thick shrubs. But it wasn't meant to be. The burdensome weight of her saturated skirt pulled her down, its fabric clinging to her legs and hampering her steps. She stumbled and fell to one knee, and in that moment, she knew all was lost. Her strength was fading fast. If he caught her again, she'd be powerless to stop him. She just didn't have the energy to fight anymore. A sob escaped her, and through blinding tears, she lifted her water-soaked skirt, intending to try once more to escape him. Coming to her feet, she staggered forward onto the sun-baked shore. As she glanced back over her shoulder, the muscles across her chest tightened instantly. He was standing at the water's edge, fists resting on his hips, his chin lowered and a slight flare to his nostrils. Water glistened in his dark hair and enriched the bronze expanse of his broad shoulders and muscular arms, and Jennifer doubted there was another man anywhere with a more exquisite form. Perhaps, if they had met at another time, in another place . . .

In the distance, a horse whinnied, and Jennifer turned her head toward the sound, new hope rising within her when she spotted the black stallion pawing the sand on the beach about a hundred yards or so away from her. A devious smile parted her lips when she looked back at the captain, her head cocked to one side, an open challenge gleaming in her eyes. She was daring him to try to cut her off before she reached the spirited animal. She had learned how to ride as a young girl. Indeed, she preferred riding bareback, and what this man didn't know was that she hadn't met a single person who could do it better than she.

Chad knew what was on her mind the instant she looked at him. Not only was she beautiful, but cunning as well, with the same wild nature as the beast she proposed to ride. He admired that in her, but at the same time he

49

wondered how long it would take for her to be thrown from the steed's back, providing of course that she reached him first. There wasn't a soul on the island the animal trusted . . . except for Chad. Enjoying their contest and oddly wishing for it to continue, he bowed slightly and held out a hand, inviting her to take the lead.

Jennifer didn't waste a second in lifting her heavy skirts above her knees, spinning on her heels, and racing off. This would be her last chance. If she failed this time . . . She looked back only once just as the pirate captain sprang into action and it suddenly became a footrace. She had a good head start on him, and the few minutes they had taken to stare at each other had given her a chance to catch her breath. Now all she needed was endurance, and to be lighter and quicker on her feet.

Her heart pounded in her ears. Her side was beginning to ache, but she never slowed her pace. The distance to the stallion had been cut in half. As long as the beast didn't bolt, she'd be able to catch his reins, swing herself up across his back, and gallop away before the pirate came within ten feet of them. That was what she thought she could do. But the plan had barely formed in her mind before she was thrown off balance by the strong hand that grabbed her arm and jerked her around. She tumbled painfully to the ground with him, rolling several times before she found herself pinned beneath him.

"Nice try," he mocked, his face only inches from hers.

Jennifer could feel every inch of his hardened frame pressed against her as his weight held her down. She gasped for air and kept her eyes squeezed tightly shut, praying that he would disappear if she did so long enough. When she felt his hand brush away a strand of her hair from her cheek, she cringed. Then, suddenly, he lifted himself from her, rose to his feet, and pulled her with him. As he dragged her back toward the water, she clawed at the powerful fingers wrapped around her wrist,

50

certain he planned to drown her. Once they reached the shallows, he yanked her forward and into the water despite her resistance.

"W-what are you going to do?" she whimpered, wondering how anyone could be heartless enough to take another's life without so much as a moment's hesitation.

"I like my women clean," he stated, heading into deeper water and the wave rolling toward them. "You have sand all over you." He glanced over his shoulder at her. "So do I."

A wall of sparkling clear water washed over them before she could correct his assumption that she belonged to anyone, least of all him, and she was knocked off her feet by the force of it. But rather than finding herself carried back to shore with the current, she was lifted above the surface by the hand that hung onto her and thrown barbarously over a wide, hard shoulder, there to dangle precariously while her captor marched back to the beach.

"No! Please . . . put me down!" she begged, kicking and pounding her fists against the broad back that blocked her view.

"That's exactly what I intend to do," he told her. "But not here. I think we'll be more comfortable on a bed of leaves."

"No!" she screamed. "You can't. Please. You mustn't do this." For an instant, she thought he had agreed when she felt him bend forward slightly and deposit her on the ground. Then his hand trapped the back of her head, his fingers tangled in the thick mass of hair at her nape; and tears burned her eyes when he tugged painfully downward, bringing her face up to meet his. She couldn't move.

"Maybe not," he whispered with a vague smile, his warm breath brushing her cheek. "But I'm going to."

His free hand grabbed the front of her dress, and

51

before Jennifer could make any effort to stop him, he curled his fingers in the tattered neckline and yanked down. The seams gave way under such abuse, but he obviously wasn't satisfied with just ripping the bodice of her dress for his hand came up a second time and seized the thin fabric of her camisole. It too was left in shreds.

"Please," she whimpered, making a futile attempt to cover herself. "Please don't do this."

But the captain wasn't listening. His eyes had already darkened with lust for the treasure he had exposed, and when Jennifer struggled to break free of him, he simply caught her arm and lowered her to the ground beneath him.

She fought to keep her arms between her and the pirate captain, to protect what modesty she had left. She had never been with a man before, never felt his kisses or the strength of his body pressed against her own, and what was about to happen frightened her. Too embarrassed to discuss such matters, her father had never taken her aside and explained what a man and a woman could share together. But somehow, this wasn't what she had imagined. She had assumed the moment would be special, a gentle coupling of two people who cared about each other. She felt nothing for this man. She didn't even know his name. Eyes wide with terror, her lips quivering and tears streaming down her cheeks, she sucked in a trembling breath.

"Why?" she asked. "When you know it isn't what I want."

Deep brown eyes held hers as he lifted a wide hand to brush the backs of his fingers against the cool, smoothness of her cheek. "You will," he whispered and lowered his head.

Warm, moist lips found hers and Jennifer closed her eyes, the sensations sparked in her taking her breath away. He kissed her with the kind of tenderness she had expected from a man who loved her, and for a moment, she was confused. He didn't care about her, so how could he pretend he did? But what puzzled her more than anything was the strange warmth his kiss aroused deep within her, and unknowingly, she relaxed, enjoying the way his mouth moved hungrily over hers. Then his hands took her wrists and pulled her arms from in front of her, and she came to life.

"No!" she cried, twisting her face away. She gasped when he pressed the hard muscles of his chest against her naked breasts, and before she could utter another sound, his mouth came down hard on hers again. He trapped her head between his powerful hands while his tongue tasted the sweetness of her lips then pushed inside, and Jennifer began to kick and squirm beneath him.

Her struggles only seemed to impassion him, and before she could stop him or even guess his intent, he had ripped away the few remaining pieces of her clothing and shed his own. The branding heat of his body touched every inch of her flesh, and when his mouth took hers again, she pounded tiny fists against his wide-rock-hard shoulders. Then his knee brutally pushed her thighs apart, and she arched her back, trying to shove him from her. It was the worst mistake she had made, and she realized it the instant his throbbing manhood was thrust deep inside her.

A bolt of searing pain shot through her whole body, and she stiffened, unable to draw a breath to scream and positive she was about to die. With her eyes squeezed tightly shut, she lay unmoving, willing her death to be quick and without further pain. But to her surprise and confusion, the captain's caresses softened and from somewhere deep inside her, a spark was ignited and flooded her body with a strange warmth, a tingling that was almost pleasurable. Suddenly, she was aware of her surroundings; the crashing surf against the shore, the

53

golden sunset, the gentle sea breeze, the distant song of tropical birds, and most of all, the strong, mysterious pirate captain who claimed her—body and soul. He had forced himself on her, taken what she didn't willingly want to give, but for some unexplainable reason, after the first wave of pain subsided, she found his touch, his desire, his insistence to possess her exciting, and she relaxed. He moved, long and sure, within her while he tenderly kissed the corner of her mouth, her delicately boned jaw, and then nuzzled her ear before burying his face in her bright golden hair. His breathing became ragged, and she could feel his heart pounding wildly against her naked breasts. And when he shuddered in ecstasy, his passion spent, she was mildly disappointed that it had come to an end. No one had ever wanted her so savagely before, and she reveled in the pleasure of knowing someone had—especially a man like this powerful, forceful stranger. But just as quickly as the emotion arose, it vanished, and in its place shame mounted to destroy the moment. Tears welled beneath her thick, black lashes, and before she could find the strength to control them, she began to weep forlornly.

A long while passed before he raised up from her and sat back on his heels, quietly, angrily staring at her. Jennifer could feel his gaze upon her, but she wouldn't open her eyes. Nor could she stop the heartrending sobs that shook her body. She was only vaguely aware that he lifted her in his arms, and it didn't matter to her where he might be taking her. Then she felt the cooling waters of the ocean wash over her as he carried her into its depth, and for a second she hoped he would leave her there. But he didn't. A moment later, he was setting her down on the torn remnants of her lavender dress, and she sat shivering while he donned his breeches.

"Why didn't you tell me?" his deep voice demanded.

She couldn't bring herself to answer. Instead, she drew

up her knees and hugged them to her, her eyes still clamped tightly shut as though such an effort could make the whole world disappear. She jumped when she felt the silky texture of his shirt, which he had draped over her shoulders. Without a sound, she quickly slid her arms into it and buttoned up the front.

"Why didn't you tell me?" he asked again, dropping down beside her on one knee.

Her tiny frame shook uncontrollably. "I-I did."

"No, you didn't. You never said you were a virgin."

The words issued forth through clenched teeth, and Jennifer was surprised by her own laughter. Eyes glistening with tears, she looked up at him. "What right do you have to be angry with me? I asked you to stop, but you wouldn't." Then she shrank back, fearful of the rage which suddenly darkened his eyes.

"That isn't the same. You should have said something."

Her own ire rose at his insinuation that this whole affair was her fault. "What good would it have done?" she snapped, glaring out across the sunlit waters of the ocean.

"I would have been more gentle," he barked, although his tone belied the statement.

Laughter erupted again. "How gallant," she scoffed.

In anger, he tried to take her arm, but she jerked away from him and scrambled to her feet. He quickly rose.

"Excuse me, pirate captain, but I'm a virgin, so would you mind taking it easy with me? After all, I have so looked forward to this, and don't want anything to spoil it." Tears started anew and spilled over the rims of her dark lashes. "Is that what you expected me to say?" she sobbed. "Well, I didn't. And there's nothing you can do now to change any of it."

The scar across his lower lip gleamed almost white. "If you're trying to make me feel guilty, don't bother. I've never felt guilty about anything in my life."

"Guilty?" She rallied despite mounting tears. "I doubt you've ever felt *anything!*" She jumped back when he reached out for her. "Don't! Don't touch me again! Ever!"

He tried again, and she quickly eluded him.

"Go away!"

"And just leave you here?" he snarled. "Look at you. What has being on your own done for you so far?"

"Until you came, I was fine!" she shouted, her chest heaving.

Dark brows lowered over smoldering eyes, and the muscle in his cheek flexed. He glared at her for several minutes, not uttering a sound, then turned and marched back to where his boots and stockings lay. Practically throwing himself down on the sand, he brushed its tiny particles from his feet and donned the rest of his attire. But rather than standing up again, he bent his knees, rested his elbows on them, and clasped his left wrist with his right hand.

"How did you get here?" he asked after a while, deep brown eyes staring at her.

By now, Jennifer had managed to pull herself together, and although she didn't like the way he looked at her, she decided not to say anything that might provoke him. He had a very short temper, and she didn't relish thinking of what might happen should he unleash it on her. Dropping her gaze, she spotted the torn remains of her clothes and frowned.

"The ship I was on got caught in a storm," she said, coming to kneel beside the garments. "It sank and I somehow managed not to." She lifted the shreds of her lavender dress.

"The *Sea Lady?*"

She glanced up at him and nodded hesitantly. He had a funny look in his eyes, one that provoked her curiosity

56

and put her on guard. "Why? Did you know the captain?"

He presented her with a rather striking profile when he turned his head to look out across the rolling surf as if he half expected to see the ship still sailing there. "No," he finally answered. A moment of silence followed, then, "Did anyone else survive?"

Jennifer shook her head. "Not that I know of. Just Kinsey and me." When he frowned, she added, "The ship's cat."

A hint of a smile touched one corner of his mouth, but he quickly turned his head away as though he didn't want her to notice. He was quite different, a complex individual, Jennifer decided, and despite what he had done to her, she was surprised to find that he interested her.

"Who are you?" she dared to ask.

This time, he did smile . . . openly, and Jennifer thought how much more handsome he was when he wasn't angry.

"A scoundrel to most women, a threat to the men who sail the Atlantic, and a black mark against my family name."

"Which is?" she pressed.

The smile vanished, and he cast his gaze upon the setting sun, the strong line of his jaw tense with emotion. "Doesn't matter. I carry my own name. Not my father's," he hissed, his thumb tracing the scar on his chin. Suddenly, he rose angrily to his feet. "It's time we started back."

Clutching the lavender dress and torn chemise to her breast, she hurriedly pushed herself up. "Back? No. I'm . . . I'm not—"

"You're not going to argue," he finished, shooting out a hand to grab her wrist. "Your days of fending for yourself are over. You're coming with me." Jerking her

57

forward, he took her elbow in a painful manner and started shoving her down the beach toward the place where the black stallion munched lazily on the green grasses at his feet.

"Please," she begged, stumbling along beside him. "Please leave me here. Don't give me to your men."

"My men?" He frowned, taking her tiny waist in his hands and lifting her onto the stallion's wide back. "I have no intention of giving you to anyone." He reached for the reins, grabbed a handful of thick mane, and easily swung himself up behind her. "I found you. You're mine. That's the law." Spinning the animal around, he kicked the heels of his boots into the horse's sides, and the magnificent beast bolted down the long, deserted stretch of beach.

Chapter Three

A light, chilling rain fell upon the dark streets of London, discouraging even the bravest of souls from venturing out of the safe haven of their homes where warm fires chased away the shadows and offered dry places in which to spend the few remaining hours before daylight forced its way through the black, dismal clouds blanketing the city. Yet even at this early hour, a carriage wound its way down the narrow avenue, heading toward Newgate prison. Its driver was already soaked to the skin while the passenger inside the coach, though warm and dry, seemed more distressed than the man who held the reins.

Charles Elliott Wadsworth II pushed himself back into the plush leather seat of the landau, his thin face twisted in a worried frown. He had business to take care of at the jail, important, secret business, and it was imperative that he complete his dealings as quickly as possible and return home before his father came down to breakfast. Above all others, his father must not learn of his trip to the prison.

For the past ten years, he had periodically heard vague reports on the whereabouts of his half brother Chad LaShelle, and up until a few months ago, Charles hadn't

59

cared where Chad was as long as he stayed away from London. But now . . . now it was urgent that Charles find him. He had to get to him before their father learned the truth.

The carriage lurched sideways as it rounded the last corner on its way to the main gate of the prison, nearly throwing Charles off the seat. Swearing under his breath, he pushed himself up, straightened his attire, and tugged his curly brown wig back into place, pale brows drawn together and a promise on his thin lips that the driver of the rig would not be paid the full amount because of his ineptness. No one treated Charles Elliott Wadsworth II in such a manner, and this imbecile would hear about it. Sliding to the edge of the seat when the carriage slowed, Charles peered out from behind the window flaps at the huge, dark stone building that loomed large and foreboding, against the gray sky, and he shivered at the thought of having to be among the wretched people who inhabited the prison. He'd finish his business as quickly as possible and leave this odious den of beggars and thieves and murderers before someone mistook him for a man who cared what happened to their kind. Unlatching the door, he swung it open and stepped down, hurriedly pulling his tricorn forward over his brow to shield his face from the rain and his identity from anyone who might be looking.

Garth Lathrop was stretched out on the straw cot in his cell, his arms folded behind his head as he stared up at the ceiling above him and listened to the steady rhythm of the rain outside the prison. Days and nights had blended into one endless span of time for Garth with only the bleak promise of death as an end to the monotony, something he chose not to think about. He had spent the last five weeks locked up in this narrow, little cell with its rats, its damp chill, and the vile smell that choked the breath from him. His meals had consisted of hardly more than a crust of dried bread, a bowl of porridge, and never anything other than water to drink, water from the bucket that had been laced with a bit of rum to keep it from souring, its purpose to both quench his thirst and to allow for what cleanliness it could provide during his imprisonment. Life behind a locked door wasn't something new to Garth. He had been in this situation many times before, but never awaiting the hangman's noose as he was now. And never caged up in a single cell away from the rest of the prisoners. A smile creased his bearded face. They weren't taking any chances this time. He wasn't going to escape the way he always had before. The fools! Did they really think he or his men would just calmly allow the guards to cart him off to the gallows? Of course not. Somewhere along the road the crew of the *Challenger* would attack and free their captain. Garth only hoped his sanity could hold that long.

From somewhere near the end of the long corridor running past his cell, Garth could hear the muffled voices of two men and footsteps on the stone floor coming in his direction. His execution wasn't scheduled for another week, but for some unexplainable reason, he sensed the pair would be paying him a visit. He was sure of it when he heard the key in the lock. Sitting up, he swung his feet to the floor and waited.

"I tell ye, gov'na, 'e ain't the kind ye want ta be alone with," the jailer warned.

"I'll decide that," the other man replied as the door creaked open, presenting Garth with an indistinct view of the man.

"Then I'll be waiting outside, gov'na," the jailer insisted. "It will be me bloody neck they'll 'ave should the bloke see fit ta murder ye."

"You'll wait where I found you," Garth's visitor

61

hissed, grabbing the edge of the door and pulling it shut behind him. Though his eyes centered on the man before him, he listened to the jailer's footsteps as the man walked away, and once he was assured of privacy, he disapprovingly glanced about the interior of the cell. "A rather deplorable place to spend one's days," he remarked, more to himself than to the prisoner who occupied that foul space.

"You get used to it," Garth replied, squinting in the dim light in an effort to discover the man's identity. Failing in that attempt, he studied the visitor's clothing, starting at the dark brown, leather shoes with gold buckles, and running his gaze up skinny legs covered in beige stockings, velvet breeches almost hidden by a full-skirted frock coat, and finally noting the mass of tiny curls on the man's wig as a plumed tricorn was removed from his head. Garth grinned openly as he fell back against the wall and drew up one knee on which to rest his forearm, for his visitor had withdrawn a lace handkerchief to hold beneath his nose. "And the smell," Garth added.

"Hmmm," his visitor replied, scanning the room as if looking for a place to sit down.

Garth jerked a thumb toward the end of the cot. "I'm not opposed to sharing."

The man's tall, thin figure straightened, as if he were offended by the thought of soiling his clothes. "Thank you, no," he said stiffly. "I don't intend to stay long."

"I wish I could say the same," Garth smiled, highly curious as to what had brought this well-dressed stranger to a place like this.

"Yes, well, maybe I can make that possible," the other suggested. "It's the reason I'm here. To offer you freedom in exchange for services to me."

"I'm condemned to hang, sir, by order of the King," Garth pointed out, "for crimes against the Crown. I don't think ol' George will—"

"Ol' George, as you call him, will never learn of it," the stranger assured him.

Garth raised a dark brow dubiously.

"I've arranged to have another take your place," the man explained. "Someone else will be buried in your name."

"You've done that before knowing if I'd agree or not?" Garth laughed.

"I honestly didn't think you'd refuse," his visitor exclaimed irately. "I can't think of a soul who would pass up living, no matter what the price."

Whatever this man wanted had to be extremely important to him, but since it was always Garth's nature to treat any situation as if it were nothing more than a game, he heaved a tired sigh and lay back down on the cot. "Honor, sir. My honor comes before all else."

"Including money?" the other squawked, his high-pitched voice cracking.

Garth's green eyes moved to look at the man. "You're offering me my freedom and money besides? What is it you want me to do? Kill someone?"

"Yes."

The quick reply provoked Garth to sit up again. "Who? Ol' George?"

The stranger shook his head and stepped forward a pace or two, moving into the dull stream of light coming in through the tiny window near the ceiling as if he were afraid someone might hear him through the thick walls of the cell. "No. But someone the King will thank you for killing, someone who's a bigger threat to the British Navy than you, my friend. Chad LaShelle."

Garth stared at his visitor for several moments, trying to remember where he had seen this dandy before as well as to figure out what possible reason he could have for wanting Captain LaShelle dead. Then it came to him. "I

63

know you. You're LaShelle's half brother, Charles Wadsworth."

"Shhh!" Charles urged. "Keep your voice down. Someone might hear you."

Garth gave the cell a quick once-over. "Who? The rats?" Frowning, he came to his feet and walked the short distance to the man, backing him up against the door. "What makes you think I can even find LaShelle, much less kill him if I do? He's not one to be caught alone anywhere, you know. And why do you want him dead? The way I hear it, he hasn't stepped a foot on Wadsworth property since the day his father threw him out. He's no threat to you. Why the interest in bringing about his demise all of a sudden?"

Charles could feel himself start to sweat despite the chill in the air. He gulped and dabbed at his brow with his handkerchief. "Why I want him dead isn't your concern, Captain. And if anyone can find him, you can." He quickly stepped aside, frightened nearly out of his wits when his companion raised a hand. This pirate, though not much taller than Charles's own six feet, weighed considerably more than he and none of it fat, but solid, well-toned muscle. For a fleeting moment, he thought that perhaps he had been wrong in sending the guard away. Then the captain casually propped his elbow on the doorframe.

"And why do you think that, Lord Wadsworth?" he mocked, wondering how a weak-kneed individual such as this could have found the courage to come to Newgate prison, to seek out a condemned criminal like himself, and talk about murdering his own half-brother as if this were a common topic of conversation. He suspected that under the lace and silk and the elaborately coiffured wig was a man with a very devious little mind. But not a mind crafty enough to cheat Garth out of the hefty purse he would demand as payment.

"I-I know what you're thinking, Captain," Charles admitted as the pirate looked him up and down. "You're wondering how someone like me could possibly know anything about someone like you. We . . . ah . . . don't exactly travel in the same circle. But I do know. I have friends who have friends . . . ." He let the sentence trail off and waved the handkerchief beneath his nose, breathing in the scent of lavender. The stench of this awful place was beginning to get to him. "You know what I mean. Anyway, I've learned that my half brother has claimed an island somewhere in the Atlantic as his own, and that the only ships allowed to anchor near its shores belong to men of his—" He caught himself before he had said too much and insulted the man. "Other pirates. No respect— I mean, no one else is allowed near it or he opens fire with cannons hidden in the bluffs surrounding the village. I've been told, however, that you've been to this island several times. You know how to find him, and more important, he won't wonder why you're there." Charles's thin lips drew back in a smile. "He'll trust you."

"You know an awful lot, Charlie," Garth mocked, grinning when he saw the man flinch over the abuse of his name, "but you don't know anything."

"What do you mean?" Charles objected, his nose raised in the air.

"Chad LaShelle doesn't trust anyone. Least of all me. How do you think he's managed to stay alive all these years?" Dropping his arm to his side, Garth went back to the bunk and lay down. "Even his half brother wants him dead." He crossed his wrists behind his head and stared up at the ceiling again, sighing, "And if you can't trust your own family . . ."

"All right, so he won't trust you. But you know where the island is. That's more than I know. And I'll pay you enough to figure out a way to get to him . . . to kill him."

"Will you?" Garth challenged.

"Yes! Whatever it takes!"

Garth turned his head to look at him. "How much?"

Excited now when it seemed the captain had agreed, Charles rushed forward to stand beside the cot. "Enough to buy a new ship," he announced, thinking the offer more than fair.

"That's a great deal of money, Charlie," Garth replied, pretending to be impressed.

"It's worth it to me." The firm nod of Wadsworth's head supported his claim.

"Is it?" Garth countered. "Then let's see if we can loosen the strings of your purse a little and find out just how much it's worth to you."

"W-what do you mean?" Charles straightened and took a nervous step backward. This wasn't going the way he had planned. The man was supposed to be grateful for the chance to save his life and earn money doing it. He hadn't expected him to barter over the price!

"What I mean, Charles Wadsworth, is that with or without your help, I don't intend to face the hangman. Therefore, your offer isn't enough to tempt me into going against your half brother. Double it, and you've got a deal. "

"Double it!" Charles exploded. "Why, that's— that's—"

"Too much?" Garth grinned.

Charles sucked in an outraged breath, fiercely wanting to turn on his heel and march from the cell. The bloody bastard deserved to hang! His upper lip twitched as he glared down at the pirate. If he didn't need him so badly, he'd enjoy seeing it happen. But his future rested in the hands of this one man, though Charles hated being in that position. He had never had to depend on anyone in his entire life, and now, being forced into doing so was almost more than he could bear. Well, maybe this

66

scoundrel had him where he wanted him, but Charles wasn't about to make it easy for the man. He turned and walked back to the door.

"All right," he concurred. "It's a deal. But there's one condition to your being paid." He faced Garth again. "You must bring proof of my half brother's death."

Rolling onto his side, Garth propped his head up on his fist and smiled. "And what shall I bring? His head?"

Charles recoiled at the thought, certain this barbarian would do just that if he told him yes. "I'll leave that up to you, Captain. But do hurry. Time is of the utmost." With that, he placed his tricorn back on his head, raised his arrogant nose in the air and pushed the door, pausing once he had stepped into the corridor. "I'll see to it that you're freed by this afternoon."

The smile on Garth's lips only lasted until the door of his cell squealed and then banged shut behind his visitor, and the gleam in his eyes was anything but humorous. Wadsworth might have left this rank cubicle under the assumption that its occupant had agreed to his proposition, but Garth was far from committed. This fool's help would free him sooner than he had planned, but as for tracking down Chad LaShelle and then murdering him . . . Collapsing back on the musty-smelling cot, Garth stared up at the tiny window high above him, at the pale shaft of light intruding upon the dismal blackness, as he contemplated the reasons why Charles Wadsworth would want his half brother dead.

Garth had first met Chad when LaShelle was not yet sixteen and he was about twenty-seven. He had noticed the boy among the crowd on a busy London street because of the nervous way Chad's attention darted from one person to the next as if he were sizing up a victim. At the time, Garth was on the sidewalk opposite Chad, and he and his first mate paused to watch. Working his way closer to a rather buxom woman in rich garb, Chad waited until an equally well-dressed man moved out to walk past her; then at precisely the right time, Chad roughly laid his hand on the woman's plump backside. Her reaction was an earsplitting shriek and a soundly placed slap directed at the poor, unfortunate fellow she thought guilty of such deplorable behavior. Her victim stopped dead center in the sidewalk to demand an explanation just as Chad accidentally bumped into him— or so it was to seem. However, this particular gentleman had been robbed in such a fashion before and he instantly felt Chad lift his purse. A meaty fist latched onto the boy's shirt collar while the man shouted for help. Seeing a ripe opportunity to finish what Chad had started, Garth nudged his companion and the two of them hurriedly crossed the street.

"William!" Garth sharply called out, grabbing Chad away from the man while his first mate stepped in behind him. "How many times have I warned you about this?" Seizing the man's purse from Chad's fingers, he handed it back. "I apologize for my brother's behavior, sir, but you see, it's kind of an illness with him. He doesn't need to steal. Our family has more than enough money to support him, but he continues to do this anyway. I hope you'll agree that no harm's been done seeing as how I've given you back your money."

The man muttered something about sending them all to prison, then straightened his attire and marched off, much to the delight of Garth and his first mate. Chad, however, wasn't as pleased.

"Let go of me, you son of a bitch," he raged, struggling to free his arm from Garth's strong grip as he was propelled toward an alley. "If you hadn't interfered, I'd be on my way by now *with* his money."

When they were sequestered from the crowd on the street, Garth gave young Chad a rough shake, then spun him around and grabbed his collar in much the same manner as the man had done. "It didn't look like that to me, you little beggar. If we hadn't interfered, you'd be on your way, all right. On your way to prison." He gave Chad a hard shove that sent him falling face down in the dirt. Laughing, he turned his back on the lad and faced his first mate. "Did you get it, Donnie?"

"Sure did, Cap'n," the mate replied with a bright smile as he pulled the gentleman's purse from inside his shirt.

"That's mine!" Chad exploded, scrambling up and catapulting himself through the air. He caught Garth around the knees, and they both crashed to the ground. Stunned for a moment, Garth didn't move, but Chad was on his feet in a flash, ready to do battle. It was the sound of Donnie's pistol being cocked that warned Chad to back off, and though his dark, brown eyes showed no fear, he froze, his feet widespread, fists clenched, and a snarl distorting his mouth.

"You all right, Cap'n?" Donnie asked, his weapon pointed at Chad while he helped Garth up.

Brushing himself off, Garth smiled at Chad and said, "Donnie, remind me never to turn my back on this young man should it ever be our misfortune to meet him again."

"Aye, aye, Cap'n," Donnie chuckled.

Just then outraged shouts coming from the end of the alley drew the attention of all three, and they looked up to spy the gentleman whose purse they had stolen waving his fist at them. Deciding it was time to make a hasty exit, Garth grabbed his first mate's shirt sleeve, gave it a tug, and then bolted off down the alley in the opposite direction Chad close on their heels. Garth and Donnie purposely lost the lad in the crowd on the next block, and hurriedly returned to their ship since that was where they had been headed before all of this began. But Garth did not forget the lad though more than two years passed before he saw him again.

Through a turn of bad luck, Garth then found himself

in Newgate prison sharing a huge cell with a dozen or so other prisoners. One of them was the lad, and Garth recognized him right off. He hadn't changed much except that he now had a hard, callous look about him, and his disposition was cold and ruthless. Wondering if the thief would remember him, Garth casually moved closer to where he sat with his back to the wall, knees drawn up and arms wrapped around them. Only his eyes moved to look at Garth, silently warning him to back off. But Garth wasn't intimidated. Dropping down onto the bed of dirty straw, Garth assumed a position similar to his companion's.

"Name's Garth Lathrop," he said. "What's yours?"

The muscle in Chad's cheek flexed, but he remained silent.

Giving him a sidelong glance, Garth smiled at his stubbornness. "You don't remember me, do you?"

Dark eyes settled on him for a moment before Chad turned his head to watch the scuffle going on between two of their cell mates. "I remember," he answered flatly.

Surprise showed briefly on Garth's face, for he knew if the tables were turned, he wouldn't be so calm. "It's been a long time since then," Garth continued, wondering if the young man was holding back an urge to slam his fist into Garth's jaw.

"Two years, three months and five days," Chad replied. He glanced over at Garth, a vague, almost frightening half-smile lifting one corner of his mouth. "But who's keeping track?"

"Obviously, you are." Garth frowned, failing to understand why.

The fight that had started as a pushing match suddenly exploded into a full-fledged brawl, and because of the lack of anything else with which to occupy themselves, nearly everyone in the cell joined in. For a few minutes, it was contained to one-half of the area. Then it began to spread, and to keep from being drawn into the ruckus, both Garth and Chad hurriedly vacated their spots near the wall. At that moment, Garth came upon an idea, for he heard the angry shouts of the guards who had come to break up the row. Grabbing a handful of Chad's tattered shirt, he yanked him closer to the cell door.

"If the fools are stupid enough to unlock this," he whispered into Chad's ear, "then you and I are out of here."

"And then what?" Chad argued. "We get beaten to a pulp for trying to escape?"

"This isn't the first time I've been here. I know a way out that isn't guarded." He pulled back when a wildly thrown punch nearly hit him in the head. "Are you with me or not?"

Side-stepping out of the way of two men who were trying to wrestle each other to the floor, Chad replied, "I guess anything's better than this."

"All right. Then I'll tell you want I want you to do." Wrapping an arm around Chad's shoulders, he pulled him closer. "Just as soon as the door's opened, I want you to hit me. And make it look good."

"That won't be hard," Chad jeered, bringing a smile to his companion's face.

"Yeah, well just make sure you don't knock me out or you'll be on your own," Garth warned. "I'll fall through the door, and I want you to follow me out. That way if one of the guards stays in the corridor, the two of us can jump him. Got it?"

A suspicious frown creased the other's brow. "Yes. But I'd like to know why you're including me in this."

Garth smiled and shrugged his wide shoulders. "For one, I need you. For another, I guess I feel I owe you."

"That you do," Chad responded, then nodding toward the guard who was about to twist the key in the lock, he took a step backward, ready to strike when Garth gave him the signal.

The door to the cell swung open, and to their satisfaction, both guards entered, swinging their clubs and shouting above the din that the fight must stop or the prisoners would suffer the consequences. Thus, Garth and Chad easily slipped out without being noticed. Their way was dark except for the flickering yellow glow cast by an occasional torch hanging on the wall. Chad stayed close to Garth, for it seemed the damp, stone passageway was taking them deeper into the prison. When they heard the hurried footsteps of two people coming toward them, Garth motioned for Chad to hide in the shadows. A moment later, two guards appeared and Garth wasted no time in jumping them. The surprise of the attack caught both men unawares and once Chad joined in, they were easily subdued and knocked unconscious. Their next encounter was with the sleeping guard at the back entrance to the prison. Garth quickly clubbed him across the back of his neck, stole his keys, and opened the door to freedom. The pair never stopped running until they had reached the docks and the safety of the crowd of workers moving about the pier.

"You—got some place—to go?" Garth asked once they had staggered to a halt, breathless and tired, but exhilarated.

Bending forward with his hands on his knees, Chad shook his head, too winded to answer any other way.

"Ever thought about—being a sailor?" Garth puffed, leaning against a barrel while he caught his breath. "Or I should say—a pirate?" He raised his brows suggestively.

"I don't know anything about—boats," Chad confessed, pressing his fingers over the ache in his side.

"Ships, mate," Garth corrected. "They're called ships—frigates to be exact. And—I could always—use another deckhand. You interested?"

Standing erect and stretching his cramped muscles for a minute, Chad gave the proposition considerable thought. At least on board a ship he'd be guaranteed a meal, and staying in London right now wasn't a very good idea—not for a while, anyway. Besides, he owed this man. A strange smile appeared on his face and he nodded. "Yeah, I'm interested."

Smiling broadly, Garth held out his hand. "Then welcome aboard, mate—or do you have a name?"

Accepting the handshake, Chad replied, "LaShelle. Chad LaShelle."

"LaShelle," Garth repeated with a frown. "I've heard that name before, but I can't place it. Seems to me some high and mighty lord had an illegitimate son by that name—"

"*Had* is correct," Chad replied bitterly, turning to look out at the monstrous ships anchored near the pier. "One of these belong to you?"

Garth's frown lingered as he pointed out the *Black Falcon*. He wondered what had happened between this young man and his father to provoke the hatred in Chad's voice when he spoke of him, but he knew he'd never find out unless Chad wanted it that way. Stepping up next to him, he draped an arm around Chad's neck and said, "Let's see if we can find someone to row us out to her."

The crew of the pirate vessel—she was flying the British flag while anchored in the Thames—greeted her captain with cheers and surprise. They had known that Garth Lathrop would somehow figure out a way to escape from prison but not that he would do it this soon, and now that he had, and he was on board the *Black Falcon* again, they realized they must weigh anchor and head out to sea as soon as possible. Someone would be looking for them and soon!

Nonetheless, Garth introduced Chad to each member of his crew, including Donnie Holman, his first mate, and Garth instantly noticed that Chad's features hardened when Donnie welcomed him on board. The young man had reason to dislike him and his first mate for what they had done two years ago, but the expression on Chad's face and in his eyes was more akin to hatred. Right then, Garth vowed to keep a close eye on his new crewman.

For the next two years. Chad sailed with Garth and the crew of the *Black Falcon,* and he proved to be an excellent student as well as a merciless pirate. He fought as well as any man on the ship, and his natural talent with a sword soon made him most dangerous. Yet, through it all, Chad stayed to himself. He never laughed and seldom joined the crew on shore at a local pub. He did, however, have an unquenchable thirst for women, and with his good looks, he was never long without one. The *Black Falcon* sailed as far north as Norway and then south to Brazil, attacking any ship she came across and stealing whatever was on board. While his shipmates squandered their share of the take on food, women, and drink, Chad never did. Whatever jewelry, rich cloth, or furs he received as his cut, he sold, and he kept his gold coins locked up somewhere among his things. No one ever entertained the thought of stealing them from him—not after what had happened to one of their mates.

William S. Ryder, better known as Blackie because of the dark circles under his eyes, had a passion for rum, so much so that he spent the better part of each day staggering drunk. Whenever his supply ran out, he'd turn mean, and most of the crewmen on the *Black Falcon* would forfeit their own bottles rather than fight him for them. Chad, however, would not. The *Falcon* had been at sea for nearly two weeks when Blackie suddenly discovered he had consumed every bottle of rum aboard, his own as well as his crewmates'. He'd even tasted the last of Captain Lathrop's, and that left only one other possibility—the quiet, dangerous Chad LaShelle.

At first, Blackie decided he'd hold out until they sailed into the next port instead of going up against LaShelle, but by the time two hours had passed, his hands were shaking and his stomach was beginning to cramp. Forcing himself to wait until it was Chad's turn to take the helm, Blackie quietly sneaked down to the crew's quarters and the bunk where Chad slept. Thinking to find a bottle of rum in LaShelle's sea chest, he stuck the blade of his knife in the lock and began to pry it loose. He had just about succeeded when he was roughly seized by his shirt collar, yanked to his feet, and hurled nearly the width of the cabin. He rolled several times before his shoulder slammed against the wall, and although the pain was almost unbearable, he ignored it to turn fearful eyes on the man before him, a plea for mercy and understanding on his lips. There wasn't much in life that frightened Blackie, but the rage glowing in Chad's eyes turned his blood to ice, and a strangled cry escaped him as he witnessed Chad pull his sword. Certain the young man could be persuaded to wait long enough for Blackie to explain, Blackie raised his hand in front of him, the fingers fanned wide, and opened his mouth to speak. But before a single word had passed his lips, Chad drew the sword to one side, then whipped it across the man's outstretched fingers, severing the first three and nicking the fourth. Blackie screamed in pain, clutched his bloody hand to his chest, and crumpled to the floor, twisting and moaning in agony. His cries brought the rest of the crew scrambling to the cabin to see what had happened. Chad waited until the last man had entered, then he raised the bloodstained sword in the air, pointing it at them.

"*No one* steals from Chad LaShelle and lives," he snarled, and much to the horror of those who watched, he stepped forward, took Blackie by the hair, lifted him up to his knees, and thrust the sword into the man's chest, killing him instantly.

Life on board the *Black Falcon* took a different turn after that. Garth could see that his crew had a new respect for the young man he had freed from prison, and although they made certain they never crossed Chad or made him angry, Garth noticed that they were always trying to win his approval. That worried him. And it worried his first mate. Both men sensed that Garth Lathrop was beginning to lose his power of command. For the two years Chad had been with the *Black Falcon*, they had sailed haphazardly wherever the winds took them, with never a destination in mind. Months could pass before they came upon a ship to pirate, and while the others didn't seem to mind, Chad thought this was a waste of time. He had told Garth so. Indeed, he'd proposed they have some sort of plan, a method of learning which vessels carried large cargos that would be worth attacking, rather than hitting merchant ships at random and sometimes coming up empty-handed. Garth had listened to the young man's suggestions, but hadn't done anything about them. He enjoyed his leisurely way of life, and what Chad proposed would take too much effort. He regretted his decision about three months later, when he was abruptly awakened by the pressure of the muzzle of Chad's pistol against his temple.

"What the hell's the meaning of this?" Garth scowled, but he did not move until Chad motioned for him to get up.

"I think it's rather obvious, don't you?" Chad smiled back, waving Garth toward the door of the cabin. "You're being replaced."

"By you?" Garth didn't have to ask. He already knew the answer. "The least you can do is tell me why. I thought breaking you out of prison and giving you a job

76

on my ship repaid you for that incident back in London."

"If that was all you owed me, it probably would have," Chad admitted.

Garth stumbled backward out the door, a frown on his face. "What do you mean if that was all? We only stole a few gold coins from you. That hardly warrants taking my ship!"

Switching the pistol to his other hand, Chad unsheathed his sword and returned the gun to his belt. He pointed the tip of the blade toward the side of the ship and the rope ladder dangling over the edge. Numb, Garth obeyed, his eyes darting from one man to the next as the entire crew gathered to watch. The seamen were silent, but approval for Chad's actions glowed in their eyes. At the railing, he glanced over the side and saw Donnie Holman waiting for him in the longboat; then he turned a confused frown on Chad.

"Why?" he demanded.

"Breaking me out of prison repays me for the gold coins," Chad coldly explained. "Your ship will make us even on the years I spent in that rat-infested hole. You see, Captain, you and your first mate managed to get away from that fat man screaming about being robbed. I wasn't as fortunate. The way I see it, I wouldn't have had to spend even a day in that prison if you and Donnie boy hadn't interfered."

"You've been plotting this out since the minute I was thrown into that cell with you, haven't you?" Garth hissed.

Chad shook his head. "No. I decided to teach you a lesson the first time you laid a hand on me there in the street. You just made it easier by giving me a job on your ship."

Carelessly, angrily, Garth slapped the tip of Chad's sword. "Then why not just run us through? Let us die like men, instead of setting us adrift."

77

An evil smile parted Chad's lips. "Because I want you to think for a while—the same way I had to think. But you'll be luckier than me. You won't last two years, three months and five days."

He nodded at the four men standing closest to Garth, and they quickly seized him by the arms and legs, lifted him in the air, and threw him overboard.

Garth thought about that now as he lay on the straw cot in his cell listening to the rain outside the prison, and he could still remember the look on Chad LaShelle's face that morning, the way he himself had laughed as he'd climbed into the longboat with Donnie.

"You were a shrewd one, Chad LaShelle," he whispered in the darkness. "But not shrewd enough. You didn't count on Donnie and me making it to land." His laughter rumbled through the stone cell, frightening two of his four-legged companions into seeking out a corner. "I'll bet you lost a year's growth the first time you saw us after that, even though you didn't act surprised." Sitting up, he leaned back against the wall, drew up his knees, and wrapped his arms around them, mentally going over Charles Wadsworth's proposal.

Although Garth Lathrop could be ruthless at times— nearly as savage as Chad—he honestly held no hatred in his heart for what LaShelle had done to him some nine years before. In truth, he respected Chad LaShelle, felt the young man had a purpose in life—although Garth wasn't sure exactly what it was—and nothing would stop him from achieving it. Chad had a brilliant mind and could catch on to anything faster than any man Garth had ever known. It would be such a waste to kill him. But then again, with Chad out of the way, the island and its people would be Garth's for the taking. A devious smile kinked his mouth. And, of course, there was Chad's treasure. No one had ever seen it, but everyone knew that somewhere on that island, Chad had hidden every coin he had ever stolen. That cache alone would be worth the risk entailed in trying to kill him. However, such a move would take a lot of careful planning, and once Chad permitted Garth's badly damaged ship to drop anchor off shore—the damage would be purposely inflicted by the crew—Garth would have to execute his plan as quickly as possible. Chad would become suspicious otherwise. And wouldn't it be fitting, after he had killed Chad, to sail off in the *Black Falcon,* the ship Chad had taken from him?

He laughed suddenly, thinking that would be most fitting, but better still, before the *Challenger* set sail this afternoon with Charlie's help, he'd do a little investigating on his own. Whatever the man's reason for wanting his half brother dead, it had to involve money, and Garth meant to have a share of it.

Yawning, he stretched out on the cot and closed his eyes, unconscious of the flea which had hidden itself in his thick growth of beard.

Chapter Four

For the past hour, Jennifer had been too frightened and apprehensive about her immediate future to speak a single word to the man whose arms encircled her as he held the reins and guided the stallion along the beach. But she was very much aware of the feel of his hardened frame, which was molded against her each time the animal took a step or pranced sideways; and the thin fabric of the shirt she wore did little to ease the turbulent emotions his closeness aroused. The white, silk garment hung from her shoulders in gracious folds, and would have complimented any man who donned it, provided he had broad enough shoulders. For Jennifer, it proved disastrous, however. Although it was long enough to reach midthigh when she stood, perching sideways on the back of a high-spirited animal forced the garment to ride up, and she was constantly tugging it back into place. If anything, she didn't want to pique the captain's interest again. She knew he'd have no qualms about reining the horse to a stop right there on the beach and taking her in the same manner as he had before. Yet, every time she pulled on the hem of the shirt, the neckline plunged downward and nearly exposed her breasts. Finally, out of desperation, she began to unfold the tattered remnants of

81

her once-beautiful lavender dress and lay them across her lap, only to have the captain yank them and the camisole from her hands and fling them out into the water.

"What are you doing?" she moaned, trying to slide off the stallion. Strong arms tightened around her, keeping her in place. "They're all I have."

"I'll get you something else to wear," he barked irritably. "Besides, there isn't enough of them to piece together. Now sit still before this horse decides to throw us off his back."

Tears quickly gathered in her eyes as she watched the pale violet cloth float along the shoreline, catch a small wave, and then wash up onto the beach. It wasn't just the dress she had lost. The garment represented her last tie with home. Giving it up was like saying good-bye to her past. Biting her lower lip, she lowered her head and tried not to think about it.

Chad's dark brows knotted as he studied the path his steed took. He couldn't understand why a simple piece of cloth meant so much to this slip of a girl. It was only a dress. There were plenty more to be had in the village. She'd forget about it soon enough. Unknowingly, his gaze drifted to the top of her blond head, then followed the bright golden strands of hair falling over her shoulders. He breathed in the scent of her. He had been with many women in his life, but none as fragile and soft-spoken as this one. A dark brow raised appreciatively. And none with the kind of courage it must have taken for her to survive all this time on her own. A faint smile parted his lips. She was special . . . this little lady who had come into his life most unexpectedly.

Jennifer could hardly believe what she saw once the captain had reined the stallion up a steep incline, through a stand of palm trees and tall ferns, and out into the open. Nestled high above the shoreline and protected on three sides by the tall volcanic-rock bluffs surrounding it lay a small hamlet, its shoppes and two-story houses stirring up images of the London her father had described. Fishing boats filled the cove, while in deeper waters a huge frigate rode at anchor, its sails hoisted and its tall masts silhouetted against the fiery backdrop of the dying sun. The sight almost made her laugh. While she was fighting to stay alive and thinking that she was doomed to spend the rest of her days in solitude, a short hour's ride away was a village. She squeezed her eyes shut, then opened one at a time, expecting all of the buildings to disappear. They didn't, and as the stallion cantered on, she sensed that something was wrong. Why would this man, a pirate and self-proclaimed enemy of principled people, boldly rein his horse onto the road leading directly into the center of the town? Could it possibly be that the captain and his band of cutthroats had seized the little hamlet and held its mayor hostage, threatening to kill him if the villagers didn't do exactly as they were told? A confused frown marred her smooth brow as they approached the first building on the outskirts of the small town. It didn't appear that way from what she could see, for there were no guards and those who walked the streets did not look frightened upon glancing up and espying the couple riding in. She tugged at the hemline of the shirt again.

Jennifer noticed something else about the town that struck her as peculiar. Each building had a clean look about it, as if it were only a few years old, some with fresh paint, others with raw, bleached wood that hadn't had time to weather. It was almost as if the place had sprung up over night. She was almost sure of it once she realized that there wasn't a single child to be seen . . . anywhere. An eerie chill raced up her spine, and she shivered, aware of the eyes fixed on her as a crowd began to grow and fall into step behind them.

"'Ey, Cap'n," one of the men in the group called out, "what ye got there? Modesty ain't gonna like it."

The proclamation was followed by a hearty round of laughter, and it made Jennifer feel as though she was about to intrude upon a very delicate situation. Was it possible that Modesty was the captain's wife? She cringed at the thought, envisioning a buxom woman dressed in suede breeches and sporting a pistol in one hand, a knife in the other; and she wondered if she'd make it through the night without having her throat slit.

The captain reined the stallion toward a large stone building at the end of the street. The sign hanging above its door read Freedom Inn, and Jennifer silently prayed that it would live up to its name, that once she stepped inside, no one could make any claim on her. More than anything, she wanted to be free—free of the man who had brought her here, free to leave the island, and free to set about forgetting everything that had happened to her.

By the time they reached the hitching post near the front door, the crowd had grown to such a size that it annoyed her. These people were behaving as if they were welcoming home a conquering hero rather than a man who deserved nothing more than a dark, damp prison cell. Wasn't it obvious to them what had happened? Shouldn't someone be demanding an explanation? Just then a man stepped out of the inn, followed by a rush of others who shoved through the doorway for a better view. He crossed the wooden sidewalk and came to stand beside the jittery horse, grabbing the animal's reins and firmly hanging onto them when the beast shied away.

"Captain," he said with a polite nod of his head. His green eyes shifted to Jennifer, quickly noting her attire or the lack of it, then returned to her companion. "We were beginning to think something happened to you." A hint of a smile twitched at the corners of his mouth and his gaze lowered to the captain's bare chest. "Apparently, it did."

A ripple of laughter floated through those close enough to hear, but Chad's quick, warning scowl instantly silenced them. He wasn't in the mood for games. Gritting his teeth, he caught Jennifer around the waist, then effortlessly lifted her from the stallion and set her on the ground before he, too, swung free of the animal.

"Where's Modesty?" he snapped.

"In her room, I guess," Jason shrugged. "Haven't seen her since you left."

Suddenly irritated by the gawking stares of those who watched, and angered even more when he couldn't explain why, he somewhat roughly took Jennifer's arm above the elbow and dragged her toward the entrance to the inn. "Have someone see to my horse, Jason," he ordered, frowning all the more once he saw the pleased smiles of the men who stepped aside for him. "And the rest of you find something to do."

Heads and eyes lowered instantly as those guilty of dawdling quickly moved away, choosing to busy themselves with whatever they could find rather than answer to their captain. Yet, a few courageous ones lingered long enough to steal one last peek at the beautiful blonde Captain LaShelle had brought back with him, and everyone was envious. Suddenly his rule giving right of ownership to the man who found something didn't seem quite fair, and a few disgruntled murmurs came from the men he had ordered back to work.

Instinct had warned Jennifer not to voice her plight and beg for help. There was something oddly different about this situation, and it was too soon to distinguish who among these people didn't support the pirate captain, who might be willing to help her. Thus, she decided it was best to keep her mouth shut and her ears open to the things going on around her. Sooner or later

85

she'd find someone brave enough to stand up to the man. She just had to.

The captain didn't slow his pace once they stepped inside, but hurried her across the room toward the staircase opposite them. Nor did anyone try to stop him. They didn't, however, escape the suggestive whistles sent their way, and although the captain acted as if that didn't bother him, she knew it had when his grip tightened around her arm. At the top of the steps was a long hallway that ran past several doors on one side. He took her to the one at the far end, catching the latch and quickly swinging the wooden barrier open. Without a word, he shoved her inside, then slammed the door behind her before she could even turn around. The sound of a key turning in the lock made her spin about in panic. Did he intend to keep her a prisoner in this room for the rest of her life? Tears suddenly filled her blue-green eyes when she realized how strong a possibility that really was. Rushing forward, she pressed an ear against the door, listening for his footsteps to fade before trying the knob.

She jumped back when the deafening crash of a door being thrown open echoed from somewhere close by, and angry voices soon followed the sound. She couldn't hear what was said except for the string of oaths a woman hurled at the intruder, and Jennifer suddenly wondered if this might be the one referred to as Modesty. Her stomach knotted, for she feared that she might be the cause of the argument and she dreaded what the repercussions could be. She turned around to examine the room. Maybe she shouldn't wait for someone's help.

The two-story drop from the window changed Jennifer's mind about using this method of escape, unless, of course, she could get her hands on a length of rope, one that would easily lower her to the ground. One corner of her lovely mouth twitched. It wasn't very likely she'd find one here—a smile danced in her eyes—but it wouldn't hurt to look. Standing in the center of the room, tiny fists perched on narrow hips, she began to study the interior from top to bottom.

It was a surprisingly large room with a huge fourposter bed standing against one wall. The rich, red velvet canopy with its side curtains pulled back and tied to each bedpost matched the luxurious spread. A hint of disapproving frown wrinkled Jennifer's smooth brow as she thought how unnecessary the heavy cloth was. The nights here proved too warm to have need of it. On each side of the bed was a night stand, one holding a water pitcher and bowl, the other a brass hurricane lamp. A gigantic armoire filled the space between the two windows in the room, and to her right stood a large dresser with a mirror hanging above it. In one corner, a rocker sat, while in another was a folding screen. The walls were freshly painted and the wood floor sparkled. All in all, Jennifer decided, it might not be too bad a place to stay in . . . for a while.

Crossing to the tall armoire, she lifted the brass latch and swung the doors wide, her tiny chin dropping once she saw the clothes hanging inside. She had honestly expected to find it empty, not filled with a man's apparel. She slammed the doors shut and fell back against them, her heart racing. And to which man did the clothing belong? She squeezed her eyes shut, knowing the answer without having to be told. This was the captain's room, and just like everything in it, she, too, now belonged to him. She raised a trembling hand to touch her fevered brow.

"This is a nightmare," she groaned, realizing the urgency of escape.

Standing erect, she glanced at the window, then back at the bed. Maybe there wasn't a rope to be had, but the sheets would work equally well. All she had to do was rip them into long pieces and tie them together, then anchor

87

one end to the leg of armoire and dangle the other out the window. With a determined gleam in her eye, she set about executing her plan.

"Where did you find her, Cap'n?" Jason asked as the two men shared a mug of ale in the commons.

Propping one booted foot up on the bench on which he sat, Chad draped an arm over his knee and stared off into the distance. "About an hour's ride along the beach. I came across her camp near where we found the wreckage of the *Sea Lady*, and followed her trail from there."

"How do you suppose she got here?"

"Believe it or not, she was one of the passengers," Chad announced, lifting the tankard to his lips.

"My God. You mean that poor little lady has been on her own for over a week?" Jason's eyes lowered to the broad, bare shoulders of his friend. "I'll bet she's thinking she was better off."

Chad's dark head jerked around and he glared at his companion. "She was living on coconuts," he snarled, "and sleeping in a hut made out of palm leaves. Do you honestly think she'd prefer that over what she has now?"

Jason hid his smile behind the mug he raised to his lips. "Probably not," he muttered into the tankard. "At least now she'll have something to wear." He took a sip of ale, then added, "Must have been horrible for her to run around the beach all this time without a stitch on."

The muscle along Chad's jaw flexed. "What is it you want to hear me say, Jason? That I bedded the wench?"

The man quickly raised both hands in front of him, fingers fanned wide. "Just making conversation."

"No, you're not," Chad remarked. "For some reason you enjoy provoking me. So, in order to bring an end to this inane chatter, I'll tell you. Aye, I bedded her . . . right there on the beach. And she was wearing my shirt because I tore her clothes to shreds." He glared off across the room muttering, "I doubt there's a person on this island stupid enough not to have figured that out by now."

"So why does the fact that you bedded her upset you?"

"It doesn't," Chad growled, rubbing the back of his hand inside the stubble on his chin. He wasn't about to tell Jason that she had been a virgin. He'd never taken a virgin before, not by force anyway.

Knowing when not to press, Jason decided to change the subject. "So what do you plan to do with her?"

"Do with her?" Chad repeated. "What kind of a question is that?"

"Well, you don't intend to keep her here against her will, do you? If she was a passenger on that ship, she was going to England for some reason or another. She's probably got someone waiting for her."

"And when the ship doesn't arrive, whoever it is will think she drowned with the rest of them," Chad irritably pointed out.

"So you are planning to keep her here." Jason frowned. "What are you going to do, lock her up for the remainder of her life? Every chance she gets, she'll try to run away."

"And go where? This is an island, remember?" He lifted the mug to his lips and downed the rest of his ale.

What had started out as good-natured ribbing suddenly had turned serious. Leaning forward against the table, Jason crossed his arms in front of him and lowered his voice so that only his captain would hear. "Chad, I've never known you to let a woman cloud your common sense. It's dangerous to keep her here, and you know it. I realize the chances are slim, but think of what might happen if she escaped, hid somewhere on the island, and signaled a passing ship. So far we've been lucky. No one knows we're here, but she could change all that. If you take her to England—"

A huge hand slammed against the table top. "Enough!" Chad roared, bringing everyone's attention to him. But he didn't notice nor would he have cared if he had. *"I'm the one who rules here, and anyone who doesn't like what I do is free to go."* He bolted to his feet, glared at Jason for a moment, then leaned his weight forward on the knuckles of one fist pressed against the table top. "And that includes you," he hissed.

An eerie silence filled the inn as each and every man there waited for the captain's first mate to reply. The two had argued before, but never so violently. In fact, Jason Bingham was the only man among them who ever dared question the captain's orders. Rumor had it that although Mr. Bingham owed the captain for getting him out of debtor's prison, as everyone on the island did, the captain owed Mr. Bingham for saving his life many years ago. Neither man would talk about it, but everyone was sure that was the *only* reason Captain LaShelle tolerated the man's straightforwardness. Had any of them spoken their minds to him, they would have had to defend themselves or find someplace else to live.

Jason's own temper flared, and he was about to stand up and tell the hardheaded renegade to do whatever he liked for all he cared, but just then Modesty's earsplitting shriek rent the air.

"Ye open this door, ye bloody bitch, 'fore I 'ave Cap'n LaShelle break it in!" The shrill words were followed by the distinct sound of something heavy striking a solid object.

Chad nearly knocked the table over trying to get around it in order to race for the stairs. Taking them two at a time, Jason right on his heels as well as half the men from the commons, Chad never lost stride as he reached the top and turned down the hall. At the far end stood Modesty, a clean dress draped over her arm, a wooden bucket in her other hand, and water spilled on the floor. Not having noticed Chad's arrival since her attention was focused on the closed door, she brought the bucket back a second time and swung it forward as hard as she could, splashing water all about, down the front of her own skirt as well.

"Ye 'ear me, Miss 'Igh and Mighty? Open this door! I ain't gonna take no blame for this." Of a sudden, she was flung out of the way by the hand that caught her elbow.

"What's going on?" Chad demanded. "How could you be locked out?"

"I don't know, gov'na," Modesty snapped. "I came 'ere with the dress like ye told me, used the key ye gave me, but the door won't budge. Ain't my fault the *liedy* don't want a bath."

Knowing the little temptress had placed something before the door, Chad motioned for the others to stand aside as he moved back a step or two. Then he turned, lowered his shoulder, and hurled himself against the wooden barrier. The door edged open a ways under the abuse, and once he could wrap his fingers around the side of it, he used his weight and strength to push it open all the way. What he saw once he had a clear view of the interior enraged him, and for several moments he just stood there glaring at the open window and the knotted length of white rope disappearing over the sill. The bare muscles across his back stiffened, the cords in his neck gleamed in the fading light of day, and everyone who witnessed his fury silently thanked God it wasn't centered on him.

He was about to turn around when he spotted his white shirt lying on the floor near the armoire. He crossed to it and picked it up, wondering, for a second, if the crazy wench had fled without anything on. Then he noticed the wardrobe's door was ajar. Opening it all the way, a brief examination told him that she had simply exchanged the shirt for something else, something that might help her escape by disguising those shapely limbs and that rich, thick, blond hair. She was a crafty one, this little sea nymph, but not crafty enough. He'd find her. And when he did . . .

Slamming the door to the armoire shut with a bang, he spun around and headed for the exit, pulling up short when he saw Jason standing in the way. He raised a finger and pointed it at the man's nose.

"Not a word," he ground out. "Don't . . . say . . . a word."

Jason hated it when he was right about something, especially when his accuracy went against his friend's grain. Dropping his gaze, he started to move aside, only to be knocked out of the way by the broad shoulder that hit his own as Chad hurried from the room. The others quickly followed their captain, leaving Jason alone to ponder the fate of the young woman once Chad caught up to her. He had never known his friend to strike a woman, but none of those he'd known had done something like this. This one had made a fool of him. And Chad LaShelle didn't enjoy being played for a fool.

Lowering herself down the knotted lengths of sheeting had been easier than Jennifer thought. The hard part had been crossing the street without attracting too much attention. The captain's clothes were much too big for her, so much so that one look her way would arouse anyone's curiosity. Although she had hidden her long, blond hair beneath a red bandana, the baggy shirt and pants she wore wouldn't fool anyone into thinking she was anything other than a woman in men's clothing. Then God had graced her with a small piece of luck. Outraged cries from within the inn had turned everyone's attention in that direction, allowing her to slip past those walking the street. Without a moment's hesitation, she had raced across the dirt road and disappeared between two buildings. Beyond them lay the protective covering of ferns, bamboo, and palm trees, and hopefully her freedom. But just as she was about to step out of the alleyway and dash across the open space to the dense woodland, a door opened somewhere close by and she froze, holding to the shadows of early evening.

"Sounds like ol' Modesty don't like Captain LaShelle gettin' 'imself a new liedy," a man's voice proclaimed. As it was followed by the laughter of another, Jennifer's knees buckled, spilling her to the ground.

Chad LaShelle? her mind echoed. Dear God, it couldn't be! Of all the places in the world, how could she have managed to find herself here—on *his* island? If he ever learned who she was, he'd kill her! Scrambling behind a rain barrel when the two men suddenly appeared in the alley, Jennifer held her breath until they had passed by. If he ever found her again, she thought. Glancing out at the growing darkness enshrouding the woods, she wondered if there was a spot anywhere on the island where he wouldn't think to look. But then, what choice did she have? She couldn't just give up and let him find her sitting behind this barrel. If nothing else, she would make certain his search would be lengthy and very exasperating. Checking the narrow passageway once more to ascertain that no one would see her, Jennifer jumped to her feet and raced toward the woods.

During the next hour, she stopped only to pick a few berries to appease her mounting hunger, paused only long enough to listen for footsteps trailing her. She took comfort from the fact that all she heard was the rolling surf splashing inland and leaves rustling in the gentle breeze. With the disappearance of the sun, a bright silver moon and a blanket of glowing stars guided her way to the top of the first hill. From there she could look back and see the lights of the town below, and she relaxed a little, satisfied with the distance she had placed between herself and the pirate captain.

As she started down the other side of the hill, Jennifer realized that she had only two choices in her selection of a place to hide out. Along the beach or in a cave. The first option would allow her to fish and have something besides berries to eat, but it would be very easy for the captain to track her footprints in the sand. Her other alternative entailed climbing the highest hill and possibly finding a cave in which to seek shelter . . . if there was a cave on this island. From such a lofty elevation she could keep an eye on the activity in the hamlet, and she would be able to spot a ship sailing in any direction. Thus, with her mind made up, she set her sights on the tallest peak.

She walked until the moon was high overhead before she contemplated taking a rest. Her bruised feet demanded it. A short way ahead, she could see a cluster of rocks, and she decided that would be a good place to sit down. Once she had reached them, she was doubly glad she had traveled this far, for just on the other side of the rocks was a hot mineral spring. Without any hesitation, she pulled the red bandana from her head, circled the boulders, and quickly stepped into the water. Its warmth soothed away the aches in her tired limbs, and not caring that she would have to spend the next hour or so waiting for her clothes to dry, she sat down and let the water swirl all around her, finding the sudden urge to rid herself of the captain's scent too strong to resist. Floating to the edge of the spring, Jennifer rested the backs of her shoulders against a rock and stared up at the moon as she let her body soak in the warm water.

She didn't know much about Chad LaShelle, only what her father had told her, and that hadn't been a great deal. While she and her parents lived in England, they had been neighbors of Sir Charles Wadsworth and his wife,

Mary Elizabeth. Although her family wasn't as wealthy as the Wadsworths, her father and Wadsworth had greatly respected each other, and the two men had enjoyed a strong friendship that had begun long before Jennifer was born.

During the first ten years of their married life, Charles and Mary Elizabeth had remained childness because she had never been able to carry a child full term. According to Jennifer's father, Mary Elizabeth blamed herself for her husband's wandering eye, and when their French maid, Martine LaShelle, announced that she was going to have Charles's baby, Mary Elizabeth had no bitterness in her heart toward the woman or her husband. When Martine died giving birth to Chad, it was Mary Elizabeth who insisted they take the child and raise him as their own. Charles was thrilled, for although Chad wasn't Mary Elizabeth's son and would never carry the Wadsworth name, at least he wouldn't be cheated out of watching his offspring grow to manhood. So pleased was he to have actually fathered a child, he went to his good friend, George Grey, and made him promise that once George married and started his own family, his firstborn girl would marry Chad. Then, two years later, to everyone's surprise, Mary Elizabeth gave birth to a healthy boy, and they named him Charles.

Ten years passed, and the Wadsworth family seemed very happy. George Grey had married Katherine, and Jennifer was a year old. Then disaster struck. George had been called out to fight a duel, his opponent claiming that he had insulted his family name. It wasn't true, but honor demanded that George defend himself. Being skilled with a pistol, a fact well known in London, George intended to merely wound the man, but he discovered too late that the sights had been filed down. Instead of hitting his challenger in the shoulder, the lead ball struck the man in the head, killing him instantly. The family of the dead man then claimed George had cheated and threatened to have him hanged. Within the week, George packed up everything he owned, sold his estate in London, and moved his family to the Colonies.

Charles and George kept in touch even though an ocean separated them, and although her father didn't tell Jennifer everything, she did learn that Charles had had a bitter argument with Chad and that the fourteen-year-old boy had left home, vowing never to return. Shortly after that, her father announced that he and Sir Charles had decided that she should marry someone of noble birth rather than a bastard child like Chad LaShelle. The engagement was broken, and she then became betrothed to the young Charles Wadsworth.

Over the next fifteen years, the name of Chad LaShelle became as well known as that of the feared pirate Blackbeard. On his ship, the *Black Falcon*, he sailed the Atlantic, seizing any merchant ship that crossed his path. It was rumored that his crew was the worst group of buccaneers ever to sail the seas, and Jennifer knew that if this man learned her identity, her life would be worthless. He would look at her and see his father, and all the old hatreds she was sure he still carried would surface. He would take his revenge on her.

Her fingers and the palms of her hands were wrinkled by the time she decided to leave the spring and find a place to lie down so she might sleep for a while. As she studied the area and discovered that there wasn't a single spot that looked comfortable, she suddenly longed for the hammock she had been forced to leave behind. With a shake of her head, she told herself that wishing wouldn't get her anywhere—if it could, she'd be back home in Virginia—and she settled for a place that was thick with grass, ivy, and ferns. She fell asleep almost immediately.

To Jennifer's aching body and troubled mind, it seemed as though she had slept only a few hours when bright sunshine pierced through the leafy overhang and rudely disturbed her fitful slumber. Groaning her disapproval, she rolled to one side, blocking the glaring stream of light with an arm, and when her stomach growled, it only added to her irritable mood. Berries just weren't appealing anymore. Her mouth watered as she thought of how delectable a roasted rabbit smothered in a rich, brown gravy and topped off with fresh bread would be. Hurriedly, she sat up, knowing she would never enjoy such a treat as long as she was hiding out on this island, and it wouldn't do any good to torture herself by thinking about it.

Stretching, she came to her feet and quickly surveyed the area to make certain no one had stumbled across her trail and followed her. To her right, she saw a clearing through the tall, stately trunks of towering palm trees and beyond that point was her destination, the tallest peak on the island. Squaring her shoulders and filling her lungs with fresh, clean air, she started toward it.

As the sun defiantly hid its bright, glowing face behind the tall bluffs surrounding the village, the quickening shadows postponed Chad's search for Jennifer, the delay intensifying his rage over her escape. He had doubted she was foolish enough to return to the place where he had found her, but once the entire village had been scoured on the chance that she might be hiding in one of the buildings, he had ordered a group of men to ride along the beach just in case he'd been wrong about her. Meanwhile, he and Jason had ridden in the opposite direction. It was completely dark by the time the two parties returned to the hamlet, both empty-handed; and while everyone else sought out some form of relaxation, whether it be a mug of ale in the pub or a soft bed for the night, Chad chose to stand by the window in his room staring out at the tall,

97

dark silhouette of his frigate anchored in the bay. There was no use in trying to track her in the dark. About all he'd accomplish would be the destruction of her trail, and by the time morning came he'd be so tired he might miss something. Thus, he had decided, at Jason's urging, to wait until dawn. Then he would begin again, and he wouldn't stop until he found her.

He stripped off his clothes except for his breeches, and lay down on the bed, intending to go to sleep. But he couldn't rid his mind of the image of a beautiful, blond-haired woman, nor could he erase the memory of how easily she had stirred his passion. In the glow of moonlight cast through the window, Chad crossed his wrists and placed them behind his head, absently staring up at the canopy above him. She had made a fool of him, of everyone in the village for that matter, when she'd so easily escaped them. His dark brown eyes softened a mite, and a vague smile parted his lips as he thought about her. She was different from the women he had known, and for some odd reason he thought of Jennifer Grey, the young woman his father had arranged for him to marry. He wondered what he would be doing right now if things had turned out differently between his father and himself, if he hadn't run away fifteen long years ago. If he wasn't mistaken, Jennifer Grey would be close to twenty years old by now, and chances were that she would have been his wife for a year or so. He might even have a child, a son—

Chad spat out an oath and angrily swung his feet to the floor. Jennifer Grey was dead. And even if she wasn't, she would be marrying his half brother, not him. *They* would be the ones with a child. It would be *their* son his father would adore.

"Damn them," he growled. "Damn them all!" His insides twisting with rage, he left the bed and returned to the window, where he leaned forward, his arms spread wide, his hands pressed against the framework as he glared out into the night. Why had God seen fit to let her die? He needed her. He wanted his father to suffer the way he had all these years. He wanted to use her, then take her back to London and flaunt that fact in his father's face. He wanted all of the man's rich friends to learn that Charles's bastard son had stolen the woman meant to marry a man of nobility—a man with a name that meant something—that he'd made a whore out of her and then dumped her on their doorstep. Jerking upright, he sucked in a deep breath and turned back toward the bed. Well, maybe he didn't have Jennifer Grey to use, but that didn't mean he wouldn't find some other way to get even. Throwing himself down upon the mattress, he rolled onto his side, tucked one arm under the pillow, and closed his eyes. He'd think more about it tomorrow. Right now he needed to get some sleep. He had a woman to track in the morning.

Chad was up and dressed before anyone else in the town, just as he had planned to be. Finding the young woman was something he wanted to do alone . . . for several reasons. It was *his* rule that gold was divided among his crew and anything else belonged to the man who found it. That included the girl. Although he had been the first to find her, now that she was on her own again there might be trouble. He had seen the lustful gazes many of the men had given her when he had ridden in with her the night before, and he was sure that if someone else got to her first, he would have a hard time reclaiming her. Taking his pistol from the top of the dresser, he shoved the weapon into the sash around his waist and quietly left his room.

He started his search behind the inn at the spot where the girl had lowered herself to the ground. The earth was dry there, and her tracks were clearly visible in the dust. They circled around to the side of the building, and once they headed toward the street running through the middle of the village, Chad stopped and looked up. On the other side of the buildings across from him was the dense foliage of the woodlands. He stood staring at it for several minutes, trying to decide which direction he would take if he were the girl. A search of the beach the night before had assured him that she wasn't stupid enough to go somewhere where she could be easily seen, and he knew that she planned to make finding her as difficult as she possibly could. Irritated, he recalled Jason's warning that should the young woman escape, she would more than likely try to signal a passing ship. In order to do that, she would have to be at a vantage point from which she could see the entire circumference of the island and the water surrounding it. His dark eyes drifted to the rolling hills and to the tallest peak among them, a sudden urgency spurring him into action. Even though a British naval vessel had never sailed within spyglass range of the isle, he knew there could always be a first time, and he had to find the girl before their luck changed.

The climb to the top of the hill hadn't been easy for Jennifer. Several times the terrain had become very steep and it was often filled with thick vines, dense weddel ferns, clusters of palm trees, and large rocks she had to go around or pull herself over. By noon, she was both exhausted and hungry, and the only things that lifted her spirits were the breathtaking view from atop the ridge and the distance she had put between herself and the village. Now, she had to find something to eat, had to stack up a pile of wood to use for a signal fire. Thank God she had had the foresight to take the flint and steel she had found lying on the night stand next to the lamp. One corner of her mouth crimped sarcastically. And his knife. It would make stripping bark off trees much easier than it had been with a broken shell. And, of course, she could use it to defend herself . . . from any two-legged or four-legged beast that might happen upon her campsite.

It took her about an hour to find and stack the wood she thought necessary for a fire that would catch someone's attention. Once that was completed, she decided to investigate her surroundings on the chance that she might find a cave somewhere close by, or at least some form of shelter against the rain. It irritated her that she had to duplicate everything she had already made, but she preferred sleeping in a hammock to lying on the ground.

She had walked about a hundred yards when she thought she heard the trickling of water. Following the direction of the sound, she came upon a narrow stream, too shallow to bathe in, but at least she had water to drink. To the right, she spotted an assemblage of huge rocks that formed a kind of protective ledge, but its discovery wasn't what held her attention or brought the smile to her face. Just beyond was a rainbow of brightly colored flowers in a wide variety of sizes and shapes, and standing tall and proud in the center of them were a half-dozen or more spiraling plants with whorl-like clusters of fruit adorning them. Excitedly, she raced across the short distance to the fruit, picked up a long stick, and reached high above her head to tap several of the lower ones loose, catching them in her hands before they hit the ground. The peels were still rather green, and she had to use the knife to cut one open, but the yellow, spearlike fruit was ripe enough to eat, so she sat down in the midst of the wild flowers to enjoy her meal.

Jennifer hungrily devoured three of these fruits before the ache in her stomach went away and she actually felt full. The trek up the side of the hill had been tiring, and with the warmth of the bright sun shining in her face, her eyelids began to droop. She knew she shouldn't lounge

101

for even a minute when there was so much work to do, but then, who was to tell her that she couldn't? Stretching, she lay back in the tall grasses, surrounded by purple orchids, pink lilies, and white fuchsias, and closed her eyes. A moment later, she had drifted off to sleep.

Only a short while passed before Jennifer's dreams brought a frown to her brow, and she mumbled incoherently. She had been walking along a beautiful sandy stretch of beach. The sun glistened on the whitecapped waters of the ocean. Sea gulls circled overhead, and a warm breeze lifted the long, silky strands of her hair. A huge ship suddenly appeared on the horizon, its sails full as it caught the wind and cut through the choppy surface of the sea toward her. At first, the man at the helm resembled Arnold Lucas, and Jennifer frantically waved her arms in the air as she called out to him. But as the ship sailed closer, he began to change. His gray hair darkened. His narrow, rounded shoulders grew wide and strong. His plump belly flattened, and the gentle expression on his lined face turned hard and angry. He was no longer the sweet man who had taken her under his wing, but the fierce pirate captain Chad LaShelle. In her sleep, she screamed, and the sound ricocheted around in her brain and brought her to full wakefulness. She sat up and touched shaky fingertips to her damp brow. Her entire body was drenched in perspiration, and Jennifer suddenly knew that these nightmares would never end until she was off this island and safely tucked away in the huge mansion that was her home in Virginia.

A twig snapped somewhere near the grouping of rocks she had decided to use as her refuge, and when she lifted her eyes to look in the direction of the sound, she numbly wondered if her dream had spilled over into the daylight hours. She blinked, glanced down at the flowers surrounding her, then back up at the tall, muscular

102

figure glaring at her. It took her a full minute or more to realize that the captain wasn't a figment of her imagination, and that if she didn't get up, right now, he'd be on her before she had the chance to run. Her hand moved to the knife lying on the ground beside her. If she couldn't escape him, at least this time she'd be able to defend herself.

Jennifer's body trembled with fear as she slowly drew herself up on to her knees, her blue-green eyes locked on the angry face above her, her hand gripping the leather-bound handle of the knife. She clamped her teeth together to stop them from rattling and guardedly came to her feet, ready to attack the moment he advanced.

Dark eyes shadowed by an ominous frown raked over her, and though he stood some twenty feet away, Jennifer could feel the heat of his fury even at that distance. She gulped and held her weapon out in front of her as a silent warning that she intended to use it. A flash of white teeth against bronze skin sent a chill down her spine when he returned the threat in an easy manner that told her he welcomed the challenge. Then his hand moved to the butt of the pistol he carried in the sash around his waist, and Jennifer gasped, thinking he planned to simply shoot her rather than fight fairly. In a panic, she dropped the knife, spun around, and raced off into the trees.

Tears flooded her eyes, blinding her. But her mind was vividly clear, for she knew that at any second a shot would ring out and a lead ball would pierce her flesh. She didn't want to be his prisoner, but she didn't want to die either. Visions of her body lying on the ground, twisting and turning in agony, of blood pouring from her wound, and of the pirate standing over her, laughing, filled her head. It was just too much. A sob tore through her and before she could get a grip on her emotions, she burst into tears. She didn't know where she was going. Everything around her was a green blur. Huge leaves

103

lashed out at her. Ferns and palm branches threatened to knock her down. Her chest hurt and her strength was failing. Finally, too weak to take another step, she stumbled to a stop and fell to her knees, sobbing hysterically.

Chad had only meant to lay aside his pistol, not shoot her as she'd obviously thought he was going to do. He had no desire to kill her, but he wasn't against giving her a few bruises which he thought she deserved for all the trouble she'd put him through. It hadn't been too difficult to track her once he'd found the footprints in the soft earth behind the village. They had headed right into the woods and had then gone in a direction that convinced him he had been correct in his assumption of where she planned to hide out. About an hour later, her tracks had led to a mineral spring, beside which he'd found a red bandana, and he'd figured this was where she had spent the night. He was sure of it when he'd noticed a place where the tall grasses had yet to spring back to full height as though the weight of some*thing* or some*one* had crushed them. That told him she wasn't very far ahead of him.

He had walked for another hour or so, climbing over roots and the fallen bamboo trees that lay in his path and wondering how a woman of her size and strength had managed to come this far. Then he'd looked up and seen her. She was still a good distance ahead of him, but he knew it wouldn't be long before he'd catch up to her.

Once he'd stood on the ridge and seen the pile of wood she had collected, he'd quickly glanced out toward sea, silently breathing a sigh of relief that he had been able to find her. From this lofty height, a blaze of the size she planned to ignite would attract the attention of the entire British Navy should it just happen to be in the area. Frowning, he'd glanced back over his shoulder in the direction he was sure she had taken. The little twit would probably never give up trying, he'd thought. What could

104

he do to guarantee that she would? An idea had come to mind, one he'd felt certain she wouldn't like, and he'd turned around to go after her.

He hadn't believed it was possible, but when he'd seen her lying there sound asleep amidst a colorful assortment of flowers, it was as if he'd forgotten how beautiful she was. His blood had stirred, and he'd been tempted to take her right there, but at that moment, she'd roused from sleep and sat up. His desire had faded, and in its place, he'd felt an odd sense of pride in the way she had taken care of herself these past days, something most women wouldn't have been able to do. Then she'd come to her feet and pointed the knife at him. She'd been ready to fight him, and he'd looked forward to it. It had surprised him when she'd dropped her weapon and run off, and when he'd caught up to her and found her sobbing like some half-crazed madwoman, it angered him. She was acting like all the other women he'd known. When all else fails, cry.

"Get up," he hissed, grabbing her wrist and yanking her to her feet. When she continued to weep, he gave her a rough shake that sent her long, golden hair shimmering around her shoulders. "And stop that damned crying before I do something that will give you good reason to weep."

Some sanity returned with his harsh threat, and Jennifer bit her lower lip, trying to regain control. She turned tear-filled eyes to look at him and swallowed hard. "Such as?" she courageously challenged. "What more can you do to me than you have already?"

Dark brown eyes returned her glare, and he was quiet for a time before asking, "What's your name?"

Jennifer's tears dried instantly and fear replaced her anguish. "M-my name?"

"Yes," he sneered. "You do have a name, don't you?"

She nodded her head while her mind raced in search of a suitable one.

"Well?" he demanded when she took too long to answer. "What is it?"

"Jennifer . . . Lucus. I am Jennifer Lucus," she hastily replied, cursing herself for not being able to come up with something a little more distant from her own name. She truly regretted her choice when he cocked his head to one side and looked as if he didn't believe her. She dropped her gaze away from him.

"Well, Jennifer," he said after a moment, "it isn't so much what *I* can do to you as what my men can do."

She could feel the blood drain from her face. "Your . . . men?"

His mouth twisted in a crazy half-smile once he realized he had her full attention. "Uh-huh. You see, Miss Lucus, there isn't a person on this island that doesn't answer to me. I set the rules, and everyone obeys them." He turned and firmly guided her back the way they had come. "Once we get back to the village, you're to do everything I tell you. If you run away again, I won't come after you. I'll send my crew to find you. And I guarantee you won't like that. You won't have one man to hide from, but twenty . . . or thirty, and you know how easily I tracked you down. Imagine how long it would take a group that size—and what they'd do once they found you." He could feel the muscles in her arm tighten beneath his fingers, and he cast her a sidelong glance. "Good. Then I guess we have an understanding . . . *Miss Lucus*."

Jennifer fixed her eyes on the path they took, wondering what kind of torture he had in store for her and how long she'd be able to endure it.

Chapter Five

Their descent toward the village had been spotted through the thick foliage of palms and ferns before Chad and Jennifer had wound their way down the volcanic rock ledges, and the moment they reached level ground, a cheer went up from the crowd that had gathered to watch. No one in the hamlet had ever defied the captain's orders so blatantly as this young woman, and while some admired her courage, most were thankful they didn't have to face the punishment Captain LaShelle would exact for her foolishness. Yet, if asked, none could name what they thought it would be. She hadn't come here from debtor's prison as they had, and therefore couldn't be sent back. The captain had been relentless as he'd half dragged, half carried her back down the hillside with him. She had stumbled several times, and that had only seemed to enrage him further. Her bare feet were bruised and cut, and when the breeches she wore had become entangled on the thorny branch of a shrub and she had stopped to free the cloth, he had impatiently jerked on her arm, obviously thinking she'd only wanted to delay their return. The rending of the seam from knee to hip had told him otherwise, and now as they moved through the throng of people pushing in around them, Jennifer's face flamed as she desperately tried to hide the long, bare thigh exposed to the lustful gazes of the men in the crowd.

As they neared the entrance to Freedom Inn, Jennifer frantically glanced back over her shoulder in search of one friendly face, someone whose eyes revealed an objection to the way the captain was treating her, and because her attention lay elsewhere, she didn't notice that he had stopped to speak with his first mate until she walked right into him. The crowd roared with laughter, darkening the color in her cheeks even more and bringing a disapproving, silencing scowl from their leader. Instantly, eyes fell away from the couple, and the crowd started to move back. Their entertainment had come to an end. It was the first mate's question that drew Jennifer's startled, fearful gaze to him.

"Do you want her locked up in the jail?" he asked dispassionately.

Her attention shifted to the tall, dark man who still held her tightly by the wrist, then her gaze dropped to the ground when he glanced over at her out of the corner of his eye.

"It won't be necessary, Jason," Chad answered lightly. *"Miss Lucus* and I have come to an understanding. She'll be staying in my room."

"Lucus?" Jason repeated with a frown, missing the horrified look that came over the young girl's face at the captain's announcement.

"Aye." Chad nodded, taking her elbow to push her through the door ahead of him. "She says her name is Jennifer . . . Lucus."

There was a knowing gleam in the captain's dark eyes as he shot his companion one final look before turning to the entrance of the pub. Jason didn't miss it. His brow furrowed as he thought about what the captain had said and the way he said it, and he lingered outside for a minute or more while he contemplated the meaning behind his gesture. Unable to come up with an answer, he shrugged and stepped into the doorway of the pub to watch the couple climb the stairs that led to the captain's room.

"I'd rather stay in the jail," Jennifer muttered sheepishly, her eyes trained upon the wooden treads they mounted.

"I'll bet you would," he agreed, smiling broadly. "But that isn't how it's going to be." Reaching the top of the steps, he turned her toward his room. "Besides, you'll be safer with me."

His statement brought Jennifer to an abrupt halt in the middle of the corridor. She jerked her arm free and stared up at him, her tiny mouth dropping open. "Safer?" she mocked. "With you? I'd be safer trying to outswim a shark."

Chad could feel the muscles in his throat tighten as laughter threatened to spill forth, but he quickly checked it. She certainly was a brazen young thing. He liked that. "Maybe. But if you ever find yourself tangling with my crew without my protection, you'll better understand what I mean." He took her arm again and started them off.

They had just about reached his room when a door on the opposite side of the hall was flung open and darkly painted, red-haired woman filled the opening, clenched fists resting on her rounded hips and a murderous look in her eyes. Jennifer sensed that the captain didn't approve of this interruption for his grip tightened around her arm and an irritable, almost throaty sigh escaped him. He stopped, lowered his chin, and glared back at the woman.

"What, Modesty?" he snarled.

"What, Modesty?" she mimicked, her brown eyes flashing rage. "What do ye think, Chad LaShelle? I ain't gonna share ye with the likes o' 'er. And I ain't gonna

109

play no chambermaid."

"All right. You won't have to share, and you won't have to be a chambermaid." His words brought a triumphant smile to her red lips, then his eyes darkened, and the muscle in his cheek flexed. "You can go back to doing what you were brought here to do . . . serve the customers their drinks. It's time you earned your keep, anyway." Her chin sagged, and when she started to object, he added, "And if you don't like that arrangement, then I'll see you're taken back to London."

Without giving her the chance to respond, he angrily guided Jennifer to his room, lifted the latch, and opened the door. His mood had changed again. He was now the dark, brooding man she had met on the beach, and although the woman he called Modesty had given Jennifer an idea, she thought it best not to do anything about it for a time. It was something that would take a little scheming on her part, but since she wouldn't be going anywhere for a while, she decided to play it out step by step. She jumped when the door slammed shut behind her, and it wasn't until the sounds of his footsteps faded down the hallway that she relaxed and suddenly became aware that fatigue sapped every ounce of energy she had. Stretching the aching muscles of her neck and shoulders, she strolled to the window to look out. Below her, in the alley, was a group of men working on an overturned fishing boat propped up on wooden sawhorses. She realized that even if she decided to try her luck again, her former method of escape would be impossible right now. She glanced over her shoulder at the bed. Besides, the thought of lying on something soft for the first time in over a week was more inviting. But first, she'd soak her tired feet in the water bowl.

Jason had just raised a mug of ale to his lips when Chad

approached the table and slammed a book down on it, startling the unsuspecting first mate so much that he jumped, shook the tankard, and spilled dark brew down the front of his shirt.

"God in heaven," he howled, making a feeble attempt at brushing away the ale that saturated his clothing. "Can't you warn a man before you do something like that?"

"She's lying," Chad jeered, ignoring his companion's reprimand.

"Who? About what?" Jason didn't bother to look up or he might have guessed the answer upon seeing the hurried way Chad was leafing through the log they had recovered from the wreckage of the *Sea Lady*.

"Miss Lucus," Chad informed him. Coming to the list of passengers, he stopped and ran a finger down the entries one at a time. "If I remember rightly, there was only one Lucus on board. And he was the captain."

His interest aroused, Jason set aside his mug and leaned closer, trying to read upside down. "Maybe she lied about which ship she was on . . . or how she got on the island."

Chad shook his dark head, his gold earring catching a stream of sunlight. "I don't think so."

Jason shrugged and settled himself sideways on the bench so that he could lean his weight on one elbow. "So, she lied about her name. What difference does that make?"

"It doesn't. But she must have a good reason for keeping her name a secret—or think she has."

"Like what? Who are we to her?" Jason argued.

Dark brown eyes glanced up from the book. "Maybe she's the daughter of some wealthy man in the Colonies, and she figures if we know, we'll use her for ransom."

"Well, do you recognize such a name on that list?"

"No," Chad grumbled disgustedly, shoving the book

111

away. "There's only one name in there that means any—" He straightened sharply, his jaw slackening, his dark eyes drifting toward the staircase. And for the first time in a long, long while, Jason saw a smile spread across his captain's face.

"What is it, Chad?" He frowned, alarmed by the other's unusual behavior. Then he, too, straightened abruptly when his companion made a quick grab for the log and hurriedly scanned its pages until he found Captain Lucus's diary. Twisting his head to one side, Jason tried to see what it was that held Chad's attention. Failing in that, he decided to wait. Chad would tell him soon enough.

"I should have figured it out the minute she hesitated to tell me who she was," Chad muttered to himself with a shake of his head. Snapping the book shut, he tucked it under one arm and then rose. "I knew she was lying, but I just didn't suspect why."

"Chad," Jason interrupted when his friend started away from the table.

"I'll say she had reason to lie. But it won't do her any good because she doesn't know I have this," he rambled on, patting the ship's log he carried.

"Chad," Jason called, rapidly coming to his feet. "Chad, don't do this to me again. Who is she?"

Hearing Jason's voice for the first time since he'd discovered his captive's true identity, Chad stopped and turned around, an almost evil look on his face. "Her name is Jennifer. But her last name isn't Lucus. It's Grey, Jennifer Grey."

"Oh, my God," Jason breathed. "Are you sure? I mean, isn't there a chance you're mistaken?"

Chad slowly shook his head, a half-smile twisting his mouth. "How much of Captain Lucus's diary did you read?"

"Not much."

112

"Well, if you had, you'd be just as sure as I am. He described the young woman of whom he was so fond— her pale blue eyes, blond hair, and the fact that she was on her way to England to marry a wealthy man."

"But there might have been another woman on board with blue eyes and blond hair, Chad. That doesn't make this little lady Jennifer Grey."

"True. But there isn't any other Jennifer listed as a passenger. And the only Lucus aboard was Arnold Lucus, the captain. And she is about the right age. Too many coincidences, friend. Too many."

He turned then and headed for the stairs, and Jason fleetingly thought to stop him. But he didn't. Once Chad LaShelle set out to do something, *no one* got in his way. He had an explosive temper and a skill with the sword that only a fool would go against. Watching LaShelle bound up the stairs two at a time, Jason sank back down on the bench, praying the young woman in Chad's room could persuade him that she wasn't who he thought she was . . . even if he was right.

Jennifer had just climbed onto the bed and made herself comfortable when she heard footsteps in the hall. She sat up when they approached the door, bolted off the mattress when the latch clicked. Eyes wide with worry, she carefully positioned herself to one side of the bed, placing it between her and whoever it was who hadn't bothered to knock before stepping into the room. The muscles in her body tensed when the captain slammed the door shut behind him, and she retreated a step when he threw something on the bed.

Raven black brows were drawn over his dark brown, piercing eyes as Chad glared over at her. His feet were widespread, and one shoulder dipped down slightly when he turned toward her and leaned his weight forward. She

113

had seen him angry before, but there was something frightening about the way he looked at her now. Her eyes shifted from his handsome face to the book lying on the bed.

"Have you ever seen a ship's log, *Miss Lucus?*" he ground out.

Hesitant, Jennifer shook her head, wondering why he'd asked and why he'd emphasized the name she had given him.

"Usually, they're only a day-to-day record of a ship's navigation, but this one is a little different. The captain of the *Sea Lady* kept a diary. Ordinarily, I wouldn't have given it much thought. I probably wouldn't even have read it. But now I'm glad I did. He'd grown fond of a young woman sailing his ship, a young woman whose father had died a few weeks before she'd boarded the *Sea Lady*. She was on her way to England to marry a man she hadn't seen since she was a child. Her name was Jennifer Grey."

The hair on the back of Jennifer's neck tingled. If she didn't do some fast talking and right now, he'd take her silence to mean she understood what he was getting at. She swallowed hard and took a breath. "What has that to do with me?"

"A lot, I think." He sneered, and started around the end of the bed toward her. "Besides the diary, the captain had a list of passengers. I found it rather interesting that Jennifer Lucus wasn't among them. In fact, the only Lucus was Arnold Lucus, the captain. Would you care to explain?"

Jennifer forced a laugh. "It's quite simple, Captain. I'm his niece. He wouldn't very well list me as a passenger when I didn't pay to be there. I sailed with him many times—"

"That's odd," he cut in, his manner almost casual as he paused near the foot of the bed and rested his right

114

forearm against one of the pots, his left hand resting on his hip. "Arnold Lucus wrote that he was so fond of Jennifer Grey because he'd never had any children of his own, nor did he have any nieces or nephews to claim. Now why do you suppose he lied?"

Jennifer's heart pounded wildly in her chest, and tears burned her eyes. He'd known before questioning her that she hadn't told him her real name. She jumped back when he dropped his arm to his side and stepped forward.

"Or should I be asking why *you* lied, Jennifer Grey?"

Positive that at any second he would lunge for her, clamp his strong fingers around her neck and squeeze the life from her, she turned and leaped up on the bed, intending to race across it to the door and what little chance she had of surviving. But Chad had expected as much, and he easily caught her by the ankle, pulled her off her feet, and dragged her back to the middle of the mattress. She let out a bloodcurdling scream that rattled the windowpane when he cruelly grabbed her arm and rolled her onto her back, then fell on top of her, his weight pinning her down in the soft feather ticking. She wriggled and squirmed beneath him, fighting desperately to push him from her and frightened nearly out of her wits. Tears quickly filled her eyes and streamed down her face. She hadn't the strength to get free of him, and she knew it, but she wasn't about to just give up and let him kill her without a struggle. Then, suddenly, he trapped her face between his hands, and when his mouth came down hard on hers, she knew he didn't plan to kill her just yet. He wanted to play with her for a while, torment her, violate her the way he had on the beach. But Jennifer wanted no part of that. She was a woman and didn't possess the physical strength he had, but that didn't give him the right to do whatever he wanted with her. With unleashed fury, she sank her teeth into his lower lip.

Chad instantly jerked himself up on his knees, and

115

straddling the little hellcat between them, he quickly touched a fingertip to the drop of blood he tasted. He could hardly believe she had actually bitten him when all he had done was kiss her. What the hell was the matter with her? And why was she looking at him as though she wanted to stick a knife in his heart? What had he done? She was the one who had lied. And she had defied him, had run off and made him look bad in front of his crew. He had every right to beat her senseless, if he was so inclined, and no one on the island would disagree. He wiped the blood from his lip and stared at the crimson smudge on his finger.

"I'd prefer it, Captain LaShelle, if you just went ahead and killed me," Jennifer bravely admitted as she struggled to push herself up on her elbows. "The thought of death is much more pleasant than what you have in mind."

Confusion and surprise wrinkled Chad's brow. "Kill you? What the hell are you talking about? Why would I kill you?"

"Because of who I am," she rallied, trying to squirm out from under him. She gasped when he caught her wrists and yanked her arms out from under her, drawing them up on either side of her head and crushing her back against the mattress.

"My half brother's betrothed, is that what you mean?" he asked, nose to nose.

Jennifer winced when he tightened his hold. "Yes," she cried out.

"That's still no reason to kill you. In fact, it's all the more reason *not* to kill you." An evil smile parted his lips as he rested his weight on his elbows, his rock-hard body pressed against her much more fragile one. "Imagine how upset my father will be when he learns you've been with me? How ashamed he'll be. All his wealthy friends will look down their arrogant noses at him because his

116

son's intended bride has been the prisoner of a pirate who used her. And not just any pirate, but the man's bastard son, the one who wasn't good enough to marry her."

"That's not my fault," Jennifer argued, tears choking her. "It was a decision your father made. I had nothing to do with it. I was only a child when you ran away from home—"

"Ran away?" he choked out, rage burning in his dark eyes. "I didn't run. I was pushed out the door! I was told to get out and not to come back!" The muscle in his cheek flexed as he gritted his teeth. "And I never did, because I had no reason to. No reason until now."

His declaration sent an icy rivulet of horror trickling down Jennifer's spine. What kind of evil plot was he hatching? Why should it involve her? And why had God seen to it that their paths crossed? Dear Lord, what had she done that was so horrible as to warrant this? She squeezed her eyes shut and clamped her teeth together, turning her face away from him and willing the sobs not to come. Crying only enraged him.

"I-I have some money of my own, Captain," she whimpered, feeling his warm breath on her cheek. "I'll give you all I have, if you'll just let me go." His scornful laughter resounded in the room and made her tremble all the more.

"Do you?" he jeered. "And where might you be keeping it? Here?" His hand quickly moved to her hip. "Or here?" He traced the shapely length of her bare thigh where the torn breeches exposed her flesh, then shifted his weight and ran his hand up the outside of her other leg to her waist.

"I don't have it with me," she shrieked, grabbing for his hand and trying to pull it away before he tugged the hem of her shirt from the breeches. "But I can get it!"

"I don't want your money, Jennifer," he hissed, taking both of her wrists in one hand and drawing them above

117

her head. "I want you."

Her scream of protest was instantly smothered when he lowered his head and crushed her lips with a fierce, hurting kiss while his fingers unfastened the buttons on her shirt front. Tears stole between her dark lashes, and Jennifer fought with every ounce of strength she had left. Where was the man who had claimed earlier that if he had known she was a virgin he would have been gentle with her? Now that he had already used her, did it mean there was no longer any need for such consideration? Did he think that she had hardened her heart as well as her mind and body against such abuse? Well, she hadn't. She was still a woman. She needed tenderness and understanding, not some brute who enjoyed taking his anger out on a defenseless woman. He popped the last button free, and when he yanked the cloth away from her naked breasts and raised up to view the treasure he had uncovered, Jennifer struck out with the only weapon she had left—the truth.

"Your father was right," she hissed, her own fury glowing brightly in her sea green eyes. "You're not good enough to marry *any* woman."

Chad's eyes narrowed as he glared back at her, his nostrils flared, and the scar across his chin gleamed white when he pressed his lips into a tight line. In a rage, he jerked himself up from the bed, and Jennifer quickly pulled the shirt around her and sat up, silently uttering a thankful prayer. Her gratitude for having the wisdom to attack his weakness was short-lived, however, when his eyes darkened even more and his hands moved to the buttons on his shirt.

"The truth, my fiery vixen," he growled, pulling the garment free of his breeches, then tugging off his boots, "is that there isn't a woman alive I would want to marry when all are for the taking."

As the shirt fell from his wide shoulders and glided to

the floor, Jennifer watched its descent, too stunned to react. Next, he tossed aside his stockings, and when his fingers loosened the fastening on his breeches, then moved to slide them from his hips, Jennifer panicked for she knew there was nothing she could do or say that would change his mind about having her. Scrambling back to the edge of the bed, she lifted her feet and swung them to the floor, bolting off toward the door once she felt the wooden planks beneath her. Grasping the ivory knob in one hand and clutching the shirt over her breasts with the other, she struggled to free the latch, unaware that Chad had bounded across the bed after her. When his arm came around her waist and lifted her from the floor, she scramed, but his relentless fingers began to undo the button on the breeches she wore.

"No! God, no!" she wailed, making a grab for the garment when he yanked it from her. Cool, crisp air washed over her bare hips and thighs, and her cries for mercy dissolved into sobs when he threw her down upon the bed. In a feeble attempt to hide her nakedness from those piercing brown eyes that devoured the sight of her, she grabbed the edges of her shirt and crossed her arms over her trembling body. She gasped when he leaned down, caught a handful of the cloth at her throat and pulled her up to her knees. His dark scowl never left her tear-streaked face while he slowly, forcefully stripped the garment from her fingers and then her shoulders before flinging it away.

Jennifer squeezed her eyes shut when his long, lean fingers closed around her arms just above each elbow and he moved back a step to let his gaze roam freely over the length of her. She could almost feel the branding heat wherever his eyes rested, and her shame mounted tenfold. Then one hand came up behind her head, the other pressed into the small of her back as he drew her body against his own.

119

"Mine," he whispered against her lips. "Whenever, wherever I so desire."

Jennifer strained against him, fighting to break free, but the explosive, scorching heat of his naked body and the rock-hard muscularity of his massive frame seemed to envelop her and steal her breath away. She was powerless to stop him or turn her head away when his mouth swooped down and covered hers. He kissed her almost savagely, forcing her lips apart with his tongue and pushing it inside until Jennifer could scarcely breathe. Wedging her arms up between them, she pushed against him, hoping to loosen his hold so that she could break the kiss, but instead, his grip tightened as he began to lower her to the bed. Her muffled screams did little good, and out of desperation, she brought up her hand and raked her nails across his cheek. Strong fingers quickly clamped down on her wrist and drew her arm in back of her while his mouth moved hungrily over hers. Crushed beneath him on the feathery mattress, Jennifer went limp in his embrace, using all her energy just to suck in a breath. Every inch of her flesh burned, every muscle ached, and she was sure she would perish from the abuse.

Then his fiery kisses trailed a burning path down her neck to the hollow at the base of her throat while he shifted his weight and thrust one knee between her thighs. She wriggled beneath him, but could not free herself, and she gasped when his open mouth found the peak of one breast. A blistering heat shot through her veins, setting her on fire, and she cried out in anguish when his tongue teased the nipple, then sucked greedily upon the tender flesh. Feeling hopelessly lost, she gave way to her tears and sobbed forlornly.

Whether her misery found a place in his heart or not, Chad didn't react. He merely raised up to kiss those luscious, tempting lips once more while his hand ran along the trim line of her hip, down her thigh, then back

120

up the inside of her leg and across her flat belly, before seeking greater treasures. Cupping her breast, his thumb gently stroking the peak, he rose up, positioned himself between her trembling thighs, and then lowered his weight upon her. At first he teased her, barely touching the branding heat of his manhood against her. He hoped to spark a flame of passion in her that would match his, to have her experience the rapture of desire, the pleasure he could give her; but for a moment his need ebbed when he saw the torment twisting her beautiful face. He couldn't understand the game she played, why she resisted, why she wouldn't allow herself to feel the ecstasy this moment could arouse. His gaze drifted across the soft arch of her brows, her high cheekbones, the flowing, golden strands of hair that fanned out around her; and his pulse quickened again. It didn't matter why. If that was what she wanted, that was what she'd have. But he wasn't about to cheat himself because of the foolish whim of a woman. Framing her face in his hands, he pressed his mouth against her slightly parted lips and thrust his manhood deep inside her.

Anger raged within Jennifer. Hot tears raced down her cheeks. Uncontrollable sobs shook her body. His stubbly growth of beard scratched her cheek and chin, and any protest she tried to voice was smothered beneath his fierce kisses. His moves were long and sleek, his breathing heavy, and Jennifer tried with all her might to block out the sounds, the feel of him, the knowledge of what he was doing and why. But each time she tried, his branding kisses sent a liquid fire coursing through her as his lips moved from her mouth to her closed eyelids, across her tear-streaked face to her ear, then down to her slender neck. She wanted to close out the emotions, the frightening sensations his touch aroused—and she didn't want him to suspect she had failed to do so. Finally, after what seemed a lifetime, his ragged breathing slowed, and

121

Jennifer turned her face away and kept her eyes tightly closed as she lay unmoving beneath him.

Propped up on his elbows, her arms trapped between them, he stared down at her. Her tousled hair and flushed face excited him even now, and though she pretended not to want him, he knew in time he could change her mind. She was meant to please a man, every woman was, but this little sea nymph held the promise of much more than casual lovemaking. She was different from Modesty—or any other woman he'd been with, willing or otherwise—and the thought of having her again brought a vague smile to his lips. Without realizing it, he gently lifted a long, silky strand of golden hair from her brow, then lowered his head to lightly kiss her temple. Jennifer came to life.

"No!" she wailed, wrenching her arms free. Long, sharp nails came up to claw his face, and it was only Chad's quick reaction that saved him from certain harm.

"You little minx," he growled, catching her wrists and foiling the attack by pinning them high above her head. "What the hell's the matter with you?"

"Please . . . no more," she begged, jerking her head from side to side, her sea green eyes closed.

"No more?" he repeated, a frown furrowing his brow. Didn't she know? . . . His anger waned. Of course, she didn't. All of this was new to her. "Stop the tears," he said, lifting his weight from her. "Even if I wanted an encore, I would have to wait a while."

Circling the bed, he picked up his breeches and quickly donned them while Jennifer scrambled beneath the coverlet and huddled up against the headboard as far away from him as possible. Thinking to pour fresh water into the bowl, then splash the cool droplets over his face and neck, he stepped up to the night stand and placed his hand on the pitcher before realizing the bowl was missing. Glancing all around him, he finally spotted it sitting on the floor near the bed, and he frowned, wondering what it was doing there. The pink hue of the water told him, and he looked up sharply to find the frightened beauty staring back at him.

"Let me see your feet," he ordered, his dark brows drawn together.

When she didn't respond, he grabbed the end of the coverlet, tugged it free, and flipped it up past her knees. Jennifer clung frantically to her corner of the velvet spread, tucking the edges underneath her while she clutched the rest up under her chin. She cringed when he sat down on the bed and grabbed her ankle.

"Bloody hell," he growled once he saw the cuts and bruises covering the tiny soles of her feet. Rising, he went to the dresser and, from the many bottles sitting on top, selected one that held a yellow salve before returning to the bed and sitting down again. Pulling out the cork, he dipped his finger into the ointment, then forcibly took her ankle when she pulled away from him. "It'll help," he barked, glaring at her until she gave in.

Jennifer could feel its soothing effect almost instantly, and if her wounds hadn't been his fault in the first place, she might have thanked him for seeing to her care. But somehow she doubted these would be the last cuts and bruises she would have to endure because of him. Even so, she found herself relaxing beneath his gentle touch, and this sudden change in his nature brought a curious frown to her brow. He could be so heartless at one moment, almost tender the next. Smiling seemed to take a great deal of effort on his part, and when that reaction caught him by surprise, he'd quickly mask it. She couldn't say why, but she sensed he didn't want anyone to suspect that he had a softer side, and she could only assume it had something to do with the argument he and his father had had many years ago. She could understand his resentment toward his father if what he had told her

123

was true—that his father had ordered him out of his home—but it didn't explain his treatment of her.

Bright sunlight suddenly flooded the room, drawing her attention to the window and the vivid blue sky that ceiled the island. It was comprehensible that he had chosen to live in such a place. It was peaceful here and offered a retreat from the harsh realities of life beyond the perimeter of the island . . . for those who *wanted* to live here. Jennifer didn't. Reminded of why, she returned her attention to the man who tended her injuries, and her breath caught in her throat when the golden glow of light coming into the room fell across him. He was a wild-looking sort, Jennifer thought, with his unshaven jaw, his thick, black hair in need of a trimming, his darkly tanned skin, and the gold earring dangling from one lobe. She smiled in spite of herself. Somehow it suited him. It was his way of openly defying what others considered to be a man's moral duty, his principles, his ethics. Chad LaShelle didn't have any.

Suddenly, warm, brown eyes were staring suspiciously at her, and Jennifer quickly lowered her gaze.

"Why were you looking at me like that?" he asked.

She glanced up at him, then dropped her gaze to her lap and shrugged one shoulder. "I've never seen a man wear an earring before," she admitted, her voice hardly more than a whisper.

Chad had forgotten all about the piece of jewelry until she'd mentioned it, and he was suddenly flooded with memories of what had happened more than five years ago, when he and his crew were sailing near Spain and came across a disabled Spanish ship. On board were a wealthy count and his daughter, Doña María, the most beautiful woman Chad had ever seen. Her flowing black hair and very dark eyes impelled him to step forward to claim her, but when he did so the count drew a pistol to

124

protect her, and Chad ran the man through with his sword. As he thought about it now, he realized he should have done the same with Doña María rather than take her aboard his ship and into his cabin. But his passion for her blinded him and nearly cost him his life. Strapped to her thigh was a tiny bejeweled dagger, and while he was busy trying to rip her clothes from her, she was freeing the blade from its scabbard. The next thing he knew, she had pierced his side with it and fled the cabin. He never did find out exactly what her fate had been, but Jason had brought him one of her gold earrings as a souvenir. And from that day on, Chad wore it as a reminder never to trust the gentler sex.

"I'll bet not," he remarked, shoving the cork back in the bottle as he stood up again. "I would imagine the men you're used to wear ruffles, drink wine, carry a pinch of snuff, and don curly wigs to hide the fact they're men."

Without caring about the consequences, she retorted, "And they're gentlemen. They'd never force themselves on women."

Surprised by her answer, he stared quietly back at her for a moment, a vague smile crimping one corner of his mouth. "Really?" he challenged, returning the bottle to its place on the dresser. "Then why do you suppose there are so many bastards in the world?"

"Like you?" The question slipped out before Jennifer had time to reconsider, and she instantly regretted it when dark, glaring eyes looked back at her from his reflection in the mirror. She quickly cast her own away, inwardly cringing when he came back to stand beside the bed, one foot propped on its edge, an arm draped across his knee, and the weight of his upper torso braced against it.

"You don't know anything about me, Jennifer Grey," he snarled.

125

The tone of his voice made her tremble, and she forced herself not to look at him. She'd made him angry . . . again.

"But I know all about you and the kind of men you call gentlemen . . . men like your father."

Jennifer's head snapped up, her tiny chin sagging in shocked dismay that he would verbally attack a man he didn't know. She took a quick breath to remind him of that fact, but he cut her off.

"He gave his word—a gentlemen's agreement, I think they call it—and then went back on it." Chad straightened suddenly, letting his foot drop to the floor, and as he rounded the end of the bed, intending to pick up the bowl of water and toss its contents out the window, he flung another indictment over his shoulder. "And then there's the matter of cheating." Dark, mocking eyes glanced over at her. "Tsk, tsk. Not a very gentlemanly thing to do—filing down the sights of his dueling pistol."

"He didn't!" Jennifer exploded. "Why would he? He was an excellent marksman. And you've no right to say he did. You were just a child when it happened. How could you possibly know—"

"And how old were you at the time?" he questioned. "One? Two? How would you know what happened? Did your father tell you?" He waited for her answer, and when all she did was snap her mouth shut and turn her head away, he leisurely strolled back to the night stand, picked up the pitcher, and filled the bowl with fresh water. "You know what I think? I think your father was deeply in debt and approached the man's wife with a deal—a share of the inheritance in exchange for killing him, but she went back on her word. Is that why your father and mother sold everything they had, bundled up their daughter, and fled England? What I don't understand is why my father financed him when he knew George Grey wasn't honorable."

126

Tears of rage filled Jennifer's eyes, but rather than give him the satisfaction of knowing how angry he had made her, she stared straight ahead, waiting for him to turn his attention away from her. Out of the corner of her eye, she saw the hurricane lamp sitting on the night stand beside her. Maybe she couldn't kill him with it, but she'd certainly try to give him one awful headache.

Chad had noticed the way the muscle in her cheek had flexed as she'd suppressed the string of oaths he was sure she wanted to hurl at him. He truly had no idea what was behind the duel her father had fought, and he honestly didn't care. He'd only said those things out of bitterness, perhaps even jealousy that his own father cared more about a friend than he did his own son. He glanced down at the water in the bowl. There was so much about his father that he didn't understand and probably never would. And it pained him even now to think the man could blame a fourteen-year-old boy for the death of his wife. Visions of Mary Elizabeth Wadsworth flared up in his mind, and he had to grit his teeth to keep his emotions in check. Didn't the man know how much he'd loved his stepmother? It wasn't his fault the bolt on the carriage broke. Couldn't he see that? Didn't he understand? Out of the corner of his eye Chad caught a movement, and he jerked his head up in time to see Jennifer make a lunge for the lamp.

"Leave it!" he roared.

The command nearly rattled the walls and brought a quick end to Jennifer's plan. Her hand outstretched, she sat perfectly still, afraid that he might take any move as defiance. She jumped when she felt his weight upon the mattress and quickly drew her arm back to her chest, her eyes wide and staring as he knelt on one knee, a finger pointed warningly at her.

"I said you were more important to me alive, Jennifer, and I meant it," he hissed. "But try a stunt like the one

127

you were considering just now, and I promise you, you'll regret it. Do I make myself clear?"

"Yes," she bravely admitted, though her chin quivered. "But I think I should tell you something as well."

His eyes narrowed, and he tilted his head to one side, curious. "What?" he asked, lowering his hand.

"The only person who ever meant anything to me is dead. The home where I lived doesn't belong to me. What little I had to call my own went down with the *Sea Lady*, and every minute I spend here with you reminds me that I have nothing to live for. I'm not a very courageous woman, Captain, and if you threaten me with physical harm, I'll do as I'm told out of fear. But if you *ever* slander the good name of my father again, somehow I'll find the courage to kill you."

Cold, dark eyes held hers for a long while, and Jennifer wondered if he wouldn't murder her right then and there. Finally, a hint of a smile parted his lips and he lifted a brow as he said, "I believe you would, Jennifer Grey. I believe you would." Standing erect, he returned to the washbowl and bent forward slightly to splash water over his face and neck.

Jennifer wanted to hate him, to find the mere sight of him abhorrent, and she even went so far as to display her disdain by raising her delicate chin in the air, hoping he would notice and then she'd turn her head away. But he didn't, and even if he had, Jennifer probably couldn't have pulled her eyes from him. The thick muscles across his shoulders flexed with each move he made, water droplets glistened in his dark hair, and the profile he presented made her heart beat a little faster. She couldn't understand why. He wasn't exactly the kind of man a woman dreamed of. Then she noticed a deep, rather vicious-looking scar just above the waistband of his breeches.

"How did you get that?" she innocently asked, suddenly wishing she hadn't when he turned a scowl her way.

"What?" he asked irritably, lifting a towel to his face.

"That scar on your side. It looks awful."

Glancing briefly down at it, Chad gave a short, sarcastic laugh. "From a woman much like you, I'm afraid," he admitted, rubbing the cotton cloth over his chest, then up across his neck before tossing it back down on the night stand. "She took objection to my . . . amorous moods, shall we say?"

Feeling no sympathy for him, Jennifer scoffed, "Unfortunately for me, her aim was off."

Oddly enough, Chad found her criticism amusing. "Actually, it was her misfortune." He grinned, casually reaching up to grasp the framework of the canopy above his head as he stared down at her. "Her foolishness cost her her life."

A chill of fear shot through Jennifer, and as though it might make a difference, she hugged the coverlet tighter under her chin. "You . . . you killed her?"

His grin widened. "No, I wasn't in much of a condition to do anything," he replied dispassionately. "I'm not sure who did. One of the crew, I imagine."

Jennifer's stomach did a flip-flop. She closed her eyes and touched shaky fingertips to her damp brow, wondering if she would faint. "God, how can you be so insensitive?"

"Insensitive?" He chuckled. "She wanted to kill me."

"Because you were trying to rape her!" Jennifer exploded, frowning at him. "You're barbaric!"

Chad shrugged a shoulder. "If I were barbaric, her death would have been slow and agonizing. I'm sure it wasn't." He dropped his arms at his sides, turned, and sat down on the edge of the bed to don his stockings and boots.

"Oh," she jeered, "so you just had someone slit her throat, instead."

He glanced over his shoulder at her. "Or someone tossed her overboard. I don't really know."

"And you don't really care," she admonished. Suddenly, being so close to him became intolerable. Yanking the coverlet free, she swung her feet to the floor and stood up, wincing a little when she put her weight on them. "And I suppose I can expect the same if I do something to displease you?"

Tugging on his boots, he came to his feet and in a relaxed manner rounded the end of the bed, then paused to rest his forearm against the bedpost and unhurriedly look her over from the top of her blond head to the bare calves and toes peeking out from beneath the velvet quilt. A lazy smile parted his lips when she nervously rearranged the coverlet around her in an attempt to restrict his view.

"I doubt you'll ever displease me, Jennifer Grey," he murmured after a while.

Her face flamed instantly, for she knew full well what he implied. She sucked in a breath and raised her chin a notch. "I'll certainly try my hardest," she promised, trembling a mite when he raised a dark brow in response.

His arm fell to his side, and he took a step forward. "Actually, her failure to kill me is to your benefit."

Frowning suspiciously, Jennifer quickly backed away when he continued to advance. "How?" she asked, bumping into the night stand behind her.

"Because if I were dead, I wouldn't be able to teach you the pleasures to be had in bed."

Jennifer heaved an exasperated sigh. "You're disgusting."

"Disgusting?" He shook his head. "No, just truthful."

"And conceited as well," she rebuked. "What makes you think I would find any pleasure whatsoever"—she

130

couldn't bring herself to say it—"with you?"

A lean, brown hand came up to lift a golden curl from her shoulder, and Jennifer pressed back as far as the night table would allow, wanting nothing to do with him. But even though he hadn't touched her, his nearness radiated a scorching heat that penetrated through the thick, velvet spread draped around her. She gasped when he grabbed her arm and crushed her against his bare chest, one hand grasping the thick mass of hair at the nape of her neck in order to draw her mouth to his. His blistering kiss seared her to the soul and made her head spin, and she wasn't even aware that he had turned with her and was lowering her to the bed until she felt the softness of the mattress beneath her. Yet, even then, she didn't react the way she should have, for somewhere deep inside, despite her closely guarded reserve, a spark was ignited and it rapidly flared up to consume her. It muddled her senses, confused her thoughts, and caught her totally unawares. It burned through every nerve in her body, melting her defenses, and swirling in a wild, blissful mass of sensation. It was as if her body defied her mind, and before she reaized what she was doing, she began answering his passionate kiss with equal fervor. Then suddenly, abruptly, Chad lifted himself from her, and Jennifer's desire erupted into mounting shame. He had only been making a point . . . and he had succeeded.

He stared down at her for a long while, not saying anything or even changing his expression. Then he crossed to where his shirt lay, picked it up, flung it over his shoulder, and walked out the door. The faint clicking of the latch exploded in the quiet room.

Chapter Six

A gentle knock on the door to her room spun Jennifer around from the window beside which she had been standing as she'd stared out at the pale blueness of the sea for the past half-hour, and at first, she couldn't understand why the captain would suddenly change his habits. He hadn't bothered to give her any consideration the last time he'd stormed into the room. Why would he now? The knock sounded again, startling her, and for a moment, she debated hurling herself out the window rather than face him again. She glanced over her shoulder at the two-story drop and resignedly decided that with the kind of luck she'd been having, she'd probably only break her leg instead of killing herself. A glimmer of hope brightened her eyes; perhaps he'd go away if she didn't answer his summons. Then the doorknob rattled, and she started to race for the bed, deciding that maybe he'd leave again if she appeared to be sleeping. But once she had taken a step, she realized what a horrible mistake lying in bed would be, since it seemed all he thought about was ripping off her clothes and seeing how he could humiliate her. Feeling terribly frustrated, she heaved a heavy sigh and remained where she was, watching the door slowly swing open. To her surprise, a young girl Jennifer guessed to be around fifteen years old peeked in, a most apologetic expression on her freckled face.

"Beg pardon, mum," she said in a tiny voice, her bright red hair falling about her shoulders. "I didn't mean ta wake ya."

Jennifer had to bite her lip to keep from shouting for joy. She didn't even know the girl's name, but she suspected the two of them would become fast friends *and*, perhaps, she would be willing to help with Jennifer's plan. So far she was the only person who had showed an ounce of thoughtfulness for her. "You didn't." She smiled warmly, rounding the bed and walking toward the young redhead. "Come in, won't you?"

The girl bobbed her head, then pushed the door open wide, and Jennifer frowned when she saw the large sewing basket the girl carried and the plain, gray woolen dress, the white petticoats and chemise she had draped over her arm.

"Me name's Megan O'Connor and me mother owns a dress shoppe here on the island. The captain sent me, mum," she explained, having seen the puzzled look on her companion's face. "He said ye be needin' somethin' ta wear. I'm ta take yer measurements, then have two more dresses made up for ya as well as some undergarments. He says he'll be tellin' ye how ye can pay for them."

"What?" Jennifer gasped. All sorts of cruel forms of payment flashed through her mind.

"Aye, mum," Megan hesitantly replied. "Captain LaShelle said he wouldn't be payin' for somethin' he don't use. I'm sorry, mum, but we've got to be paid."

"Oh, I understand," Jennifer quickly assured her. "It's the captain who doesn't."

"Mum?"

Pulling the young girl further into the room, Jennifer

134

then closed the door behind her. "He owes me one dress, and if you'll ask him about it, I'm sure he'll agree. And one dress is all I want right now. I won't be in debt to him."

"But Miss Grey, he'll be very angry with me if I don't do as he told me," Megan argued.

"How can he be angry with you when I'm the one who refused?" Jennifer asked. "Just tell him that I said I wouldn't buy anything until I could pay for it first." A perplexing frown crimped her brow. "Of course, the way things are now, I'm not sure I'll ever be able to buy anything." She straightened and took the basket from Megan and set it aside. "So show me what you've brought with you. If everything fits, then the captain can consider his debt to me taken care of."

Megan frowned worriedly for a moment, then shrugged and turned toward the bed, obviously deciding there wasn't much she could do to change Miss Grey's mind. That would be up to the captain to do. Bending, she spread the garments out on the mattress for Jennifer to examine.

Jennifer was pleased with the dress Megan had chosen for her. Although she would have preferred the neckline to be a little higher, she was sure a lace handkerchief artfully placed would cover up anything that might interest the captain. The full, puffy sleeves extended to the elbow, and had white eyelet trim. The snug bodice buttoned up the front, and the modestly full skirt had a white dairymaid apron sewn in at the waist. The simple design and the reserved color certainly wouldn't attract too much attention. If she wore a lace cap and tucked her thick, blond hair underneath it, perhaps she would be of no more interest to the men in the village than any of the other women. The hopeful expression quickly faded from her lovely face. Her problem had nothing to do with the men in the village. It was Captain LaShelle she must

135

consider, and no one else.

"I can be takin' them in if they don't fit proper, Miss Grey," Megan offered, her auburn brows drawn together in a rueful frown. "I just wish me mother had somethin' better to offer ye, but it was all we had on such short notice. Ye can be wearin' it until she can make ye somethin' else."

"Oh no, Megan," Jennifer smiled excitedly. "This one is perfect!"

"But, mum," Megan objected, "the sleeves are too long, the bodice is too tight, and the skirts will get in the way. Very few of the women on the island wear dresses like this. It will be too hot. Ye should wear what I have on, Miss Grey."

Glancing at the girl's attire for the first time since she'd come into the room, Jennifer instantly recognized the danger in wearing something as loose and flowing as what Megan had on. The lightweight, white cotton blouse had short puffy sleeves and a low-cut, gathered neckline held in place by drawstrings tied in a bow just above her bosom. Although it was opaque enough to prohibit seeing what Megan wore underneath it, its ballooned bodice accentuated her shapely curves and highlighted her narrow waist. The skirt, though full, came only to her ankles with a single layer of petticoats beneath it, and the sandals she wore were hardly the style a genteel lady would wear. But Jennifer had to admit the outfit looked comfortable compared to the dress she had decided on, and if it weren't for the captain and her fear of him once he saw her in such garb, she would have agreed with Megan.

"Thank you, Megan, but no," she said quietly, lowering her eyes. "It would be better for me to wear the one you've brought with you."

The young redhead opened her mouth to question Jennifer's reasoning, remembered her mother's teaching not to be nosy or they both would pay the consequences, and bobbed her head in reluctant agreement instead.

The dress, petticoats, and chemise fit Jennifer perfectly, and a bright smile spread across her face when she stepped up to the mirror to examine her appearance. Now she need only hide her hair. With Megan's help, she braided the long strands of thick, golden curls, then wound the braids into a knot which, with the hairpins Megan provided, she fixed to the top of her head.

"Megan, you didn't happen to bring a cap with you, did you?" Jennifer asked, turning sideways to look at her profile in the mirror.

"No, mum," Megan replied, "but I can be gettin' ye one. And shoes and stockin's, too."

Smiling at her from the reflection in the silvered glass, Jennifer added, "And collect your fee for it all from Captain LaShelle. All right?"

"Aye, mum," Megan nodded, picking up her sewing basket and starting for the door.

"Megan, wait," Jennifer called. "Stay a while, can you?"

The girl was about to say that she had a lot of work waiting for her at the shoppe, but when she saw the pleading look in Jennifer's blue-green eyes, she decided it could be done later. After all, she had planned on spending an hour or so altering the dress she had brought to the newest arrival on the island. She smiled, set down the basket, and walked to the bed.

Jennifer motioned for her to sit beside her. "Tell me about this place, Megan."

"The island, mum? Isn't much to tell. It's just an island."

"I mean, how do you happen to be living here? Unless I'm mistaken, you sound English."

A sadness came over the young girl's face, and she

137

dropped her gaze to her hands which were folded in her lap. "Aye, mum."

Sensing that her observation had stirred up painful memories, Jennifer reached over and touched Megan's arm. "I'm sorry, Megan. I didn't mean to make you sad."

"Oh, ye didn't, mum. It isn't yer fault I can't go home."

"What?" Jennifer gasped. "Are you saying Captain LaShelle is keeping you a prisoner here?"

"No, mum." Megan quickly corrected her. "If it weren't for the captain, me mother would still be in Newgate. He's the one what paid ta free her, and then he gave her and meself a place to live."

Jennifer's tawny brows came together in a puzzled frown. "I—I don't understand, Megan. What do you mean he freed your mother and gave the two of you a place to live?"

Twisting on the bed so that she could look directly at Jennifer, Megan smiled. "Me father owned a tailor shoppe in London. Me mother was his seamstress. He died about two years ago, and all the creditors came knocking on our door wantin' what me father owed them. We didn't have it, so me mother was put in debtor's prison, and I went ta live with me aunt. About a year ago, Captain LaShelle's first mate, Mr. Bingham, came ta me aunt's door and told me that me mother sent him, and that I was ta be comin' with him. I don't mind tellin' ye, I was scared. But when I saw me mother, everything was all right."

"Had Captain LaShelle already known your mother that he felt compelled to help her?"

"Oh no, mum," Megan said, shaking her head. "All the captain knew about me mother was that she was a seamstress, and he needed her on the island." Megan laughed at the confused expression that came over Jennifer's face. "I guess I should be explainin' it from the

138

beginnin'." She smiled and settled more comfortably on the bed. "Ye see, this island belongs ta Captain LaShelle. Some time ago, he decided ta build a village here, but he didn't have the carpenters. He could steal the lumber and nails, so he figured he could be stealin' the carpenters, too. That's when he came up with the idea of takin' people from debtor's prison. In exchange for their freedom, they were ta live on the island and work at their trade. Everyone here gets paid, just the way it was in London, only there's no credit. Ye pay first."

"But for how long?" Jennifer asked. "How long must you work here before you can go home?"

"Oh, no one goes home, mum," Megan said. "This is our home. The only way ye go back ta London is if ye do somethin' wrong. And then ye are sent back to prison."

"But—but that's the same as being in prison. You're not free to go where you want," Jennifer argued. "And who decides if you've done something wrong?" She quickly raised a hand when Megan started to answer. "No, don't tell me. I already know. Captain LaShelle."

"It's his island, mum."

Jennifer bolted from her place on the bed beside Megan and began to pace the floor. "And you people willingly go along with whatever he decides?"

"He's never been unfair, Miss Grey," Megan told her. "And every one of us on the island agrees that livin' here is better'n dyin' in debtor's prison."

Jennifer spun around to face her. "Everyone who was *in* prison agrees. But what about you, Megan? What do *you* think about spending the rest of your life here? Is there a man among the villagers that catches your eye, one you'd consider marrying? Don't you want to have children? And speaking of children, why haven't I seen any? Or doesn't the captain approve of them?"

Stung by this outburst, Megan couldn't bring herself to look Jennifer in the eye. "There's only two married

139

couples on the island, mum, and they be too old to have children."

"But there are plenty of young people, including yourself. Are you trying to tell me that the captain's men—pirates—haven't forced themselves on you?"

Tears glistened in Megan's eyes. "No, mum. Captain LaShelle won't allow it. That's why he brought prostitutes to the village. If his men have need of a woman, they are to come to the inn. Captain LaShelle says the others are to be left alone, that we're needed to work, not fulfill a man's pleasures."

The muscles across Jennifer's chest tightened, an awful dread building up inside her. "Come . . . to the inn?" she repeated weakly. "Here?"

Megan nodded. "Aye, mum. All the women living here are—" She caught herself before she had finished, the blood draining from her freckled face. She came to her feet and rounded the bed to take Jennifer's hands. "Not you, mum. I didn't mean you."

Tears welled in Jennifer's eyes. "And why not me? You said everyone here works at their trade. I don't have one. My papa and I lived on a plantation . . . with servants to do most of the work. I only supervised and took care of the sick. I learned how to do needlepoint and tapestries, and occasionally, I would help papa with his books and play hostess at the parties he had. I don't know how to do anything else!" A sob shook her slender frame. "And he's already made me his . . ." Tears flowing freely now, Jennifer pulled away from Megan and plopped down on the bed. "This is all so horrible. I didn't want to come here. I don't want to stay. Oh, Megan, I have to get off this island!"

Feeling totally helpless, Megan sat down next to Jennifer and gently put her arms around the woman's trembling body. Word of the blond-haired beauty's arrival had spread very quickly among the townsfolk, as

140

had the knowledge that Captain LaShelle had made his claim on her. Everyone accepted it, since they all felt they owed the captain too much to interfere. They also realized that if they tried, they'd be sent back to prison, so no one gave much consideration to the plight of this young woman. Megan, however, had questioned such treatment, but her mother had quickly reminded her of what would happen to the two of them should either voice an objection to the captain. But that didn't settle the matter in Megan's mind, and now that she had met Jennifer Grey and heard her speak of the injustices forced on the people of the island, injustices Megan ofttimes argued about with her mother, she knew she was right in questioning them.

"I don't know what I can do ta help ye, mum," she whispered, a tear streaming down her cheek. "None of us are ever allowed on Captain LaShelle's ship and any other vessels that anchor here are searched before they can set sail. His first mate says it's because they don't trust the other pirates, but I think it's ta make sure none of us are stowaways. But—" A glimmer of hope sparkled in the girl's green eyes, and Jennifer quickly dried her own.

"What, Megan? Have you an idea?"

"Have ye kin in England?" She smiled.

"Not really. My only relative was my father, and he died more than a month ago. But I was on my way to London to meet my betrothed. Why do you ask?"

"Might he be a wealthy man, mum?"

"Yes. But—"

Excited now, Megan left her place beside Jennifer and hurried to the door. Pressing an oar to it, she listened for a moment then opened it to peer outside into the hallway. It was important that no one—especially Modesty—heard what she had in mind. Closing the door again, she faced Jennifer and smiled brightly.

"If he be wealthy and ye his betrothed, he might do *anythin'* ta free ye from this place."

"But he doesn't know I'm here, Megan."

"Aye, mum. Not now, he doesn't. But if ye were ta send him a message—"

"How? Who would give it to him?"

Returning to the bed, Megan sat down beside Jennifer again. "I don't think we can trust one o' Captain LaShelle's men. But . . . every now and then, another pirate ship docks here for repairs or supplies or some other reason, and I think if ye tempt a man, he would be willin' to take yer message to London."

"Tempt him?" Jennifer repeated, failing to understand. "With what?"

"Money, mum. If ye be willin' ta pay him—"

Jennifer moaned forlornly. "I don't have any money. You know that. I can't even pay you."

A devilish grin danced in Megan's pale green eyes. "Aye, mum, ye don't. But I do." She giggled at the surprised expression on Jennifer's face. "I know what ye are thinkin', Miss Grey. Why would I be willin' ta help when we've only just met? A little while ago, ye asked if I was happy here. I'm happy, but I don't want ta spend the rest of me life here. And I don't think me mother does either. I'll give ye the money ye need if ye promise ta help us get off the island, too. We can't be goin' back ta London. Ye'll have ta see that we're taken ta the Colonies . . . in America—someplace the captain will never find us."

Tears of joy glistened in Jennifer's eyes. "Megan, I'd see to it that you and your mother were taken anywhere in the world you want to go." She threw her arms around the young girl and hugged her very tightly. "Thank you, Megan. Thank you so very much for being my friend."

Laughing, Megan said, "I think ye should wait until we're away from here before ye thank me. 'Tis only an

142

idea right now, one that might not work."

"But it's a chance," Jennifer smiled, brushing at her tears. "And it's more than I had a minute ago. Even if it doesn't work, I'll always be in debt to you."

Squeezing Jennifer's hand, Megan stood up. "Now don't be impatient, mum. It could be months before another ship sails in. But when it does, I'll come for yer note. I think the captain will be keepin' a close eye on ye for a while, so ye mustn't be seen talkin' ta any strangers." Reaching for her sewing basket, she started for the door. "I'll be back later with the other things ye need. Will ye be all right until then, mum?"

"I'll be fine, Megan, and please . . . call me Jennifer."

Smiling broadly, the young redhead nodded, gave a short curtsy, and then pulled the door shut behind her as she stepped into the hall. Her new friend had given her the courage to rebel against the way things were supposed to be on the island, and although her mother would strongly disapprove of her trying to help Jennifer Grey, Megan didn't care. Both of them wanted to leave, and if it were in her power, Megan would see that they did. Reaching the top of the stairs, she paused, sucked in a breath, and squared her shoulders, knowing that Captain LaShelle would be waiting for her in the commons below. It would be her pleasure to tell the man exactly what Jennifer had told her to tell him about the dress, and Megan wouldn't leave until the captain had handed over the money he owed her for Jennifer's clothes. Megan only hoped there were a lot of witnesses to hear what she had to say. It was about time someone stood up to him.

It was very easy for her to spot him sitting with Jason Bingham and three other members of his crew at a table in the far corner. His rugged good looks always set him apart from anyone else in the room, and Megan's courage slipped a little. Those dark, piercing eyes could set a person back on their heels without so much as a single

143

word from the man, and as Megan walked closer to the table, she wondered what kind of impact Jennifer's declaration would have and more so what the result would be. She knew she'd be unable to stop the captain should he decide to beat some sense into his captive for defying him, and that was very likely what he'd do if her announcement angered him enough, but Megan took a little comfort from the knowledge that he had never killed anyone for showing a stubborn streak. He had more convincing methods of dealing with insubordination . . . like sentencing an offender to a few days in the jail or, worse, a humiliating week in the pillory. Yet, Megan thought, if the captain chose to sentence Jennifer to one or the other of these forms of punishment, the entire town would sympathize with her once they heard the reason she was there. Megan's eyes suddenly glowed with mischief. And she'd be the one to tell them.

"Captain LaShelle," she said, drawing his attention to her and away from the other men at the table. "Miss Grey says ye owe me two shillings."

A deathly silence fell over the room with Megan's statement, and she gripped the handles on her basket a little tighter when the captain slowly lowered his mug of ale back down on the table, his eyes never leaving hers.

"She told me to remind ye that ye owed her the cost of one dress, and that she wouldn't be buyin' any more until she could pay for them first. She prefers, sir, not to be in debt to ye."

Jordon Stuart and Andrew Tranel, two of the men sitting with Chad, quickly cast their gazes elsewhere rather than on their captain. It was bad enough that the impudent woman had made a fool out of Captain LaShelle by managing to escape his room without them staring at him when he was confronted with another show of open contempt for his orders. Another of his men, Marc Bartell, didn't feel the same way, however.

144

"Saucy little wench, ya got fer yerself, Cap'n." He laughed, his bald head gleaming. "And a bit too much for ya ta handle. Maybe ya should be givin' her ta me. I could tame her down a mite."

"Marc, shut up," Jason warned, scowling. It wouldn't take much for Chad to split the man's skull with the barrel of his pistol, and Jason knew it. The two men had never liked each other from the first, and it was only a matter of time before they settled their differences. Only Jason knew Marc wouldn't be the winner.

"Ahh, mind yer own business, Bingham," Bartell snarled. "I'm talkin' ta the cap'n."

"And I'm his first mate. You're nothing more than a deckhand, which means that if I give you an order, you'll obey it." While he spoke, Jason casually leaned forward and braced one arm on the table while his other hand went for the pistol stuck in his belt. Withdrawing it, he pointed the muzzle at Bartell's stomach from under the table where the man couldn't see it.

"Yeah?" the man challenged. "And what'll ya do, if I tell ya ta go ta hell?"

The clicking of a hammer being cocked answered him, and Bartell's suntanned face whitened and sweat dotted his brow almost instantly.

"Do you really want to know?" Jason grinned, daring the man to say yes. "Now, suppose you find somewhere else to finish your ale. The captain has business to discuss with Megan, here, and it doesn't concern you. Understand?"

Reluctantly, Bartell came to his feet, mug in hand, but he glared back at Jason for a long moment. "Someday, Bingham, you and me is gonna have this out. And it's gonna be the sorriest day of your life."

Smiling, Jason nodded his head. "I look forward to it." Then all humor vanished from his face. "Now get out of here."

Once Bartell had turned to leave, Jason motioned for the other two at the table to go with him, and after the three men had settled at another table a good distance away, Jason carefully released the hammer on his gun and returned the pistol to his belt. It wasn't until after he was satisfied that Bartell would not cause any more trouble that Jason turned his thoughtful frown on Chad, ready to listen to whatever his captain decided to do about the rebellious young woman sentenced to share his room. He expected to see a black, angry scowl on the man's face. Chad's expression was anything but ill-tempered, however, and Jason quickly registered surprise.

"You really enjoyed that, didn't you?" Chad asked, nodding toward Bartell who sat staring at them.

Jason hadn't given it much thought until Chad mentioned it, and now he had to admit that he did. "Bartell's a bully, and everyone lets him get away with it. I just thought it was time he realized not all of us will. Besides, he's a good deckhand, and if he had kept crowding you, you would have blown his head off, and we'd be looking for a new crewman. I was just saving us a little work, that's all," he said with a shrug of one shoulder and a sportive gleam in his eye.

Chad quietly stared at his companion for a moment or two. "You hardly resemble the kind of man most people would picture as a lawyer, Jason. You've changed quite a bit since you joined up with me."

"Yeah, well, I guess I just wasn't meant to practice law," Bingham replied with a half-smile, though his eyes betrayed him. His father had been a lawyer, and for as long as Jason could remember he'd wanted the same profession. Only when his father had died, had he learned of the elder Bingham's weakness for gambling. At that time, Jason had just started his practice, and when all of his father's debts fell on him, he hadn't had the money to pay off the creditors. Thus, he wound up in prison, doomed to spend the rest of his days there. Chad LaShelle had freed him from that horribly depressing existence, but Jason never forgot those months in Newgate, nor did he ever give up the idea of doing something to change the way the place was run. He blinked when he realized he had drifted off into thought and then smiled at the man watching him.

"You're wrong there, Jason," Chad said. "You are meant to be a lawyer, and someday you will be. You've just put it aside for a while, that's all. I know this island isn't what you had in mind as a place to practice law, but when I paid to free you from prison, you decided to sail with me as my first mate. You're good, the best I've ever had, but I'd understand if you changed your mind."

Jason couldn't ever remember Chad talking to him in this way. Their conversations usually consisted of a sentence or two, and most of the time, they were heated. Smiling to himself, he dropped his gaze and toyed with the mug of ale sitting in front of him on the table. Maybe Chad LaShelle had a soft spot after all.

"I realize that, Cap'n. And someday I probably will." He tilted his head and looked at LaShelle out of the corner of his eye. "But not until I've seen you find what it is you're looking for."

Masking his smile, Chad shifted on the bench and reached into a pocket to withdraw the two shillings Megan had said he owed her. Handing them over to the girl, he dismissed her by jerking his head toward the door, but not before he had noticed the somewhat gloating expression on her young face. His eyes darkened as he watched her walk away, for he sensed that perhaps the beauty who waited in his room had made an ally. And that could be troublesome. But it wouldn't be hard to correct. His gaze shifted toward the stairs. Then he glanced back at Megan just as she stepped through the front door of the inn, her bright red hair catching the golden streams of sunshine. Not too difficult to handle. Grabbing his mug of ale, he swallowed the rest of it in one gulp and stood. Without saying a word to Jason, he turned his back on him and headed for the stairs. He'd put an end to this friendship before it had a chance to grow.

At the top of the stairs, he paused and absently touched the tender spot on his lip, where Jennifer had bitten him. He couldn't quite reason why, but he felt differently about her than any other woman he'd been with. A devilish smile crimped one cheek. Maybe that was because he enjoyed making love to a woman of quality rather than a whore. The sparkle in his eyes disappeared. Or maybe it was because of who she was, because of the part she innocently played in his life. For a very brief second he felt guilty at having subjected her to the kind of treatment he'd imposed upon her.

"Careful, Chad," he whispered. "You've come too far to start feeling guilty about anything." His eyes darkened suddenly when he thought that that was exactly what he'd been doing since the day his stepmother died. The accident hadn't really been his fault, but he couldn't help feeling to blame for it anyway. If he'd just taken the time to check over the carriage, maybe . . . He shook off the thought and started toward his room. What did it matter anyway? Mary Elizabeth Wadsworth hadn't really loved him. If she had, she never would have lied to him . . . or to her husband.

He didn't bother knocking before he turned the knob and opened the door to his room, and once he saw Jennifer, he was glad he hadn't. He had caught her by surprise as she stood by the window absently staring out at the sea, the late afternoon sunlight reflecting the golden shades in her hair, and the startled, frightened look on her face when she spun around to confront him

148

added a special beauty to her already flawless face. Although her hair was braided and piled high on top of her head, whereas he preferred to see it hanging loose and free about her shoulders, the severity of the style accentuated the delicate bone structure of her cheek and jaw and the sea green shade of her eyes. Then he saw the dress she wore, and he frowned, suddenly realizing why Megan had seemed pleased. Its billowing sleeves and full skirts hid practically everything from view, and what the neckline would have revealed, Jennifer had carefully concealed with a handkerchief. Fighting the smile that threatened to lift the corners of his mouth, he casually turned, closed the door behind him, and then leaned back against it, his arms folded over his chest.

"I remember that dress," he said dryly. "Or I should say I remember the girl who wore it."

Jennifer's face paled even more, yet she somehow managed to pretend that he didn't intimidate her in the least. She raised her nose in the air and again glanced outside. "I suppose you had her killed, too, when she resisted."

Chad honestly had no idea whose dress it had been or who had worn it last. He merely wanted to frighten her into doing whatever he wished without argument . . . like everyone else on the island. Yet, he found her tenacity refreshing. He expected it of men, but never of a woman. They usually fell apart whenever they were faced with no other alternative, resorting to tears in the hope of winning his pity. But tears only made him angry because there was no way of talking sense into someone who was hysterical. His dark eyes traveled down the slender length of her.

"No, she wasn't killed," he said with a vague smile. "She just spent a week in the stocks as punishment for disobeying me."

Jennifer's head snapped around to stare at him in wide-eyed surprise. "The stocks? What had she done that deserved such punishment?"

"She wore that dress," he stated simply, forcing himself not to laugh out loud.

Jennifer's tiny chin sagged, and she glanced down at the full skirts billowing out around her ankles. "What's wrong with this dress?"

"Nothing," he replied with a shrug of one wide shoulder. "I just happen not to like it, so I bade her not to wear it. She decided she didn't care what I liked and wore it anyway. As a result—"

"You sentenced her to the stocks," Jennifer finished with a disgusted sigh.

Chad nodded and stood away from the door, his arms still folded over his chest. "But you aren't going to be that foolish, are you?" he asked, walking toward her.

Jennifer's heart thumped loudly in her chest, and she took a step sideways, hoping to elude him. But Chad quickly shot out a hand and caught her arm, pulling her close.

"You wouldn't last a day in it. It's made of wool, and the days here on the island are hot. You'd break out in a rash, all over your body, and I like your skin the way it is." His eyes lowered to her heaving bosom and the lace handkerchief covering it. With slow deliberation, he reached out and pulled the square of lace free.

Though his fingers never touched her, Jennifer's flesh burned with anticipation, for she was certain he intended to do more than alter her neckline. In a burst of courage, she yanked her arm free and quickly backed away from him. "And that, Captain, is just the point. It's *my* skin and *my* dress. Whatever I choose to do with either of them is no concern of yours." She could feel her body tremble and hoped he wouldn't notice. She knew it wouldn't take much of an effort on his part to make her change her mind, but perhaps if he thought she was stubborn enough to contest his authority, he might respect her and relent. She knew differently when she saw the half-smile that kinked his mouth, and she took another hurried step backward when he started toward her again.

"I hate to think how uncomfortable you'd be locked up in the pillory," he said, continuing his advance. "And how humiliated you'd feel with everyone staring at you, grinning and making comments." The smile disappeared from his lips, but it still sparkled in his eyes as he backed her into the corner and brought her retreat to a quick end. "But I admire your determination to stand up for what you think is your right." His ebony eyes lowered to examine the dress. "I admire it, but I can't allow it." Without warning, he seized the neckline of her dress and ripped the garment all the way to the waist in one merciless sweep, ruining it beyond repair.

"Damn you!" Jennifer exploded, her rage foregoing her concern over what he might do in retaliation. He had victimized her for the last time! Bringing up her hand, she struck him with her open palm, snapping his head to one side as the sound of the well-placed slap reverberated throughout the room.

Surprised more than hurt by the blow, Chad stood perfectly still. He couldn't remember the last time a woman had slapped him, though what he usually did to them warranted more than this mild form of reaction. Jennifer Grey was treating him as if he were a gentleman who had said something to offend her. He smiled in spite of himself. She had a lot to learn about pirates . . . and about Chad LaShelle. He rubbed his smarting cheek and looked at her.

"Take it off," he calmly ordered.

Jennifer's face flamed, and she stiffened her spine. "I will not!" she declared, clutching the tattered remnants of her dress to her bosom. "I don't know who you think

151

you are, but I'm not about to bow down to your every whim. I won't always be your prisoner, and when I'm freed of you, I'll see justice brought down upon your head, so help me, God!"

Chad's brown eyes softened as he stared back at her. "Oh? And how do you plan to go about doing that? No one knows where this island is, and even if someone did, he wouldn't get within a half-mile of the shore before we blasted him out of the water. And who do you think would be stupid enough to try? Charles? My half brother is a snob, Jennifer. When he learns you've been with me—and I mean in a most intimate way—he'll renounce your betrothal, and our father will agree. You don't have any money to hire someone to help you, and there's no way off the island unless I decide to take you." He raised both hands and leaned forward to brace them against the wall on either side of Jennifer's head. "So the way I see it, you'll enjoy your stay here a little more if you do everything I tell you to do without arguing. You really have no choice, but doing so willingly will make things easier on you. Now take off the dress or I'll be obliged to do it for you."

Jennifer glared at him for a long moment, her teeth clamped shut to keep her chin from trembling. Tears burned the backs of her lids, and she blinked several times to stop them from welling in the corners of her eyes. She wasn't afraid of him. She wanted to kill him. But being trapped between his outstretched arms gave her no other option at the moment but to give in . . . at least until he stepped away from her. Lowering her arms, she started to slip the dress off one shoulder, waiting for him to drop his guard. She knew that he'd win eventually. But her defiance of his orders would be a victory for her, one he'd remember.

A twinge of mild disappointment wrinkled his brow when the little minx appeared to relent, and he dropped his arms and stepped back, intending to watch. But the instant he did, Jennifer bolted toward the bed, fell upon it, and rolled off the other side, grabbing the hurricane lamp from the night stand before she landed on her feet again. "I've met a few ogres in my life, Captain LaShelle, but you are by far the worst. You seem to get some distorted pleasure out of preying on helpless women. If you weren't truly a coward, you'd treat us the way we're supposed to be treated. But you can't. You feel threatened by us because we have the ability to think and to reason . . . and because the majority of us find you appalling. It bruises your ego to think one of us might not want anything to do with you, so you force yourself on us before we have the chance to decide for ourselves."

The corner of his mouth twitched as he fought back a smile. With cool casualness, he slowly rounded the bed and leaned his shoulder against one of its posts, staring at her with one brow raised. "Are you trying to tell me that if I played the part of a gentleman, you'd welcome my advances?"

"No!" she rallied, the lamp rattling in her hand. "It's too late for that."

He shrugged and stood erect. "Then I guess it doesn't matter how I treat you. Does it?"

A wicked grin parted his lips, and Jennifer knew she was about to pay for her foolishness. She raised her weapon higher. At least she wouldn't give in without a fight.

"And before you throw that at me, I think I should tell you what will happen to you if you do."

Jennifer's upper lip curled. "You'll put me on public display."

Chad nodded his head. "Without the dress."

Fear shot through every muscle in Jennifer's body, making it impossible for her to draw a breath. She had very little doubt that he would do exactly that, so rather than find out for sure, she quickly set the lamp back on the night stand.

"Now take the dress off," he ordered again. When she hesitated, he glowered at her. "On your own or with my help."

Her hands quickly moved to her shoulders when he took a step toward her, but her eyes never left his face. Dropping the dress to the floor, she stepped out of it, then stooped to pick it up. But rather than politely handing it over, she found enough courage to fling it at him.

"You still owe me a dress," she spat.

"What I owe you is a piece of advice," he growled in return, no longer amused by her spunk. "If you're thinking to win Megan's sympathy so she'll try to help you get off this island, don't bother. I have ways of dealing with people who go against me, and helping you would be just that. You wouldn't like being the reason she's punished, nor would you like my method." Wadding the dress up into a ball, he turned and stormed the door. "Now I suggest you think about that for a while. And I suggest you take a good hard look at your situation here. You can either make it rough on yourself by continuing to defy me or have it relatively easy by doing as you're told!"

"By being your whore?" she courageously blurted out through mounting tears. "Or do you intend for me to earn my keep by prostituting myself to any man who stumbles up here?"

A brief frown wrinkled his dark brow as he wondered what had given her such an idea. Then he decided perhaps the threat of it would tame her down. "That might not be such a bad idea. At least then you'd be too tired to give me any trouble." He glared at her for a second longer, then yanked open the door and marched out, jerking it shut behind him with a loud bang.

Tears instantly filled Jennifer's eyes. How would she ever survive this ordeal when she had to contend with him? He had taken away her only hope of getting off the island, and if she didn't do whatever he wanted, he'd make her pay for that in a most humiliating way, either with her head and wrists trapped between two boards where everyone could laugh at her or here, in his— She squeezed her eyes shut, thinking the former punishment would be more tolerable than enduring the shame of having everyone know what went on in this room. God, if she were only fat and ugly and old, maybe then he wouldn't even look at her. With a groan, she plopped down on the bed. Her looks had nothing to do with it, and she knew it. He had openly admitted that he was doing this out of revenge against his father and half brother. Damn him! Damn his rotten soul! Right now it seemed impossible, but if there was a way to make him pay for this, she'd find it. Overcome by hopelessness, she collapsed against the pillows and wept.

"Stuart." Chad called out to his second mate as he descended the stairs into the commons.

"Aye, Cap'n," the man replied, quickly coming to his feet.

Without breaking stride, Chad headed toward the table where Jason sat watching him, barking out orders as he walked, "Find Megan and tell her I want to see her right away. I'll be waiting over here."

"Aye, aye, sir." Stuart nodded, then hurried off.

The angry expression on Chad's face told Jason that his captain's meeting with the young woman hadn't gone well, but he didn't understand why Chad wanted to speak with Megan again. He took a sip from his mug and waited until Chad was close enough to hear his question. "Is there a problem?"

Tossing the torn dress onto the table at which his first mate sat, Chad growled. "Not anymore." Straddling the bench, he motioned for the barmaid to bring him a mug of ale.

Jason gave the garment a quick once-over, noticing that the bodice was in shreds, and frowned. "What's this?"

"It's what I paid two shillings for."

"But it's ruined," Jason observed. "Surely Megan didn't think you'd—"

"Megan had nothing to do with it. And it wasn't torn when she gave it to Miss Grey." He took the mug the serving girl brought him and downed a long swallow before he shifted around on the bench and leaned forward on his elbows, a dark scowl drawing his black brows together. The scar on his chin gleamed white.

"You're not saying Miss Grey deliberately—"

Chad cut him short. "The only thing Miss Grey does deliberately is provoke me. She didn't ruin it. I did." He waved a hand at the pile of cloth. "Look at it, for Christ's sake. It's wool. How long would it take for her to faint from the heat wearing something like that?"

Jason shrugged, confused. "So why—"

"She picked it because she knew I wouldn't approve." He slammed his palm against the table top. "Damn! That woman is infuriating." He glared into his mug for a moment, then heaved a disgusted sigh and glanced up at his friend, a finger pointed at him. "If I didn't need her . . ." He let the sentence go unfinished, curled his hand in to a fist, and then glared at it as if he'd like to smash it against something.

Jason cleared his throat and quickly rubbed his thumb along his lower lip, praying he wouldn't burst into laughter. He hadn't said two words to Jennifer Grey, but he liked her without having had the opportunity to get to know her. She had a lot of nerve where the captain was

156

concerned, and it would be very interesting to see who broke first.

"You know," he said, leaning back against the wall behind him, "you can't exactly blame her. She doesn't strike me as the type who's used to being treated like a prisoner. She's bound to rebel simply out of a need to survive."

Only Chad's dark eyes moved to look at his companion from beneath lowered brows. "Are you suggesting I give her a room of her own, allow her total freedom of the island, a personal maid, and the promise that as soon as my ship is repaired, I'll take her to England . . . or anywhere else she'd like to go?"

Jason couldn't hold back the smile that parted his lips. "No. That isn't what I meant. I'm just saying that unless you come to some sort of compromise, she'll defy you whenever she can—whether she does it on purpose or unintentionally. She isn't a whore, and I doubt you'll turn her into one. Choosing that dress wasn't necessarily done to provoke you, Chad, perhaps it was a frantic attempt to save her dignity."

"Dignity?" Chad barked. "From whom?"

"Everyone on this island. I'm sure she's learned by now who's in charge and why, and that everyone thinks of her as your 'property.' I'm sure she realizes that she can't stop the gossiping, but she can show the rest of us that she isn't going to do what you want her to do just because you demand it . . . the way everyone else does. She isn't here of her own accord, and that's what she's trying to prove to the rest of us. To you."

"And if I let her get away with it, if I relent one tiny bit, the others will think they can defy me, too," Chad reminded him.

"I know that," Jason replied. "And it's why I'm trying to tell you that if Miss Grey is a prisoner, she has to be treated as such, and that you can't expect anything less than obedience from her. If she's a thorn in your side, lock her up in the jail until you're ready to sail with her to England . . . or wherever you plan to take her. But if you decide to keep her in your room, you're going to have to be willing to put up with her defiance."

A lazy smile spread across Chad's handsome face. "Put up with it or break her." He grinned into his mug before taking a drink, a devilish gleam sparkled in his eyes when he looked back at his friend.

Sighing, Jason shook his head and smiled, wondering if he shouldn't warn Chad that there was always a chance he might not win. Beauty coupled with a sensitive nature could have a devastating effect on a man, especially if a woman knew how to use those traits to her advantage . . . and the man on whom she centered them was too sure of himself. Deciding that it was time his friend learned a long-overdue lesson, Jason waved at the barmaid, intending to order his supper. Maybe Chad thought of the conflict as a challenge, but Jason knew *he'd* be the one to enjoy it.

Chapter Seven

"Oh, dear God in heaven," Jason moaned, tears of frustration welling in his eyes. "Who would do such a thing?" Turning angrily away from the group crowded around the dismembered remains of a young girl's body, he buried his face in his hands, trying to regain control of his emotions and hoping the star-filled night wouldn't allow the others to see his grief. He had always liked the little redhead.

"Who found her?" Chad asked, dropping the blanket back over the mutilated corpse once he'd confirmed the report that it was Megan. Her clothes had been torn from her, indicating that she had probably been raped. But the worst of it was that both legs had been severed at the knee, and one arm at the elbow. Chad bitterly wondered if her attacker had killed her first and then proceeded to chop off each limb with an axe or whether he was the kind of vermin who got some sort of sick pleasure out of simply torturing his victim.

"Tranel found her, Cap'n," Stuart replied. "After her mother told me that she hadn't come back from her visit to the inn, I asked some of the crew to help look for her."

"Ely Brown said he saw her walk past his blacksmith shop, that was shortly after she left the inn," Tranel explained when Chad stood up and turned to him. "She was heading toward her mother's shoppe. So that's where I started, at the blacksmith's, since no one saw her after that. Can't tell ya why I decided to look here, Cap'n, bein' so far back in the woods and all, but I did. Gut feelin', I s'pose. Anyway, I saw this here axe." He held up the weapon and used it to point back toward a stand of trees. "It was stuck in the trunk of that palm, and when I got close enough, I noticed all this blood on the blade and handle. Gave me a real funny feelin', it did, almost like I knew what to expect. Anyway, I walked on a little ways further and that's when I found her. Cap'n?' he frowned. "None of us ever thinks twice about killin' someone, but we'd never do somethin' like this. Especially to Megan. Everybody liked her."

Chad had been thinking the same thing. But it didn't erase the fact that someone on the island had murdered Megan O'Connor . . . brutally. He shot a quick glance up toward the bluffs surrounding them. Either one of his men had done this or there was an intruder hiding out there somewhere.

"No one heard her scream?" he asked thoughtfully.

" She's got an awful lump on her head, Cap'n," Stuart remarked. "I'd say whoever did this knocked her out first. Megan was a feisty little gal; she would have put up a good fight. And she wasn't one to go wandering off."

"What are you saying?"

"Simply that the man responsible for this had to have been right here in the village. And she probably knew him. Otherwise she would have screamed loud enough to bring the entire place down around the bastard's ears."

"But Jordon," Andrew Tranel objected, "if that's what really happened, then there's no question but what one of us done her in." His face whitened suddenly, and he staggered back a step. "Ya ain't thinkin' it was me, are ya? I'm the one what found her."

"No," Jordon quickly assured him. "I know you better than to think that."

"Then who?"

"I'm not going to accuse anyone until there's more proof." He frowned and glanced down at the dark shape covered by a blanket. "If there ever is . . ."

"Andrew, let me see that," Chad said, nodding at the ax the man held. After studying the blade and making a thorough examination of the wooden handle, he asked, "Anyone have any idea who this might belong to?"

"Hard to say, Cap'n," Stuart answered. "Ely makes them for us, so they're all pretty much the same. Could even have come from his place. I know he has several lying around. It would have been very easy for anyone to pick one up."

"Without being seen?"

"Aye. He's got a back door to his shop, and he usually keeps it open in the day—to let out the heat from his fire."

Chad handed the ax back to Tranel. "Take this to him and see if he recognizes it. It's the only lead we have." He turned to Stuart as Andrew hurried away from them. "Has anyone told her mother yet?"

"No, Cap'n. You want me to?"

Chad shook his head and glanced back toward the village. "No. The people on this island are my responsibility. I'm the one who should tell her."

"What about Willard? Someone ought to tell him. He cared an awful lot for Megan, and I'm afraid he's going to take this pretty hard."

Chad envisioned the huge, but gentle young man the moment Jordon mentioned Willard Anderson's name. He had found Willard wandering the streets of Pembroke, a small coastal town in western England, about three years ago. Willard had appeared to be in a daze, and if someone were to ask Chad why he had stopped to help

161

the boy, he probably couldn't say. He had guessed that Willard had been close to nineteen years old, yet he'd had the mind of a twelve-year-old child, and something inside Chad had snapped when he'd seen the way people were making fun of the boy. Having assured Willard that he wasn't going to hurt him, Chad had taken him to his ship, given him food and something to drink, then he'd encouraged the lad to tell him what he was doing wandering about. Willard had broken down in tears as he'd told his new friend that his mother had just died, and that his landlord had thrown him out of the back room he'd shared with her. He had been such a pathetic sight that Chad hadn't had the heart to send him on his way. And besides, the *Black Falcon* could always use a strong hand to mend her sails and scrub her decks.

Chad had realized his mistake in taking Willard along with him the first time the pirate vessel had attacked a merchant ship sailing toward France. But it wasn't until after his crew had killed all those on board, ransacked its cargo, and set sail for the island, that Chad had learned Willard's tender nature couldn't handle the brutality of piracy. He had found the boy hiding beneath the canvas of the longboat, his eyes filled with tears, nearly frightened out of his wits. At that moment, Chad had decided that Willard would never sail with him again, but would live on the island and earn his keep repairing the *Black Falcon* whenever she limped into the harbor.

His size and oddity had scared most of the people in the village, and at first, it had been very difficult for Willard to adjust. Then Chad introduced him to Megan, a bright, kind hearted young girl who fell in love with Willard the moment she saw him. Megan was only twelve at the time, and she had no playmates. Willard took care of that, and they became good, fast friends. She always looked out for him, and he for her. Her death would come as a terrible shock to him, and Chad wasn't sure how he'd react.

"No, Jordon." He sighed. "I'll tell Willard, too. Perhaps he'll accept it a little easier coming from me." His dark brows drawn together in a troubled frown, he looked back one more time at the tiny shape covered in a blanket. "Take care of her for me, will you, Jordon?"

"Aye, Cap'n," Stuart quietly assured him.

A long moment of silence followed while Chad continued to stare at the body that had once been a lively, sparkling young girl. It angered him that despite all his rules and precautions to insure the safety of his people on the island, someone had blatantly undermined him. This was *his* village, these were *his* people, and he would see to it that someone paid for what had happened.

"Chad." Jason interrupted into his captain's thoughts. "I'd like to go with you when you talk to Megan's mother."

Dark brown eyes settled on the man. "All right," Chad concurred. "But then I'd like you to start questioning everybody in the village. I want to know what they saw or heard and where they were at approximately the time Megan was killed. And they'd better have someone to back up their claims. Those who don't—I want their belongings looked at. Whoever did this got blood on his clothes. We'll find her murderer, and he'll be executed the same way Megan was . . . only he won't be unconscious beforehand."

As Chad walked back toward the inn, a bundle tucked beneath one arm, he kept reliving the scene with Megan's mother, marveling at the woman's outward show of self-control. She had even thanked him for his promise to find Megan's murderer. It wasn't until she had gathered up most of her daughter's clothes and handed them to Chad, instructing him to give them to someone who could use them, that he realized the impact of his news

163

hadn't truly hit her. Jason had sensed that, too, and when he'd offered to stay with Mrs. O'Connor for a while, Chad hadn't objected. His features softened a mite as he thought about the pair, for Chad had noticed some time ago that his first mate had more than a casual interest in the dressmaker. She was still a very comely woman in her mid thirties, and she had obviously attracted Jason's attention, though he tried very hard not to show it. That was probably why he'd taken Megan's death so hard. At least Marya O'Connor had someone to comfort her. Willard didn't.

Chad had spent the last hour talking to the young man, trying to assure him that just because Megan had died didn't mean Chad was going to send Willard away. The poor lad associated the death of someone he loved with having to lose his home as well, and before he broke down in tears, he had begged Chad not to die, too. Chad found that he couldn't lie to Willard, and he attempted to explain to him that everyone had to die sooner or later, but that he didn't plan on doing so for a long, long time. That seemed to relax Willard a little, and Chad left him only after he had promised to go to bed for the night because there was nothing either of them could do for Megan right then. Chad stood outside Willard's little hut at the edge of town for a long while, remembering his stepmother's death and the pain he'd suffered because of it, thinking how similar his situation was to Willard's. Chad had lost his home, too, when someone he loved had died. Finally, pushing aside thoughts of his past, he forced his attention to the matters at hand. He'd locate Stuart and Tranel, two of the few crew members he trusted, and he'd instruct them to ride the beach in opposite directions until the entire perimeter of the island had been searched. If an unwelcome ship had dropped anchor, he wanted to know about it.

The commons was empty when Chad entered the inn.

Obviously, word of Megan's brutal death had quickly spread through the village and anyone who didn't live at the inn had decided it was safer to be at home than to roam the streets at this late hour. He crossed to the stairway and started to climb it. As soon as he collected his pistol and dropped off the clothes Mrs. O'Connor had given him, he'd look for Jordon and Andrew.

Only ashen moonlight trickled into his room to light the way when Chad opened the door and stepped inside. His thoughts centered on what he'd do next, he didn't see Jennifer at first until she stood up suddenly and backed away from the bed, taking the sheet with her to wrap around her slender frame. In all the excitement he had forgotten about her, and he silently cursed his stupidity in doing so . . . for several reasons. The obstinate little wench might have seized this opportunity to run off again, unaware of the dangers that lurked right outside the door. She could have been killed in the same manner as Megan, and the fear that already gripped the village would have been intensified. More important, he would have lost a very powerful means of exacting revenge. He closed the door behind him and crossed to the night stand to light the lamp, tossing his bundle onto the bed as he did so and grinning secretively. And, of course, he wouldn't have had the lively vixen to warm his bed anymore. A soft glow of amber light flooded the room, and he turned about to take from the dresser the pistol he had hidden in the bottom drawer under some of his things.

"What are you doing?" she asked worriedly when he stood erect again, his back to her, and proceeded to check his gun.

Dark brown eyes shifted up to look briefly at her in the reflection of the mirror, then returned to the pistol he held. "Nothing that concerns you," he said dryly.

Jennifer had been unable to think of anything since he

165

had stormed from the room earlier, other than the conversation they had had. She didn't want harm to come to Megan because of her. Megan had told her that anyone on the island who did something very wrong was sent back to London to serve out his or her time in prison. But the captain hadn't found Megan in prison, so Jennifer assumed he would lock the young girl in his jail or sentence her to the pillory. Either punishment, to Jennifer's way of thinking, was unfair. Megan shouldn't be treated like the others on the island since her only crime had been wanting to be with her mother. Of course, trying to explain that to the captain would be pointless. He wasn't the sort who could be reasoned with. He'd more than likely slit a person's throat for simply trying. A shiver ran through her when her gaze absently lowered to the knife and scabbard looped through his belt and hanging from his left hip. And more than likely he'd use his own knife. Hugging the thin coverlet around her, she took a deep breath, and hoping he wouldn't suspect her real reason for wanting to talk with Megan, she lifted her eyes to watch his reaction in the mirror.

"Will Megan be by in the morning to take my measurements?"

Satisfied that the weapon was ready for firing, Chad stuck it in his belt and picked up the pouch of gunpowder from the dresser top. He had only been half listening to her, and without giving any thought to how it might sound, he growled, "Megan won't be going anywhere."

Jennifer feared it was already too late. "You haven't locked her up, have you? She hasn't done anything."

Dark eyes, shadowed by a fierce frown and reflected in the looking glass, glared up at her. "She's dead."

The bluntness of his seemingly callous declaration and the shock of such news caught her so completely off guard that she didn't respond at first. Megan couldn't be dead. The two of them had talked only a few hours ago,

166

and they were just getting to know each other. How could she be dead? What had happened? Had there been an accident? A chilling thought ran through her mind. Had Megan died because of her? Had another pirate vessel docked as she had said one would, and had she gone to the ship to talk with someone about taking a message to Charles? Had he taken advantage of her? Murdered her? Even raped her? Tears gathered in Jennifer's eyes, and she opened her mouth to voice her worries when the captain turned around to face her. The light from the lamp fell across him, and she instantly saw the bloodstains on one knee of his breeches.

"Oh, my God!" she screamed. Every word of his pledge to punish Megan should the girl think to help Jennifer escape the island exploded in her mind. *You wouldn't like being the reason she's punished, nor would you like my method,* he had vowed. She stumbled backward several steps when he started toward her, a confused look on his handsome face. "You killed her! You animal! You heartless cur! You murdered a child!"

Chad's own ire rose. "What the hell are you talking about?"

The backs of Jennifer's legs bumped the night stand, and the bowl and pitcher sitting atop it rattled. In a panic, she cowered into the corner, wanting to get as far away from him as possible yet managing only to trap herself when he stepped before her. "You said you'd punish her if she tried to help me. You said I wouldn't like your form of punishment." Tears spilled over the rims of her dark lashes and raced for her chin. "Dear God, you killed her because of me!" Wide, fearful eyes filled with tears darted first from his face to the pistol in his belt, then to the dark stain on his clothing.

Unable to understand why she was accusing him of murdering Megan, he absently followed the direction of her gaze and, for the first time, saw the blood smeared on his breeches. He must have knelt in it when he'd examined the girl's remains. Suddenly, he realized how it must look to Jennifer, but awareness didn't soften his mood. More than anything, he hated being blamed for something he didn't do. The muscle in his cheek twitched with his irritation, and without offering an explanation—he didn't feel he owed her one—he jerked his head toward the bundle of clothing he had brought with him.

"You'll find some things in there to wear. Take care of them. They're all you'll get until you can earn your keep." He strode away from her then and went to the door, where he paused and looked back at her. "I'm going to lock this and post a guard outside the window," he told her as he unhooked the scabbard from his belt and tossed it and the knife onto the bed. "Use this if anyone other than my first mate, Jason Bingham, or I attempt to get in here. And I do mean use it." He glowered at her. "If you hesitate, you'll be dead."

Jennifer's tiny body shook uncontrollably once the captain had exited the room and slammed the door shut behind him. She wasn't even sure if he'd turned the key in the lock as he'd said he would do. Too many emotions gripped her for her to deal logically with anything. Megan was dead. She had accused him of killing her, and he hadn't denied it. Yet, somehow, somewhere deep inside her, she sensed that that wasn't what had happened. He was angry—he always seemed to be angry—but the root of it stemmed from something else, something he wouldn't share with her. If he had killed the young redhead for trying to help Jennifer, then why hadn't he come back and told her what he'd done, warned her that if she tried to find someone else to take Megan's place, he would kill that person, too?

"Oh, Megan," she whispered through her tears. "I'm so sorry."

Maybe Captain LaShelle wasn't guilty, but the

168

atrocities he inflicted upon the people of this island had to be stopped. Her father had told her years ago about the debtor's prison in England and how ridiculous it was to lock people up because they couldn't repay what they owed. How would locking them up help? It made more sense for them to work it off. Then everyone would benefit. Debtors weren't really criminals . . . just victims. What the captain was doing for those people was humane, but he only did it for his own gain. He wasn't thinking of them when he freed them and brought them to this island. He needed them. If the captain had set up a sytem in which these people were allowed to pay back what they owed to him for freeing them, and if they then had the option of staying on the island or returning to England or going anywhere they chose, then Megan and her mother would have been gone, and Megan would still be alive.

Jennifer's chin quivered, and she slowly sank down on the bed. Maybe it wasn't by Captain LaShelle's hand that Megan had died, but in a sense he was responsible for her death. *He* was the reason she was here on the island. Her gaze absently drifted to the knife and the scabbard, and she reached out to trace a fingertip along the leather handle. If there were only some way for her to get off the island, she would do everything in her power to see that Chad LaShelle got what was coming to him. Suddenly, an idea came to her. She straightened, briskly wiped the tears from her face with the back of her hand, and stood up to hurry toward the window. Peering out, she could see the figure of a man below, the guard Captain LaShelle had placed there, and a devious half-smile lifted her lips. Whirling, she returned to the bed and quickly unfastened the strings tied around the bundle of clothing he had given her. She would get off the island, and she was going to do it with Megan's help.

A disapproving scowl darkened Jennifer's sea green

eyes once she saw the attire from which she had to choose. The skirts and blouses were all patterned after the outfit Megan had worn, and there was even a pair of sandals with leather straps that tied across the foot and up around the ankle. Possibly these garments would be more comfortable in the heat than those she was used to wearing back in Virginia; nonetheless, she still didn't think them proper attire for a lady. But then, who in this village planned to treat her like one? Captain LaShelle?

"Ha!" she laughed sarcastically. "He wouldn't know how."

Standing erect, she shimmied out of the petticoats Megan had brought her, and kicked them aside, knowing that their cumbersome weight would only slow her down. She had no idea how long she would have to be in hiding or how quickly she'd have to move to keep from being spotted or, worse yet, caught. She picked up one of the white cotton blouses and put it on. Perhaps wearing the customary garb of the village women would have advantages after all. She'd blend right in should it become necessary for her to move about in the daytime. She smiled as she secured the skirt around her narrow waist, thinking how frustrated Chad LaShelle would be when he searched the entire island for her while she remained hidden right here in the village. Then, just as soon as a ship dropped anchor in the harbor, she'd swim out to it and board it when no one was looking. But first she'd have to steal enough money to convince the captain of the ship to take her to England. And that could be a problem, she thought, as she sat down on the edge of the bed to don her sandals. But it would certainly be worth the effort.

Satisfied with the way she looked, she leaned forward, grabbed a petticoat from the floor, and proceeded to rip off a long, thin strip. Threading the piece of material through the loops on the scabbard, she tied the weapon to her thigh. Once she dropped her skirt, no one would see it. Then she stood up. Now all she had to do was trick the guard into unlocking the door, and she already had an idea of how to accomplish that. Crossing to the window, she cautiously peered down at the man to make sure he hadn't left for some reason or another. Then she returned to the side of the bed and picked up the water bowl from the night stand. Captain LaShelle had said not to let anyone other than himself or Jason Bingham into the room. She didn't know why. Previously, he hadn't cared whether or not anyone came into her room. What difference did it make now? Shrugging that off as unimportant, she held the bowl out in front of her and let it go. It hit the floor with a thunderous crash and shattered into a hundred pieces.

"No! No, stay away from me," she shouted toward the window, her voice frantic and loud enough for the guard to hear. She waited a moment, then grabbed the pitcher and slipped over to the window to peek down. A pleased smile touched her lips when she saw that the guard had left his post; she could only assume he was on his way up to save her. Darting across the room, she positioned herself beside the door, the water pitcher held high above her head. If the fool didn't catch on to her scheme when he discovered that the door was still locked, she'd club him over the head when he broke in. She closed her eyes, mumbled a prayer, and then held her breath as she heard footsteps racing down the hall.

Her heart pounded so loudly in her chest, she was sure he would hear it. The palms of her hands were wet. Every muscle in her body ached, and for a moment, she was afraid she was going to faint. It seemed to take the man an hour to cover the distance to her door, and it suddenly dawned on her that perhaps it wasn't the guard coming to rescue her but Captain LaShelle! A whimper escaped her quivering mouth, and she bit down hard on her lower lip

171

to stop from screaming out loud. She jumped when the doorknob rattled.

"Miss Grey!" The voice called to her. "Miss Grey!"

For a split second she thought it was the captain until she realized he would have unlocked the door and rushed in without calling to her . . . and he wouldn't have been so formal! She sucked in a quick breath and shouted, "Please help me! He's trying to kill—" She purposely allowed the plea to go unfinished, hoping that would be enough to convince the guard of the urgency of the moment so he wouldn't think there was time to get the captain. It worked. Only a second later the door came crashing open when the man put his shoulder to it, splintering the framework around it. He stumbled in off balance and before he could catch himself, Jennifer hit him with the water pitcher. The impact of porcelain against the man's skull numbed her fingers, but she jumped over the body lying in the way and raced out into the hall, heading for the stairs and escape. Yet, before she had traveled ten feet, a door to her left, just a few steps ahead of her, was thrown open, and Modesty Copeland appeared before her.

"What the hell's goin' on?" she shouted, fumbling with the sash of her robe.

Her hair was a mess, and it was quite obvious to Jennifer that the woman had been awakened out of a sound sleep for she buried the knuckles of her hands in the corners of her eyes and blinked repeatedly in an effort to clear her head. If Jennifer worked quickly enough, she could dispose of this threat before the woman knew what hit her. Without any hesitation, she grabbed Modesty's arm, spun her around and shoved her back into her room.

"Go back to bed, Modesty," Jennifer instructed with a smile, as she reached for the key that protruded from the lock in the door. "The captain says we are to stay in our

172

rooms." Without giving the woman a chance to ask why, Jennifer grabbed the knob, pulled the door shut behind her, and locked Modesty in. A delighted smile curled her lips as she purposely dropped the key into the bucket of dirty wash water sitting on the floor near her. Then she whirled around and headed for the stairs. Either the captain would have to have two doors repaired or Modesty was in for a long, lonely stay in her room until a locksmith could be summoned.

"Hey, ye bloody bitch," she heard Modesty scream after her. "Let me out of 'ere! I'm gonna tell the cap'n what ye done!"

"I'm sure you will," Jennifer mumbled to herself once she reached the top of the stairway.

For a moment she paused, wondering whether anyone would be around to spot her, and her heart beat a little faster as she cautiously descended the stairs to the commons. Luckily, the large room was vacant, and she wasted no time in crossing to the front door. Peering out into the street, she noticed a group of men at one end, but they seemed to be involved in a discussion of some sort, thus freeing her to slip out unnoticed. Hurriedly leaving the inn, she started off, heading in the opposite direction from the men and keeping to the shadows in case one of them should happen to look her way.

Upon her arrival in the village two days ago, she had noticed a huge building located near the pier and had assumed it was a warehouse. If she was fortunate, it would offer the refuge she needed until a ship sailed into port, and it would certainly be the last place Captain LaShelle would look for her. It was much too close to the village. She was sure he would send his men into the hills to search for her, and while they were off chasing shadows, she'd be helping herself to the food and water she needed to stay alive—and to the money that would see her on board the next ship bound for England. A devilish gleam lighted up her eyes. If she could manage it, she'd be sure to take some of his.

Sticking close to the buildings, she ducked into the first alley she came to and hurried in the direction of the shoreline, toward the place where she recalled seeing the warehouse. To her delight, its tall, dark shape loomed promisingly before her when she stepped out from behind the corner of the last building. Guardedly, she scanned the space between her and her destination, the area around the pier, then back over her shoulder for anyone who might stumble out of a doorway or step from behind a leafy palm tree or cluster of ferns, and all the while she was listening for voices or footsteps close by. Satisfied that she was alone and that she could reach the warehouse without being seen, she bolted off, running as quickly and as noiselessly as possible.

Upon reaching the dark side of the building where moonlight couldn't brighten it and the glow of street lamps fell short, Jennifer pressed her body up against its rough wooden exterior and paused a moment to catch her breath and calm her nerves a mite, her gaze hurriedly surveying the area she had just traveled. She could hear faint voices some distance away, but their tone held no urgency, and she relaxed a little, knowing that so far her plan had gone well. Glancing to her right, she decided to try the door she was sure was around the corner, and started toward it. If it was locked, she'd be forced to use one of the windows.

Platinum streams of light filtered down through the broad palm leaves shading the entrance to the warehouse, and Jennifer stopped to examine the area. A long wooden walkway ran from the pier directly to the double doors at the front of the building. These were closed, but appeared to have no lock barring her from entering. At the end of the pier was the only ship in port. Its tall masts jutted skyward like black sentinels standing guard over

174

the cove and the people of the village, and Jennifer shivered when she realized the ship must belong to Captain LaShelle. If only there were some way to sail the vessel alone, she'd weigh anchor and take an easterly course toward England. She sighed inwardly, knowing how ridiculous it was to even think of doing such a thing, and rounded the corner of the warehouse.

The huge wooden door moaned a little when she took the handle and pulled, but it swung open on well-oiled hinges. A chill shimmied up her spine as she looked at the mammoth, black cavity before her, imagining it to be the gaping mouth of some gigantic monster waiting to devour her. She hesitated, then stepped inside, telling herself that the real monster lived at the inn and before very long, he'd be breathing fire—just as soon as he returned to his room and found it empty.

Along the wall to her left and midway into the enormous room, she could see two windows, the pale silver light from outside funneling in through them and falling on a stack of large crates sitting in front of them. It took her eyes a few minutes to readjust, but once they had, she noticed that the place had a loft at one end and that the ladder leading to it was next to the last window. Since the rest of the warehouse appeared to be empty save for the crates, she decided to hide in the loft. That way she'd have a clear view of anyone coming in through the front doors and possibly enough time to figure out an escape route should she be seen. After pulling the door shut behind her, she carefully made her way to the ladder and started up it.

The air changed. No longer simply humid, it now had a musty smell as well once she swung herself onto the floor of the loft. But that didn't bother her as much as being reminded of her fear of heights. She crawled away from the edge and collapsed on her back, her breath coming in labored gasps as she tried to assure herself that she was

175

perfectly safe now. For as long as she could remember, she'd been afraid of being more than five feet off the ground—something she couldn't understand. As a child, she had been a bit of a hoyden, running foot races and hunting snakes with the slave boys instead of remaining inside the manor mastering the art of needlepoint. Her father claimed that her fear had started when she'd fallen out of an apple tree she had climbed while playing hide and seek, but she could never quite accept that. She loved riding horses bareback, and though she had been thrown several times, she'd always gotten right back on. Sitting astride one of her father's huge stallions, she was a good distance off the ground! Yet, whatever its cause, her fear was very real, and she knew climbing back down the ladder would be a challenging feat. She closed her eyes and released a heavy sigh. Of course, being hungry could force a person to do just about anything.

She hadn't realized until now just how tired she really was. Nor did it take her long to figure out how stiff she'd be in the morning from lying on a hard, wood floor. Sitting up, she tried to focus on her surroundings, and noticed the square outline of moonlight peeking in around the closed loft door. She grinned excitedly. Not only would she get some fresh air by opening it, she'd also be able to see if there was anything in the loft out of which she could make a comfortable bed. On hands and knees, she crawled over to the door, fumbled for the catch, and slowly swung it open. Cooler air rushed in and she sat back on one hip to enjoy it for a moment. From here, she had an unrestricted view of the village off to the right, and on her left, she could see the long stretch of white beach as it curled around the perimeter of the island. Considering all that had happened to her since her arrival and how she came to be here, she reluctantly had to admit that this small piece of land with its palms and hot springs, its wide assortment of flowers and fruits, and its moonlit nights was truly a paradise. Her expression saddened as she thought about her father and how he would have liked this island. He'd always told her that he didn't truly enjoy living in the Colonies because of all the rules and regulations the Crown imposed on them, and that he wasn't really cut out to be a planter. But he hadn't wanted to return to London either. Jennifer decided that this little island would have been the perfect solution—her lovely brow knitted—if it weren't for the pirate captain, for he had turned this tiny piece of heaven into nothing more than a prison without any bars.

Absently, her gaze drifted upward, and she briefly took note of the rope and pulley hanging from an extension. Obviously they were used to lower heavy crates from the loft to the ground outside. Now that she thought about it, she realized that Chad LaShelle had turned a deserted plot of land into a functioning and productive village or at least doing so had been his idea. The townsfolk were the ones who had done the actual work. A yawn caught her off guard and reminded her that she had opened the small door to let in the light and enable herself to examine the loft, and she casually swung around to begin her search, one hand still covering her mouth. The square shaft of light fell across a long section of the floor, revealing nothing, and Jennifer's shoulders drooped. Just as she decided she would have to be content with the hard, wooden planks, a man suddenly stepped out of the shadows and half into the light, his bloody trouser leg and left shoe all that she could clearly see of him. A scream lodged in her throat, and she sat perfectly still, paralyzed with fear and unable to pull her eyes away from the dark crimson stain on the man's clothing.

"Hello, Miss Grey." His deep, unfamiliar voice was mocking. "You're a very hard person to catch alone. I've been trying now for some time." His evil laughter

177

bounced off every knot in her spine. "Then you go and make it easy for me. Almost like ya knew I was up here, waiting."

He took a step toward her and placed the lower half of his torso in the light, but his identity was still shielded by darkness. Yet, Jennifer didn't have to see his face to know what he intended to do. It was quite simple to figure that out. He planned to kill her, with the knife he'd pulled from in back of him. When the steel blade caught the light and flashed in Jennifer's eyes, she bolted into action. Coming up on her knees, she jumped to her feet and threw herself out the loft's tiny door, her arms fanned wide, fingers groping for the length of rope tied to the extension. One hand missed, and if she hadn't been so scared, she might have screamed. The rough cord burned into the palm of her hand as her weight pulled her down a notch, but for an instant she thought it was the most wonderful pain she had ever endured. Then, when she felt her body start to fall, the realization of what she had done hit her. Frantic, she grabbed the rope in both hands and looked up. She could only vaguely make out the top of the block and tackle, but that look told her she would plummet earthward for another five feet or more before the knot in the rope hit the shackle and stopped her rapid descent. She had barely come to that conclusion when she was jerked to a halt and bounced roughly upward. She lost her grip and fell the rest of the way to the ground.

Luckily, Jennifer landed on her feet, but in the process, she twisted her ankle. Excruciating pain shot up her leg as she tumbled onto one hip. She wished she could take a moment to make sure she hadn't broken anything, yet she knew she couldn't afford to waste even a second. If she had managed to lower herself from the loft in this manner, then her assailant would most assuredly use the same method. Glancing up at the small

178

opening in side of the huge building as she struggled to rise on one foot, she could see his dark shape preparing to lunge for the rope, and she limped off as fast as she could, ignoring her pain and forcing herself not to cry.

Jennifer never looked back over her shoulder once she had rounded the corner of the warehouse, but she half hopped, half ran toward the cluster of buildings about a hundred feet ahead of her, seeking the hiding places they offered. Captain LaShelle had warned her about what would happen if any of his men ever caught her alone, although she had imagined he'd meant some form of intimate abuse, not murder. Maybe he hadn't treated her the way a gentleman should, but at least, with him, she hadn't feared for her life. He needed her to fulfill his plan, and for a brief second she considered taking her chances with his rage and returning to the inn. But his rage wasn't the only thing she'd have to face. Mentally shaking off the notion, she darted into the first alley she came to and dropped down behind one of the rain barrels sitting near the entrance, praying the man who followed had lost track of her in the darkness. A mixture of pain, fear, and frustration brought tears to her eyes as she curled her legs beneath her and huddled against the weathered side of the wooden drum, and her heart pounded so loudly in her chest that it was difficult for her to listen for the crunching of pebbles. She wondered if the man had chased after her, if, indeed, he was close by.

Several agonizing minutes ticked away, during which panic threatened to send her racing off, screaming at the top of her lungs. And she might have done just that if her body hadn't started to shake so uncontrollably. Drawing up her knees, she wrapped her arms around them and buried her face in the thick folds of her skirt, angrily telling herself that if she wanted to survive this, she would have to be in full command of her emotions and her body. Her silent reprimand worked, and within a moment or two, the tremors had ceased and she was breathing easily again. Fear still rode high, but Jennifer managed to overcome it with rational thinking. She reasoned that the man wouldn't be foolish enough to chase her through the middle of town where his crewmates could see him . . . or, worse, Captain LaShelle. She was sure the man valued his life more than that.

Only the gentle lapping of waves came to her ears, and after a few minutes, she was fairly certain he hadn't followed her into the alley. Now all she had to do was figure out another place to hide, one that would give her a view of the harbor and would allow her the freedom to move around a bit. It could be months before a ship sailed into port.

Coming up onto her knees, Jennifer peeked over the top of the rain barrel, her eyes seeking the mouth of the alleyway. She could still hear faint voices some distance away, which could be the reason the man had given up on trying to catch her, and she silently thanked those people for being nearby. Yet, she also knew that she must not head in their direction. Pulling herself up, she balanced her weight on her left foot and gingerly tested her right ankle. Relieved to find it didn't hurt as much as before, she cast a last glance toward the end of the alley, then turned and quickly limped off the opposite way.

Jennifer's mistake, she would come to realize later, had been in assuming too much. Perhaps the man who wanted to slip a blade between her ribs had lost his courage when faced with the possibility of witnesses, but that didn't mean others weren't walking the streets in this part of the village. If she had taken a moment to think things through, she might not have been so careless. As it was, she didn't hesitate in the slightest once she reached the end of the narrow avenue, but blindly turned the corner and collided head-on with the biggest, burliest, strangest-looking man she had ever seen. The impact took her breath away, and she would have fallen if his huge hands hadn't clamped onto her arms and held her up. But none of that frightened her as much as the odd, childlike expression that came over his face. Her head began to spin, and she was certain a meaty fist was about to crush her skull in one devastating blow. Her vision clouded and she surrendered to the peaceful escape of unconsciousness.

Chapter Eight

Jennifer's eyelids fluttered open, then drifted shut again before memories of what had transpired earlier arose and flooded her mind with awareness. She stiffened, but kept her eyes closed as she listened to the crackling blaze in the fireplace, felt its warmth, and smelled the aroma of something cooking in the hearth. She knew someone had to have carried her here since she couldn't remember anything after crashing into that giant of a man on the street, and the only thing that kept her from bolting off the bed in a fit of hysteria was the whirling image she saw of him in her mind—of his face with its innocent look. She couldn't say why, but for some reason she sensed he wouldn't harm her. Yet, she couldn't be absolutely positive that he was the one who lived here. Forcing herself to lie perfectly still and create the illusion that she hadn't come around yet, she listened for a noise that would indicate where he was at the moment, then courageously opened one eye to peek when she didn't hear anything. Aided by the glow from the fire, a tiny lamp sitting on a crude-looking table in the middle of the room shed light into every corner, and Jennifer sat up once she discovered that she was alone. A curious frown drew her tawny brows together as she carefully studied the place, wondering how a man of his size could live comfortably in such quarters . . . if, indeed, he did. The only chair in the room didn't appear to be large enough to hold his tremendous weight or bulk, and the bed on which she sat was better fitted for her than for him. She remembered having to tilt her chin up to look at his face which meant he was more than a head taller than she, and after glancing at the only door in the room, she felt safe in thinking he probably had to stoop down just to walk through it. Yet, the most interesting aspect of the tiny cubicle wasn't its dimensions, but the lack of items usually found in a man's room. There wasn't a rifle, pistol, or knife; no razor, mug, and brush to shave with; no pipe or cheroots; no bottle of whiskey or rum or even a hint that there ever had been. Nor was there any indication that a woman looked after the place. There were no curtains on the window. No vase of flowers rested on the table, no tablecloth. The floor wasn't swept, dirty dishes sat in a pile, and all in all it seemed that an unchaperoned child inhabited the hut. Especially so when she spied the bamboo fishing pole propped up in the corner and the wooden bucketful of mud sitting next to it—undoubtedly full of worms. This was the oddest discovery she had ever made. But then, it shouldn't have been. Everything about the island was odd—a worried look suddenly came to her face as she glanced at the door again—and everyone on it answered to Captain LaShelle.

Knowing she hadn't a minute to waste, Jennifer quickly left the bed and limped to the cupboard. The meal she had been given at the inn much earlier hadn't been enough to satisfy her appetite, and once the captain discovered that she had escaped again, everyone in the village would be looking for her, which meant she would probably have to wait until tomorrow night to steal food. Hungry as she was now, that would be a very long wait.

She'd take whatever she could find here to eat, settle herself in hiding for the daylight hours, then take her chances again after the sun went down and most of the villagers retired to their beds. However, her shoulders dropped disappointedly once she'd opened the cupboard doors and found only a few cooking utensils, bowls, and plates inside. Then the delicious smells coming from the pot hanging over the fire in the hearth drew her attention, and she smiled. She'd simply take the stew.

Grabbing the towel that had been haphazardly thrown over the back of the chair, she awkwardly crouched before the fireplace and reached out to take the kettle from its hook. With it gripped in both hands, she rose, turned back to the table, and was about to set it down when she sensed someone was coming even though she had heard no footsteps. In a rush, she deposited the iron pot on the table, threw down the towel, and grabbed the hem of her skirt. Yanking it high, she frantically fought to free the knife from its scabbard, her pulse racing wildly as she listened to booted heels crush loose rock just outside the hut. The narrow confines of the room seemed to close in on her, and in a panic, tears filling her eyes, she clumsily jerked the weapon from its leather holder just as the door to the hut was viciously thrown open. Then she froze, unable to breathe, for Chad LaShelle stood haloed in the door's crude frame. His dark eyes were filled with rage, the scar through his lower lip gleamed white against his bronze complexion, and the expression on his face chilled Jennifer to the bone. He was every bit the swarthy pirate, from his ruffled, raven black hair to his unshaven jaw and the tiny gold earring dangling from one lobe, and for a moment, she thought she would perish beneath the penetrating glower he bestowed upon her.

The knife slipped from her fingers and thudded against the floor when he lowered his chin and stepped over the

185

threshold. Her heart drummed in her chest as he continued to advance, and she hurriedly backed away, making sure the table stood between them. But that tiny piece of furniture wasn't going to stop him. Reaching it, he angrily flung the table out of the way, spilling the kettle of stew onto the floor. Positive now that he intended to strangle her, she threw herself back against the wall and crossed her arms in front of her, planning to thwart the attack for as long as she could. But he simply shot out a huge hand, grabbed her wrist in a painful and unrelenting grip, and jerked her forward. She stumbled and fell against his broad, hard chest, and for several long moments, they stared into each other's eyes, neither blinking nor saying a word. Then a voice from the doorway broke the trance.

"Cap'n Chad? Ya won't hurt her, will ya?"

Until that moment, Jennifer hadn't cared whether or not the captain had come here alone. She had been too frightened of him to even consider that someone else might object to the way he treated her. Although she doubted it would make a difference to LaShelle, she was grateful, at least, that someone had the courage to speak up for her. Hopeful that perhaps this man was the exception she sought and that he could persuade his captain to take it easy with her, she turned her gaze upon him and instantly recognized the face of the last person she had seen before she'd fainted.

He was everything she had remembered and more. To see him in the light was even more awesome than what she had conjured up in her mind. She had been right in assuming he couldn't walk through the door without stooping down, but now as she looked at him standing just outside, she wondered if his massive bulk wouldn't hamper his entry as well. His size would surely worry even the most savage of pirates if he were ever to carelessly untether his anger, but Jennifer doubted that

that happened very often. There was a boyish look to his face with its freckles and blond, tousled hair, and the childish expression in his eyes that told her he was different . . . special . . . and that difference made people protect him rather than fear him. Her anger flared up again when Chad squeezed her arm and gave her a rough shake.

"I think she deserves it, Willard. Don't you?" He sneered. "After all, she disobeyed the captain's orders. Everyone else on this island has to follow the rules. Why shouldn't she?"

"But ya ain't gonna hurt her, are ya, Cap'n Chad?"

Jennifer's worried gaze shifted back and forth between the pair as they spoke, and she anxiously awaited LaShelle's answer just as Willard did.

A threatening, half-smile lifted one corner of Chad's mouth. "No," he said after a while. "I have something better in mind." Yanking her along with him, he turned without giving Willard or her a chance to ask what it was, and stormed from the hut out into the moonlit night.

"What ya gonna do, Cap'n Chad?" Willard asked, hurrying to keep up with the quick pace of the couple walking ahead of him. "Ya gonna put her in jail?"

Jennifer's ankle still hurt, and being dragged along didn't help. She tried hopping, then touching just the toe of her sandal on the ground, but nothing made it any easier. And the shock of Willard's question made her lose her concentration. She stumbled and went down on one knee. Tiny rocks cut into her flesh, and her temper flared.

"No!" she snapped, jerking free of Chad as she rolled onto one hip and glared up at him. She had had enough. All of her life she had been told what to do and when to do it without the slightest consideration for her feelings. Her marriage had been arranged before she'd been born, and then when her betrothed hadn't turned out to be

187

what her father had wanted for her, she'd been given to someone else . . . as if she were a prize broodmare, and the stallion had turned out to be incapable of siring offspring. She hadn't argued with her father because she'd loved him deeply and would have done anything he wanted. Then, when he'd died and she'd found herself on a ship sailing for England and the man she was to marry, a man she had never met, she had had second thoughts about going through with the arrangement, and she had just about made up her mind not to marry Charles when the vessel had encountered the storm. While floating aimlessly along on a piece of wreckage from the *Sea Lady*, she had felt that she was being punished for her defiance. She was almost convinced of it when she'd drifted to the shore of what she'd assumed was a deserted island. And she might have excused the captain's treatment of her there on the beach as payment for her rebellion. But this . . . this was too much!

"Don't touch me!" she shouted, jerking out of reach when a huge hand came down to seize her arm again. "I haven't done anything. In fact, the only crime I'm guilty of is being engaged to your half brother. But that isn't my fault. I had nothing to do with it. And I don't want to marry him if he's anything like you!" Sea green eyes sparkling with unshed tears glared at dark, scowling orbs. "You have no right to treat me like the rest of the people who live here. Maybe they don't mind being slaves, but I do!"

"They're not slaves," Willard argued, his soft blue eyes round and confident.

"Oh? Then ask your captain why no one is allowed to leave the island? Ask him why the islanders live in fear of being sent back to debtor's prison if they disobey him? And what does he call disobedience? What rights do any of these people have? They were simply taken from one prison and thrown into another . . . one without bars!"

188

Willard's pudgy face crimped in a thoughtful frown. "But they owe him," he finally said, though his words lacked the assurance they had before.

"Maybe." Jennifer relented, untying the straps of the sandal that cut into her swollen ankle. "But I don't owe him anything." Hostile eyes glared up at Chad. "Megan didn't owe him anything, and he killed her."

Willard's freckled face paled considerably. His chin quivered, and he shifted his attention to the man who had silently stood by and listened to it all. "Cap'n Chad?"

Since the day Chad had walked out on the argument he had had with his father nearly fifteen years ago, he had not explained his actions to anyone. No one had meant enough to him for that to be necessary. He had never let anyone get that close. But Willard was different. The man standing before him and waiting for an answer wasn't one who thought rationally. He was a child . . . in a man's body. And for nearly five years, Willard had put complete trust in Chad, so Chad knew that if he didn't give this man-child a logical answer, Willard's faith in him would crumble. There was even the chance that Willard might become dangerous if he thought his captain had murdered the only friend he'd ever had. Gritting his teeth, for it sorely enraged him to be forced into doing something, he sucked in a breath and looked the young man squarely in the eye.

"I'll answer all your questions, Willard," he said. "But not here." He quickly raised a hand when the boy opened his mouth to object. "Wait for me at Freedom Inn. We'll talk there."

Feeling a bit slighted as well as distrustful, Willard looked long at him. "Promise?" he said.

Chad nodded reassuringly. "I promise. Now go to the inn and see if Mister Bingham is there. Tell him we found Miss Grey. All right?"

His confidence in Captain LaShelle restored, Willard

189

smiled brightly. "I'll tell him I found her."

"You do that," Chad nodded with a vague smile. His dark brows lowered in a sympathetic frown as he watched Willard's huge body hurry off toward the inn, for he was thinking how unfair life had been to the boy. Yet in a way, Willard was blessed by ignorance. He didn't know he was different from everyone else, and because of his twisted kind of fate, Willard would never have to endure the hardships being an adult would force on him. Chad reached up and absently tugged on one earlobe. He rather envied him that.

"I don't suppose you plan to tell him the truth, do you?"

The question brought him out of his reverie rather abruptly. If it weren't for this little chit, Willard wouldn't have doubted him. The muscle in his cheek flexing beneath his mounting rage, he cast her a look over his shoulder and seriously considered laying the back of his hand to her jaw for all the trouble she'd caused him. But that wouldn't do any good, and he knew it. She had a stubborn streak in her that needed to be broken, and hitting her would only intensify it. Suddenly, the vision of his father flared up in his mind. He could see rage gleaming in the old man's eyes, the ring on his finger, and the hand that was descending upon a fourteen-year-old boy. Chad stiffened, reliving the pain he had felt when that ring had torn into his flesh and opened a bloodied wound on his mouth. Striking him hadn't done any good either. He had simply walked out and never looked back. Clamping his teeth together, Chad closed his eyes and struggled to force those thoughts from his head. The deep gash on his lip had healed, but the wounds he felt now never had.

Jennifer had meant to ridicule him in front of someone who was innocent enough to question his authority, but the result of her effort hadn't been exactly what she had thought it would be. Moonlight graced his rugged profile and enabled her to see the torment etched on his handsome face, and it confused her. His confrontation with Willard couldn't possibily have had this kind of effect on him. It must stem from something else . . . conceivably something in his past. Her own brow furrowed when a tinge of sympathy shot through her. Why should she care if he suffered? Hadn't he been the cause of her own misery? She gasped when he suddenly turned on her, reached down, caught her wrist, and hauled her to her feet. But rather than being dragged along behind him, she was roughly thrown over his shoulder with no alternative but to be carried wherever he wanted to take her.

"Put me down," she demanded, beating tiny fists against his broad back. "You have no right to make me your prisoner. Put me down, I say!" Tears began to well in her eyes with each step he took. "Let me go!" Her demands turned to pleas once she realized that if he intended to jail her as Willard had suggested, she would be unable to sneak aboard the next ship that sailed into port. "Please don't lock me up. I promise not to run away." This could very well be the end of her scheming if she couldn't persuade him. Praying she could follow through with her pledge should he agree and take her back to his room, and before she could change her mind, she quickly added, "I'll do *anything* you say."

Perched on his shoulder as she was, she couldn't see his face and so learn whether he believed her or not, but when his pace slowed, she took that as encouragement. Then she heard a metal door swing open, and in a panic, she twisted around to see where they were. "Nooo!" she wailed as he plucked a burning torch from its holder and carried her into a small, one-room stone building, then unceremoniously dropped her on a narrow straw cot. Before she could scramble to her feet, he turned, strode

191

from the place, and slammed the door shut behind him, taking the only source of light with him. Darkness closed in around her almost instantly, and she would have screamed had it not been for the soft yellow glow that seeped in through the tiny barred window in the door. But the sound of the key turning in the lock sent her racing toward it.

"Captain LaShelle, please!" she cried out to him as he placed the torch back in its holder and started to walk away. "Please don't leave me in here. It frightens me! Please!" The last was wrenched from her throat in a scream, but as tears flooded her eyes and spilled over her dark lashes, she knew he had made up his mind. She would spend this night, and possibly many to come, here in this dark, tiny prison made of stone.

"Damn you." She wept, pounding a fist against the metal door as she watched the ebony curtain of night enshroud his broad-shouldered figure and steal away the last sight of him. "Damn you."

Overcome with hopelessness, she sank to the floor, buried her face in her hands, and cried.

Jennifer was jolted awake when something furry darted across her outstretched arm. She sat up, then jumped to her feet once she saw what it was that shared her prison. She had gone on snake hunts as a child, but she had always detested mice. Shivering, she rubbed her arm and backed across the small room to the cot, keeping her eyes on the deplorable little rodent until he had slipped through a small opening between two of the stones in the wall. Satisfied that he was as scared of her as she was of him and that he wasn't going to come out for a while, she sat down on the straw mattress and shoved a fist into the small of her back, stretching. She hadn't meant to fall asleep on the floor, and if she had known

192

beforehand what kinds of creatures roamed around in the darkness, she most assuredly would have chosen to sleep on the bed.

As muted light of early sunrise filtered in through the tiny opening in the door, Jennifer leaned back against the wall to study the interior of her cell. There were no windows in the place, but there appeared to be a trap door in the ceiling from which a metal bar hung down. Curious, she stood up and moved to the center of the room, then raised a hand to grab the bar, pushing upward. The trap door lifted to let in fresh air as well as sunshine, and to allow the sweltering heat of midday to escape the tiny dungeon. But that was all that would escape from it. Even if she could hoist herself up to the opening, it was too small for her to climb through. Leaving the trap door open, she returned to the bed and sat down to continue her examination of her cell. The only other furnishing besides the bed was a chamberpot, and Jennifer's mouth crimped disgustedly once she realized that the captain didn't intend to let her out of the jail even to satisfy basic needs. He was such a callous man! He probably wouldn't even feed her! The thought had barely crossed her mind when she noticed a slot in the door sealed by a sliding panel. No doubt this was how an inmate was served food. She leaned her head back against the wall and closed her eyes, sighing heavily. The captain had thought of everything. Unless he decided the prisoner could go free, there was no means of escaping this place, and she wondered how many had gone insane here before release was granted.

A noise outside distracted her, and Jennifer quickly left the bed to investigate its origin, only to discover yet another aspect of Captain LaShelle's ingenious scheme. The one-room jail was located more than one hundred feet past the last building of the village, in an open spot void of shade trees, brush, or anything else that might hide a person who intended to help a prisoner break out. Of course, the people living on this island didn't have the courage to do something like that, but the captain obviously wasn't taking any risks.

Judging by the pale coloring of the sky, she doubted anyone was up yet which meant it would be some time before her breakfast was served. She'd only been awake for a few minutes, but boredom had already set in— boredom and frustration. She didn't deserve to be locked up, but the only person who could decide on that was Captain LaShelle. And *he* was the one who had jailed her. Her hands gripping two of the bars in the window, she rested her temple against the third and stared out toward the shore and the majestic frigate bobbing rhythmically in the vivid blue waters of the cove, losing herself in the beauty of the scene.

Suddenly, from out of nowhere, a man's face loomed up in front of her, startling her, and before his identity could register in her brain, Jennifer screamed and jumped back from the door.

"Good heavens, Willard," she moaned, touching her hand to her chest to ease the pain. "You nearly scared me out of my wits! What are you doing here?" She stepped to the door to get a better look at him.

The long-legged trousers he wore hardly reached his ankles, and he had tied them up around his thick waist with a piece of cord. He had donned a billowy-sleeved white shirt that needed to be washed, and hadn't bothered to put on shoes. His strawberry blond hair was ruffled and in need of a good trim—she wondered if he had attempted his last haircut on his own by the uneven lengths of it—and his lower lip quivered as if he were about to cry. The pathetic sight of him touched Jennifer's heart.

"Willard, I'm sorry for hollering at you," she quickly apologized. "But you should have called out to me so I

194

knew you were there. You understand, don't you?"

One broad shoulder jutted upward in a boyish shrug. "Yeah," he said, his eyes lowered. "I won't do it again, Miss Grey."

"Call me Jennifer." She smiled encouragingly. "Miss Grey makes me feel old."

His freckled face brightened instantly, and the smile he gave her in return made Jennifer laugh.

"So tell me why you're here, Willard." Her gaze darted past him toward the village. "Does Captain LaShelle know you are?"

"Naw," Willard replied, shoving his fists deep into his pockets as he swayed side to side. "Cap'n Chad's still asleep. But he won't care. He says I can do whatever I want around here." The sparkle in his clear blue eyes disappeared. "He didn't kill Megan, ya know."

It would take a lot of convincing to persuade Jennifer to believe that. She decided not to discuss Megan's death in view of their obvious difference of opinion. "Did you know Megan very well?"

"Yeah. She was my best friend." The corner of his mouth twitched. "My only friend 'sides Cap'n Chad." He glanced over his shoulder then back at her again, a look of desperation on his innocent face. "Will you be my friend . . . Jennifer?"

She could sense Willard's pain, both in losing a friend and hoping to gain another, though she couldn't understand his uneasiness in asking. A soft smile broke the serious line of her mouth. "I'd be honored, Willard. Will you be mine?"

"Oh, yeah!" he beamed, "I'll take real good care of—" His round blue eyes widened in dismay as if he'd said something wrong. Dropping his head, he ambled closer to the building and disappeared from Jennifer's view when he fell back against the stone wall.

"Willard," Jennifer called to him. "Willard, what's

wrong?" When he didn't answer, she leaned as close to the bars of the window as possible in an effort to see him, to make sure he hadn't left. "Willard. Talk to me. Tell me what's wrong," she coaxed.

"I was supposed to take care of Megan," the trembling voice admitted. "I didn't. Maybe you shouldn't be my friend. I'm not very good at being one."

"Oh, Willard, that's not true. You couldn't have stopped—" She wanted to say Captain LaShelle but decided that would only upset Willard all the more. "Him," she said instead, "from doing whatever he pleased. No one could."

"Ya don't mean Cap'n Chad, do ya?" His face suddenly appeared before her again, and she cast her gaze back into the darkness of the cell. "He didn't do it," Willard urgently continued. "He swears! And Cap'n Chad never lies to me."

Had Willard's mind enabled him to think logically— the way an adult would think—Jennifer would have argued the point. But because he couldn't, she didn't feel she had the right to put doubts into his head about someone he cared so much for. And she had noticed the way Captain LaShelle had acted toward Willard. The captain seemed to like the young man.

"Tell me why ya think he did it, Jennifer," Willard begged, curling his thick fingers around the bars in the window and pressing his face between them. "I know I'm not too smart. Everybody's always tellin' me that, but I ain't real stupid. I can understand a lot of things. And if ya think Cap'n Chad did it, I can tell ya why I know he didn't."

"Then tell me, Willard," she said softly. "I'd like to hear his explanation."

"Well, first off, he was having supper at the inn when Megan disappeared. Mister Jason was with him. Then he went to the *Black Falcon*—his ship," he offered when

196

Jennifer frowned questioningly at him. "He was check-ing on her repairs. After that he went to his cabin to work on his 'papers' as he calls 'em, and two of his crew said he never left there until Mister Jordon came lookin' for him to tell him they'd found Megan."

"He had blood on his clothing," she pointed out. "Did he explain where it came from?"

Willard nodded his head. "He said he knelt down beside her." Even in the obscure light, she could see the tears lining the rim of his lashes. "I went to see her before Mister Jordon buried her." His chin trembled. "The awful man who hurt her chopped off her legs."

Jennifer's knees buckled at the grotesque vision she saw. Her stomach churned, and she quickly backed away to sit down on the cot, certain she would faint. "God. How could anyone do such a demented thing?"

"Cap'n Chad's finding out. He's askin' everybody where they were last night, and they've got to prove it. He's real angry, Jennifer. This ain't never happened here before, and I've lived on this island for three years."

Bracing her elbows on her knees, Jennifer cradled her face in her hands, fighting not to cry. She had to be strong . . . for Willard's sake. But in her mind, she kept going over how horribly young Megan must have suffered. Had her murderer at least killed her before he— She bolted to her feet and began to pace the floor. No! She mustn't think about it!

"Jennifer, how did you get on the island?"

Her trek came to an abrupt halt. "What?"

"There ain't been no ships dockin' here for a long time. How did you get here?"

Thankful for the chance to put her thoughts some-where else rather than on Megan, she came to stand next to the door and leaned a shoulder against it. "Didn't you ask Captain LaShelle?"

"Yeah, but he wouldn't tell me. Said he had more

important things to think about and couldn't spare the time talkin' to me." He smiled weakly, trying to hide the fact that his feelings had been hurt.

What better way not to lie than to simply avoid the subject? she thought sarcastically. "It's a long story."

"I ain't got nothin' to do. And I like stories."

"You might not like this one, Willard. You and I have different feelings toward the captain."

"You mean you don't like him?" Willard frowned, unable to understand how anyone couldn't. Cap'n Chad had always been kind to him, but other people had been mean for the most part.

"I guess you could say that. I know I don't have any respect for him. He steals from defenseless people to satisfy his own needs."

"Did he steal from you?"

Jennifer could feel a hot blush rise in her cheeks. She wasn't about to tell the young man yes. He'd most assuredly ask what, and that wasn't something she wished to discuss with anyone. Least of all someone with the mind of a child. He wouldn't understand what she meant, and then he'd ask her to explain it. But she didn't want to lie to him either. Her smooth brow wrinkled in a perplexed frown as she tried to think of a way to get around the situation and still tell the truth.

"He stole my freedom, Willard. I'm a prisoner here "

The corner of his mouth wrinkled as he thought about it. "Why would he do that?"

"Captain LaShelle's father and mine were friends a long time ago when we still lived in London. Before I was born, my father promised Mister Wadsworth that I would marry his oldest son, Captain LaShelle. We moved to the colonies while I was still a child, so I can't tell you exactly what happened, but the captain and his father had an argument . . . a bitter argument . . . one that made the captain so angry he left home and never talked to his father again."

"Are you still supposed to marry Cap'n Chad?"

"No. His father called off the engagement and, together with my father, decided I should marry Charles, the captain's half brother. A month ago, I booked passage on a ship sailing for England. I was to meet Charles and we were to be married. But the ship encountered a bad storm at sea and it sank. I managed to drift here to the island."

"Then why do ya think Cap'n Chad stole your freedom, Jennifer? He didn't bring you here."

"Because after he found out who I was, he decided to use me to get even with his father and half brother. He won't let me go to England, and he was keeping me locked up in his room. Why do you suppose he put me in here?"

Willard's pudgy face wrinkled with thought. "For punishment," he finally answered.

"What have I done to deserve punishment, Willard?" she challenged, turning to look him squarely in the eye. "All I was trying to do was escape him so that I could find some way to get off this island. I don't owe him anything. I'm not like the rest of the people here. He didn't save my life. I don't owe him money. He has no right to keep me here against my will."

Willard's attention fell away from her, but Jennifer could see from the expression on his face that he hadn't liked what he'd heard. He took two steps in the direction of the village, paused, glanced back at her, then started off again.

"Willard?" she called out to him. "Willard, where are you going?"

He continued on as though he hadn't heard her, and Jennifer suddenly regretted telling him all that she had. It was thoughtless of her to vent her anger on a person such as he. Her shoulders drooped, and with a sigh, she turned around and went to the cot to lie down. But even a child would suspect something was wrong sooner or later, and Willard had admitted that he wasn't stupid. Rolling onto her back, she stared up at the opening in the ceiling. Perhaps it was better he'd learned the truth from her. Captain LaShelle might have lied at some point, and Willard's trust in the man would have been destroyed once he'd found out.

The rest of the day dragged by, one long, endless span of time. An old man Jennifer had never seen before brought her a tray of food at noon, and again at sundown. She tried to get him to talk to her, but it was as if he were deaf. He wouldn't even respond when she thanked him for bringing her something to eat. Willard did not come back.

The tiny cell, though dark and damp, became so humid by late afternoon that she had to spend most of the time sitting on the cot fanning herself with her skirt. Her white cotton blouse clung to her, and perspiration dripped from the tip of her nose until she thought it would drive her crazy. Even her four-legged companion never came out of its hole, and for a moment Jennifer wished she were small enough to fit into that crack. It certainly had to be cooler in there than in the cell.

Once the sun went down, she thought her misery would cease for a while, but it only seemed to worsen. Her clothes were drenched in perspiration and when the heat of the day finally filtered out of the small room, she began to shiver from the cool night air. Trying to sleep was nearly impossible, for the captain hadn't seen fit to give her a blanket or even a pillow for her head, and by the time she managed to doze off, the early light of dawn trailed in through the window, streamed across the floor, and fell upon her face. Growling, she rolled over and put her back toward the door. But by now the villagers were ready to begin their day. The early morning breeze carried their voices and the sounds of their labors all the way to her cell, denying her the chance to fall back to sleep. Resigning herself to the fact that her day had begun, Jennifer sat up and leaned back against the wall to listen to the laughter, the pounding of hammers, and the crashing of surf. She wondered how long she'd have to spend her time in this manner.

The old man came with her breakfast, and when he unlocked the panel and slid it aside to slip the tray through the slot, Jennifer asked him if he would be kind enough to bring her a blanket, explaining that the nights in the cell were cold. His tired green eyes shifted to look up at her for a moment before he guardedly glanced over his shoulder toward the inn, and Jennifer suddenly realized that the man had been forbidden to speak with her, no doubt at Captain LaShelle's order. Without answering, he concentrated on closing the panel and locking it again. But before he stepped away, he told her that he would try to get a blanket to her somehow—he wasn't sure how or when, but he'd try—and as he turned to start back toward the village, Jennifer thanked him for at least offering to help.

He returned about a half-hour later to pick up her tray, and once he had unlocked the panel and slid it to one side, he discreetly pulled a bottle from inside the loose folds of his shirt and handed it to her. It contained water, he said, and made her promise to hide it under the cot should the captain pay her a visit. She wasn't to have anything more than three meals a day, but he said he knew how hot it could get in the cell in the middle of the afternoon since he had spent some time there himself. Jennifer assured him that she would do as he wished, and before he turned to leave, he smiled at her.

After that, the day seemed to pass more quickly for Jennifer. She looked forward to another short conversation to break the monotony. And during the old man's next visit, he unknowingly gave her a ray of hope. He told her that many of the villagers disagreed with the captain's treatment of her, and that several of the men were considering telling him so. A pained expression deepened the wrinkles around his eyes as he told her that he doubted it would do any good. Since Captain LaShelle owned the island, he'd do whatever pleased him, but at least the men were beginning to feel like men again rather than spineless cowards who hadn't the courage to stand up for something they believed in.

Jennifer's eyes filled with tears as she watched him walk away, his rounded shoulders seeming to straighten a little as though he took pride in being able to talk to her when he'd been ordered not to, and she suddenly decided that maybe the captain had made a very big mistake in placing her in the jail. In doing so, he had stirred up unrest among his people . . . or at least he had reminded them that they weren't mindless animals brought here to work and not think. Trouble was brewing, and Jennifer was glad she was the cause of it. Though this might be subtle retaliation, it was some revenge for the way he'd behaved toward her.

The sun had been down for about an hour before she heard a noise just outside the cell door, and she bolted from the cot to investigate, praying the old man had been able to find a way to smuggle a blanket to her. She was already beginning to shiver.

Wrapping her fingers around two of the bars, she leaned in and called in a harsh whisper, "Is someone out there?" She tilted her head, straining to hear anything that would give her a clue. Nothing. She called again. Still no reply. Finally, when she was about to return to the cot and her fantasies of going home to Virginia where she could forget this nightmare, she heard the sound of pebbles being kicked about. "Who's there?"

"Me, Miss Grey. Willard."

Tears sprang to her eyes the instant she heard his

202

voice. "Willard? Willard, come here where I can see you. Please?" A moment passed before his tall, massive build moved into view, and Jennifer thought he was the most beautiful sight she had seen in a long time. She had to bite her lip to keep from crying once she saw the blanket he carried wadded up and tucked under one arm. "Oh, Willard," she moaned happily. "I was so worried I'd never see you again. I was afraid I'd made you angry with me."

Shifting the blanket from under his arm, he hugged it to his chest and stared down at the ground. "I ain't angry with ya, Miss Grey," he mumbled. "I'm angry with Cap'n Chad."

"What?" She could hardly believe her ears. "Why are you angry with him?"

"'Cause he won't let ya outta there. Says ya gotta stay until he decides ya've 'learned your lesson.'" He glanced up sheepishly at her. "And it's my fault ya're in there."

"Your fault? How did you come to that conclusion, Willard?"

"'Cause I'm the one who told him where to find ya," he half whispered, half whined. "If I'd known what he was gonna do with ya, Miss Grey, I wouldn't have showed him where ya were."

"I don't blame you, Willard. Honestly, I don't. And why are you calling me Miss Grey again?"

He shrugged his broad shoulders and stared down at the ground again. "'Cause I don't deserve to be your friend no more."

"Willard," she tenderly replied, "if you won't be my friend, then I won't have any. I *want* you to be my friend, I *need* you to be my friend. You're the only one I can talk to. Everyone else on the island has been forbidden to speak with me. Say you've changed your mind."

Willard wiggled his big toe, disturbing the pebbles under his feet. He glanced shyly at her and then back

203

toward the inn, smiled brightly, and said, "Yes. I've changed my mind." A startled look came over his face when he remembered the blanket he had brought her. "Oh, I almost forgot. Mr. Sullivan said for me to give this to ya." He stepped closer to the door and held up the brown, woolen coverlet to shove it through the barred window.

"Who's Mr. Sullivan?" she asked, eagerly accepting his gift. Its warmth chased away the chill the instant she tossed it over her shoulders.

"He's the cook at Freedom Inn. He's the only one 'sides me that Cap'n Chad will let come here," Willard replied, jamming his hands into his pockets. "I think he likes you."

His statement brought a smile to Jennifer's lips. "Is he the one who brings my meals?"

"Uh-huh."

"Well, I like him, too. Tell him I said thank you and that I hope he doesn't get into any trouble with the captain for giving me this." She nodded at the blanket.

"He won't," Willard said with a shake of his head. Then he smiled. "We agreed to tell the captain that I was the one who decided to give it to ya. He don't get angry with me . . . much."

"Tell me about yourself, Willard, where you came from, why you're here."

Turning slightly, he leaned a thick shoulder against the door and stared off toward the shoreline. "Me and my mother lived in this little room behind the tailor's shoppe in Pembroke. When she died, Mr. Kempt said I couldn't live there no more and locked me out. Cap'n Chad found me and said I could be one of his mates." His sandy brows came together in a distressful frown. "But I didn't like what they did on the *Black Falcon,* so he gave me a job here. Whenever his ship gets hit, I fix it up."

"What did they do on the *Black Falcon* that you didn't

204

like, Willard?" Jennifer asked out of curiosity, but before he could answer, she was sorry she had. It didn't take much imagination to figure it out.

"They killed people," Willard said, appalled. "Cap'n Chad told me they had to or they'd be killed, but I didn't like it anyway."

"I don't blame you, Willard. I wouldn't like it either."

"Ya know what I think?" he blurted out in a sudden change of mood. "I think Cap'n Chad likes you."

The shock of his statement took Jennifer's breath away, and as she gaped in wide-eyed surprise, she firmly shook her head, denying the possibility.

"Yeah. He does. Know why I think that?" When she continued to stare at him without uttering a sound, he giggled as if what he knew was a secret. "He don't let Modesty come in his room no more since he put you in here. And he used to kiss her a lot. Now he shouts at her and tells her to get away from him." His smile faded as he considered why. "Did ya ever kiss him, Jennifer?"

Her face flamed instantly, and she turned away from the window, praying that he wouldn't notice in the pale light of late evening.

He took her silence to mean that she had. "I'll bet that's why," he observed excitedly. "Ya kiss better than she does." Willard's upper lip curled as he imagined what it would be like to kiss Modesty's overly painted red mouth. Then another thought struck him, and he added, "He likes to kiss girls. He told me so." He smiled weakly and stared down at his feet. "I ain't never kissed a girl, but Cap'n Chad said I will someday." He turned and stuck his face between the bars to look at her. "Do ya think I'll like it, Jennifer?"

Her heart pounded so loudly in her chest that she feared it would explode. She felt faint, confused and embarrassed, and she knew that she couldn't explain that to this poor, innocent young man who hadn't the slightest idea of how his words had affected her. She sucked in a deep breath and concentrated on what he had asked her. "Well," she began, her voice weak and shaky, "it depends on who the girl is and how much you like her." She rested her shoulders back against the door and closed her eyes, praying he was satisfied.

"Hmm," he murmured. "Then I guess I'd like it if ya kissed me."

His reply brought a smile to her lips. "Oh, Willard." She grinned, turning to look at him. "You're the sweetest man I've ever known."

"Ya mean that?" he gasped, standing erect again. "Ain't nobody ever told me that before. Usually they tell me to go away." He sighed unhappily. "Everybody but Megan." One corner of his mouth crimped. "I woulda liked to kiss her," he admitted, then added ruefully, "but it's too late now."

"And she would have loved it, Willard. I know she would have. Those other people—the ones who tell you to go away—they're the stupid ones. They're cheating themselves out of having you as a friend."

He grinned boyishly. "They are, aren't they?"

"Yes, they are," she agreed, chuckling. "Now, I suggest the two of us go to bed. It's late, and you probably have work to do tomorrow."

Willard nodded his head. "But I'll come by to see ya every chance I get. Ya want me to bring ya something?"

"If I thought you could, Willard, I'd ask you to bring me the key to this door," she mocked, slapping an open palm against it. "But I know you can't, and I really wouldn't ask you to. You'd only get in trouble with the captain."

"It ain't nice being in there, is it?"

"No, Willard, it isn't. And you remember that. You do whatever the captain tells you, so he won't have reason to lock you up, too." She forced herself to smile at him.

206

"Now go home and get some sleep. I'll see you tomorrow."

"G'night, Jennifer."

"Good night, Willard," she replied, and watched his huge frame turn and amble off.

Once he had disappeared from view, a chill embraced her, and she hugged the blanket tighter around her slender shoulders, knowing that the sensation had nothing to do with the cool night air. She had been thinking about what Willard had told her—that he thought Captain LaShelle liked her. That was absurd, of course. The man was incapable of feeling any kind of emotion other than hatred. But what really worried her was Modesty. If the woman felt that Jennifer had stolen her man's affections, she could be very dangerous. Sighing, Jennifer strolled to the cot and sat down. If she was ever allowed to leave this cell, she would have to find a way to befriend Modesty, prove to her that she had no interest in the captain, and that all she wanted to do was get off the island . . . anyway she could. Leaning back against the wall, she hugged her knees to her chest, laid her chin on them, and contemplated how she would go about winning the redhead's help.

Chapter Nine

Three days had passed since Megan O'Connor had been murdered, and Chad wasn't any closer to finding her killer than when he had started. But that wasn't what brought the dark scowl to his face. There was dissension among his people, and it pointed directly at him. The young girl's brutal death was a part of it, but the root of the problem was truly their disapproval over Jennifer Grey's imprisonment. Although no one other than Willard had spoken openly about it with him, he had overheard some comments about how unfair he was being with her. The only one who agreed with his decision was Modesty, and Chad knew that was simply because she wanted the beautiful blonde out of the way. Even Jason had offered his opinion once he, too, had felt the tension growing among the villagers, for he had realized the danger should the islanders somehow find the courage to go up against the captain. But Chad wouldn't relent. Nor would he tell any of them why. Jennifer Grey had to learn to obey him. But more than that, he knew if he turned her loose just because everyone objected to her being locked up, the townsfolk would suddenly think that any time they didn't like something he did, they'd tell him so and expect him to heed their complaint. Well, he wouldn't, and that was why he had called this town meeting—to tell them so in no uncertain terms. This was *his* island, and everyone who resided here would live by his rules or he'd send them back to England!

The gentle rapping on the door to his room turned him away from the window through which he had been thoughtfully staring out at the *Black Falcon* for the past hour, wondering how many more days it would be before she was repaired and ready to sail. He had never liked being in port for very long, and with her mainmast needing to be replaced before he could weigh anchor again, he felt trapped and somewhat helpless. In addition, the situation with Jennifer and the townsfolk was beginning to aggravate him. Grabbing his pistol off the dresser, he went to the door, and as he opened it, he stuck the weapon into the sash around his waist.

"Everyone's waiting outside, Cap'n," Jason told him as he stepped out of the way to let Chad pass him. "But would you mind telling me what this is all about?"

"You'll find out soon enough," Chad replied, without breaking stride as he headed for the stairs. "Is Willard there, too?"

"Aye. He was the first one I told, just like you ordered. The only one missing is Modesty."

Chad came to an abrupt halt, did a turnabout, and marched back to the woman's door. Banging a fist against it, he shouted, "Modesty Copeland get your worthless rear end out of that bed and downstairs this instant before I kick in this door and throw you down them."

The sounds of someone rushing about inside the room brought a satisfied smirk to Chad's lips as he glanced over at his first mate and nodded. Then, moving to one side, he rested the weight of his upper torso against an elbow braced on the wall, and waited. A moment later, the door was jerked open, and the hot-tempered redhead filled its frame. Presenting him with a vicious glare, she yanked the belt of her robe into a knot around her waist, but she wisely decided not to voice her resentment at having been so rudely awakened, and stomped off toward the stairway, both men following closely behind her.

"Mind a piece of advice, friend?" Jason asked quietly as the trio stepped out into the street and headed in the direction of the jail where a crowd stood waiting for them. He knew Chad had chosen this particular spot so that Miss Grey would be able to hear every word from inside her cell.

"I'd say yes," Chad grumbled, "but you'll give it anyway. So you might as well speak your piece. I'll try to pretend I'm listening."

Jason seldom lost his temper with the man, but this was one time he couldn't control it. "You'd better listen," he barked, grabbing his companion by the arm and jerking him around so they were face to face. He ignored the black scowl he received in return. "You've got a very touchy situation here, Chad, and I don't think you realize just how touchy it is. Not only are the people of this town dissatisfied with your decision to confine Miss Grey to jail, a punishment they feel is undeserved, but the little blonde herself is a threat . . . possibly a greater one. There isn't a single man in your crew who wouldn't like to take your place and jump into bed with her, and she knows it. If you make her angry enough, she'll use that advantage to turn every one of them against you. Stack them up with the villagers, and you'll find yourself afloat in a rowboat."

"Does that include you?" Chad growled, his black eyes snapping pure fire.

Jason opened his mouth to flatly deny it, but bit off his reply. Arguing with Chad LaShelle wasn't worth the effort. He'd learned that long ago. Whether he was right or wrong, LaShelle would win. Yet, his pride had been

211

wounded and he couldn't let the gibe pass. "Someday, Chad, your grudge against all of mankind is going to lose you the only real friend you have." He brushed past him and went to stand with Stuart and Tranel at the back of the crowd.

Chad stood perfectly still, feeling the bite of Jason's words. He'd been right, of course, about everything . . . even the point he'd made about losing him as a friend. Drawing in a breath slowly and deeply, Chad exhaled in the same manner, then gazed out over the choppy waters of 'the sea, his dark brows drawn together thoughtfully. For fifteen years he had plotted a way to have revenge against his father, and now that it was so close to becoming a reality, he failed to notice what went on around him. He was losing his perspective because of his obsession with getting even. He swallowed the knot in his throat. God, how he wished things hadn't turned out as they had.

The noise of the crowd stilled, awakening him to their presence, and without looking their way, he sensed everyone was watching him. Shaking off his moment of remorse, he turned and strode to the decaying tree stump often used as a speaking platform, then stepped up on it. With feet apart, fists clenched and perched on his hips, he faced them, his dark eyes taking in each face as his gaze swept the throng. The majority looked back sheepishly at him, but there were those who plainly showed their dissatisfaction with him by the frowns on their faces. It was to them he chose to direct his statement.

"It's been quite a while since the last time I was forced to remind you people about the rules you must follow if you wish to continue living here. They're *my* rules because this is *my* island. There will be no exceptions. Whatever I decide is the way it will be, and if any of you find that you're unhappy with that, I'll be very willing to see that you're returned to London . . . to debtor's prison where I found you." He paused a moment, letting his threat sink in, and he noticed that a few of those who opposed him had lowered their gazes. The rest still needed convincing. "Miss Grey has found herself where she is now because she chose not to do as I told her. That is the only reason she has spent the last three nights locked behind a barred door, and she's going to stay there until I decide she can come out. It could be this afternoon . . . or it could be a week from now. *That* depends on all of you." A buzzing of voices filtered through the crowd as many questioned what he meant, and Chad smiled to himself. He had them right where he wanted them. "If I hear one complaint about her imprisonment after this meeting, I'll add a day to her sentence. If the complaints total seven, then for each additional complaint I hear, a week will be added. Her fate, people, is in your hands." He cast them all one long, final glance and then stepped down.

All eyes watched him as he walked away, but only one pair had tears in them. Jennifer had heard every word he had said and she'd clearly understood his intent. Yet, she didn't weep for herself, but for the people of this island. He was using her to keep them in line, setting her up as an example of what to expect should any of them revolt, and at the same time he was telling her that trying to win their sympathy was useless. If anyone tried to help her, she would be punished. If she asked for help, the islanders would be punished. Turning away from the door where she had stood watching him, she fell back against the cool stone wall with a sigh and wiped the tears from her cheek. He was a very shrewd man. He thought of everything . . . even to where to hold the meeting so that she would hear what he had to say. Well, he wasn't going to beat her down. Maybe he had frightened his people into submission—they had no hope of ever leaving the island—but

213

he hadn't scared her. He had forgotten one very important fact. She knew he wouldn't harm her because he needed her. He could make her time here quite miserable, but in the back of her mind, she knew it wouldn't last forever. Feeling much better, she pushed away from the wall and went to the cot to lie down. She'd pretend to give in to him, while in her heart she'd be just biding her time. She could play his game, and probably win, for the simple reason that he wouldn't expect it of her. Smiling triumphantly, she closed her eyes and, before very long, drifted off to sleep.

Strange, indistinct visions whirled about in her dreams, and she stirred when none of them made any sense—the flash of shiny metal, the vague image of two people struggling, the muffled scream, the vicious laughter. But the sight of bloodstains on a man's clothing jolted her upright on the cot. She was drenched in sweat and her body trembled violently, but when she could finally make some order out of her nightmare, she realized that the man hadn't been Captain LaShelle. He'd been the one she had confronted in the warehouse. Her heart began to thunder in her chest. There had to be only one reason why that man had been hiding in the loft and why he had had blood on his clothing. *He* was the one Captain LaShelle was looking for! Springing off the bed, she raced for the door, cursing herself for not having thought about that earlier. In all probability the man had long since fled the warehouse and had destroyed the only evidence that could link him to Megan's murder, but Jennifer had to tell someone about him. She owed Megan that much!

"Is anyone out there?" she screamed through the bars. "Please! Somebody tell Captain LaShelle that I have to talk to him. It's important. I saw the man who killed Megan!" Angry tears filled her eyes when no one responded or stepped into her view. "Did you hear me? I

214

saw the man who killed Megan!" Still no one answered her. "Willard! Someone. Anyone. Answer me, damn you! Stop being such cowards!"

Her temper flaring, she gripped two of the bars and shook them, but they held steady, only slightly rattling in the huge, metal door. She gritted her teeth and whirled away, frantically searching the interior of the cell for something she could bang against the door loudly enough to draw someone's attention ... even the captain's. Sunlight filtered in through the trap door in the ceiling and flooded the tiny space with a bright glow, so she instantly noticed a loose stone in the wall near the floor, obviously the result of some prisoner's futile attempt at escape. Rushing to it, she wedged her fingers into the narrow crevice and wriggled them from side to side, pulling as she did so. Several moments later, the stone came free with a jerk, nearly tumbling her onto the floor. It was about the size of a coconut and twice as heavy, and she knew it would do nicely.

"I want to speak with Captain LaShelle," she shouted, beating the fragment of stone against the door. "I want to talk to him right now! Do you hear me?"

The vibration of rock against heavy metal rattled her teeth and stung her fingers, but Jennifer wouldn't quit. Over and over again she hit the door, the reverberating sounds carrying all the way to the other side of the village. She kept it up until the muscles in her arms ached and the palms of her hands were rubbed raw, and only then did she relinquish her endeavor. But her voice was still strong, so she continued to shout at the top of her lungs. Finally, when it seemed no one in the village cared or believed her, she spotted Willard's bulk. He was walking toward her from the direction of his hut.

"Willard!" she screamed. "Willard, go find the captain and tell him I *have* to speak with him. Hurry!" Tossing aside the stone, she wrapped her bleeding fingers

215

around the bars in the window and watched him clumsily rush to do as she asked, tears gathering in her eyes. "Tell him I saw the man who killed Megan," she whispered with a sob.

A tear trickled down her cheek and when she raised a knuckle to wipe it away, she saw the cuts on her fingers. Stumbling back from the door, she stared at her hands, at the blood covering them, and the horrible vision of Megan's mutilated body flared in her mind. Why had the girl been killed? Had she known her attacker and been silenced? And who was next? A chill raced up her spine. It was all so very clear to her now—why the captain had locked her in his room, given her his knife, and told her not to let anyone in except himself or his first mate. He had done it to protect her. Not because he cared about her. Only to protect his own interests. He feared she would be the next victim, and if she were dead, he couldn't take revenge against his father. Feeling weak, she turned for the cot and sat down. LaShelle had probably jailed her for two reasons, not as punishment for defying him but as a way of telling her that he didn't have to explain his actions and as a means of insuring himself that Megan's murderer couldn't get to her. Leaning her head back against the wall, she closed her eyes. Chad LaShelle's way of doing things might appear to be hard-hearted, but now that she thought about it, she realized it wasn't that way at all. It simply wasn't his nature to discuss his decisions with anyone . . . least of all her. A faint smile parted her lips. And from the look of things, she was the first to defy his orders, and he didn't quite know how to handle it. Suddenly, Willard's voice penetrated her thoughts. Jumping to her feet, she hurried back to the door.

"He's comin', Jennifer," Willard called out excitedly as he ran toward her. When he neared the jail, he staggered to a stop, too breathless to say anything more.

But if he had, Jennifer probably wouldn't have heard him. Her attention was already focused on the tall, muscular man who followed him, and even at this distance, she could see the suspicious look in his dark eyes. Yet, to her surprise, that wasn't what set her heart thumping or made her flesh tingle. It was as though she were seeing him for the first time, and she quickly lowered her gaze, hoping that would calm her rapidly beating pulse, while she told herself that he wasn't the sort of man who should excite her. It didn't help. In fact, the image of him on the beach, when he had chased her down and then made love to her, flared up hotly in her mind, and she could feel a blush warm her cheeks. She shivered as imaginary fingertips traced the smooth line of her jaw and sensed warm, demanding lips pressing a kiss to her throat. She blinked, sucked in her breath and looked up, startled to find him standing only a few feet from her, his chin lowered and his eyes searching her face for some clue to her odd behavior. She blinked again when his tiny gold earring caught the sunlight and flashed in her eyes. Thinking it best not to look directly at him, she glanced past him and swallowed hard.

"There was a man," she began very slowly, praying he couldn't hear the quaver in her voice, "in the loft of the warehouse. I went there to hide. He stepped out of the shadows with a knife in his hand. I didn't know until Willard told me yesterday that you were looking for a man who probably had blood on his clothes. This one did." Her gaze shifted back to him. "On his breeches and shoes."

"Would you recognize him if you saw him again?"

The deep timbre of his voice seemed to caress her every nerve, and it was all Jennifer could do just to answer him. "He never moved fully into the light, so I didn't see his face."

"You said he spoke to you. Did he sound familiar?"

217

Jennifer shook her head. "I was so frightened I doubt I'd know his voice if I heard it again."

Irritation and disappointment were etched clearly on Chad's face as he turned and stared out across the cove, and Jennifer took the opportunity to study his profile for a moment. His raven black locks were worn longer than most men wore their hair, and a two-day growth of beard merely added to his rebellious air. The tiny gold earrings symbolized his contempt for authority, and the scar through his lip was evidence of it. Yet, for some reason, Jennifer sensed that deep inside this man wanted nothing more than to prove he was deserving of someone's love and trust, even capable of returning them, while at the same time he was afraid to take the first step toward winning them. She jumped when his dark eyes suddenly turned on her, and she backed away from the door a step or two, worried that he might read her thoughts and become angry when he realized someone had guessed the nature of his well-guarded feelings.

Chad cursed his decision to lock Jennifer up in jail the night Willard told him where to find her. If he hadn't, he might have learned then about the man in the warehouse, and thus had time to look for him before he got away. As it was, the murderer had probably rid himself of the clothing that had Megan's blood on it, and had set up an alibi that would put him somewhere away from the scene of Megan's death. Something like this had never happened before on his island, and it enraged Chad. Not simply because a young girl had been murdered, but because it had happened right under his nose and he'd been powerless to stop it. Furthermore, he hadn't even given a thought to the possibility that such a thing would occur. He had assumed that because this was his island, his village, and these were his people, no one would be stupid enough to think of going against him. The murder was an act in blatant disregard of his authority, and the repercussions of it were just beginning to be felt. The whole situation boded ill, and if he didn't find the man responsible and have him executed, there very well could be some troublesome times ahead.

A movement before him brought him out of his thoughts, and he blinked once he realized he had been staring at the beautiful blonde watching him from behind the bars. And Jennifer Grey was another matter entirely. In the few days she had been here, nearly everyone—including his first mate—had taken it upon themselves to speak out on her behalf and to object to his treatment of her. The muscle in his cheek flexed. Everything was beginning to fall apart, and what infuriated him more than anything was that he couldn't do a thing to stop it. Turning abruptly on his heel, he stomped off without a word, heading toward the inn.

An hour later Chad was sitting alone in the commons, a black scowl marring his handsome features and his right hand gripping the mug of ale resting on the table top. With one foot propped up on the bench, he laid his left elbow across his knee and glared at his fingers as he worked that hand into a fist and studied the tense cords running up his arm each time he tightened and released it. He could feel his power beginning to slip and knew something had to be done. The problem was that he didn't know exactly what he should do. Using Jennifer Grey as a warning had only made matters worse.

His gaze drifted across the room to where Henry Sullivan struggled with the two steaming kettles of water he was carrying toward the stairs. No doubt Modesty wanted to take her afternoon bath, Chad decided with a raised brow, and lifted his mug of ale to his lips. The brew tasted good, so he took a second sip of it as he watched the old man mount the steps, his shoulders slumped beneath the weight he carried. It never ceased to amaze him that Hank, as everyone called Sullivan, continually bowed down to Modesty's demands. No one else did. But whatever she wanted, Hank did. But then Hank was that kind of man. There were few people on the island that he didn't like, and that was probably why everyone liked him. Only lately had he shown a different side to his nature, evidenced by the disapproving scowls Chad had received every time Hank came back from giving Jennifer a meal. Chuckling softly, Chad was starting to take another sip of ale when he was suddenly struck by an idea. If everyone liked Hank, then it stood to reason that whatever Hank approved of, the rest would view in a favorable light. He hurriedly set down his mug and left the table to race up the stairs after the old man.

Jennifer couldn't be certain, but she vowed this was the hottest afternoon she had spent in her cell. Not a single breath of air drifted in through the tiny window in the door or the opening above her in the ceiling. The only comfortable place she could find was on the stone floor, where she sat with her skirts pulled up around her hips so that her bare flesh lay against the coolness of the rocks beneath her. But even then perspiration continued to dot her upper lip and brow, and to streak down her neck and dampen every inch of her clothing. During the first day of her confinement, she had pledged not to let her will crumble, since Captain LaShelle had put her in this place to see that happen. He wanted her to break, to beg him to let her out, and he would do it only if she agreed to do everything he told her to do. Her firm determination had seen her through two days, but now as the sun climbed to its highest, brightest peak on the third one, she thought she'd do just about anything for a bowl of cool water to splash on her face. Remembering the fresh bottle of water Mr. Sullivan had brought with her breakfast tray, she crawled on hands and knees to the cot. She had wanted to use it only as drinking water, but the heat and the humidity were beginning to wear her down and give her a headache, so she decided to squander a little by pouring it over the back of her neck. She had just taken the bottle from under the bed where she kept it hidden at Mr. Sullivan's request when the clinking of the brass key in the lock made her bolt to her feet. It was the most gratifying sound she had heard in a long while. Joyous tears filled her eyes as she watched the huge metal door swing inward, and it took a great deal of effort for her not to throw her arms around the old man who was about to give her her long-awaited freedom.

"Captain LaShelle said I was to bring you to the inn, Miss Grey." Hank smiled, offering his hand to her.

Presenting him with a playful curtsy, she touched her fingertips to his and eagerly followed him outside. The bright sun made her squint, but the discomfort didn't bother her. Anything was better than staying in that jail, and if it were at all possible, she would see to it that she never had to go back.

Apparently, the people of the village had learned about her release before Hank Sullivan had come for her. They were already beginning to line the street, and as the couple headed toward the inn, the crowd moved closer. At first, they only stared. Then a few bravely offered congratulations to her, and by the time Jennifer and Hank reached the front door of the inn, they were hailed with applause and uproarious shouts as if the people thought of her as their queen and she was returning home after years of exile. It was certainly a change from the last time they had greeted her.

Jennifer's gaze quickly surveyed the commons once she and Hank had gone inside, for she was half-expecting Captain LaShelle to be sitting in the center of the room

221

waiting for her. To her surprise, the place was empty. A knot of worry found its way to the pit of her belly. Something wasn't right. She sensed it. But she couldn't say what it was.

"Where's the captain?" she asked nervously as Hank guided her to the stairs.

"Don't know for sure, miss," he replied nonchalantly. "Said he had something to do and told me to fetch you from the jail." He smiled enthusiastically at her and tried to hurry her up the steps. "I've got a surprise for you."

"A surprise?" she echoed with a chuckle. "What kind of a surprise?"

At the top of the stairway, he let go of her arm and rushed on ahead to the last door on the left, quickly turned the knob, and swung the portal open. Jennifer's steps faltered. The room was just across the hall from Captain LaShelle's. The eerie feeling pricked her nerves again, but she tried not to show it. Whatever Hank Sullivan wanted her to see must be important or he wouldn't be motioning so frantically for her to approach. She shoved aside her uneasiness and went to stand beside the man.

Jennifer could hardly believe her eyes when she glanced into the room and saw the brass tub filled with bubbles, smelled the sweet fragrance of rosewater. In a daze, she stepped toward the bath, afraid that if she blinked, it would disappear.

"The captain ordered it, Miss Grey," Hank offered, following her into the room. "Gotta admit, it surprised me." He turned suddenly and went to the dresser, then laid his hand on the pile of clothing atop it. "Everything you need is right here. Something to dry yourself with, a change of clothes, everything. And he said you could take as long as you liked. No one is to come up here until he says so." He chuckled softly as a thought crossed his mind. "Guess maybe he decided he was being too hard on you after he saw the way the rest of us reacted." He laughed again and started toward the door, shaking his head as he went. "If he keeps this up, he'll have me believing he has a heart after all."

Jennifer continued to stare down at the ocean of white bubbles in the tub while she listened to the door shut quietly behind Hank, a suspicious gleam in her eyes. Maybe he believed the captain had done this for penance, but she didn't. Not more than two hours ago Chad had warned the people in the village not to offer her any help or they would suffer. Now he had done a complete turn around and had fooled them all. Everyone except her. Frowning, she shifted her attention to the stack of clothes on the dresser and gasped when she caught sight of her reflection in the mirror hanging above them. Dirt smudges covered her nose and chin. The beautiful braid she had labored over had come loose and now hung lopsided. Stray tendrils of golden hair fell across her brow and down the back of her neck. Her white blouse was soiled and torn, and she had a bright red scratch on her arm. Even her face was drawn and tired looking. No wonder everyone had taken pity on her. At first glance, she looked like an orphan in desperate need of a good meal. A thought flashed through her mind and she spun around to glare at the door. That was probably why Captain LaShelle had ordered a bath and clean clothes! He planned to make the islanders think she was being well taken care of so they would lose interest in her. She looked at the tub again. The arrogant rogue! As much as she longed to soak herself in that water, she knew that she mustn't. If she did, she'd be helping him rather than herself. She squared her shoulders and walked away from the tub. He was so mean. He probably realized how difficult it would be for her to resist. But she would. She wasn't going to give in.

A gentle breeze floated in through the open window,

stirring up the aroma of roses, and Jennifer moaned agonizing as she collapsed on the huge, fourposter bed. What good would it do to fight him? Mr. Sullivan knew LaShelle had ordered the bath drawn and he had his own opinion as to why it had been done. If she refused to bathe, she would merely be playing into the captain's hand. *He'd* be the one everybody felt sorry for. It would seem that she was being stubborn and ungrateful when Captain LaShelle was only trying to apologize. Damn! She was caught right in the middle. Tawny brows came together sharply. That was exactly the way he wanted it!

"I wonder what other little surprises he has for me," she growled, yanking the pins from her hair and undoing the long braid. Rising angrily, she loosened the strings on her blouse and slipped it off. Next came her skirt, petticoats, and chemise. "Well, whatever they are, at least I'll be clean," she spat out. Grabbing the piece of linen from the dresser, she dropped it beside the tub and climbed in.

A devilish grin kinked Chad's mouth as he sat on his bed, shoulders braced against the headboard, arms folded over his chest, ankles crossed. He had listened to the conversation in the hallway and had waited patiently to hear Hank Sullivan's footsteps on the stairs. All he had to do now was give the tenacious little blonde time to shed her clothes and get in the tub. His blood warmed as he envisioned long, slender limbs, a tapered back, and luscious golden hair. She was the liveliest wench he had had in a long while, and he wondered if he would ever tire of her. His smile softened. Probably not. She wasn't the type to give in, and that was the way he liked his women. If they weakened toward him, it meant they had grown fond of him, and that kind of attachment was the last thing he wanted. Absently, he traced a thumb over the scar in his lip. Nothing good ever came out of such a relationship. He jerked his hand away when he realized he was thinking of the past, and hurriedly left the bed. No, it was best Jennifer Grey continued to hate him. She must obey him, but hate him. Crossing to the door, he yanked it open and stepped into the hall.

He paused to look toward the stairway. He had given strict orders that no one was to come to Jennifer's room, and had seen to it that his crew was busy elsewhere. The kitchen, where Hank Sullivan worked, was at the other end of the building, too far away for anything to be heard. As for the other women who lived at the inn, he had simply told them to get out and stay out until he said they could come back. He had the entire place—and Jennifer—to himself. Moving closer to the door of her room, he tilted his head to listen for any indication that she might not have gotten into the tub, and smiled crookedly when he heard water splashing.

Sinking low in the tub after she had washed her hair, Jennifer sighed and closed her eyes. This was the most glorious feeling in the whole universe as far as she was concerned. She hadn't realized until this moment that this was the first real bath she had had since before boarding the *Sea Lady* so many weeks ago. There was something about soaking in perfume-scented water, it made one's troubles disappear. The expression on her lovely face saddened as she recalled having gone to her room after her father's funeral to do just this. It had relaxed her tired body, but hadn't eased the pain in her heart. But then, it wasn't supposed to. It was only meant to take one's mind off things for a while . . . as it was doing now.

Sitting with her back to the door, Jennifer neither saw the knob turn nor heard the latch click, but a sudden chill

225

brought her out of her reverie, and she opened her eyes. The golden light of late afternoon flooded the room as she took a moment to study her surroundings. The décor was simple: white painted walls, frilly lace curtains on the single window—they trailed all the way to the floor and matched the bedspread's soft shade of pink—a mauve-colored rug, and a tapestry in complementing hues that hung above the headboard of the bed. The furnishings consisted of a bed, a tall armoire, a night stand, and a rocking chair. The room had a woman's touch, right down to the vase of cut flowers sitting on the dresser, and Jennifer decided that if she had her pick of places to stay, this would be it.

Reaching for the piece of soap floating at the other end of the tub, she lathered up her sponge and began to scrub her arms and her chest. The water was getting cold, and she knew she'd have to hurry if she didn't want to look like a shriveled-up old lady. Leaning back in the tub, she raised one leg at a time and vigorously washed them clean. Then, tossing the sponge aside, she cupped her hands and splashed sudsy water over her face and down her neck and arms, rinsing away the foamy lather. A bright smile lit up her face as, feeling totally refreshed, she grabbed the towel from the floor and stood up to wipe herself dry. She doubted that she'd actually be able to thank the captain for his generosity no matter what his reason, but she was glad she had changed her mind about the bath. Blotting most of the moisture from her hair, she wrapped the towel around her and stepped from the tub. It was then Jennifer first noticed the ivory-handled brush lying on the dresser, and her delicate mouth dropped open in joyful surprise. It seemed a hundred years ago since she had had such a luxury. Hurrying to it, she tenderly picked it up. Not only was it made of ivory, but on its back were tiny pearls clustered in the shape of a flower and the handle was made of gold. It must have cost an awful lot. For a moment she thought it was too elegant to use simply to brush one's hair. But the temptation to run its soft bristles through her long, golden curls was too great to ignore, and before she looked up at her reflection in the mirror, she pulled the thick, damp mane off her neck and laid it across her shoulders, ready to begin. Then she saw him.

Chad had never enjoyed anything as much as watching this golden-haired beauty leisurely taking her bath in the brass tub. Her suntanned skin glistened with moisture and challenged him to shed his clothes and join her. And he would have, had he not realized what her reaction would be. In all probability, she would more than likely have tried to drown him. So he was content to watch and derive pleasure from the shapely curve of her back. Yet, when she raised a long, tapering limb to scrub away the dirt, his pulse quickened and his passion mounted, forcing him to suck in a quiet breath and calm his desires . . . momentarily. And when she stood up and gave him a full view, his lust soared until he had an ache in his loins, and he had to grip the doorknob on which his hand rested to bring himself under control. She was the most devastatingly beautiful woman he had ever seen, and for as long as he wished, she was his.

Paralyzed with a flood of emotions, Jennifer merely stared back at him in the reflection of glass, wondering just how long he had been there, watching. She hadn't heard him open the door nor sensed that he was in the room. Yet, from the way his dark eyes slowly traveled down the length of her and took in every curve, every inch of bare flesh before settling on her face again, she knew it had been long enough. Although he stood quite casually—one hand resting low on his hip, the other gripping the doorknob—she recognized the burning lust that shone in his deep, brown eyes and the danger she was in. Hairbrush in hand, she slowly faced him.

"This is what you had planned all along, isn't it?" She was amazed at how calm she sounded. "To get me alone." She swung a tiny hand out to indicate their surroundings. "I suppose you told everyone at the inn to leave for some reason or other so no one will hear anything. Even Mr. Sullivan thinks you're off somewhere or he wouldn't have seemed so pleased about leaving me alone." When LaShelle didn't reply but simply stared back at her, she voiced her opinion. "Everything you've done—setting me free, the bath—was for appearance's sake. What I don't understand is why. You haven't gained anything. In fact, the villagers now think of me as a martyr, and if you misuse me in any way, they could possibly turn against you. What did you hope to prove?" She jumped and took a step backward when he stood erect suddenly, dropped his hands to his sides, and started toward the bed.

"You surprise me, Jennifer." He smiled wickedly, his voice low and confident. "You've guessed correctly so far. I would think the rest would be obvious." He sat down on the edge of the bed and pulled off his boots. "The people of this village are like the sheep that graze on the hillside. They want someone they can follow—look up to—trust to tell them what they should do. With my help, they've chosen you." He began to undo the buttons on his shirt. "Right now, they'd throw themselves off a cliff if you told them to do it."

Jennifer suddenly understood. "But I won't, will I? Whatever I tell them to do will be what *you* tell me to tell them."

He didn't reply, but slid the shirt off his broad shoulders and tossed it over the arm of the rocking chair that stood beside him.

"Well, you're wrong," she fumed. "I'm not going to lie to them, pretend that I have their best interest in mind whenever they come to me for advice . . . if they do.

228

Why should they?"

"Because they think you have nothing to lose by going against my orders whereas they do." The smile returned to his lips but never reached his eyes. He stood up and slowly rounded the end of the bed. "But you and I will know differently."

A chill raced down her spine. "What—what do you mean?"

He paused at the foot of the bed and leaned a shoulder against the tall, wooden post. "They've made you a martyr, and that's exactly what you'll be. You're going to sacrifice yourself for them."

Jennifer's first thought was that he planned to murder her. Then her gaze dropped from his handsome face to the wide expanse of his bare, muscular chest with its matting of dark curls that tapered to a narrow line and disappeared beneath his breeches, and his meaning became quite clear once she saw the evidence of his desire. Her knees threatened to give out from under her, so she quickly grabbed the edge of the dresser behind her for support.

"N-no." Her denial came out in nearly a whisper as she moved along the piece of furniture toward the door. "No. I won't do this. There's no reason why I should."

"Really?" he questioned smoothly. "Maybe you should hear what I have to say before you decide."

Jennifer's chin quivered, and although she truly wanted to race from the room with no particular destination in mind, his warning gnawed at her conscience. He hadn't come to own this island, his ship, and everything around her purely by accident. Whatever he did was for a reason, and obviously for his own gain. Moreover, his methods always worked. She stepped to the side of the dresser and backed up to the wall, mildly satisfied that the brass tub separated them.

He grinned triumphantly. "Very wise choice, Jennifer." Pushing himself away from the bed, he walked around the tub, then half sat on the edge of it. Arms folded over his wide chest, he stared quietly at her for a moment. "If you fail to do whatever I want—and that means staying in your room when I tell you to without explaining why, or any other little thing I might want from you—those *sheep* will be punished. One of them will spend a week in the jail not knowing why, and if you really get out of hand, I'll start shipping them back to London. You know now what it's like being locked up, so imagine how horrible it would be to spend the rest of your life in debtor's prison, knowing that the only way you'd be able to leave would be in a pine box."

His dark brows lowered, his gaze was intense. Jennifer should have been scared out of her wits. But she wasn't. Her body still trembled, and she would have preferred to be elsewhere, but his callous, shocking recital of the rules he expected her to follow, and of the consequences if she didn't, overshadowed her fear of him, and she said the first thing that came to mind.

"Now I understand why your father renounced you as his son. You're not worthy of being in the same room with him."

From the moment Chad had walked out of his father's house fifteen years ago, he had trained himself not to let his emotions get in the way and cause him to say or do something he'd regret. But no one had ever stung him quite so deeply as this minx had just done, and his anger reigned.

"He has a son whether he wants to admit it or not."

"Yes!" she rallied, failing to hear the innuendo in his statement. "Charles! The man I'm going to marry instead of you, you cold-hearted bastard!"

Livid and unable to control his rage, he flew at her and took her roughly by the arms. She cried out in pain when his fingers dug into her flesh, and the brush she still held

230

in one hand dropped from her grip and thudded on the floor. He crushed her to him, and a long moment passed as he glared into her tear-filled eyes, his own shooting sparks of rage. When he spoke, his voice was filled with undeniable hatred.

"Aye, bastard is the only title which I can rightfully claim, and I'm proud of it. At least my mother never tried to hide the truth from anyone. She confronted my father before I was born, told him that she carried his child so that he would acknowledge me as his son. And he did, until fate played a cruel trick on both of us."

Jennifer's anger cooled a bit with his announcement, for she sensed there was more to his words and that confused her. What did he mean by saying fate played a trick on them? Her curiosity vanished, however, when she saw the expression on his face slowly changed from bitter indignation to unmistakable lust as his dark eyes left her face, to run over her neck and then seek the valley between her breasts. The towel offered little protection should he decide to tear it from her.

"And then fate brought you to me," he whispered, his parted lips descending upon hers.

Jennifer quickly turned her head away, avoiding his branding kiss and trying to break his hold on her by pushing her arms out against his. But his grip only tightened, and he chuckled softly as he pulled her against the rock-hard muscles of his bare chest.

"Why fight me, Jennifer?" he asked quietly. "I've already proven to you that it doesn't do any good. If I want you, I'll have you. It's that simple." The faint smile on his lips faded as he lowered his mouth to the tempting flesh just below her ear.

"You'd like that," she hissed through clenched teeth, straining to get away from him, "wouldn't you? You'd love to be able to tell Charles that I gave in willingly. Well, I won't. Never! I'll never enjoy having you touch

231

me. You're a vile, heartless man, Chad LaShelle. You never think of anyone other than yourself." Jennifer's courage grew when he ceased nibbling on her ear and looked her in the eye, his head cocked to one side, waiting for her to continue. "I'm a woman, in case you've forgotten. And not the kind you find in this place." She jerked her head toward the door. "I wasn't put on this earth merely to pleasure a man. I have feelings, needs, desires of my own, and they don't include having to tolerate yours."

"Really?" he grinned, enjoying her tirade. "And what would your needs be, exactly? Flowers? A kind word? A carriage ride in the country? A walk along the beach? If I did all that, would it change anything?"

"It would be a start," she rallied, knowing he only mocked her. "But then it would just be wasted. Underneath it all, you'd still be a bastard."

The muscle in his cheek flexed. "And you'd still belong to Charles."

"Yes!" she shouted.

"Then why go to all that trouble?" he growled, swooping down to lift her in his arms.

"Damn you, no!" she wailed, kicking and fighting him as he carried her across the room to the bed. Then her anger suddenly turned to tears. "Chad, no. Please!"

She gasped when he threw her roughly down upon the mattress, her linen wrap coming loose. She made a quick grab for it, but before she could grip the cloth in both hands, he had torn it from her fingers and hurled it away. In a panic, she rolled, thinking to get off the bed, but he easily caught her by the ankles, yanked her toward him, then threw himself down between her parted knees, his mouth coming down hard against hers. Every inch of Jennifer's flesh burned where he touched her, and his ardent kiss stole her breath away. His lips moved savagely, hungrily against hers, muffling her cry of

232

protest. She squirmed frantically beneath him, desperately trying to deny the raging fire that had erupted within her. This wasn't how it was supposed to be. She should detest his kisses, the way his fingers scorched the flesh along her neck as he fanned them wide to cradle her jaw and hold her steady. She gasped when his mouth trailed a moist path down her chin, across her throat and onto the firm mound of one breast, his tongue teasing the taut nipple while he gripped both her wrists to prevent resistance. She could feel herself weakening beneath his onslaught, and knew that if he sensed it, she would be lost. He must not know how his caresses affected her. She steeled herself against the rapturous sensation he aroused as his tongue dotted across the valley between her breasts to sample the second rose-hued peak, only to find that she had to bite her lip to keep from moaning in sheer ecstasy. Then, suddenly, he lifted himself from her, and Jennifer's face flamed with guilt over her wanton desires. Her eyes closed, she expected to hear his callous laughter, for she was positive that he had discovered her unwilling surrender. But only a moment of silence passed before she felt his weight upon the bed again, and a second later, she realized he had left her only to shed the rest of his clothes.

"Don't fight me, Jennifer," he whispered tenderly against her throat, sending a shiver through her whole body. "I won't hurt you, if you'll yield to me." He kissed the soft flesh beneath her ear. "I'll take you beyond the limit of earthly desires to a heaven you never dreamed existed. Open your eyes, Jennifer. Look at me. Deny the passion I've aroused, if you can, and I'll stop. I'll leave you right now, and you'll never know the pleasures that are just within your reach."

Jennifer's chin trembled, and although she didn't want to respond by opening her eyes, being certain he would know her answer the moment she looked at him, she did

233

so anyway. Everything he had said was true. He had touched upon a part of her that begged for fulfillment and went against the gentle teachings of her father. He had sparked a flame of passion in her and fanned the fire with curiosity. She didn't want him to stop. She didn't want to be left wondering to what heights he could take her and if, indeed, they were pleasurable. Yet, what disturbed her wasn't her desire to learn, but the man she wanted as her teacher. She wanted this fierce pirate captain who threatened her very existence and who made no promise of a future. She knew this, and yet she didn't care.

Braced on his elbows, his face only inches from hers, Chad watched the many emotions reflected in her beautiful blue-green eyes, and his blood turned to liquid fire. He hadn't truly believed he had ignited anything in her except loathing and contempt, but the naked lust glowing hotly in their murky depths told him otherwise and his passion soared nearly out of control. Dropping his gaze to her slightly parted lips, he impatiently covered her mouth with his in an explosion of unleashed desire while one hand eagerly followed the contour of her waist and hip before he slid his arm beneath her and pulled her up to meet his first thrust.

The branding heat of his manhood pressed deep within her filled Jennifer with a shocking wave of unfathomable urgency, and while her body craved all he could give her, her mind suddenly screamed out for her to bring their coupling to an end. Words formed in her mind, but never reached her lips. The mystical power that had spun its web around her and drawn her to him now cast a spell upon her conscience, numbing it, infecting it with titillating cravings, and her clumsy uncertainty—her innocence—melted away with each sleek movement of his body against hers. She arched her back to welcome him. Her nails dug into the hard muscles across his back. Her fevered kisses responded to his, and just as he had promised, he carried her from one plateau of ecstasy to another, higher and higher with mounting glory until her world careened dizzily and she thought her mind would explode. She could hear his ragged breathing, the thunderous pounding of his heart against her breast, and she marveled at the joy such a union could bring. Her mind whirled, her pulse raced, and the blending of their desires touched her very soul with a fiery splendor that left her weak and exhausted. All too soon, it ended, and Jennifer smiled shamelessly to herself, wishing that it hadn't. But only a moment passed before the full impact of what she had done hit her with more force than the gale winds that had torn apart the *Sea Lady*, and when he raised up from her, intending to lie beside her so he could stroke her velvet skin, she flew off the bed, grabbed the linen wrap from the floor where he had tossed it and awkwardly covered her slender frame, shielding it from his piercing dark stare.

"What the hell!" He scowled, his ebbing passion turning to anger once he saw the tears of rage streaming down her lovely face.

"You're detestable, Chad LaShelle," she spat out before he could question her sudden change of mood. "You don't care about anyone but yourself. You take whatever you want without a promise of . . . of . . ." Words failed her, and she gave way to sobs.

"What?" he snarled, failing to understand the tender, turbulent emotions that tore at her heart. "Promise what? Marriage?" Furious, though he didn't know why, he slid to the edge of the bed, picked up his breeches, and jerked them on. "You're damned right I take what I want without a promise," he announced, drawing on the old wounds of his own suffering. "And I don't explain why. Nor do I ask forgiveness." He jammed his feet into his boots, stood, and picked up his shirt. "But I will promise you this." He pointed a finger at her. "I won't change just because of you. So get used to it, wench. Until the day I hand you back to Charles, *this* is all you'll get from me." He glowered at her a moment longer, then stormed from the room, slamming the door shut behind him with a thunderous bang.

Her face streaked with tears, Jennifer stared at the closed door, the linen wrap drawn up beneath her chin, her body shaking. Even though he had left her, she could still feel the warmth of his touch, his kiss; the strength of his arms encircling her. Yet, in her heart, she knew an emptiness that took her unawares and totally confused her. What had happened to her? It wasn't the shame of allowing her passion to rule her mind that brought her tears, but something else, an emotion she'd thought she would never feel for a man. She was drawn to Chad, and not out of pity or sympathy, but something much deeper.

"No," she sobbed, and flung herself across the bed. "It's not meant to be!" Burying her face in the pillow, she gave way to her sorrow. Chad LaShelle was too filled with hatred ever to allow the tender seed of love to grow.

Chapter Ten

Jennifer viewed the morning from the comfort of her bed, bright yellow streams of light coming through the window. She took in the pale blueness of the sky with its sprinkling of white clouds, and the gentle movements of the lace curtain where the soft breeze filtered in and flooded the room with the sweet smell of flowers. It was a cheerful morning, yet it failed to bring a smile to her lips or to chase away the sadness reflected in her blue-green eyes. Her discovery the night before of how she felt about the pirate captain had lingered in her thoughts, making it impossible for her to sleep.

She had spent most of the evening standing by the window and staring out at the hillside until the shrill laughter of a woman in the commons had reached her ears and reminded her of what went on in the various rooms on the second floor once the price was met. Mr. Sullivan had told her that Captain LaShelle had ordered everyone to stay away from her chambers until he said otherwise, but that had been before she had made him angry. And since he had yet to announce what her duties would be during her stay on the island, she'd feared his rage had decided that question for him. After all, hadn't he given her a room at the inn, the place where the prostitutes lived? That thought had sent her flying to the door in the hope of finding a key protruding from the lock so she could assure her safety for the night. When there had been none there, she had tried the knob, praying that Chad had locked her in on his way out. But to her dismay, the latch clicked and the door opened easily to her touch. In a panic, she had slammed it shut and hurriedly moved the night stand in front of it, knowing the tiny piece of furniture wouldn't be enough to stop anyone who wanted to get in, but thinking the noise of it being shoved out of the way would awaken her and give her a chance to defend herself—if she could fall asleep.

Feeling a little better, she had gone to bed. But sleep hadn't come, and she had lain there listening to the loud voices of the men in the commons, trying to decide if Chad's was one of them. An hour later the gaiety having increased, she had assumed that the patrons of the inn were getting drunker by the minute. She had been sure of that when she'd heard the uneven, staggering footsteps of a laughing couple who'd climbed the stairs and started down the hall toward her room. She had sat straight up in bed, inched back against the headboard, and stared at the door, fearing that at any moment, they would burst into her room. Only after recognizing Modesty's voice and realizing the woman's room was next to hers, did Jennifer relax. Yet, as she listened to them stumble about, bumping into furniture, giggling, knocking over something that shattered on the floor, and then finally falling onto the bed that squeaked a protest, tears had sprung to Jennifer's eyes for she had wondered if Modesty's companion for the night was the captain. Willard had said that Chad had been ignoring the woman lately, but after what had transpired between Jennifer and him a short time earlier, it was quite conceivable that he had changed his mind. Sinking low in the bed, the coverlet drawn up over her head, she had tried to block out the sounds passing through the thin wall separating her from the couple next door. But, in the darkness, her mind had conjured up visions to accompany the laughter, the moans, the squeaking bed; and out of frustration, she had grabbed her pillow and clamped it over her ears. Much later, she had fallen asleep, only to be awakened at dawn by the slamming of a door somewhere down the hall.

Jennifer had never been one to lounge about in bed all day, and although she had no idea of what to do with her time, she decided that perhaps she should go downstairs and look for Mr. Sullivan. Maybe Chad hadn't determined what job best suited her, but given half a chance, she was sure his need to satisfy his anger at her would result in her spending each day and night right here in bed. She cringed at the thought of having to allow a man—any man—to touch her just because he had paid for the privilege, and she swung her bare feet to the floor. How could a woman do such a thing? Didn't she have any pride in herself? Shrugging it off as something she truly didn't care to learn, much less discuss with someone, Jennifer went to the dresser and picked up the brush. As she began to pull the tangles from her hair, she spotted a corner of the brass tub reflected in the mirror. The sight of it flooded her with memories, and she slowly laid down the brush and turned around to stare at the tub.

Soaking in it had brought her such pleasure, how was it possible now for her to feel sad simply because it was in the same room with her? The answer wasn't that difficult to figure out. It reminded her of Chad, of what they had shared, and like the water filling it, their passion had cooled and no longer held any pleasure. Her gaze drifted toward the wall that separated her from the redhead everyone on the island had considered Chad's woman before Jennifer arrived, and a knot formed in her throat. He was probably lying in that woman's arms right now,

239

sleeping off the effects of a night spent drinking ale in an attempt to forget what he and Jennifer had shared only a short time before. The thought stung her pride, but it also gave her self-esteem a nudge. If he could see her now and know what she was thinking, he'd laugh at her. He didn't care if he hurt her feelings or not. Why should he? She was nothing to him—nothing but a tool he planned to use against his father. So why should she allow what happened to get the better of her? Feeling sorry for herself wouldn't change any of it, but he certainly would enjoy seeing her suffer. She raised her delicate nose in the air and straightened her shoulders. Well, he wouldn't see that. She wouldn't let him. If last night meant nothing to him, then it meant nothing to her. She'd prove that by finding Mr. Sullivan and asking him if he needed help in the kitchen. Turning back to the dresser, she finished brushing her hair and slid a fresh blouse and skirt on over the chemise she had slept in. Then she put on sandals and went to the door.

Once she'd found her way to the room where Mr. Sullivan worked, Jennifer smiled and greeted the old man.

"Miss Jennifer," he responded, obviously surprised by her presence. "What are you doing here?" He wiped his hands on the apron he had tied around his narrow waist and came to meet her at the door.

"Willard told me you were the cook here at the inn, and I decided that maybe you could use some help," she told him. "I think my talents do not lie in standing behind a stove, but I could carry trays or wash dishes or do something. I might even be able to peel potatoes without cutting off my finger."

The lines around Hank's eyes deepened with his laughter. "I think you probably could." He nodded and pointed toward one of the cupboards. "You'll find an apron over there. Would you happen to know how to cook eggs? I usually just scramble them." He chuckled and went back to the stove. "Nobody's really too finicky this time of day."

"I think I can handle that. At least I don't have to worry about breaking the yolks." She grinned playfully and hurriedly took down one of the aprons hanging on a hook. "How many people do you usually serve breakfast to, Mr. Sullivan?" she asked, tying the strings around her waist and then lifting the basketful of eggs off the table and carrying it to the stove.

"The name's Hank," he corrected. "Only those who spend the night, so it varies."

She tried not to laugh at what he said, for he had made it sound as though the village had travelers coming and going at all hours of the day and night, which was not the case.

"Did I say something funny?" he asked, smiling over at her as he finished cutting up the ham and placing slices of it in a frying pan.

"Oh, I'm sorry," she apologized. "I was just having trouble imagining who would spend the night when everyone on the island has their own place."

"A few of the men stay from time to time, along with the captain's crew."

"But why don't they go home? Don't they have to pay to stay here?" She was busy cracking eggs into a bowl and missed the surprised look on Hank's face.

"Yes'm," he quietly replied, then concentrated on taking the freshly baked loaves of bread out of the oven, too embarrassed to explain further.

Jennifer shrugged a shoulder and glanced up. "Seems like a waste of money to me when—" Suddenly, the reason why the men spent a hard-earned coin for the right to sleep at the inn became perfectly clear, and her face flamed hotly. She quickly turned her attention back to what she was doing. "I'm sorry, Hank. I wasn't thinking

241

or I wouldn't have said anything."

"That's quite all right, Jennifer. I understand," he assured her. "I rather doubt a lady such as yourself has ever lodged in a place like this before." Turning with the steaming loaves of bread in hand, he laid them on the table and tapped them free of their pans. "Where are you from, Jennifer?"

Grateful for the chance to change the subject, she reached for a fork and began to beat the eggs as she replied. "My father and I lived on a plantation near Jamestown, Virginia, in the Colonies. But I was born in London." The delicious smells of breakfast drifted over to her. "Hank, where did you get the ham?" she asked, nodding at the stove. "And the eggs, now that I think about it."

"Oh, we have everything we need. Sheep, pigs, chickens, cattle, and several milk cows. We grow our own wheat, grain, and potatoes, and a few vegetables. What we don't have are things like sugar and spices, tea, coffee, rum, and ale. You know, things we can't grow ourselves. But the captain takes care of those."

The corner of Jennifer's mouth crimped. "By stealing them."

"Well, I don't imagine he pays for them," Hank laughed. "We're even trying to grow cotton so we can make our own clothes. We have a fishing fleet—nothing big, just small boats. And we've already built our own mill. Yes, ma'am"—he smiled, turning back to the stove—"we have ourselves a little piece of heaven here."

Taking down one of the skillets that hung on hooks suspended from the ceiling, she set it on the stove and poured in the beaten eggs. "It would be, if everyone here had the choice of whether or not to stay," she mumbled.

"Yeah, I suppose you could say that," he agreed. "But I know that if I had the choice, I'd stay. Don't have anything back in London worth going back to. My wife

242

died years ago, and we never had any children." He stabbed a fork into the ham and flipped each slice over. "And there isn't the stealing and cheating going on here like there was in London." His gray brows came together suddenly. "This thing with little Megan is the first time there's ever been any real trouble here."

Jennifer had to bite her tongue to keep from telling him why there hadn't been. The captain knew. He had called these people sheep who followed without question. A smile suddenly lit up her eyes as she thought about that. Maybe they did. But not for long. Given the right idea and a few pushes over time, by someone they looked up to as the captain put it, they would soon realize that what they had here—their little piece of heaven—had a few dark clouds hanging over it. She forced her attention on the eggs she stirred, not wanting Hank to notice her glee. She didn't want to have to explain it. That would ruin everything because she wanted these people to believe that what they did was based on their own decisions. The sparkle in her sea green eyes disappeared. She had to accomplish her goal before the captain decided to take her to England. Maybe she wouldn't have the honor of being here when it was reached, but simply knowing that it would be, would be her payment. She'd show these people that the way of life Captain LaShelle had forced on them wasn't necessarily the way things should be. As far as she was concerned, they had paid their debt, and he had no right to keep them in bondage.

"I understand from Willard that at one time you were engaged to Captain LaShelle. Is that true?" Hank asked, placing the fried ham on a platter and setting uncooked slices in the pan.

"When I was a very young child, yes. But not anymore."

"Had you ever met him before now?"

Jennifer shook her head and then reached for a clean

243

bowl in which to put the cooked eggs. "Not really. I was too young. I was only about a year old when we left London, so I don't even remember him. But my father talked a lot about him. Papa thought he would make a fine husband for me. But that was before—well, before the captain left home." Turning, she placed the bowl on the tray sitting on the table. "Has he ever told you anything about the argument he had with his father?"

"Me?" Hank laughed. "Never. I doubt he's even told Jason—Jason Bingham, his first mate and his only real friend. No, Captain LaShelle doesn't say much of anything to anybody." He flipped the ham over and laid down his fork, then faced her. "He's a very troubled young man, that captain of ours. I have no idea what it is that disturbs him so much, but there's a hatred in him that's eating away any chance he might have to be happy. I have noticed, however, that there's been a slight change in him since you came to the island. Not much. But a little."

"You mean he was worse than he is now?" she jeered, picking up a knife to slice the loaves of warm bread. "That's hard to imagine."

"He seems pretty bad to you, I'm sure. But deep down inside, he's an honorable man. He's always been fair with us, and we respect him." He quickly raised a hand to silence her when she opened her mouth to argue, certain he already knew the point she was about to make. "Yes, he's a pirate. He steals everything he needs, but only from people he doesn't care about . . . doesn't even know."

"And then he kills them," Jennifer finished, slamming the knife back down on the table. "And you respect him? He keeps you a prisoner here. You must abide by his rules or you'll go back to prison, yet you respect him. I'm sorry, Hank, but I can't understand how you can."

Hank's wrinkled brow furrowed as he thought about what she said. "When you put it that way, it does seem foolish. But I guess, maybe, we don't allow ourselves to see the way he is when he's not here on the island. We only go by the way he treats us and the kind of life we have. It's peaceful here. We're never hungry or cold. We're never beaten, and if we have a complaint about someone in the village, we take it to him and he holds court . . . just like it would be in London. Only this judge isn't out to take our money. He never has. What's ours is ours. He's not taking a share of our profits for himself, and I don't think he ever will."

"But that doesn't make any sense," Jennifer objected. "Why wouldn't he? He steals from everyone else. Why not you?"

The pot of coffee on the stove started to boil over, so Hank paused a moment to lift it from the fire and then pour two cups of the rich, dark brew. Handing one to Jennifer, he motioned for her to sit down on one of the stools near the table.

"It's only a guess on my part, but I think he's doing this to prove something. To himself, not anyone else." He smiled softly when he saw her confused frown. "I never met his father while I lived in London. He was a member of Parliament; I was a baker. But I knew of him, and of the kind of wealth the man has. Rumor is that Captain LaShelle, being the oldest son even though illegitimate, was in line for a considerable inheritance once his father died, and because of the argument they had, he will no longer receive it. I feel he's trying to prove that just because his father wasn't married to his mother doesn't mean he's any less important. Have you taken a good look at this island, at the village, Jennifer? Doesn't it remind you of London? I think he's building his own little empire here, and he's the king. You should see the house he's building for himself."

"House?" she repeated, surprised. For some reason she had never thought Chad LaShelle intended to spend

245

the rest of his life living on a small piece of land cut off from the rest of the world by hundreds of miles of ocean.

"Yes. Only I should call it a castle. It's about a ten-minute walk along the beach, and it's built on a plateau that's surrounded by sheer rock bluffs. The only way one can get to it is to climb the stone stairs he had carved out of the side of the hill, and at the top, there's a huge iron fence and a locked gate. Nobody gets in and nobody gets out unless the captain permits it." His attention was suddenly drawn away when he smelled the ham burning, and he hurriedly left the stool to take it from the fire. Adding the cooked meat to the stack already piled on a platter, he turned back to the table, the ham held in one hand. "To be quite honest, I'm surprised he hasn't moved in yet. It should be ready to live in by now."

As Jennifer had quietly listened to everything Hank had told her, her curiosity about Chad had deepened. Piecing together the bits of information she had learned about the man, she decided that the key to his dark side lay in the argument he had had with his father, and to understand Chad LaShelle, one had to know what had caused his father to disown him. Rising, she lifted the scrambled eggs and the tray of bread from the table and followed Hank to the door. "Have you any idea what the argument was about?" she asked as they carried the food into the commons.

Hank quickly glanced around the large room to make certain no one was about who might overhear him. "Not exactly," he answered quietly, nodding for her to set the food on the first table they came to. "But I do have my own theory."

"Will you share it with me? I'd like to understand what it is that makes him the way he is. My father knew, but he'd never talk about it. I think Chad's father made him promise to keep it a secret."

"Well, don't take it as fact, Jennifer. I'm really only

246

guessing," he warned. "But I think it has something to do with Mrs. Wadsworth's death."

"Why do you say that?"

"Because Captain LaShelle left London the day she was buried, and I think the accident had something to do with it."

"Accident?"

"Yes. The carriage mishap that killed Mrs. Wadsworth and her maid. And then, of course, there's the gossip about Maida Tanner." He turned away from her to go to a cupboard and take down a stack of plates.

"Who's Maida Tanner?" she inquired, helping him place the dishes around the table.

"Housekeeper to the Wadsworths. From what I've heard, she's a very shapely, beautiful woman, and there was some talk that Mr. Wadsworth and she were . . . involved."

"I don't see the connection." Jennifer frowned as she followed him back to the cupboard to take a handful of silverware from the drawer.

"His affair with the woman wasn't much of a secret around London. Everyone discussed it, him being a member of Parliament and all, so it only stands to reason that his wife knew about it. When her carriage was found in the ravine, it was filled with luggage so everyone assumed she was leaving him. I think the man honestly blamed himself for her death—his unfaithfulness—but he took it out on his illegitimate son simply because the lad was a vivid reminder of his infidelity."

"How horrible," Jennifer moaned, envisioning a boy of fourteen being confronted by such rage and such an undeserved punishment.

"Now mind you," Hank gently warned her, "it's only a theory. I have no proof, but it would certainly explain—"

Footsteps on the stairs brought their conversation to

247

an abrupt end, and although Hank busied himself with setting out the rest of the dishes and silverware as if he and his companion had been merely talking about the weather, Jennifer paused to look up and see who was about to join them. Her heart thumped a little harder as Chad came into view, and she quickly lowered her gaze. She had never been very good at hiding the truth from anyone, and if he happened to look at her right then, he'd suspect that he had been the topic of discussion on this bright, early morning by the guilty look in her eyes. A sense of panic filled her when Hank handed her the rest of the knives and forks he held, telling her to finish setting them out while he went back to the kitchen for the pot of coffee. Inwardly, she cursed the old man for leaving her alone with Chad.

"What are you doing?" the deep voice at her side questioned.

Jennifer's hand shook so badly that she dropped the flatware onto the floor. "Helping Mr. Sullivan," she replied nervously as she stooped to retrieve the utensils.

"At his request?"

"No," she said, rising and turning away from him to go back to the cupboard for more silverware. "I couldn't sleep, and I thought I might be of some use down here. Besides, if I do a good job, he might hire me. I could use the money." She had managed not to look at Chad, but she knew exactly where he stood. She could feel every inch of his muscular frame.

"You already have a job," he informed her, his tone flat. "Only you won't be paid."

Jennifer's long, blond hair tumbled about her shoulders in a brilliant spray of gold when she jerked her head around to stare at him, mouth agape. "What do you mean I won't get paid? Everyone else does."

His dark eyes raked over her slender form from head to toe, taking in the sight of her heaving chest and the low-cut blouse that fell off one shoulder, before settling on her flawless face once more. "You'll be working for the food you eat and the bed you sleep in. You won't be here long enough to need any money." His gaze dropped away from her as he reached for a plate and began to fill it.

"And what kind of work will I be doing, dare I ask?" she demanded as he turned away from her and selected a place in the far corner of the room where it was dark and he could put his back to the wall. Yet, even in the muted light, she could distinguish his handsome face and broad shoulders, the flexing of muscles in his forearm when he picked up a knife and cut into the ham on his plate, the way his black hair shimmered to a purplish hue each time he moved his head. Her pulse quickened a little. She wanted to shut off the excited tingle his presence aroused in her every time she saw him, but she couldn't, so she silently damned her weakness, certain it would interfere with her attempt to present a disinterested mien. She watched him a moment longer as he casually chewed his food, ignoring her question, and she was about to ask it again, when Hank returned from the kitchen, carrying the huge pot of coffee in one hand and several mugs in the other.

"See that Captain LaShelle gets a cup, will you, Jennifer?" he whispered, setting everything down on the table. "I have to tell the others that breakfast is ready." He turned quickly and headed for the stairs before she had a chance to object, missing the irritable frown that drew her tawny brows together as she watched him go.

"You'd be wise to learn from him."

Jennifer's head snapped around. "Oh? And what would I learn? How to tremble in fear whenever you walk into the room?"

Dark eyes glanced up at her, then returned to the plate of food.

"Do you get some sort of pleasure out of watching

people cower? I would think you'd get tired of it after a while," she added disgustedly, and lifted the pot to pour his coffee. Mug in hand, she went to stand before him, leaning in to roughly deposit the coffee on the table near his elbow. "You didn't answer my question. What kind of work will I be doing?"

He didn't grace her with his full attention, but finished cutting up the slice of ham as he commented, "I don't know. What are you good at doing?" Stabbing a piece of meat with his fork, he popped it into his mouth and glanced up. "I mean besides being a bitch."

Highly insulted, Jennifer couldn't find the words to express her rage, which was heightened when he concentrated on his breakfast again as if what he had said only voiced a well-known fact. All she could do was stand there and fume while he finished off his meal.

"You'll be working for me," he finally admitted before taking a sip of his coffee. Shifting, he leaned back against the wall, propped a booted foot on the bench and laid his arm over his knee as he looked her up and down. "I need someone to take care of my house. I'm sure Mr. Sullivan told you all about it."

"Yes, he did," she managed to reply, deciding his earlier remark wasn't worth discussing. "But the answer is no. I'll find employment elsewhere . . . someplace where I'll be paid." She leaned forward and reached out to take his empty plate from the table, then gasped when he jerked himself up from the bench and grabbed her by the elbow, nearly pulling her across the table toward him.

"You don't have a choice, Jennifer," he snarled. "You belong to me. Where I go, you go. If I want to pay you, I will. If I don't, you'll work for nothing."

"By being your whore or your housekeeper?" she retorted though tears were welling in her eyes.

Chad's anger lessened a bit. "Either one," he half whispered. "Or both."

250

Hearing Hank's footsteps on the stairs as he returned to the commons gave Jennifer an idea, and she wrenched her arm free and turned around. "Mr. Sullivan," she called. Stopping at the bottom of the staircase, he looked back worriedly at her. "Captain LaShelle says he'll pay me five shillings a week to be his housekeeper, but I'd prefer to work for you. However, I'd have to take the best offer. Can you beat it?" She could almost feel the heated glare of her companion on her back, and was certain of his reaction by the startled, fearful look on Hank's face when his gaze moved past her to the man standing behind her.

He gulped, then shook his head.

It was what she expected. No one had the courage to challenge Chad LaShelle face to face. But she wasn't finished. She knew she'd have to do whatever he wanted, but he was going to pay and Hank would, unknowingly, see to it.

"Oh, that's too bad," she calmly replied, feigning disappointment. "Then perhaps you'd do me a favor." She watched his green eyes shift from her to Chad and back. "I'd like you to keep my earnings for me. I've never been very good at saving, and I really would like to have something to give to my fiancé when I return to England. Would you do that for me?"

Not knowing that there had never been such a bargain made between the captain and this young woman, Hank could see no harm in agreeing. He silently questioned his judgment in doing so, however, once he saw the furious look in the captain's eyes and the pleased, somewhat triumphant smile in Jennifer's eyes before she turned to face the man.

"Then I guess you've hired yourself a housekeeper, Captain LaShelle." She grinned sarcastically and reached for the plate she had tried to take when Chad had grabbed her arm. "When would you like me to start?"

Chad's dark glare told Hank to make a hasty exit, and once the man had gone back into the kitchen and left the couple alone, his angry scowl turned on her. "Very shrewd, Jennifer, but have you decided what you'll do at the end of the first week after I refuse to pay you?"

"Oh, I don't think that will happen," she confidently replied. "The whole idea behind setting me free from jail and giving me a bath and a room of my own was to prevent the people of this village from revolting . . . or at least thinking about it." Her blue-green eyes hardened a bit. "Your mistake was in using me to achieve that end, and it's too late now to do anything about it. You wanted them to look at me as their leader. Well, they do. And the minute you do something to me that offends them, you'll be right back where you started."

"Obviously, you've forgotten our earlier discussion," he pointed out, his nostrils flaring with his rage. "About shipping them back to London one at a time with no explanation whatsoever. And the first one to go will be Hank Sullivan."

Jennifer's stomach churned a little, but she knew she couldn't back down now. "You'd never get him on the ship."

Chad laughed mockingly. "Oh? And would you care to explain why not?"

"His friends wouldn't allow it. I believe they outnumber your crew." She could feel her knees start to shake, and she decided it might be better if she didn't look at him anymore. She turned and headed toward the kitchen.

"You have a lot to learn about these people, Jennifer Grey." His tone was smooth and confident. "When faced with a choice, you'll see that even though they might outnumber my crew, they'll decide not to take a chance on losing their freedom. That's what would happen if they tried, and they know it. They might win a battle, but

252

they'd certainly lose the war."

"And how would that happen?" she challenged, whirling around to glare at him.

In that moment, Chad thought this little vixen had never looked so beautiful. Bright sunlight streamed into the room through the open door, and bathed her golden hair and skin with a rich, healthy glow. The snowy white blouse she wore hung loose over her bosom, but it failed to completely disguise what lay hidden beneath its gauzy fabric. She was a tempting vision that Chad had to force from his thoughts. He'd have her again, but right now, there were more important things to think about. He rested a hip on the table, crossed his wrists, and leaned forward to return the angry glare she gave him.

"Weapons, Jennifer," he calmly answered. "It takes weapons to win a war, and these people have none. Unless you consider hoes, skillets, and rakes as deadly weapons, they'd have to face my crew with empty hands." He grunted sarcastically. "They don't even know how to fight, and half of them are women. What chance would they have going up against even a small group of men who wouldn't hesitate to shoot them or run them through? If you really want to do these people a favor, Jennifer, you'll leave well enough alone and concentrate on your own troubles."

Her blue-green eyes narrowed, and a vague smile lifted one corner of her mouth. "There are other ways to win a war, Captain," she gallantly replied, "and they don't entail using firearms."

A brief frown wrinkled his brow, and he tilted his head to one side, contemplating her meaning. "Such as?"

Her smile widened. "You'll see," she said, and turned around to disappear into the kitchen.

Chad's dark eyes stared at the empty doorway for a long time as he wondered just what it was that she had in mind. He'd have to stay alert from now on. The little

253

minx would more than likely try to stir up trouble in any way she could, but oddly enough, he found the challenge stimulating. Earlier, she had asked him if he ever got tired of people cowering at his feet, but hadn't allowed him the chance to answer. Aye, he got tired of it. He disliked seeing people too afraid to stand up for their own rights, and it usually made him angry. To his way of thinking, people on this earth had a right to live in the ways they wanted. But if they were too cowardly to fight for that right, then he'd use their weaknesses to his advantage. He reached up and ran the knuckles of one hand along his unshaven jaw. It would be interesting to see what method Jennifer would use to change these spineless milksops into men . . . if she could. But then, it would be more interesting to see if she wanted to do so once he was finished with her. A flash of white teeth showed briefly in a smile before he turned and hurriedly strode from the inn.

Jennifer didn't see Chad again for the rest of the day, but by early evening, she was wishing he would return to the inn. She had offered to work for Hank, serving drinks and food, until the captain notified her that she could begin her new job as housekeeper. Hank had been very reluctant to agree, and at first Jennifer couldn't understand why. Then Modesty and the other girls who lived upstairs made their grand entrance. The minute the ill-tempered redhead saw Jennifer trouble began. And it worsened when Marc Bartell and two of his friends came to the inn for mugs of ale, each man in possession of the coins needed to buy the right to spend the night with one of the prostitutes. No matter what Jennifer did for them, whether it was refilling their mugs or serving their dinner, they complained. She was too slow, the ale was flat, or the food was cold or overly cooked. Jennifer never argued with them, knowing that they only wanted to provoke her into doing something she'd be sorry for, and she was near tears by the time Jason Bingham entered the commons to have his supper. The surprised look on his face told her that Chad hadn't ordered him to see how she was doing, and the discovery stung her a bit. But then, what had she truly expected. She had defied him, and done so in front of a witness whether Hank Sullivan was aware of what she'd been doing or not.

"Did the captain approve of this?" Jason quietly asked as she had neared his table with a bowl of stew and mug of ale.

She blinked back the rush of tears that threatened to spill down her cheeks. "He knows I'm here, so I guess he approves."

Jason's green eyes quickly scanned the crowd of patrons in the room, taking note of the hate-filled glare Modesty aimed at Jennifer's back while the pretty, little blonde set the dishes down on the table in front of him. He couldn't imagine Chad leaving Jennifer as open game for the likes of Marc Bartell. The man had made it perfectly clear that he wanted Jennifer Grey whether his captain liked it or not, and he would seize the first chance he got to take her. Allowing Jennifer to work the commons in any way—even sweeping floors—was asking for trouble. Frowning, Jason shifted his attention to the deck hand, watching him guzzle down his ale, slam the mug on the table, and in a loud voice demand a refill. Sober, Bartell's disposition was sharp edged. When he'd had too much to drink, he was easily moved to violence, as two of the four women sitting at his table could attest. Both Pearl and Ruby had sported black eyes because of him. But they were used to it. It came with the job. Jennifer Grey, on the other hand, wouldn't know how to handle such violence. And there'd be hell to pay if Marc Bartell laid a hand on her. Chad would see to it.

"Come on, ya arrogant bitch," Bartell shouted at Jennifer. "Bring me another ale, and be quick about it."

Jason's gaze moved to the young woman standing at his table. He could see the frightened look in her eyes and noticed that she trembled. He caught her hand and pulled her down on the bench beside him. "Get your own ale, Marc," he said evenly. "Or have one of your girls get it for you. This one's busy with me."

"We ain't no bloody servin' wenches," Ruby shouted in return, her darkly painted face pinched into an angry scowl. Plopping her rounded shape into Marc's lap, she wrapped her arms around his neck, giving him an unrestricted view of her bosom, which was almost totally exposed because of the low cut of her blouse, and then she laughed. "Are we, 'oney?"

"Ya sure ain't," Bartell guffawed, burying his face in the valley between her breasts and bringing a squeal of delight from the woman.

Jennifer cringed at the sight and lowered her eyes, unable to watch and feeling a little faint.

"What's a-matter, Miss 'Igh and Mighty?" Modesty's voice rang out. "Is yer liedyship too good fer the likes o' us?" Rising from the corner of the table on which she had been perched on one hip, she sauntered over to Jason's, her hands on her waist and her glare centered on Jennifer. "Ye ain't no better'n us, lovey. Not no more. Chad saw to that. Yer a 'ore . . . just like us."

"That's enough, Modesty," Jason warned.

Her brown eyes narrowed as they turned on him. "Not talkin' about it ain't gonna change the fact, Mr. Bingham. She's a 'ore and everyone 'ere 'as a right to 'er." Her red lips twisted into a sneer. "Even you, gov'na. But I guess ye already know that or she wouldn't be sittin' next to ye now, would she?"

Jason ignored her last comment, knowing she had only said it to further upset his companion. "Correct me if I'm

256

wrong, Modesty, but didn't Captain LaShelle tell you that since he no longer had any use for you, you were to do the job you were brought here to do—serving drinks?"

Modesty's spine stiffened instantly, and her nose went up in the air, but she refused to answer.

"I suggest you fetch Mr. Bartell his ale before the captain hears you're not living up to your part of the bargain and ships you back to England."

The smile he gave her glowed threateningly in his eyes, and when he jerked his head back toward her friends, dismissing her, Modesty clamped her teeth together, biting back the string of oaths she wished to hurl at him. Jason Bingham had never liked her, and she knew it. In fact, he didn't like any of the prostitutes on the island, and she had many times wondered if he had a preference for boys since he never paid for female company. She longed to question him about it right here in front of the blond-haired bitch he tried to protect, but thought better of it. It would only anger him, and then she'd be the one who'd have to answer to Chad. And Chad was furious enough with her as it was. Presenting them both with a hostile glower, she turned and stormed off.

"You'll have to watch out for her, Miss Grey." Jason sighed resignedly. "She has a very nasty side to her, and I'm sure she'd like to show it to you. Whether or not you wanted it that way, you've stepped in between her and her man, and she's not the forgiving sort."

Guardedly, Jennifer glanced in Modesty's direction, then quickly averted her eyes when she discovered that the woman was still watching her. She mumbled, "I'd be very willing to give him back to her if I thought I could."

"Aye," Jason chuckled. "I imagine you would." Reaching for the bowl of stew, he pulled it closer and picked up his spoon. "So, suppose you explain to me how it is you happen to be working here with the captain's approval. I'm interested in knowing why he would give it."

She watched him stir the meat, potatoes, and broth for a moment, then lift a spoonful to his mouth, wondering if he would like the stew or not. She hadn't made it entirely on her own. Hank had supervised its preparation very closely, but it was her first attempt at making a meal. A soft smile parted her lips when he moaned delightedly and commented on Hank's ability to turn something simple into a feast. He took a second bite and straightened suddenly when it dawned on him that perhaps Jennifer had prepared the stew.

"Or has Hank been getting lessons?" he asked, looking at her.

A light blush rose on her cheeks. "Not really. I just told him about the way Camille used to fix it."

"Camille?" he questioned, chewing on another mouthful.

"She was our cook."

"You mean you ate like this every day?" He grinned, hoping to ease the tension he was sure she was feeling.

Jennifer shrugged one delicate shoulder. "I guess."

"Maybe we should fire Hank and have you be our cook," he teased, smiling broadly when Jennifer vigorously shook her head. "Is that why the captain decided to let you work here? He always was complaining about the food."

"I'm only helping Hank out for a while," she admitted, glancing at Modesty's table when the group burst into loud laughter.

"Really? Then what?"

"Captain LaShelle said I'm to be his housekeeper." She missed the shocked expression that came over Jason's face, but her attention was drawn back to him when she heard his spoon clink against the table top.

"Are you telling me that the captain didn't give his permission for you to be in here?"

258

Jennifer's finely arched brows knitted. "Well, he never said I couldn't. Not really. I mean he said that I wouldn't be able to work for Hank because I'd be working as his housekeeper."

"All right," Jason interrupted with a raised hand. "Let me ask it this way. Does he know you're serving tables today?"

"I don't think so. He left right after breakfast, and I haven't seen him since."

"That's what I thought," he grumbled, pushing the bowl of stew away from him. Rising, he left the mug of ale untouched and bent slightly to take her elbow. "Come on. I'm taking you out of here."

"Why?" she objected. "I promised Hank that I'd wash—"

"Hank will have to do the dishes himself," he said crossly. "You're going to your room where you should have been all along."

"But I don't want to go to my room," she snapped, suddenly irritated that everyone wanted to do her thinking for her. She yanked her arm free. "I have a right to work if I want to, and Hank said—"

"Hank said," he shot back at her. "In all of your conversations, did he once warn you how dangerous it is for someone like you to be down here?"

"Dangerous?" she echoed. "What could be dangerous about—"

A movement to her right caught her attention, and when she looked up to find Bartell and his two companions casually walking in her direction, she knew exactly what Jason meant. Sensing that the trio hadn't come to pass the time of day with their first mate, Jennifer covertly placed Jason between her and the men.

"Havin' trouble, Bingham?" Bartell grinned evilly. "Maybe me and me mates here can help."

"Back off, Marc, before you do something you'll

259

regret," Jason cautioned, his gaze darting from one tar to the next as the three men spread out around him.

Bartell's smile widened. "Regret? Havin' this piece of fluff isn't somethin' I'm gonna regret. I'm gonna enjoy it. We all are, ain't we, mateys?"

The other two laughed and moved in slowly.

Panic filled Jennifer when everyone else in the place stood up and backed away from them. Jason Bingham was on his own, and she knew he'd never be able to stop these three all by himself. "Mr. Bingham?" she whimpered.

One hand came out to quickly shove her directly behind him, while he pulled his knife with the other. "I don't care who's first," he growled, "but all of you are going to feel my blade."

Jochum and Saunders, Bartell's friends, showed a glimmer of worry as they exchanged hesitant glances. Not as easily intimidated, Marc pulled his own knife from the sash around his waist.

"It will be my pleasure to go first, Bingham," he challenged. "I've been waitin' a long time for this." Crouching slightly, his weapon gripped in his left hand, he told the other two to grab Jennifer the minute she was clear and then moved in.

She screamed the instant Bartell swung his knife and nearly slit Jason's arm, but Bingham deftly moved out of the way and evaded injury. Yet, as he did, he left Jennifer free for Jochum to grab, and she screamed again when his callused hand roughly seized her wrist and yanked her toward the door of the inn.

"No!" she wailed, kicking and fighting to claw at the arm that had suddenly encircled her waist and crushed her back against his hard chest.

"Get her legs," he shouted to Saunders. "We'll take her to Willard's place. The big dummy ain't there right now."

"Aye," Saunders agreed with a toothless grin, as he

twisted and turned in an effort to snatch Jennifer's ankles yet avoid being kicked. "Him and the captain are up at the house."

"Not anymore," a deep voice announced just as the muzzle of a pistol struck Jochum across the back of the head.

The blow instantly knocked the man unconscious, and tumbled him to the wooden floor, pulling Jennifer with him. She landed with a thud even though she fell on top of her erstwhile captor, but it didn't take her more than a second to scramble away, her eyes wide and her breath coming in painful heaves. The click of a weapon being cocked drew her attention to the man who had saved her, and she froze on hands and knees as she watched Chad aim his pistol at Marc Bartell. Black rage distorted his rugged features, and Jennifer thought she had never seen anyone as angry as he in her entire life. Even Saunders recognized how close to dying he was, and he fell to his knees, hands held high and a prayer for mercy on his lips.

"You have one chance to see another sunrise, Bartell," Chad snarled, his pistol leveled on the spot between the man's brows. "Hesitate, and you're dead."

"No, Chad," Jason shouted, his own rage darkening his green eyes to an emerald hue. "It's been coming to this for a long time, and I'm going to see it finished."

He tossed his knife from his right to his left hand and back again, ready to lunge and strike the fatal blow. But Bartell wasn't willing anymore, and dropped his own weapon to the floor. He knew he could beat Jason Bingham in a knife fight, but he also realized he wouldn't live long enough to enjoy his victory. Chad LaShelle would see to that.

"Throw him in jail, Jason," Chad ordered, "and let him think about this for a while. Him and these two friends of his."

"Jail?" Bartell wailed. "We don't deserve no jail. Bingham's the one what started this, didn't he mate?" Saunders nodded vigorously. "All we wanted was our turn with the girl and Bingham pulled his knife. It's the law—it's *your* law. Any woman workin' here is for the crew. We abide by your rules and leave the other women in the village alone. Now you go and change 'em to suit your friend."

"That's right, lovey," Modesty spoke up, sashaying toward Chad. "Your little woman 'ere was workin' tables, and that makes 'er one o' us."

Chad's deep brown eyes darkened all the more as they turned on his first mate. "Jason?"

His concentration never wavering from the man who had wanted to kill him, Jason replied, "That's the way it appeared, Cap'n, but I knew it wasn't done with your knowledge. I came here to eat supper and found Miss Grey serving drinks. I asked her if she had your permission, and she said no. I was merely taking her to her room where she'd be safe, and then I planned to find you."

"Ain't true!" Modesty shouted, seizing the opportunity to even the score a little with the blond-haired bitch who had stolen her man. "'E was takin' 'er to 'is room fer a toss and wouldn't pay the price. 'Tis why they were arguin'! We saw it. We all did."

Although no one had actually heard the conversation between the pair, what Modesty suggested was quite possible. Jason Bingham had made his claim on the girl when he'd pulled her down on the bench beside him and refused to allow her to serve Bartell. Modesty had even pointed it out in a loud, clear voice, and he hadn't denied it. Then when the couple had started for the stairs, the girl had become angry, had jerked away from him. To all appearances, what Modesty said was true, and everyone in the place who had witnessed the scene agreed and

262

voiced their opinions enthusiastically.

Jason's confidence slipped a little. "Chad?" he frowned, lowering the knife he'd still held ready as he turned to look directly at his friend. "I wouldn't lie to you. I never have, and I never will. On my honor, what I've stated is the truth."

One of Chad's most frustrating traits was that it was nearly impossible to know what was going on inside his head when his expression remained stony and unfathomable . . . as it was now. Only his dark eyes moved—from Modesty to Jason to Bartell—and even they gave no clue to what he was thinking. The only ray of hope Jason held was the fact that Chad hadn't aimed the pistol at his heart. If Chad hadn't believed his first mate, he would have shot him by now.

"Take your friends, Bartell, and go to the *Black Falcon,*" he finally said. "I want all the decks scrubbed down and the brass polished. When you're finished, you can turn in . . . but not here. You're banned from Freedom Inn until I say otherwise. If you feel that's unfair punishment for mistakenly thinking you could have what's mine, then say so right now, and I'll end it."

No argument came from Bartell, and no one could blame him for that. Chad's pistol hadn't lowered in the slightest, nor had he taken his finger off the trigger. Whether Bartell counted himself lucky or not, no one would ever really know, for without hesitating, he motioned for Saunders to help him drag off their unconscious cohort and quickly left the inn. Yet, the tension didn't ease once they were gone, for there was still the matter of Jennifer Grey.

It was hard for Jennifer to admit to herself that she was thankful Chad had rescued her from a most degrading and frightening situation, but she was. However, her gratitude only lasted until Bartell and his group disappeared from sight, for then she had turned her full

263

attention back on Chad. The chilling look he gave her set her nerves on edge, and for a moment she wondered if he wouldn't point the gun at her and squeeze the trigger just to rid himself of the nuisance she had become. She gave a breathless sigh as she watched him release the hammer and jam the weapon into the sash around his waist, deciding that perhaps he didn't blame her for the incident after all. Then he started toward her, and she knew by the way his nostrils were flared and the whiteness of the scar across his lip that that wasn't true. She shrank away from him as he reached down to grab her wrist, which only seemed to enrage him further, and she opened her mouth to point out to him that none of this would have happened if he had bothered to tell her why she shouldn't be alone in the commons.

"Not a word," he seethed. "Don't say one word."

The men's eyes focused on their captain as he took the young woman's arm, yanked her to her feet, and hauled her off toward the door of the inn. The entire group, led by Jason, crowded through the aperture and stepped out into the street to watch the couple head away from the village.

"Mr. Bingham?"

Glancing to his left, Jason spotted Willard edging his way toward him through the throng of people. "Aye, Willard?"

"Cap'n Chad ain't gonna hurt her, is he?" he asked, his pudgy face wrinkled into a fearful frown.

Heaving a deep sigh, Jason turned his attention back to the departing pair. "I don't know, Willard. This time, I really don't know."

Chapter Eleven

For nearly a quarter of an hour, the couple walked along the beach at a rapid pace, neither speaking nor looking at one another, and if they had headed away from the village in the opposite direction, Jennifer would have thought Chad was taking her back to the place where he had found her to leave her there. But he wasn't, and with each hurried step they took, she wished he would. His rage hadn't lessened in the least, and she was beginning to imagine all sorts of vengeful punishments he might impose upon her, the worst being tied to a rock twenty feet out in the water and left there to wait for high tide. He had no sympathy for women, least of all her, so he'd probably find himself a comfortable place beneath the spreading leaves of a palm, then watch and laugh as she screamed for help.

Chad's stride was twice as long as Jennifer's so she practically had to run to keep up to him. Her legs were beginning to tire, and the pebble that had lodged itself between the leather strap of her sandal and the side of her foot brought tears to her eyes. Finally, more out of frustration than anything else, she yanked her arm free of him and plopped down onto the sand to remove the pesty rock.

"Get up," he growled, his mouth drawn into a tight line.

Jennifer shot him an angry glare of her own as she plucked the tiny piece of granite from her shoe and, in a fit of temper, threw it at him. It bounced off his chest as harmlessly as a snowflake, but her show of defiance was what made him grit his teeth, bend down, and grab her by the hair at the nape of her neck. Jennifer shrieked in pain as he wrenched her to her feet and crushed her to him, his mouth only inches from hers.

"You're the most obstinate woman I've ever known," he snarled, giving her a shake. "And the most foolhardy. What the hell did you think to prove back there in the inn? That men are willing to die just to have their turn with you?"

Tears burned the backs of her eyelids, and she squeezed her eyes shut to keep them from spilling down her cheeks. "I wasn't trying to prove anything!" she snapped, tugging at the fingers entwined in the long, golden strands of hair tumbling down her back.

"Then why were you in the commons?"

"To help Mr. Sullivan!" she shouted. "He's an old man, in case you hadn't noticed, and he single-handedly cooks, serves tables, washes dishes, and does anything else those heartless half-wits tell him to do."

"He gets paid for it," Chad answered sharply.

Jennifer's eyes flew open in rage, and without a care, she slapped the heel of her hand against his chest. "That's all you ever think about. Money! Doesn't an old man's life mean anything to you at all? Too much heavy work could kill him!"

Chad's eyes narrowed and he lowered his head. "If I thought like that, nothing would ever get done." He jerked his head toward the village. "They'd all be lying around from sunup to sunset and still expect to get paid."

"You're hopeless," she barked, wincing when he

266

yanked on her hair. "And you're a bully! Let go of me!" She had had enough, and decided to let him know it. Doubling up her fist, she pounded it against his chest, and when he merely caught her wrist to thwart the attack, she sank her teeth into his arm. He yowled in pain and released her. "I hope I drew blood," she announced, stumbling away from him. "That's assuming, of course, you have any. But I really don't see how that's possible without a heart."

Gripping his injured limb with his other hand, he stared back at her in surprise. Any other woman he'd treated that way would be in tears, begging for mercy. He'd never come across one who'd stood up to him—except for Doña María, and she had tried to kill him. His frown deepened. And this one certainly had good reason to want to see him dead. He glanced up the long stretch of beach toward the cover where his house had been built. Maybe it wasn't such a good idea to allow her the freedom of his home. There was a good chance she'd sneak into his room during the night and murder him in his sleep. A wicked smile parted his lips as he turned his head back to look at her. He could always lock her in her room . . . or tie her to the bed . . . or better yet, lock her in with him. His eyes darkened lustfully as he took in the tempting sight of her standing on the white sandy beach, the golden sunlight of late evening shining in her hair, and haloed against a backdrop of crystal clear, blue water. She was a most fetching sight and he doubted that at her worst she'd be anything less than beautiful. A glimmer of his past flared up to remind him that she could have been his wife had things not turned out the way they had. Suddenly, his body and mind ached from fatigue. He was tired of fighting for everything he wanted, tired of hating, tired of having to constantly prove himself. Without further comment, he turned and stared down the beach, away from her.

"Since we still haven't found the man who murdered Megan, I suggest you hurry up," he threw back over his shoulder. "I'm through rescuing damsels in distress for one night."

Jennifer's anger vanished instantly with his declaration, and she stood dumbfounded, watching the casual stride of the tall, muscular man as he walked on without her, unable to believe the sudden change in him. She glanced back toward the village, but the idea of returning there lasted only a moment. Maybe Bartell and the other two had been ordered to stay on board the *Black Falcon*, but the rest of the crew had not, and she decided that fending off one man would be easier than attempting to cope with a dozen. She looked back at Chad. Or would it? A soft breeze rustled the dense growth of ferns lining the beach, and Jennifer started, a frightening chill darting up her spine as she imagined an evil pair of eyes watching her from within the growing shadows. Her heart thundering in her chest, she concentrated on the dark underbrush and what might be hiding in it as she hurriedly took a step sideways, intending to do as Chad recommended and stay within his protective reach.

A strange emotion came over Chad once he felt Jennifer's presence beside him and realized she was there because she needed him. She might not care much about him, but she needed him, and it felt good to know someone did. It reminded him of a time long ago when a young blond-haired, green-eyed little boy followed him wherever he went. There were occasions when Chad would have preferred not to have to take his little half brother with him when he went to play with his friends, but on the whole he never got tired of Charles. He loved him . . . just as he loved his stepmother. A sadness was reflected in his dark eyes. If it hadn't been for him, Mary Elizabeth wouldn't have died, and they would all still be living together.

Chad was brought out of his thoughts about the past when he realized Jennifer was no longer walking beside him, and he stopped and turned around to learn why. The instant he saw the look on her face, he knew the reason, and he smiled softly.

"I've never seen anything like it," she breathed in awe, as she stared up at the huge, stone mansion nestled high upon a ridge and secured on three sides by sheer rock bluffs. "It looks like a castle." She turned bright, approving eyes on him. "Is it yours?"

Chad didn't know why, but it pleased him to know that she liked his house. "Aye," he replied quietly, simply.

"But it's so big," she moaned, glancing back at the mansion. "Do you plan to live alone in it?"

An unexpected pang of loneliness crept through him, something he hadn't felt for a long time.

"But of course not." Jennifer laughed before he had a chance to answer. "You'll have to have dozens of servants just to keep it clean." Spotting the narrow stone stairway leading up to the iron gate high above them, she started toward it. "If word of this ever gets around London, you'll find yourself fighting off marriage proposals." She stopped at the bottom of the steps and looked back at him. "There won't be a woman in the world who wouldn't want to live here. It's beautiful, Chad."

The sound of his name on her lips tingled every nerve in his body. It was the first time she had called him by his given name without her voice being laced with anger or fear, and that touched a part of him that had ached for years to be caressed. Unaware, he came to stand before her, lift a silky strand of golden hair off her shoulder, and entwine it about his finger. He hadn't realized until this very moment how much he needed to have someone care about him. He'd never known the love of his mother, for Martinique LaShelle had died giving birth to him. Mary

269

Elizabeth had cared for him, but even so, that kind of caring wasn't truly what he longed for. It was the love of a woman he yearned to know. He blinked suddenly when he realized where his thoughts had taken him, and jerked his hand away as if the lock of hair had burned his finger. Angered by the discovery that this mere slip of a girl had stirred emotions that he had tried so hard to smother, he brushed past her and started up the steps without a word.

Jennifer stood for a long moment, watching him climb the stairs and wondering at the pain she had seen in his eyes, at its cause. Had she said something that reminded him of the past? She recalled their conversation. She had mentioned marriage, but was that what had upset him? Why should it? He didn't strike her as the type who wanted such a commitment. Her finely arched brows crimped in a thoughtful frown. Of course, that opportunity had been taken out of his hands when his father had decided Chad wouldn't marry the woman he'd chosen for him. Jennifer didn't think it mattered who that woman was, just that Charles Wadsworth didn't feel Chad worthy of marrying someone. Suddenly, she understood. Here was a man who had had to accept the fact that the one person in his life who should have stood beside him had turned his back on him and had announced to the world that he no longer cared what happened to him. Chad LaShelle was alone. His mother and stepmother were dead. His father wanted nothing to do with him, and more than likely, he hadn't seen his half brother since the day he had left London. To Chad, it must seem as if Charles didn't exist. How painful it must have been for him to have the one person who would remind him of the past suddenly show up here on his island after all these years. The muscles in her throat tightened. How unfair it was that she had no control over any of it! It had all been decided before she had even been conceived.

270

The breeze rustled the thick growth of ferns and wild flowers around her, reminding Jennifer of the danger in being alone. "Chad, wait!" she called out to him, and raced up the steps to catch up with him. There was nothing she could do to change what had happened those many years ago, but, given the opportunity, maybe she could do something about the future.

The climb to the top seemed endless, and by the time they reached the iron gate, Jennifer's legs ached and her heart was pounding so loudly that she wondered if it might explode. Chad, however, looked as though he had only gone for a short walk, and the smile he gave her as she collapsed on the last step to catch her breath was rewarded with her smile of self-mockery. Unlocking the gate, he pushed it open, then extended his hand to her.

"Or perhaps I should carry you," he offered with a grin.

Jennifer's tawny brows lowered over her sea green eyes. "I can manage on my own, thank you." Having rebuffed him, she pushed herself to her feet. She had a pain in her side, and would have liked to press her fingers against it, but out of pride she refused to let him know how much the trek up the long stairway had bothered her. Chin raised and shoulders squared, she moved past him and stepped into the courtyard.

All of her discomfort vanished the moment she had a full view of the grounds and the manor house laid out before her. The lawn had been perfectly manicured, and clusters of white orchids lined both sides of the winding stone path with the tiny arched bridge that led to the entrance of the huge house. Tall palm trees offered shade, and to her right was a waterfall that cascaded into a small pool surrounded by rocks and fern. A narrow stream trailed off from it, wound its way across the courtyard, and disappeared into the thick underbrush on the opposite side. Hank Sullivan had said he had a little piece of heaven here on the island, but from the look of things, Chad had taken a bigger cut. Her only regret was that the sun would be going down very soon, for that meant she'd have to wait until morning to enjoy the peaceful splendor she had found here.

Chad had walked on ahead and was waiting for her on the bridge, his arms folded over his chest and his hip leaning against the handrail. Although he tried to hide the pride he felt about his accomplishment, it was evident in his dark eyes and in the way his mouth curled upward slightly. It was a shame his father couldn't see this. He would be amazed . . . and proud.

The stand of palms had restricted her vision of the manor until she and Chad had nearly reached the small veranda with its brick floor and wrought-iron settee and chairs. But once it was in plain sight, she came to an abrupt halt, her tiny chin sagging. She was simply too astonished to think of words that could possibly express how she felt. She had always considered the house in which she had lived with her father to be the most beautiful one in the world, but it paled in comparison to what stood before her now.

The face of the two-story stone house was covered in ivy except where the stained-glass windows peeked out from beneath their dormers on the second floor. The double front doors were haloed by two immense pillars that rose all the way up to the roof line, and huge granite planters filled with flowers of all colors dotted the entryway. It was an awesome sight, but not nearly as breathtaking as the panorama she encountered once she and Chad had stepped onto the black marble floor of the foyer. Three gigantic doors led from the entry hall. The remainder of the first floor was one enormous chamber with a cathedral ceiling, white marble fireplace, ceramic tile flooring, and, at the opposite end, a monstrous stairway that jutted off to the right. Elegant paintings in rich gold-leaf frames hung from every available space. A

272

medieval suit of armor stood in one corner. A harpsichord graced another. Luxuriously upholstered wing chairs and a matching settee were set in the middle of the room, and alabaster figurines and vases complemented the minutely carved tables on which they sat. To the left and away from the fireplace stood a mammoth oak desk and a leather chair, and although the walls were simply painted white, Jennifer felt as if she had stepped into another time, into a paradise different from the one she had found beyond outside its doors.

"Chad, this is incredible," she breathed, descending the pair of steps that led from the foyer to the main floor. "I can't imagine King George living better than this. Where did you get all of these beautiful things?" Whirling, she glanced up at the high, arching ceiling overhead, and noticed the two balconies overlooking the spacious room. "Can you see the ocean from there?" she asked excitedly, moving back a step to better see the tall, narrow windows that graced each balcony.

"You can see almost anything from up there," he murmured, thoroughly enjoying her enthusiasm. He couldn't remember the last time he had done anything that pleased someone else, and liked the way it made him feel. Swinging the door shut behind him, he followed her into the room, then went to the wine decanter sitting on one of the tables. Pouring himself a glass, he sat down in one of the wing chairs to watch Jennifer stroll about the room, examining each work of art—the numerous statues, figurines, and vases he had collected; the armor, and finally the harpsichord he was so proud of.

"Can you play it?" she asked, turning to look at him, one hand resting on its shiny dark finish.

Chad shook his head and took a sip of wine. "I always wished I could. Especially after hearing George Handel play." He raised one hand and wiggled his fingers. "Too large to fit the keys."

"You heard George Frederick Handel play the harpsichord?" she exclaimed. "When? Where?"

Chad chuckled. "A long time ago in London. My stepmother took me."

"Oh, it must have been marvelous," she sighed enviously, sinking down on the bench. "I always dreamed of meeting him someday." She blushed and looked at her hands. "I wanted him to hear me play. Papa thought I was good enough to study under him, but—" She shrugged one shoulder and let the thought go unfinished.

Chad straightened in his chair. "You know how? To play the harpsichord," he added, when she looked up at him and frowned.

Feeling a little embarrassed, she smiled weakly and nodded. "It probably sounds awfully selfish, but after Papa died and I knew I'd be going to London, I was hoping Charles would somehow get me an audition." The smile disappeared when she saw him stand up suddenly and hurry across the room toward her.

"Play something," he ordered, setting down his wine goblet on a nearby table. "No one here knows how, and I've never heard it played since I brought it off the ship."

For a moment, Jennifer saw him as a man of wealth, the kind she'd expect to find living in London, a man raised with the finer things in life; and it suited him. "All right," she conceded, turning on the bench to face the keyboard. "But I warn you. I'm a little out of practice."

Clipped, staccato notes issued from the delicate instrument, filling the room with music, and Chad closed his eyes, reveling in the sound of it. Music had been the one thing from his former life that he had truly missed, and now because of Jennifer, he had it back again. Her fingers moved gracefully over the keys, hitting each note clearly and precisely, and adding a flare of her own. Her father had been right, he decided. She was worthy of

Handel's attention. Then, all too soon, the piece came to an end, and Chad was like a man dying of thirst. He had to have more.

"Is that the only composition you know?"

Jennifer smiled brightly at the look in his eyes. It was better than any compliment he could have given her. Without answering, she began to play again.

Chad lit a lamp, and for the next hour, she performed every opus she could remember, surprised at how easily it all came back to her, at how effortlessly her fingers moved up and down the keyboard. Music had been her salvation, easing the boredom of living on a plantation so many miles away from other young women her age; and having the chance to play again brought back many fond memories.

Memories flooded Chad's thoughts, too, as he stayed right beside her, watching her face, the way she moved her body as if she were caressing a particular passage, and noting her masterful execution of each piece. Mary Elizabeth had played the harpsichord, but not nearly as well as Jennifer. In fact, he couldn't recall hearing anyone play it as well. But that wasn't what brought on the sad look in his eyes or why he picked up his wine and returned to his chair to drink it. He was remembering the last time he had seen his stepmother sitting before the harpsichord and struggling to perform one single piece without a mistake. It had been the day before she had died, the same day he and his father had argued, and the day he'd found her Bible. Swiftly drinking the remainder of his wine, he poured another glass and took a sip. . . .

For as long as Chad could remember, Maida Tanner had been their housekeeper. As a young boy, he hadn't really paid much attention to her. But as he'd grown older, reached the age where he began to take an interest in girls, he'd seen Maida differently. Although she was too old for him, the seductive way she swayed her hips whenever she walked by him, her laughter when she caught him looking at her, made him realize that a man closer to her age must surely find her attractive. He couldn't understand why she wasn't married or why she had no beau. He learned the reason late one night. It had been too hot for him to sleep, and he had gone downstairs to the parlor, where he could open the French doors and cool off a bit without disturbing the others who occupied the house. He could still hear her laughter and the shocking sound of his father's voice bidding her good night in a husky whisper, footsteps going from her room up to his father's, and the gentle click of the latch as Maida closed her door behind her lover. . . .

The wine goblet shook in his hand as he remembered the pain he'd felt that night. For fourteen years, he had looked up to his father, respected him, admired him, foolishly thought that whatever his father did was right and just. But in a few brief moments, his father had destroyed it all, had betrayed him, made a mockery out of a young boy's trust.

The tinkling of the harpsichord ended, and fearing Jennifer would notice the look on his face, Chad quickly left his chair and went to the fireplace to stare down into the darkened hearth as he motioned for her to continue.

He had waited for more than an hour that night before he'd returned to his room. What he had learned about his father and the housekeeper was something he would never tell anyone . . . especially Mary Elizabeth. In the morning, he planned to discuss it with his father, make him swear to fire Maida and never do anything like that again. Chad's stepmother deserved better than that. The whole family did. But by the time he had gotten up, dressed, and gone to look for his father, Mary Elizabeth had already found him. They were in the study, and they were engaged in a bitter argument.

"Yes, I made love to her," he had heard his father

shout, and the frightened fourteen-year-old had hidden beside the lowboy in the foyer to listen. "And yes, it wasn't the first time! What did you expect? I'm not a monk. You shut me out of your bedchamber months ago, feigning an illness that only God can name, and then you turn on me in a rage because I'm unfaithful. You drove me to it, Mary Elizabeth!"

"Perhaps this time I did," she'd retorted. "But what about all the other times? You've been with other women since the day we married. I've raised your bastard son as proof of it! How much more do you expect me to take? Everyone in London is laughing at me, and I will not stand for it any longer!"

"Mary Elizabeth wait!" Charles had called out as he'd rushed to the foyer to stop her from ascending the stairs.

"For what?" she had shouted, jerking away from him when he'd tried to take her arm. "To hear you promise that you'll be faithful . . . again! To have you beg my forgiveness so that you can whore around behind my back! That's what they are. All of them. The women you've been with are nothing but whores!" A movement to her left had caught her eye, and her face had paled considerably when she'd spotted Chad hiding in the foyer for she'd been certain he had heard every word, that he had assumed she had referred to his mother as a whore.

"Now look what you've done," Charles had raged, for he too had seen Chad. "You've hurt the boy with your careless tongue."

"*I've* hurt him?" she had sobbed, unable to control her tears any longer. Whirling about she had turned and raced up the stairs, and a moment later the slamming of her bedroom door had echoed through the house.

Chad hadn't waited for his father's explanation. He hadn't wanted to hear it. He had simply bolted past the man, out into the yard. He'd spent the night in the stables, trying to decide what to do, where to go. His presence in the Wadsworth home would be a constant reminder to Mary Elizabeth of her husband's infidelity, and she had suffered enough without his adding to it. But then, just before dawn, he'd been awakened by lantern light that flooded the stall where he hid.

"Chad, my darling," he'd heard his stepmother cry. "I so feared you had run away before I could apologize and ask your forgiveness." Tears glistening in her eyes, she had hooked the lantern over a nail and then had sat down on the straw beside him. "I didn't mean that your mother was a—a— Well, I said those things only to hurt Charles, and I fear I hurt you instead. I knew what kind of a man your father was before I married him, but now I've reached a point where I can't take it anymore. You understand, don't you?"

"You don't mean you're going to leave him?" he had asked, tears welling in his eyes, too.

"Only for a while. I need time to think. Charles needs time to miss me, to decide if I'm the one he really wants, if I'm worth fighting for."

"But where will you go?"

"We have property in southern England. I'll spend a few months there. But you must promise me that you won't run away. He needs his sons to help manage this place." She had cradled his chin in her hand and drawn it up so he would look at her. "Promise?"

"If that's what you want."

"And do you forgive me?"

Crying openly, he had thrown his arms around her. "Yes. Yes, I forgive you."

They had embraced for several moments before Mary Elizabeth had put him from her to brush away his tears. "Now be a good son and harness up the carriage for me. I'm taking Corliss with me, and we want to be gone from here before your father awakens."

Chad recalled doing as his stepmother bid, but with

278

some reservation. He hadn't wanted her to leave and he'd told her so as he'd helped load the carriage with her luggage. She had smiled at him, then had kissed his cheek and assured him that it was for the best, promising that she would return when the time was right. That had been the last he'd seen of her. At noon the same day, the constable had come to inform Mary Elizabeth's family that she, her personal maid, Corliss, and her driver had all perished in a carriage mishap.

Overcome with grief, and blaming himself for her death since he felt he should have stopped her from leaving, Chad had gone to her room, hoping to find comfort there. Instead he had found the Bible she had hidden away in the trunk that held the baby clothes that had belonged to her son. He hadn't meant to pry, and once he'd read what was written within in her own handwriting, he was sorry he had. Just then his father's voice had seemed to fill every inch of the huge manor house as he'd called Chad's name, and fearing he would be beaten for snooping around in his stepmother's things, Chad had hurriedly stuffed the Bible back into the trunk before leaving the room in search of his father.

Sir Charles Wadsworth, a man of rank, never allowed himself to overindulge in drink, but that day had been an exception. And when his illegitimate son had appeared before him, the wine he had consumed ruled his thoughts and actions. In a rage, he'd demanded to know why Chad had not tried to stop his stepmother from leaving, then not letting him answer, he'd continued with his tirade.

"When your mother came to me and told me she was carrying a child, I should have asked her if it was mine. I didn't. I just assumed she was telling me the truth. But you French are all alike. Liars and cheats! I didn't want to raise you, but Mary Elizabeth said it was my obligation. It was *her* kindness that brought you into this house and it was her *kindness* that killed her!"

279

Chad could remember how deeply his father had hurt him by saying that, and how as a young boy of fourteen he had reacted.

"Maybe if you'd spent more time with her instead of sleeping with other women, she might not have left!"

Chad could still see the black rage that had come over his father's face at that moment, he could still feel the pain that had been inflicted on him when Charles had raised his fist high above his head and then had smashed it against Chad's mouth, the diamond ring he'd worn tearing into Chad's lip and opening a deep wound. . . .

A cold sweat seeped out of every pore as Chad envisioned for the thousandth time the way the force of that blow had hurled him halfway across the room and sent him crashing into the wall. His hand trembled as he stared down at the wineglass he held, his anger flaring anew, and his grip tightened until the delicate piece of stemware shattered under such abuse.

Jennifer hadn't been paying much attention to the man who shared the room with her. She was too caught up in her dream of someday meeting the great composer George Frederick Handel. But the sound of glass breaking instantly brought her out of her thoughts, and she stopped playing to see what had happened. The back of her hand flew to her mouth and stifled her gasp once she saw the broken pieces of a wineglass lying on the floor at Chad's feet and the blood dotting the palm of the hand he held out in front of him. He seemed to be in a daze.

"My God, Chad," she exclaimed, going to him. "What happened?"

The sound of her voice affected him like a bucket of cold water thrown in his face. He stiffened, shook his head, and clenched his bloody hand, jerking it away when Jennifer tried to examine it.

"Chad, please," she begged, touching his arm. "Some of those cuts are deep, and there might be glass in them.

280

Let me take care of them for you."

Reliving that day fifteen years ago had drained Chad of his strength. He looked at the woman responsible for stirring up those memories, and he wanted to hate her, use her over and over again, and then hand her back to his father. But there was something about Jennifer Grey that made him reluctant to pursue his plan. His dark brows came together sharply in a perplexed frown. He wanted to keep her . . . here on the island with him . . . forever. He turned away from her. Or at least until he tired of her. His hand was beginning to throb, and because of all the wine he had drunk, exhaustion caused his shoulders to slump and made his steps heavy as he slowly ambled across the room toward the staircase. He'd think more on it tomorrow. Right now, all he wanted to do was sleep. Without a backward glance, he mounted the steps and disappeared around the corner at the top.

Jennifer couldn't imagine what it was that she'd seen in his dark eyes before he'd turned from her. It was a mixture of emotions, really, and none were clearly distinguishable. Agony, remorse, even defeat seemed to be reflected in those black depths, and if she wasn't mistaken, her music had brought it on. He had said that his stepmother had taken him to hear Handel play. Was it possible he was thinking of her? Hank suspected that Chad's father had blamed him for his wife's death. If that were true, anything that reminded Chad of that day had to be painful for him, especially if the accident that killed her hadn't really been Chad's fault. Sighing, she absently glanced down at the floor and saw the shattered pieces of the wine goblet.

Perhaps I could find a way to make him trust me, she thought, as she stooped to gingerly pick up the fragments of glass. Then maybe I could help him if he'd be willing to talk about what happened. Her gaze drifted toward the top of the stairs. A man shouldn't be made to suffer so long. The kind of hatred he carried around inside him would surely be the death of him.

"What do ye mean 'e's taken 'er to 'is 'ouse?" Modesty snapped, grabbing Willard's arm when the young man started for the door of the inn, the tray of food he carried rattling noisily.

"Don't, Modesty," he barked. "Ya'll make me spill this."

"I'll shove yer bloody face in it, ye 'alf-wit, if ye don't answer me question."

Even though Willard was twice the size of Modesty Copeland, her temper always frightened him. Pouting disgustedly, he faced her. "All I know is Cap'n Chad woke me up this morning, and told me to fetch Jennifer's breakfast from Hank. I'm to take it to her at the house, and then stay with her while he works in his cabin."

The redhead's brown eyes narrowed. "Then 'e's made 'er 'is prisoner."

"No!" Willard strongly objected. "He told me she could go anywhere she wanted just as long as I'm with her." He smiled sarcastically at Modesty. "I'm gonna take her to my favorite place to swim this morning, if she wants to go. I've never showed it to nobody before, but Jennifer's my friend and I'll take her. You can't go." With that, he turned and hurried from the place before Modesty could say another word.

"Looks like the captain's found 'imself another woman, Modesty." Pearl laughed. Seated at a nearby table, she had listened to the conversation.

"Shut up, ye bitch," Modesty raved. "If I wanted yer opinion, I woulda asked fer it."

The other made a face at her, then went back to devouring her breakfast. She was glad the captain had dumped Modesty for someone else. It was time the redhead learned she wasn't any better than the rest of the girls who lived at Freedom Inn.

From the first moment Modesty had seen Jennifer Grey perched atop Chad's horse, she'd known the young woman would be trouble. The blonde had a natural beauty that didn't need the help of rouge, and she was probably ten years younger than Modesty. What man wouldn't want a woman like that? Modesty's lips curled into an unflattering snarl, as she headed for the stairs and her room. Well, there was one way to eliminate the problem, and thanks to Megan's murderer, no one would suspect that she had had anything to do with it.

Jennifer had risen early in the hope of seeing Chad before he decided to leave the house, only to discover that he had already gone. Last night, after she had cleaned up the broken glass, she had found a rag in the kitchen and had rinsed away the spilled droplets of wine from the floor. Then carrying a lamp, she had toured the rest of the house. The kitchen was ready to be used, but there was no food in the cupboards, nor were there utensils with which to prepare it. The dining-room walls were painted, and there was a beautiful oriental rug on the floor, but no furniture. What she'd assumed was the servants' quarters wasn't even livable, and rather than spend the night on the settee, she had gone upstairs to see if there might be one room with a bed in it.

The first door she'd come to was Chad's, and she had paused in the open doorway to watch him for a while. He hadn't bothered to take off his clothes before falling across the bed, but she'd known by his slow, steady breathing that he was asleep. Concerned about the cuts on his hand, she had tiptoed across the floor to his bed and, without touching him, had noticed that he had washed away the blood and that the wounds were not oozing. Thinking that perhaps they had not been as serious as she had first thought, she'd quietly left him, deciding not to disturb him by trying to help him disrobe. Stepping out into the hall, she had continued her search for a place to sleep.

The door to the room next to Chad's stood ajar, and the moment Jennifer peeked inside, her mouth dropped open in silent admiration. The décor was a tasteful blend of whites and soft yellows, and the soft glow of the lamp revealed French doors on the opposite wall. But what caught and held Jennifer's attention was the tall, fourposter brass bed, made up with lace pillowcases, silk sheets, and a beautifully crocheted spread. That alone would make a woman's heart beat a little faster, but the bright yellow hibiscus lying on one of the pillows brought tears to her eyes. It hadn't gotten there accidentally. Chad had to have put it there himself. Maybe he was a rogue, she decided, but he had proven that there were times when he could think of someone other than himself.

After finding a white cotton nightgown draped over the arm of the rocker, she had slept most peacefully, intending to rise as soon as the sun came up so she could thank Chad, although she didn't know if that would be the right thing to do. Given his abrupt changes of mood, he might not want to be thanked . . . or even reminded that he had done something that was a bit out of character. But Jennifer didn't care. It was a start, a way of melting down the ice that encased his emotions. She had quickly donned her blouse and skirt, and not bothering with sandals, had raced downstairs, thinking to find him at his desk or in the kitchen since he wasn't in bed. But after searching both places and finding them empty, she wandered back into the elaborate front room and sat down on the bench before the harpsichord, wondering if she would be spending the entire day alone. For the next half hour, she listlessly ran her fingers up and down the keyboard until the click of the front door latch brought her excitedly to her feet.

"G'morning, Jennifer." Willard beamed as he opened the door all the way and saw her standing there. "Cap'n Chad told me to bring you somethin' to eat. Are you hungry?"

Hoping her disappointment wasn't reflected in her voice, she nodded and asked, "Where is the captain?"

"Workin' on the *Black Falcon*," he told her as he swung the door shut behind him and carried the tray to one of the tables near the settee. "He wants her repairs finished so he can set sail again real soon." He motioned for her to sit down, then poured a cup of tea from the pot and handed it to her. "Ain't this the prettiest house ya ever seen, Jennifer?" he asked, looking all around him before he settled his huge frame on the floor beside her and leaned back against the settee. "Cap'n Chad said he'd bet you'd like it."

"He did?" Jennifer smiled, strangely pleased to learn that Chad had even thought about it, much less voiced his opinion to someone. She set down her cup and reached for the plate of bread and ham. "Who put the flower on my pillow?" she asked, hoping to sound indifferent as she concentrated on cutting up the piece of meat.

"Me," Willard exclaimed. "Did you like it?"

Jennifer's hands trembled, and she quickly blinked back the tears that formed in her eyes. It would be too difficult to explain to the young man why his thoughtfulness had made her sad. "Oh, yes," she replied without looking at him.

"Cap'n Chad told me to pick the biggest one I could find and put it there. He really likes you," Willard stated matter-of-factly as he twisted around on the floor so that he could look at her. Folding his arms and laying them on the thick-cushioned seat, he rested his chin across his wrists, and asked, "Do ya like him, Jennifer?"

Unable to even think about food any longer, she pushed the plate away and fell back against the settee, a bright smile lighting up her eyes. She had been right about Chad after all. "I like *you*, Willard." She grinned and glanced over at him. "You're the sweetest person I've ever known."

His face glowed with happiness. "You mean that, Jennifer?"

"Yes, I mean that," she assured him, gently touching his cheek with her fingertips. "My only regret is that I'll probably never see you again once Captain LaShelle takes me to England."

Willard's brow wrinkled as he considered her statement. "You wouldn't have to go to England. You could stay right here. I could ask Cap'n Chad—"

"No, Willard," she softly cut in. "It isn't a matter of wanting to go to England. I have to go there. I have commitments to fulfill." She smiled when she saw that he didn't understand what she meant. "Promises I have to keep."

"What kind of promises?"

"I promised Captain LaShelle's father and my own that I would marry the captain's half brother. Remember? I told you that already."

Willard frowned again, thinking over what she had said. Pushing himself up to his feet, he ambled away from her as he scratched his strawberry blond head with one finger, and only a moment passed before he whirled back to face her, a bright smile lifting the corners of his mouth. "Yeah, but he don't know you're alive, does he?"

"Charles?" she questioned. "You mean the captain's half brother?"

"Uh-huh," Willard nodded vigorously. "If your ship don't sail to London, he'll think ya died with everybody else. See? Ya don't have to go back 'cause he won't think

286

you're coming anymore."

"That's true, Willard," she quietly agreed, then reached to pick up her tea. "But I'd know. It was the last thing my father and I talked about before he died. I promised him that I'd honor his wish and marry Charles. So you see, Willard, even if Charles thinks I'm dead, I'm honor bound to go to him."

"Oh," Willard pouted, his wide shoulders drooping.

"Maybe you'd like to go with me? I'm sure Charles wouldn't mind your living with us."

"And leave Cap'n Chad?" he gasped. "I couldn't do that. He needs me. He told me so." His upper lip curled in a disapproving manner as he came back to sit down next to her. "'Sides, I didn't like livin' in England. Everybody's mean to me."

"I understand," she replied, patting his knee, and decided to change the subject. "So, what are you going to do today?"

Willard's face brightened instantly. "Cap'n Chad said I could take ya anywhere I want to, and I want to show ya my secret place to swim. You'll like it! Wanna go?"

"I sure do." She laughed, then finished off her tea and set the cup back on the tray. "How about right now?"

"Yeah!" Jumping to his feet, he grabbed her hand and excitedly pulled her up. "It's down the beach a ways where nobody can find us. If ya want, we can stay there all day."

"Sounds like fun." She hurried to keep up with him as he rushed to the front door. "But shouldn't we pack something to eat, if we plan to be gone that long?"

Willard shook his head and twisted the latch. "Naw. I got stuff hidden there to eat. Fruits and coconuts, and things."

"Won't it be spoiled?" she asked, stepping out onto the veranda.

"Naw. I take fresh ones with me every time I go, and I

287

was just there last night. Come on!" Slamming the door shut behind them, he took her hand again and hurried her along beside him, pausing only long enough to unlock the iron gate, usher them through it, and then relock the fortress against intruders. Laughing merrily, he led the way down the long, winding set of stairs, unaware of the hate-filled brown eyes watching their every move from behind the palms below them.

"So," Modesty snarled, watching them descend the steps toward her, "the nitwit is takin' 'er to 'is swimmin' 'ole, is 'e. Well, it will be the last swim either of 'em is gonna take."

Her eyes remained trained on the couple as they stepped off the stairway and headed down the beach. Modesty knew she would have to stay close to the cover of ferns and rocks at the edge of the shore in case one of them should turn around for some reason. She'd follow them until they were far enough away to prevent anyone from hearing, then she'd sneak up behind Willard, club him over the head, and stab the bitch with her knife. It wouldn't be too hard to do. Chad's precious little whore was a lot smaller than she was. Pausing a moment, she lifted the hem of her skirt to make sure the knife she had strapped to her thigh hadn't come loose and fallen out. Giving it a pat, she smiled evilly and looked up, ready to continue. But before she had taken a step, a thick-fingered hand came around from in back of her, clamped itself over her mouth, and brutally dragged her deeper into the woods.

Chapter Twelve

"Willard, this is beautiful," Jennifer breathed, staring down at the small cove below them. The entire place was encompassed by huge boulders except for one narrow opening that faced the sea and let in the ocean water. To their left and above them was a waterfall that tumbled noisily into the cove, shooting out a fine mist that caught the sunlight and produced a bright rainbow.

"Ya really like it?" He grinned, his face beaming with pride.

"Oh, yes. Very much." Moving slowly and carefully, she stepped down on the next rock, wanting to get closer to the water's edge. "But isn't it dangerous swimming here?"

Willard shrugged a thick shoulder and stayed close behind her as they descended to a spot where they could sit and dangle their bare feet in the water if they wished. "Sometimes. The undertow is pretty strong."

"How deep is it?" she asked, sitting down, Glad that she hadn't bothered to wear her sandals, she stuck her foot in the water and was surprised at how warm it was.

"Right now, it's real deep 'cause of high tide," he answered, and sat down beside her. "I only touched bottom once."

"The water's so clear, it must be like taking a bath. Look!" She pointed a finger at the huge, red lobster scurrying to hide between two rocks just to her right.

"Yeah, there's a lot of them in here. That's why ya gotta watch your toes."

Jennifer instantly jerked her foot out of the water and hugged her knees to her chest as if she expected the creature to jump out after her.

"He ain't gonna hurt ya, Jennifer." Willard laughed. "They only get mean when ya try to catch 'em or ya step on their tails." Twisting his huge frame around, he stood up and asked, "Ya hungry? I got some stuff hidden up there." He jerked a thumb over his left shoulder toward the bluff above them.

"Not really," she admitted. "But you can eat something if you want. I'd just like to sit here for a while. It's so peaceful."

Willard's face puckered. "All right. But ya promise to stay right here? Cap'n Chad said I wasn't to leave ya alone."

"You aren't going far, are you?"

He shook his head. "Just over the top. But I won't be able to see ya."

"Well, don't worry. I'll sit right here, and if somebody should come, I'll scream and you'll hear me."

Willard thought about it for a moment, then shrugged and turned around.

Jennifer's eyes sparkled as she watched him awkwardly climb the rocks, for she was thinking how much she was going to miss him after she left the island. There were a lot of things she'd miss. Hank Sullivan was one of them. The peacefulness of this tropical isle was another. She sighed and absently glanced back at the waters swirling and lapping around the rocks of the cove. And Chad . . .

Deciding not to allow herself to become depressed, she stubbornly affixed her attention on the scenery around her, then spotted a tiny wild flower growing in the crevice of a rock not ten feet out of reach. Wondering what kind of fragrance it had, she got up and started toward it, picking her footing very carefully since the waterfall showered everything in its wake and made her progress a bit treacherous. She slipped once, caught herself and laughed at how scared it made her. It was rather foolish on her part to be frightened. She knew how to swim. Hadn't she drifted all the way to the island clinging to a piece of wood? If she fell in, she'd just float back to one of the rocks and pull herself out. But as soon as that thought crossed her mind, she stepped on some loose pebbles. Her foot slid out from under her and she lost her balance, and rather than land on jagged edges of rock, she twisted, pushed herself off and dove into the water head first.

Her belief that she could easily swim back to her perch proved to be misleading. The strong undertow pulled her down, and before she knew what was happening, she was being swept toward the side of the cove and huge rocks were coming at her. Forcing herself to stay calm, she spotted an opening between the rocks, one big enough for her to swim through. Praying that it was merely an underwater tunnel that would lead to the open waters of the sea on the other side, she let herself be drawn through it. If nothing else, she might escape the force of the current for a moment, renew her strength, and try for the surface again. But once she had entered the mouth of the aperture and slipped, under the surface, into the calm waters inside, she could see that it was only a cave. Panic started to set in, for she feared she would drown here where she could get no air. Then, for some strange reason, she glanced up. Sunlight sparkled in the waters overhead, and she could vaguely make out a large hole in the ceiling of the cavern. Knowing there must be air where there was light, she began to kick her legs and claw at the water with all the strength she had left. Gasping for

291

air when she broke the surface, she closed her eyes and silently thanked God for sparing her. She wasn't ready to die. There were things she wanted to do. Suddenly, she thought of the huge yellow tomcat that had shared her first turbulent adventure upon the sea, and she burst into laughter.

"Kinsey, I'm beginning to think I have as many lives as you." She chuckled, pushing back heavy tendrils of wet hair from her face and opening her eyes. Her smile vanished instantly.

The cave had a ledge around its perimeter about a foot higher than the water level, and nestled safely back from the edge, where nothing could reach it, was the largest array of gold and silver Jennifer had ever seen in her life. There were candelabrums, a tea service, bowls, goblets, an open wooden chest heaped with coins, jewelry boxes overflowing with necklaces, pearl earrings, and diamond stickpins. There was more wealth contained within the walls of the cave than a person could spend in a lifetime, and the moment Jennifer saw it, she knew to whom it belonged without having to be told.

Pulling herself up, she rested her arms on the ledge to examine the box of precious stones. The diamond ring she found left her speechless, unable to understand how a woman would have the courage to wear such a valuable piece of jewelry. It would surely tempt even a basically honest man to steal it. A bright smile lit up her face.

"And a dishonest one would do anything to have it," she grinned, slipping it on her finger. "I thank you, madam, whoever you were. Your loss will help me gain my freedom. This and the promise of more."

Letting go of the ledge, she floated on her back while she studied the walls and ceiling of the cave, wondering if there might be a way out other than the way she'd come. But the only opening was the hole above her through which sunlight filtered in, and even if it had been large

292

enough for her to crawl through, it was too far out of reach with no means of getting to it.

"Well, Jennifer," she sighed. "I guess you're left with no choice." Taking two deep breaths and exhaling one rapidly, she drew another and then dove beneath the surface.

The swim to the mouth of the cave was relatively easy. But once she reached it, she could feel the tug of the current outside trying to suck her into it. For the briefest of moments, she hesitated, thinking that perhaps she should wait in the cave until the tide went out. She decided against it. Willard would miss her long before then and go back for help, and she didn't want Chad to know she had found his treasure. The cache was going to get her off the island. Knowing that she must get back, she told herself she would survive this, and swam out of the cave.

Realizing that her only hope of reaching the surface lay in having enough strength, she didn't fight the current, but rode with it. Her lungs were beginning to burn, and every muscle in her body ached, and she decided that the treasure wasn't worth this torture. Then her hand struck something, and in a frantic effort to save herself, she hung onto it. It was the decayed trunk of a tree. She dug her fingers into the soft bark and pulled herself upward. It seemed to take forever, and just when she thought she wouldn't make it, a strong hand gripped her wrist and yanked her out of the water.

"Jennifer! Jennifer!"

Willard's voice was like music to her ears, and the pain she felt as he lifted her by one arm onto the safety of a rock didn't bother her. She was alive! Between fits of coughing and gasping for air, she managed to smile up at him and saw the tears streaming down his face.

"I thought you had drowned," he groaned, collapsing on the ledge beside her. "And it would have been all my fault."

"No!" she quickly assured him, reaching for his big hand and giving it a squeeze. Several moments passed before she was able to breathe easily again, and when she could, she pushed her wet hair back off her face and said, "I fell in. It wasn't your fault."

"But I never should have brought you here," he declared. "I never should have lied to you."

Jennifer straightened and looked at him, frowning. "Lied to me? What did you lie about?"

His shirttail had come loose from his pants, and he was ringing the hem of it around his finger. "I don't go swimming here much. Cap'n Chad told me not to."

His answer confirmed her belief that the treasure belonged to Chad, but she knew she mustn't let Willard suspect that she knew Chad was familiar with this place. "Why would he tell you that? Has he been here?"

Willard nodded his head, and Jennifer noticed the way the sunshine added golden highlights to his strawberry-blond hair. He was such a sweet, trusting man that she hated using him as everyone else seemed to do . . . even Chad.

"He told me the undertow was too strong to be swimmin' in here, so I usually only fish or catch lobsters. I'm sorry, Jennifer. I shoulda said something so ya would have been more careful."

"Well, that's all behind us now, Willard. Let's just forget about it." She smiled and rubbed his back with her hand.

"Are ya gonna tell Cap'n Chad what happened?"

"No!" she exclaimed, wiping the tears from his face. "I'm all right. Just a little wet. There's no need to upset the captain when we don't have to. Besides, my clothes needed to be washed." Somehow, she managed to keep a straight face when he looked up at her with a frown, but the twinkle in her eyes gave her away, and he laughed.

"You're supposed to take them off first," he said, shaking his head as if telling her that anyone with any sense knew that.

"I am?" she teased. "You mean I've been doing it wrong all these years?"

"Oh, Jennifer." He laughed and reached for her hand. "Come on. Ya better go home and change 'em before ya get sick."

Laughing merrily, they climbed up the huge boulders and down the other side to the beach, and it pleased her that once they had, he never let go of her hand. For as long as she lived, she'd never understand how anyone could abuse a dear, loving soul like Willard Anderson.

By the time Chad's mansion came into view, Jennifer's clothes and hair were practically dry. Even if they hadn't been, it wouldn't have mattered to her or Willard. The crowd that stood near the steps was of greater interest, and Jennifer sensed there was trouble the instant she saw Jason Bingham step away from the group, his head down, one hand on his hip, the other rubbing the back of his neck.

"Something's happened, Willard," she observed.

"Yeah," he concurred. "Cap'n Chad looks real angry."

She hadn't noticed that he was there until Willard pointed him out to her, but now she had to agree. Chad's mouth was set in a hard line. His dark eyes were shadowed by a fierce frown, and every muscle in his body was tense. And when he glanced up and saw them, her steps faltered, for she wondered if the look he gave them meant they were the cause of his rage.

"Did you really have the captain's permission to let me leave the house, Willard?" she asked nervously. "He looks like he's angry with us."

Willard gulped but he didn't answer.

"Willard, did you have permission?" She repeated her

question with a bit more strength this time.

"I asked him. He didn't say no."

"But he didn't say yes either. Did he?"

Willard's lower lip quivered. "He wasn't paying much attention to me. He was thinkin' about something."

"Oh, Willard," she moaned, and looked back at Chad. His gaze hadn't left them, and when he raised a hand to motion them closer, a knot formed in her belly. She wasn't afraid for herself, but Willard, certain Chad would mistake their early morning stroll as something she had planned. "I think you're going to have a lot of explaining to do," she sighed, taking his arm and starting them off. "And whatever you do, don't lie to him. Tell him exactly what you told me. Let it be his fault. All right?"

Willard nodded sheepishly, his round, blue eyes affixed to the man who watched him and his companion.

Once they were close enough to clearly see everyone's face, Jennifer noticed that some of the villagers looked frightened, some seemed to be relieved, and she couldn't imagine that such emotions had been brought on simply because she and Willard had left Chad's house—with or without permission. It was something else . . . something that didn't concern her or Willard.

"What's going on?" she bravely demanded, staring into Chad's dark eyes without the slightest concern that his temper would explode because of her boldness.

"I was about to ask you the same thing," he snarled.

He directed her attention to the woods with a jerk of his head, and Jennifer gasped the instant she saw Modesty's bloody corpse lying on the ground about ten feet away from her. The woman's clothes had been torn from her, and her throat was slit. Feeling sick, Jennifer clamped a hand over her mouth and turned away, squeezing her eyes shut and praying she wouldn't vomit.

"Jennifer?" Willard whined, his huge body shaking. The sight was almost more than he could bear.

Gulping down the bile that had risen in her throat, she grabbed his hand and squeezed as she faced Chad again and asked, "Do . . . do you know who did this?"

Chad's expression didn't soften. "Aye. This time we do. I had ordered Mr. Stuart to keep an eye on the two of you today just in case Willard forgot why it was that I wanted someone with you at all times. As close as we can figure out, he saw the man who attacked Modesty and tried to stop him. In the process, he got himself killed, but he did manage to finish this one off before he died."

"Mr. Jordon's dead?" Willard whined.

"None of us know him," Chad went on, ignoring the huge bulk of a man whose eyes had filled with tears. "I thought perhaps you would."

"Me?" Jennifer could hardly believe her ears. Frowning, she turned around to look at him. "Why would I know him?"

"Because he's a stranger to the island . . . just like you."

She didn't like the insinuation that laced his words, and her temper started to simmer. "So?"

"So take a look at him and tell me you don't know him."

Jennifer's blue-green eyes narrowed. "And what happens if, for some bizarre reason, I do know him? What then? Are you implying that he and I might have plotted this out? It's a big island, Captain, and unless you have a patrol guarding every inch of its shoreline day and night, *anyone* could sail in here without your knowing it . . . the same way I did."

The muscle in his cheek flexed, and he extended his hand toward a spot about twenty feet away from where Modesty's body lay.

"You're not making any sense!" she exploded. "What would I achieve by having Modesty and Mr. Stuart killed? And Megan? If this man did that to Modesty, then

297

it's rather obvious he was responsible for Megan's death as well." She jumped back a step when he reached out to take her arm. "I liked Megan!" Tears sprang to her eyes at the unsympathetic look her gave her. "I had nothing to do with this!"

"Then prove it," he growled, seizing her arm and yanking her forward.

Jennifer's stomach churned as he dragged her toward the two bodies. Jordon Stuart had been stabbed repeatedly and apparently had bled to death. The other man had a bullet wound in his chest. But Jennifer didn't really pay much attention to that fact once she saw his face. She did know him! She remembered seeing him on the *Sea Lady*. He was a deckhand, one who'd made her skin crawl. Every time she had gone topside, he'd been there . . . watching. Late at night on two separate occasions she had been awakened by the sound of someone rattling the doorknob of her cabin, and when she had called out asking who was there, no one had answered. Frightened of him, she had asked Captain Lucus about the man's background and had learned that he had just been hired on at Jamestown and that no one truly knew anything about him. From that point on, she had made sure that she was never alone on deck with the man, or anywhere else. Her body trembled violently when she realized that her first week on the island, she had been entirely on her own, that at any time he might have found her and killed her as he had Megan and Modesty. Feeling weak and unable to stand on her own two feet, Jennifer leaned heavily against the man at her side.

Chad hadn't really thought she had had anything to do with the murders, but his short temper and his frustration over this turn of events had made him accuse her. He had been unfair with her—even cruel—and he knew it. Swooping her up into his arms, he ordered Jason

298

to see that the bodies were buried, then he turned, and started up the steps to his mansion.

"He . . . he was a deckhand on the *Sea Lady*," she admitted, her throat tight as she clung frantically to him. "I don't know his name. Captain Lucus told me he had only just hired him for the voyage to England. If I had known he'd survived along with me, I never would have run away from you."

Chad's brow furrowed briefly, and he forced himself to concentrate on the steps he took to keep from looking at her. What a strange thing for her to say. Hadn't he taken her against her will, forced her to come to the village, thrown her in jail, and threatened to shame her in front of her own betrothed? Aye, the man who'd murdered Megan and Modesty had a very twisted mind, but had he treated Jennifer much better? An odd feeling came over him as he paused by the gate to unlock it. What was happening to him? He had never questioned his behavior before, had never cared what people thought of him. He nudged the gate open and stepped through it. Not bothering to secure it behind them, he carried his light burden down the stone path toward the front entrance to the house. There were a lot of things about himself that he had come to regard more closely, and he knew it was because of this woman. In her own subtle way, she was forcing him to see himself differently, and he wasn't sure that he liked what he saw.

He tried not to think about it anymore as he opened the door, stepped into the foyer, and kicked the portal shut with the heel of his boot. He had a mission to fulfill, and now that his ship was nearly ready to sail, he'd see it done. A dull ache suddenly stabbed at his heart as he carried Jennifer across the front room and up the wide staircase. Of course, that meant taking her to England and leaving her there. He clenched his teeth as he headed toward her room. Why should that bother him? There was no time in his life for a woman. Crossing with her to the bed, he gently laid her down, unaware of the sea green eyes that watched him. Jennifer Grey wasn't meant to be his. Everyone knew that. His father had made sure of it. An old hurt rose within him, and he turned to leave.

"Chad?"

The warmth of her honey-smooth voice made his heart pound. He stopped, but wouldn't turn around to look at her.

"Thank you for the flower."

He had forgotten about the hibiscus he had told Willard to find. And he had forgotten about his plan to woo her—not because it was what she wanted, but because he had thought of it as a way to break her spirit, to win total domination over her. He closed his eyes. It had just been another deceitful act on his part.

"It was Willard's idea," he lied. "Thank him for it."

A soft smile parted Jennifer's lips as she watched him storm from the room. That was what she had expected him to say.

The western sky burned with the setting of the sun by the time Chad rode back toward the village. He had taken his black stallion and galloped off down the beach alone, wanting to spend the rest of the day by himself to clear his thoughts and put his mind back on the things that were important to him. He had failed miserably. Only an hour out he had come across the place where he had first found evidence of a stranger on the isle and had remembered a piece of lavender cloth with lace trim snared on a bush. He would have turned back, but the vision of a golden-haired beauty had driven him on so he had kicked the stallion's sides with nearly as much urgency as he had that day weeks ago. When he'd arrived at the spot where he had seen Jennifer for the first time, he'd reined his horse to a stop and dismounted to stroll along the beach where they had made love. It was foolish, he knew, but this was his way of saying good-bye to her. Even if he wanted to keep her here, he knew he couldn't. The kind of life he led wasn't meant to have a woman in it. And certainly not Jennifer. He wasn't deserving of her. Modesty Copeland was more the type for such an existence. Suddenly angered, he had caught the stallion's reins, swung himself up into the saddle, and raced even farther away from the village. He was on the opposite shore before he realized how far he had ridden, halfway around the island, so he continued on, deciding to investigate the entire perimeter. What Jennifer had said—anyone could reach the shore without his knowledge—was true. He hadn't posted a watch for nearly a year, and he decided that perhaps it was time to tighten up their security again.

Once the buildings at the edge of town came into view, Chad made up his mind to find Jason and instruct him to send a few men up into the hills for the night, then return to his house and get a good night's sleep. His plans changed, however, when he was told that his first mate was at the inn having supper, and he recalled that he hadn't eaten all day. It was dark by the time he climbed the long set of stairs to the iron gate, a distance that seemed to have doubled because of the ale he had drunk, and he didn't even notice that the gate stood open. Nor did it strike him that the front door was unlocked. What finally penetrated his slightly intoxicated state was the sight of the white linen cloth draped over one of the tables in the front room. On it were a single place setting, a bottle of wine, flickering white tapers in a candelabrum, and a sterling silver, covered dish. Suddenly, he felt guilty for having come home late when she had obviously gone to a lot of trouble for him. He burst into laughter at the absurdity of it. He didn't owe anybody anything!

Descending the few steps a bit unsteadily, he crossed the room to the table and picked up the lid on the dish to examine its contents.

"Chad?"

The voice seemed to come at him from all directions, and he noisily dropped the piece of silver back onto the table before he looked up and glanced around for an indication of where she stood.

"Chad, are you all right?"

He shook his head, hoping to clear his thoughts as well as his vision when he recognized Jennifer's voice and realized she was on her way down the stairs toward him. Wishing he hadn't been so careless and awakened her, and that he didn't have to talk to her at that moment, he grabbed the bottle of wine by the neck and went to the settee. "Were you expecting someone?" he growled, sprawling upon it.

"Just you," came the soft reply.

Her shadow fell against him as she crossed between him and the light from the candles. Frowning, he raised the bottle to his lips.

"Have you eaten?"

Closing one eye, he squinted up at her, then awkwardly leaned forward and set the bottle on the tea table before him.

"I could probably warm it up a little, if you—"

"I ate," he crossly interrupted. "Just go back to bed. I don't feel very sociable right now." Closing his eyes, he laid his head against the back of the settee and rudely ignored her.

"All right," she quietly replied. "But if you change your mind, I'll be in my room."

Her kindness irritated him. "Do you have to be so damned nice about it? I ruined your dinner, for God's sake, and you act as if it doesn't matter."

When he hadn't returned home before sunset,

Jennifer had assumed he was at the inn. Now she was sure of it. "You didn't ruin my dinner," she gently pointed out. "You ruined yours. But since you've already eaten, nothing's really lost."

"Damn it, woman!" he raged, hurling himself off the sofa. "Why don't you whine and cry and complain the way you're supposed to? The way any other woman would?"

Jennifer shrank back, startled by his outburst, and her hand flew to her mouth as she watched him cross to the neatly set table, grab the linen cloth by one corner, and yank it and everything upon it to the floor.

"You're supposed to hate me, Jennifer Grey." His voice was low and frightening. "The way I'm supposed to hate you."

He started toward her, and although she was sure it was only the amount of ale he had drunk that made him behave like this, she feared he might strike her. She quickly turned on her heel and fled up the long staircase as fast as she could go. At the top, she glanced back over her shoulder only once. Upon seeing that he was chasing after her, tears sprang to her eyes, and she sped to her room, raced inside, and frantically tried to swing the door shut behind her. But Chad was already there, his huge hand coming up to slam against the door and stop its forward movement. She stumbled back as he stepped into the room, and she trembled when the moonlight trickling in through the open French doors fell upon his angry face.

"Hating me will make it that much easier, Jennifer," he snarled, his eyes never leaving hers as he advanced. "Every time you hear my name, you'll curse it. Charles will curse it. My father will curse it. That's the way it's meant to be!"

"No, Chad!" she sobbed, bumping into the dresser. In a panic and blinded by tears, she hurried around the

303

bulky piece and backed into the corner. "It doesn't have to be."

"Aye!" he shouted. "It must!"

"But I don't hate you. I never will." She shrieked and darted out of reach when he tried to grab her. "I understand your pain. Really I do. If you'll let me, I can help you forget."

"Forget?" he growled, shadowing her steps. "I'll never forget how my father blamed me for my stepmother's death. I'll never forget how ruthlessly he struck me. Every time I look in the mirror, I'm reminded of it. Can you make this scar vanish, Jennifer?" he asked, rubbing a knuckle across it. "Can you erase the scars I carry inside?"

"Only you can do that," she answered quietly.

"How?" he demanded. "It's been fifteen years, and I still bleed as badly as the very day it happened. How can I erase that?"

Jennifer gulped down her fear and replied, "By forgiving him."

Her suggestion stopped him cold. No one had ever proposed such a simple solution before. His eyes shifted away from her. But then, was it truly so simple? Forgiving his father was only part of it. Chad needed to be forgiven as well. He needed to hear his father tell him that he honestly didn't blame him for Mary Elizabeth's death. Yet, how could he expect such a thing when he himself felt guilty about the accident. He should have stopped her from going, and he hadn't. All the forgiveness in the world wouldn't change that.

"It isn't that easy," he said solemnly.

Sensing that this was the opening she had waited for, Jennifer moved closer to him. "But it would be a start. And wouldn't it be worth the risk, Chad? Finally, after all this time, you'd be able to lay to rest all the hatred you've

304

had boxed up inside you. You'd be able to start living again."

His dark eyes settled on her once more. "I'm a pirate, Jennifer. I'm wanted by the Crown. Do you call that living?"

She had no answer for that one.

"Since I turned fourteen, I've stolen everything I ever needed. But none of these things were what I wanted. Do you know what that is, Jennifer? Can you honestly say that you know what it is that I really want?"

She chose not answer. It was better he admit it on his own.

"I want my father to love me."

Jennifer's tears started anew. But this time, they were tears of sorrow. "Everyone wants that, Chad," she whispered.

"But not everyone is deserving of it." He smiled sarcastically. "Isn't that so?"

Before she could answer him, he had caught her by the back of the head and the waist and had crushed her against his hard chest, his lips swooping down to fiercely take hers. Instantly a bolt of fiery electricity seared through every inch of her. Without hesitation, she brought her arms up to encircle him, and returned his kiss with all the passion he inspired in her. Her lips moved hungrily, wantonly against his while his hands explored the sensuous curves of her body. She moaned when his tongue dotted a moist path down her throat to the pulse beating rapidly at its base.

"Hate me, Jennifer," he whispered into her ear.

"Never," she replied, her nimble fingers opening the buttons on his shirt, "I will never hate you."

His deep brown eyes darkened lustfully as they stared into hers while her smooth open palms glided upward over his chest to slip the garment from his shoulders.

"I can never love you," he said, his voice husky with desire.

"I know," she answered, cupping his face in her hands and drawing his mouth to hers. "But I can love you," she murmured against his lips.

His passion soared once their bodies touched, the thinness of her nightgown allowing him to feel the full, firm curve of her breasts. He kissed her mouth, then nibbled her ear, her neck and her shoulder, catching the thin strap of her gown in his teeth to pull it out of the way before his lips found hers again. Warm fingers glided along the smooth contours of her throat, then slid beneath the second strap and freed the thin garment, which floated lazily to the floor. Lifting her in his arms, Chad gently carried her to the bed, their lips still clinging, her arms locked around his neck.

Jennifer was reluctant to let go of him as he laid her on the soft, feather mattress, fearing he would change his mind and leave her. But once he had shed the rest of his clothes and pressed a knee on the bed, she raised up, trapped his face in her hands and pulled him down, rolling with him so that he lay beneath her. She kissed his temple, each eyelid, the tip of his nose, his mouth, and tickled the scar on his lip with her tongue. He had awakened in her an insatiable desire to fulfill all the cravings of her womanly body, taught her how to enjoy them, freed her of her shyness; and now she wanted to share his teachings with him. Shifting, she lay on one hip and entwined her legs around his while her fingers explored the muscular curve of his thick shoulder, the sinewy ripples on his chest, his flat, hard belly, his hip and thigh; smiling to herself when she heard him moan. This fierce pirate captain had a weakness, and Jennifer had found it.

Rising above him, she straddled his hips and let her

306

long, golden hair fall over her shoulders to restrict his view in the ashen stream of moonlight. But he would not be denied. Catching the silky tresses in his fingers, he pushed them away with one hand, seized her arm with the other, and pulled her down until his mouth covered the taut peak of one breast. The caress sent a raging fire through her veins. She no longer wanted to play, but needed to sate the burning passion that had exploded within her. Trapping his face in her hands, she drew his mouth up to hers and kissed him savagely as they tumbled to the bed, eager to sample the sweet nectar of their desires.

Braced on his elbows, Chad stared down into the blue-green eyes watching him, the slightly parted lips, the golden hair fanned out on the pillow; and he experienced a pang of remorse. She was his for this night, this moment, and she had come willingly to him. But on the morrow, he would order his crew to set sail for England. This would be the last time he made love to her, and he prayed to God it would be enough, that once he had fulfilled his plan, he could return to this island, this house, this room, and never think of her again. Lowering his head, he kissed the tempting lips and thrust his manhood deep within her, his thoughts of the future vanishing in a blaze of rapture.

The tiny room became a universe of its own as they were transported high above the earthly world to a heaven only lovers shared. Carried on the wings of ecstasy, they explored the celestial spheres as one, in a blending of bodies and souls and passion until, at last, they reached the summit of their desires and shuddered in the sweetness of their release.

A long while passed before Chad raised his head and turned with her in his arms so they lay nestled in each other's embrace. Inhaling the soft fragrance of her hair as he nuzzled her ear, he closed his eyes and relaxed, feeling the exhaustion of the day and the tranquillity of their lovemaking seep into every muscle, and only a moment or two elapsed before he let himself drift off to sleep, vowing to rest for only a short while.

Jennifer listened to his steady breathing and felt the faint beating of his heart beneath her hand as she stared across the room at the platinum streams of light coming in through the open French doors. A sadness was reflected in her eyes, and she knew that if someone were to ask how it came to be there, she wouldn't be able to explain when or why she had fallen in love with this man. She also realized that her feeling for him would have to remain her secret. There was no hope of their ever being able to share any kind of life together. They were two very different people—from two separate worlds.

He stirred, bringing her attention back to him, and she noticed that even in his sleep, he frowned. Was he never at peace? she wondered. A light breeze floated into the room, billowing the curtains on the doors and chilling her naked flesh. Careful not to awaken him, she slid off the bed and donned her gown before coming back to draw the spread up over his lean, handsome frame. She would remember this night for as long as she lived, but if it were within her power, she would use the diamond ring she had found to buy her way to London. She would leave Chad before he had the chance to do something he'd regret. He'd already admitted what he really wanted was his father's love. How could dumping her on Sir Charles's doorstep with the announcement that he had used her accomplish anything but a widening of the gap between father and son? A tear trickled down her cheek as she stood there watching Chad. He'd be furious when he learned she had escaped him, but she prayed that after he'd had time to think it over, he'd come to realize why she had deceived him. As for herself . . . she'd let Chad's

308

half brother decide. Once she arrived in London, she'd tell Charles that she had fallen in love with another man, and that if he chose to call off their marriage, she would understand. Turning, she absently strolled out onto the balcony overlooking the waterfall in the courtyard and stared off into the distance, never having felt so happy and so sad.

Chapter Thirteen

Morning dawned clear and bright, flooding the room with warm sunshine. A soft breeze carried a fragrant mixture of wild flowers and salt air into the room, along with the turbulent sound of the waterfall in the courtyard, none of which disturbed the sleeping couple in the fourposter bed. Below, in the foyer, thick-soled boots hurried across the marble floor, through the front room, and up the long staircase on the way to Chad's room, coming to an abrupt halt. Indecision delayed further investigation once Jason found Chad's bed empty, but the urgency of the moment brought a frown to Bingham's face. He knew where Chad had spent the night, and wished he could turn around and make a quiet exit. He liked Jennifer Grey. He didn't want to embarrass her. But the sighting of the ship headed toward the island was more important than the woman's feelings. He stepped closer to the door of her room, and silently praying she would understand and forgive him, he called out to Chad.

"Sir, it's me, your first mate." He decided to keep things formal as a way of letting Jennifer know it was only business that brought him here at this early hour, not some twisted need to pry into other people's lives. "I

thought you should know that a ship's been sighted."
Interlocking his fingers, he stared down at his hands,
which dangled in front of him, while he listened to the
sounds of someone moving about in the room. A moment
later, Chad appeared in the doorway shrugging into his
shirt.

"Any idea who it is?" he asked as he buttoned up and
stuffed the shirttail into his breeches.

For a brief instant, Jason's brow furrowed with
disapproval over Chad's seemingly indifferent attitude
toward Jennifer. But then, when had Chad LaShelle ever
cared about a woman's honor? Mentally shrugging off
the urge to tell him that this little lady deserved more—
Chad would only remind him that it was none of his
business anyway—he took a deep breath, exhaled
quickly, and looked him straight in the eye. If nothing
else, at least Chad would sense his first mate's irritation
by the look on his face.

"We won't know for sure until they dock. But it
appears to be the *Challenger*, and from the looks of
things, she's in need of repair."

A vague smile lit up Chad's dark eyes as Garth Lathrop
came to his mind. He hadn't seen his former captain in
over a year, and although Chad had every right not to
trust the man, he looked forward to an exchange of wit
for he enjoyed Garth's subtle humor. Absently playing
with the tiny gold earring in his lobe, he wondered what
had brought Garth Lathrop and his crew to the island.
Knowing the man as well as he did, Chad suspected the
damage to the *Challenger* hadn't been caused by a storm
she'd encountered at sea. Blinking, he glanced at Jason,
and smiled.

"Then I guess we'd better find out what it is Captain
Lathrop really wants from us." A fist resting on each hip,
he looked away from his mate. "Order the men to man
the cannons until after the *Challenger* drops anchor.

312

Once she has, post a guard. Somehow I don't think her captain has given up the idea of taking back the *Black Falcon*."

"Aye, aye, Cap'n," Jason replied stiffly. "Anything else . . . sir?"

A confused expression replaced the smile on Chad's face before he turned to look at Bingham again. Obviously, something was bothering his friend, but Chad doubted it would do any good to ask what it was. Not just yet, anyway. If it gnawed at Jason long enough, he'd say something sooner or later. He always had in the past. "No, Mr. Bingham. That will be all." Chad's frown deepened as he watched his first mate nod and click his heels before turning abruptly and walking away. As usual, he had done something Jason didn't like, but for the life of him, he couldn't figure out what it was. Shrugging off that thought, he headed for his room, thinking it was best to meet Garth armed with a pistol, but he stopped dead in his tracks when he suddenly realized what had upset his first mate. He didn't approve of the place where Chad had spent the night. But why? Jennifer wasn't the first woman he'd ever bedded, nor was this the first time Jason had ever found him in such a situation. It had never concerned him before, why now? He raised one dark brow thoughtfully. Maybe it was because Jason liked her. But of course! Jennifer Grey was a lady, and he wasn't treating her as one in Jason's way of thinking. Chuckling to himself, he started for his room again, concluding that perhaps it was time for Jason to retire, settle down, and leave the pirating to him.

Standing by the door but out of sight, Jennifer listened to Chad's footsteps fade as he headed to his room. She had heard every word he and his first mate had said, and she knew this might be the chance she was waiting for. It sounded as though this Captain Lathrop and Chad had had a few confrontations in the past, and they had left

Chad distrustful. But if he was allowing this man to drop anchor in the cove, that could only mean Lathrop was a pirate, too. A hopeful smile lifted the corners of her mouth. If he was a pirate, he could be bought! Her problem now was to find an opportunity to speak with the man alone. As she tiptoed back across the room to the armoire to get a change of clothes, she decided maybe Willard could help.

"Well, Cap'n, so far so good," Donald Holman remarked as the two men stared at the dark figure awaiting them on shore. "What next?"

Garth smiled lopsidedly, a devilish twinkle in his green eyes. "We accept Captain LaShelle's hospitality for as long as he's willing to give it—and wait for the right moment." Nodding to one of the deckhands, Garth silently gave an order for the longboat to be lowered, and moved to the side of the ship to watch its execution.

"And have you decided what kind of proof you'll take back to Mr. Wadsworth?"

"I'd like to cut out Chad's heart and drop it in the bastard's lap." Garth chuckled. "But if the milksop managed not to faint, I'm sure he'd tell me it wasn't enough and would refuse to pay us." Double-checking the load in his pistol, he stuck the gun back in his belt. "It would almost be worth it."

"So how will you prove LaShelle's dead?"

Draping his arm around his first mate's neck, he yanked him closer and winked. "How about letting Jason Bingham tell Wadsworth? Providing the son of a bitch is still alive."

"Oh, he's alive, all right." Donald grinned, liking his captain's idea. "He's the first one I recognized through the spyglass."

"Aye? And what about Marc Bartell? Did you see him, too?"

"Aye, Cap'n. I did."

Letting go of Donald, Garth turned back to stare at Chad and the others who had joined him. "Good. Maybe we can trick the greedy drunkard into helping us."

"How?"

Standing with his feet apart, Garth crossed his arms over his chest and cocked his head to one side, smiling. "It's common knowledge how Chad came to have the *Black Falcon*. Just as it's common knowledge how much Bartell dislikes his captain. Promise the man this ship in exchange for the *Black Falcon* and command of what's left of Chad's crew, and he'll probably do just about anything we ask."

"But you don't intend to uphold your end of the bargain, do you, Captain Lathrop?" Donald chuckled.

Garth's smile widened. "I'm a pirate, Mr. Holman. I never live up to my word." Cradling his elbow in one hand, he stroked his chin thoughtfully. "In fact, I doubt Mr. Bartell will even be alive after we get through with this little scheme." Told that the longboat was ready to go ashore, he did a turnabout, bowed deeply, and playfully extended his hand, indicating that his first mate should precede him. "Shall we go, Mr. Holman?"

"Aye, Cap'n," Donald agreed, taking a similar stance. "But after you."

Laughing loudly, he caught Donald around the shoulders and dragged him along to the railing and the ladder that led to the boat below them.

"Ahoy there, Chad, my friend," Garth called out once he and Donald and five men from his crew had drifted into shore.

"Friend?" Chad questioned, watching the man agilely jump into the knee-deep water. "Since when have we

315

become friends?" His dark eyes lowered to the pistol Garth had stuck in his belt. "Friends don't arm themselves."

A silly smirk wrinkled one corner of Lathrop's mouth. "Well, we could be, if we trusted each other."

"And why would we want to do that?"

Smiling, Garth shrugged. "Safety in numbers . . . as they say." Deciding to change the subject since both men knew this little tropical isle would sink before they trusted each other, he jerked his head back toward the *Challenger*. "Ran into a bit of a storm a few days out. Damaged some of her sails and riggings. Did most of her repairs already, but since we spotted a brigantine flying French colors off our stern, we decided maybe you'd allow us to dock here 'til she's ready to sail again." His green eyes sparkled as he smiled back at his companion. "'Sides, I thought you might be runnin' low on rum and the like, and we just happen to be carrying some of the best." He wrinkled up his face when he suddenly remembered Chad had never had a taste for rum. "Sorry, mate. I forgot. Ya favor ale to rum, don't ya?"

If Chad had learned one thing about Garth Lathrop in the thirteen years he'd known him, it was that the man seldom stopped talking, and even though he knew he could never turn his back on Lathrop, he still liked him—he didn't trust him, but he liked him. Lathrop had a way of turning a dull situation into an exciting one whether by the devilish manner in which he pirated a merchant ship or by his comments as he merely sat around a table sharing a drink or two. It truly was a shame they couldn't join forces. Between the two of them, they could rule the Atlantic.

"Actually, I prefer wine," he answered with a soft smile. "But it's harder to come by these days."

"Ahh, that's what you think, my friend," Garth corrected, wiggling his brows before he turned back to one of his mates. "LaRue. Bring the case of wine from the hold for our gracious captain."

"Aye, aye, sir," the man replied, hurriedly jumping back into the longboat and reaching for the oars.

"I was saving it for a friend of mine in Brazil—where we were headed before the storm hit us—but he'll never miss something he didn't know he was gettin' in the first place, now will he?" Not really expecting an answer, Garth moved away from Chad and walked further up the beach toward the village, his knotted fists resting on his hips as he looked the place over. "She's really growing, Chad. Reminds me of Liverpool. How many people ya got livin' here now?"

Chad knew Garth wasn't truly interested in the village's progress. He merely wanted to study its layout, size up his opponent's stronghold, and check for any weaknesses. It might be some time yet before it happened, but Chad knew there'd come a day when Garth Lathrop would decide to take back what Chad had stolen from him—plus a little extra. He was sure of it when the man didn't wait for a response but faced him again and asked, "How's old Modesty? Haven't seen her in a long time. Still takin' good care of her?" The lines around Lathrop's eyes deepened with his suggestive grin.

"Modesty's dead. Buried her last night." Chad didn't offer more but started up the beach past him toward Freedom Inn.

"Dead?" he echoed with a laugh. "Ya overwork her?" He motioned for his men to follow, and started after Chad. "You're a helluva man, Chad LaShelle. But then I always knew that. Could tell it the first time I laid eyes on ya there in the street in London." Careful not to get too close, he fell into step a safe distance from Chad.

"She was murdered," LaShelle declared, realizing Garth might as well hear the details of her death from him. That would also serve as an explanation for the

317

guards he had posted—even though it wouldn't be the true one.

"Here?" Garth wailed. "In Paradise? Who did it? One of your men? Was it Bartell? I'll wager a gold coin it was Bartell. You and he never got along. Sounds like something he'd do—just outta spite."

Chad glanced at his companion from out of the corner of his eye. Garth Lathrop might be more than ten years older than he, but he still behaved like a boy at times. That was what made him so dangerous. If a man wasn't careful, he'd let down his guard around Garth and wind up being stabbed in the back. Smiling to himself, Chad studied the path they followed, wondering again why Garth—a man who had had everything as a boy: a loving mother and father, wealth, the promise of a high-ranking position—had chosen to become a pirate. If Chad had had such a life, he wouldn't be walking along this beach right now.

"No, Bartell wasn't the one."

"Who then?" Lathrop glanced around them as if he were actually afraid the killer would jump out at him and try to slit his throat. "Do you know? Or is he still running loose?"

"We don't know his name, but he was a survivor of a shipwreck that happened over a week ago."

"*A* survivor. You make it sound like there's more than one." Garth's humor faded. He was already thinking up ways to put this fact to good use.

Chad shrugged, pretending not to notice Garth's sudden, serious interest. "Aye. If one made it here, there's always a chance there are others." He pointed a thumb toward the edge of town, then nodded at the men he'd stationed near several of the buildings. "It's why I've posted guards." He grinned over at Garth. "Can't be too careful. You never know who might try to slip a blade between your ribs when your back is turned."

318

An understanding gleam brightened Garth's eyes. "Aye. Ya never know," he agreed with a devilish grin, and followed Chad into the inn.

They took a table in the far corner, away from the windows. From this position, both men could keep an eye on the door should trouble start. Donald and the others who'd come with Garth sat at a table between their captain and the only entrance to the place, cutting Chad off from escape just in case Garth wanted to make their stay short and finish up his business without wasting too much time. What they didn't know was that Chad had already ordered Jason, Andrew Tranel, and Ralph Murdock to wait upstairs until after Garth and his crew had settled into the commons. Now when that trio showed themselves, Garth's men would have to stay put or tip their hand, which would convince Chad that the repairs on the *Challenger* weren't necessary.

"So," Garth began once he and Chad had ordered breakfast, "where's that foul-tempered first mate of yours?"

Picking up one of the cups of coffee Hank had brought to the table, Chad took a sip, then said, "He should be coming down pretty soon."

Garth unintentionally gave away his surprise at learning his companion had things well covered when his gaze darted from Chad to the stairway. Realizing what he had done, and that Chad's abilities were as keen as they had always been, and knowing it was foolish to pretend otherwise, he smiled and tugged on his earlobe. "You always think of everything. But then you always did. It's why you're still the captain of the *Black Falcon*."

"And why I've managed to stay one step ahead of the authorities." Chad smiled and took another sip of coffee. "I heard you weren't as lucky."

Chuckling, Garth leaned forward, bracing his elbows on the table. "Aye. Got a little careless. I do that from time to time. But only where women are concerned. I take shrewd men very seriously." The two stared silently at each other for several moments, and more passed between them in that one look than would have been said in a thousand words.

Hank unknowingly interrupted the exchange when he came to their table with a tray of food, and Garth just as quickly slipped back to his gay, light-hearted mood—outwardly anyway. He wasn't through with Chad LaShelle just yet.

"I met your half brother a week or so ago, Chad," he said, sliding his plate in front of him as though he was simply making conversation. "Have you ever gotten a look at him since you left home?" He picked up his knife and fork, and cut into the piece of ham. "Nobody'd believe the two of you are related by looking at him. He's quite the dandy." Garth knew Chad's one real weakness was his family. Any mention of them, and Chad's expression always changed. His eyes darkened. His nostrils flared, and the scar through his lip whitened when he set his mouth in a hard line—just as it was doing now. "I don't think ol' Charlie's too fond of you, friend." He popped a piece of meat in his mouth and chewed while he stared over at his companion.

Chad knew right away what Garth was up to. He would have done the same thing if he were in Garth's place. Find your enemy's vulnerable side and attack—relentlessly. He concentrated on the food sitting in front of him and didn't say a word. He didn't have to. Garth wouldn't let the topic die.

"Want to know why I think that?" Garth continued, sounding as though they were discussing the latest trend in men's powdered wigs. "He's trying to find someone he can hire to hunt you down and kill you." He watched Chad a moment, then stuck another piece of ham in his mouth. "Can't imagine why, can you? I thought you two were close as boys."

His news honestly surprised Chad, but he tried not to show it as he smeared jam over a piece of bread. "Suppose you tell me," he remarked dispassionately. "You're the one doing all the talking."

"Kind of hard to say," Garth admitted, smiling to himself. Chad was interested. He could feel it. "Charlie's too important a person just to want his half brother dead because he's a black mark against the family name. Besides, you're wanted by the Crown, and sooner or later you'll get caught. We all do. He can just sit back and wait for it to happen and not be involved. So my guess is that money's got something to do with it."

Chad's dark eyes glanced up at Garth. "Money?"

"Aye. Like an inheritance."

Chad studied his plate again. "My father disowned me. Remember?"

"Aye," Garth replied after taking a drink of his coffee and setting the mug on the table. "But maybe he changed his mind. You haven't talked to your father in—what?— fifteen years."

"You're straining your imagination, Garth."

"Perhaps. But money usually is the reason a man would want another dead."

Chad smiled crookedly though no humor sparkled in his eyes. "And who did Charles find to execute his plan? You?"

"Me?" Garth wailed, straightening on the bench. "Why would I agree to that? Killing you would end my fun. Besides, you still have the *Black Falcon*."

"I wouldn't have, if I were dead. And whoever killed me could take it over. I'm sure you've thought of that." He finished off his breakfast and pushed the dishes away. "Is that why you're here?"

Garth grinned openly. Chad was no fool, but he'd play the game out to the limit. It was part of his nature.

"Needed repairs, Chad. I told you that." He took a deep breath and exhaled slowly while he stretched the kinks out of his back. "I just thought you ought to be warned is all."

Now Chad smiled in earnest. "Your concern is touching, Garth. But questionable." Without giving the other a chance to reply, Chad stood and left the table to talk with Jason, knowing full well Garth watched his every move.

A chill tickled the hairs on Garth's arms once he noticed that Chad's first mate and two other crewmen had joined them without his even being aware of it. Either he was getting too old for this way of life or too confident. Whatever the reason, though, he figured he wouldn't have to worry about it much longer. Once he'd disposed of Chad, the *Black Falcon*, his treasure, and this island would be his. Along with the sizable reward Charles Wadsworth had agreed to pay, Garth could retire right here on Paradise and never have to leave the island again. Spotting his first mate, he grinned at Donald's worried expression. They knew this job wasn't going to be easy; that was what made it exciting. And what Chad didn't know was that Garth had hired on extra crew, all of whom were below decks on the *Challenger*, ordered not to come topside until they were needed. If everything went as planned, that would be tonight. A smirk wrinkled his cheek as he reached for the coffee pot to refill his cup. They'd talk with Marc Bartell this afternoon and learn from him where the cannons on the hillside were located and how many, find out how many men in Chad's crew would be loyal when given a choice. Then they'd set their plan in motion. But first, Garth wanted to walk along the beach. From a mile or more at sea, he had spotted what he thought was a huge mansion built among the bluffs on the east shore. That hadn't been there the last time he and his crew had visited the island. Knowing Chad as he did, he was certain the house belonged to him, and was filled with furniture, paintings, and hundreds of other valuables worth having. And there was always the possibility that LaShelle had hidden his treasure inside. Forgetting about the coffee he had poured, Lathrop left the table and motioned for his men to stay put. If his suspicions were right, he didn't want to have to share any of his find with anyone.

Jennifer stood on the small balcony outside her room, still angry as she watched Willard's cumbersome body amble down the winding path toward the iron gate. Chad had instructed him to bring her breakfast and inform her that she would not be allowed to leave the house or the courtyard on that day, but with no explanation as to why. All Willard would tell her was that Captain Garth Lathrop and his crew had dropped anchor, and that Willard thought it was too dangerous for her to be seen by any of the newcomers. She had tried to reason with the young man, had told him that she'd stay right by his side, and when he'd shaken his head, refusing to give in, she had decided to play on his sympathy. But even after she had told him how much she wanted to go back to the secret cove to fish a little and just dangle her feet in the water, he had flatly rejected her idea. It was then she understood exactly how much Chad meant to Willard. No matter who asked, the young man wouldn't go against his captain's orders.

"I wish I had your loyalty for one minute, Willard," she muttered as she watched him balance the tray in one hand and open the gate with the other. "I wish I could tell you why I need your help. But I can't. You wouldn't understand. And if I did try to explain, you'd tell Chad what I was planning to do so that he could stop me." She glanced off to her left and shook her head, knowing that it was impossible for her to scale the tall, rock bluffs surrounding the estate, and the iron fence was too high, and had sharp, pointed spears at the top. The only exit was through the gate. She looked back at it again. And Willard had locked— Jennifer's blue-green eyes widened, and her tiny chin sagged once she saw that the gate stood ajar. Certain he hadn't left it like that on purpose, she decided to act quickly before Chad asked him about it and Willard came back to double-check. Spinning around, she hurried back into her room and went to the dresser. She had hidden the diamond ring in a bottom drawer. Willard was probably right about it being dangerous for her to be caught alone by one of Chad's visitors, but it was a chance she had to take. Slipping the ring on her finger, she decided that once she showed it to anyone who stopped her and told him she had more valuables to exchange for passage to England, the man would be insane to harm her. But just in case, she paused a moment, whispered a brief prayer in which she asked for God's protection, and then raced from her room.

Because of the way the stone steps wound through the rocks, the dense growth of ferns and huge palm trees toward the beach, it was impossible for her to know if she would meet someone on the way up until it was too late. But that didn't slow her descent any. So far her luck was running better than it had when she'd first arrived, and she figured she deserved a little more good luck. But as she neared the bottom of the stairs, she cautiously decided to move off the rock treads and into the cover of the trees from which she could observe the stretch of beach toward the village and make certain no one was there. Yet, before she did so, she heard a rustling in the thick underbrush near her feet and she froze, imagining that the island might be inhabited by gigantic, poisonous snakes, and fearing that one was about to slither out and sink its huge fangs in her ankle. Despite the warm sunshine filtering down through the leafy canopy overhead, a chill raced up her spine as she watched the tall ferns part for this creature, and she would have turned around and raced back up the stairs if her feet would have moved. Her chin quivered, and she could feel a scream building up inside her, ready to explode once the animal came into view. Then, just as it neared the edge of the ferns and panic threatened to send her flying, she saw a yellow-striped tail pop up from within the foliage.

"Kinsey!" she called out excitedly when the huge tomcat stepped into full view. "Oh, Kinsey, you nearly scared me out of my wits! Where have you been all this time, and how did you find your way here?" Stooping, she gathered the big feline in her arms and sat down with him on one of the steps. He began to purr the instant she scratched him behind the ears. "I didn't think I'd ever see you again," she murmured, rubbing her cheek over the top of his head. She laughed when he squirmed around, practically crawled up her, and stuck his wet nose under her chin, nudging her as if to say he had missed her, too. Then, all of a sudden, he stiffened in her arms, his ears came up and his eyes widened into dark, alert circles; and before she could tighten her grip around him, he sprang off her lap and raced back into the underbrush. "Kinsey!" she called, quickly coming to her feet. "Kinsey, what's wrong?"

"I'm afraid I frightened him," a voice to her right announced, startling her.

She jumped back, nearly stumbled over a step, lost her balance, and plopped down again before she could catch herself. From her perch on the steps, she studied the stranger who smiled back at her. He appeared to be about twice her age, and he had dark brown hair and green eyes, a square jaw, thin lips and nose, wide-set cheek bones, and darkly tanned skin. He wore beige-colored breeches

325

and knee-high boots, and an ivory-hued shirt with billowing sleeves. A pistol was stuck through his belt. He was a fairly handsome man, and from the twinkle in his eyes and the smile that kinked one corner of his mouth, she sensed he wouldn't hurt her. She gulped and lowered her gaze. Not just yet, anyway.

Staring at the beautiful, blond-haired young woman, Garth decided right then that he had been right about Chad hiding a treasure in his house. In all his travels he had never seen a more exquisite face. This woman's features were delicate, her bone structure was fine, and skin was smooth and flawless. As far as he could see, her lithe form was perfectly proportioned. He glanced back down the shore toward the village to make certain he hadn't been followed, positive that if he had been seen by one of Chad's crew, LaShelle would appear in a flash, ready to defend his woman. The sandy beach was deserted, but he discreetly stepped up onto the first stair and out of sight in case he'd been spotted and Chad was on his way.

"The name's Garth Lathrop, and I'm the captain of the *Challenger*." He nodded his head in the ship's direction, though it couldn't be seen from where Jennifer sat. "And who might you be?"

Jennifer's chin came up. This was too good to be true! He was just the man she was looking for, and he had walked right to her. "Jennifer Grey," she quickly answered with a bright smile. "Does anyone know you're here?"

Garth hadn't heard her question. He was too busy trying to answer some of his own. Wasn't that the name of the young woman Chad was to have married? And wasn't she engaged to his half brother now? What was she doing here? Had Chad kidnapped her and brought her here? Did Charles know it and was that the reason he hired him to kill Chad? But if it was, why hadn't Charles said something about her? It was all too confusing to sort out without help. Blinking, he concentrated on the lovely face staring back at him and said, "Jennifer Grey. It's a pretty name. But then, so are you."

Jennifer didn't have time for niceties nor was she in the mood to play games. "Captain Lathrop," she said, descending several steps so that she could lower her voice in case someone who might overhear their conversation happened to come along, "I'd like to hire your help."

Garth didn't try to hide his surprise. "My help? To do what, Miss Grey?"

"How well do you know Captain LaShelle?"

Apparently, Chad hadn't mentioned Garth to her or she wouldn't have asked. Smiling, he reached up and scratched his temple. "I've know him for thirteen years. I guess you could say I know him about as well as anybody can. He isn't much of a talker."

"Has he told you about his past? His family, I mean."

Garth shrugged. "A little," he replied, deciding to let her do the talking.

"I'm engaged to his half brother, Charles Wadsworth. I was on my way to England when the ship I was on encountered a bad storm at sea—about two or three miles from this island. It sank and I, somehow, managed to make it here. If you know anything about Captain LaShelle at all, you know how he feels about his family. When he learned who I was, he decided to keep me his prisoner as a way of securing the revenge he feels he deserves. Well, I don't want to stay here, and I'll pay you to take me to Charles."

A vision of the English fop materialized in Garth's head, and he nearly laughed out loud. Why would any woman in her right mind *want* to be with that dolt? Especially, a woman with Jennifer Grey's enticing looks and luscious curves. His gaze absently traveled the length of her. She was meant for the kind of man who could

327

appreciate such fine, rare beauty, not some dandy who cared more about soiling his hose. His attention settled on her lovely face again and on the thick mane of golden hair falling about her shoulders. But then, given the circumstances, *this* particular lady would probably prefer *anyone* over Chad LaShelle. A hint of a smile tugged at his mouth. Maybe even him.

"Do you have any idea what you're asking me to do?" he queried, moving past her as he headed up the long staircase. "If Chad wants to keep you here, it will be quite impossible to get you away. And if what you say is true—about the ship sinking—I don't see how you can pay me anything." With his back to her, he smiled broadly. He had already decided to take her along when he set sail again. She was all the proof he'd need to show Charles that Chad was dead. But if she wanted to pay him . . . well, he wouldn't argue.

"Oh, but I can," she guaranteed, racing up the stairs after him as she tugged the ring from her finger. "Look."

He stopped when a tiny hand gently touched his arm.

"I found this—in a cave right here on the island—and I give you my word it's only a sampling of what's there." Jennifer bit her lower lip while she watched him examine the huge stone. From the expression on his face, she couldn't tell whether or not he believed her, and she was beginning to wish she had taken something else—like the gem-studded goblet she had seen. The ring, as he might see it, could very well belong to her, not come from some cave filled with valuable treasure.

"Where?" he asked, his green eyes lacking the merriment she had seen in them before. He believed her.

Jennifer had to grit her teeth to keep from smiling. But this would be the difficult part, and she prayed she had the courage not to give in if he threatened her. "It's a down payment, Captain. I'll tell you where to find the rest *after* I'm on English soil. You're a pirate, Captain

Lathrop, a man who cheats and steals for his living. Therefore, I can't trust you. If I told you now, you'd take the booty and leave me behind."

The young woman's spunk greatly amused him, and he threw back his head and guffawed until his sides hurt. "And you, dear lady, are worth more than any treasure. It's a bargain." Pulling a small leather pouch from inside his shirt, he stuffed the ring into it, then extended his hand toward the remaining stairs. "And up there, I assume, is Chad's house. Would you be so kind as to show it to me?"

Jennifer glanced nervously along the beach. "I really don't think that's wise, Captain Lathrop," she warned. "If Chad found us together, he might get suspicious. Don't you agree?"

Chad, is it? he thought. A moment ago she talked about escaping him, and now she uses his name with a hint too much familiarity.

He smiled crookedly. But what did he honestly expect? Chad loved women, and it never mattered to him that they were engaged or even married. Yet, what raised Garth's curiosity was Miss Grey's attitude. It seemed to him that she might want to escape Chad for a very different reason than the one she had told him. Was it possible the little lady had fallen for that rogue of a pirate? And what about Chad? Was there even the slightest chance he felt the same toward her? Lathrop hoped so! It would make his task so much easier. Well, there was one way to find out. He'd ask Marc Bartell.

"Aye," he finally agreed. "Captain LaShelle might wonder what the two of us were talking about all alone, and then he'd keep a very close eye on both of us." Looking up the steps one more time and wishing he didn't have to give in, he grinned back at her and said, "Besides, I'll see it sooner or later." Giving her a nod, he stepped past her and descended the stone stairs.

A puzzled frown kinked her dark brows as she watched him go. As she wondered just what he'd meant by that last comment, her stomach knotted unexpectedly. Maybe this hadn't been such a good idea after all.

Jennifer had spent the rest of the day alone, except when Willard brought her something to eat, and even then she might well have been by herself. The young man stayed only long enough to leave the tray, wouldn't answer any of her questions about Captain Lathrop, and left before she had the chance to see what it was that he had brought for her to eat. When he appeared with her evening meal, he behaved in the same way, and she could only assume that Lathrop's presence had everyone on guard.

By the time the sun started to set, Jennifer's nerves were on edge. She and Captain Lathrop hadn't discussed how he would smuggle her on board his ship or, for that matter, how he planned to free her from the house, since Willard had remembered to lock the gate after his last visit. Unable to bear the solitude of the manor a moment longer, she went out into the courtyard, thinking that perhaps she might be able to hear something that would give her a clue as to what was going on. But the roar of the waterfall ruined any chance of that, and suddenly the beauty of the gardens turned ugly. She strolled about the place for the next hour or so looking at the various flowers but not truly seeing them, and she had just decided to go back into the house when something soft and furry rubbed against her leg, startling her half out of her wits.

"Kinsey," she laughed once the pain in her chest subsided. "Are you trying to see how badly you can scare me?" Bending, she scooped him up in her arms and carried him into the house, hugging him tightly against her chest. "I think you're the only real friend I have, Kinsey," she said, scratching his neck and listening to him purr as she walked up the stairs to her room. "Whenever I'm in trouble, you always come around. But do you know what I like best about you? You never argue with me." She laughed again and sat with him on the bed, content to simply pet him until, curious about his new surroundings, he bolted from her lap. She smiled as she watched him sniff the rug and then the hem of the coverlet before he poked his head beneath it and disappeared from sight under the bed. Then she swung her legs up on the mattress, rolled across it, and lay on her stomach, waiting for him to reappear on the other side. Only a moment or two passed before the coverlet moved and a pink nose and white whiskers peeked out.

"Kinsey, you're silly," she giggled when he darted back behind the bedcover as if he wanted her to play with him. Dropping off the bed, she got down on her hands and knees and lifted the edge of the bedspread to see where he had gone. He was on the far side near the wall, crouched low and obviously frightened of something. "What's wrong, sweetheart?" she murmured softly, patting the rug and trying to coax him out from under the bed. Then she saw the tips of dark brown boots on the doorsill at the other side of the room, and she quickly came up to her knees to see to whom they belonged, her heart pounding in her chest.

"I assume that's a cat you're talking to and not a man," Chad remarked with a vague smile. He stood in a relaxed way, his arms folded over his broad chest and one shoulder bucked against the doorframe.

Jennifer's face flamed instantly, not because of the comment he'd made, but because she feared that he might know about her conversation with Captain Lathrop and that he had come to demand an explanation. Averting her eyes since the mere sight of him stirred her blood, she stood up and halfheartedly straightened her attire. "He was on the *Sea Lady*. He belonged to Captain Lucus." Thinking she could reach the tomcat from the other side of the bed, she rounded the end of it and knelt down to grab Kinsey by the scruff of the neck. Having pulled him out, she rose, cradling him in her arms. "He and I spent our first week together here until you . . . found me." She glanced up sheepishly at Chad then back to Kinsey, wondering if the cat was as nervous as she. "I was hoping you'd let me keep him. He's really the only friend I have."

Chad didn't miss the subtle sarcasm in her words, but he knew it was directed at Willard. The young man had told him how upset Jennifer had been when he wouldn't go against Chad's orders and take her fishing. Chad had issued the order for her own good, even though she couldn't see it, but he'd also had an ulterior motive—to keep her away from Garth Lathrop—for he didn't trust either one of them. She wanted to get off the island, and if Garth learned her identity, he'd use her to blackmail Charles. Not that Chad cared what happened to his half brother, but he had his own plans for the man.

"Willard was only doing what I told him, Jennifer," he explained on the young man's behalf, and frowned once he realized what he had done. It was the first time he had ever defended someone, and although it felt good, it surprised him how easily he had done it. Pushing himself away from the framework, he came to stand beside her so that he could scratch Kinsey under the chin. "We had a dog when I was a young boy, but never a cat. They always seemed to make my stepmother sneeze whenever she was around them." He chuckled softly, a faraway look in his eye as he said, "I remember one time when Charles tried to smuggle a cat into the house. Mary Elizabeth knew it the minute she walked into his room." He laughed and shook his head. "We certainly got into a lot of trouble for that one."

Jennifer could hardly believe what she was hearing. Chad was like a different man. "We?" she dared ask, praying he would continue. He was so at ease, and she liked him that way.

"Of course, we. I was the one who put him up to it. I told him that as long as he kept it hidden, she'd never know he had it." He smiled brightly at her. "That boy would have believed anything I told him." He chuckled again as he recalled the time he had tricked his ten-year-old brother into trying their father's snuff by guaranteeing that it was something pleasurable. It turned out to be quite the opposite, and poor Charles had coughed and snorted for nearly ten minutes. Then their father had come into the study and caught them. The smile on Chad's face faded. That was one of the rare times his father had gotten truly angry with him over a prank he'd played on his half brother. He had received a well-deserved thrashing and had spent the next two days in his room. He hadn't even been allowed to eat in the dining room with the rest of the family. At the time, Chad had thought his punishment too harsh. His dark brows came together in a troubled frown when he realized how mild it had been in comparison to what happened two years later. Stroking the scar on his lip, he wished that just once he could remember something about his childhood without being reminded of how the pleasant times had come to an end.

He was brought out of his thoughts when the big yellow tomcat squirmed around in Jennifer's arms and then jumped to the floor to continue his snooping. "You may keep the cat, if you like," he said, watching Kinsey disappear through the doorway into the hall. "I guess we all need a friend at one point in our life." Returning his attention to her, he started to smile, but frowned instead at the sympathetic look she gave him. He cocked his head

333

to one side and raised a dark brow at her, questioningly.

"I'd like to be your friend, Chad," she answered softly. "If you'd let me."

The absurdity of the idea made him laugh. "You? We could hardly be friends, Jennifer. Not after all that's happened over the years. Our fathers have put us at odds."

"Only if you want it that way," she corrected. "I don't. And as for our being friends, I think it's truly possible. I know more about you than anyone else. I understand your pain. I've lost my father, too."

He glared crossly back at her. "Your father's dead. Mine isn't. It's hardly the same."

"But yours might as well be, Chad. For the last fifteen years you've treated him as though he were. Isn't that how long it's been since you've seen him?"

His dark eyes snapped with rage. "You're walking on very thin ice, Jennifer. I suggest you leave it alone."

"Why?" she demanded, stopping him when he turned to make an exit. "So you can go on feeling sorry for yourself for the rest of your life?"

The scar across his lip whitened. "I'm not feeling sorry for myself," he growled, his chin lowered.

"Aren't you?" she challenged, hoping he wouldn't notice how she trembled. "Then explain to me why you haven't gone back to London in all these years. Tell me why you feel you have to get even with your father by using me, if that isn't a way of covering up the hurt you've suffered. How do you know your father hasn't been suffering just as much as you? How do you know he hasn't wished he could take back every word he said to you the day you left his house? Tell, Chad? How do you know?"

The muscle in his cheek flexed, and his nostrils flared with each angry breath he took. "I think you're living proof of it." He laughed mockingly when she frowned.

"Correct me if I'm wrong, but weren't you on your way to London to marry my half brother? And until the day Mary Elizabeth died, weren't you supposed to marry me? Didn't my father decide differently? Now why do you suppose he did? Was it his way of showing me how sorry he was for the things he'd said to me? For striking me? Or was it his way of telling me that I'd never be welcome in his home again for as long as I lived? Explain that to me."

"That was decided shortly after your stepmother's funeral, Chad," she argued. "I'm talking about now."

"You're talking," he caustically agreed. "But you don't know what you're talking about. He blamed me for his wife's death, and he was right in doing so. I didn't stop her from going, and if I had, she wouldn't have died. He blamed me then, and I do not doubt that he still blames me."

Jennifer wasn't about to give up. "Why did she leave?"

"What?" Her question caught him off guard.

"I asked you what it was that made her get into a carriage and ride off?" she demanded, her fists resting on each hip, a determined look on her face. "Was it something you did?"

"No! She was leaving her husband, not me!" Infuriated, he stormed away from her and went to stand by the open French doors so he could stare out at the sea, something he always did when he was upset.

"Then she left him because of something your father did." When he wouldn't answer her, she followed him across the room and purposely stood in front of him, forcing him to look at her. "What did he do that made her so angry she decided to leave him?"

Dark brown eyes glared back at her for several long, tense moments, and while he stared at her, Jennifer could see some of his anger fade and she knew that he finally understood what she was trying to prove to him.

"He was unfaithful to her right under her own roof. She left him because she could no longer bear the shame of it. But that doesn't change the fact that I didn't stop her from going!" He quickly raised a hand when she opened her mouth to say more. "You can talk all you want about it, Jennifer, but she is dead, my father disowned me—for whatever reason, justified or not—and as long as I live, I'll blame myself for her death to some degree." He inhaled deeply and cast his gaze out across the choppy waters of the sea.

Jennifer's heart ached for him now that she understood the whole of it and knew what it was that made him so full of hatred. He was right in saying that nothing would bring back his stepmother or lessen the guilt he felt. But his hatred didn't have to be. "Chad," she said quietly, touching his arm, "your father and my father were best of friends. And to be good friends, two people must think alike. My father might have reacted the same way yours did at the loss of his wife, especially if he had been unfaithful to her and she left him because of it, even died as a result of her decision. But once the pain of his loss had eased and he could think clearly again, he wouldn't have blamed you. That's why I think you should go to your father and have it out with him. The time for hating and for torturing yourself is over."

A half-smile twitched at one corner of his mouth. "And what if you're wrong?"

"And what if I'm not?" she rallied stubbornly.

Amused by her tenacity, he looked at her again and grinned. "And why does it matter to you, Jennifer Grey? What would you get out of it?"

It was something she didn't want to answer. If he knew, he might laugh at her and she wouldn't be able to stand it. She lowered her eyes and stepped away from him.

"Wait a minute," he said, catching her arm and

336

drawing her back against his chest, a frown marring his handsome brow. He had meant only to tease her with his question, and hadn't expected her to react the way she had. He couldn't name it, but there was something in her eyes—a sadness maybe—that hinted at the possibility that she honestly cared about him. In all the years he had spent sailing the Atlantic as a pirate, no one had ever shown an ounce of tenderness toward him, and to think that this woman, who had every right to hate him, might actually feel something for him other than scorn raised his curiosity and played upon his emotions. "You didn't answer me. Why does it matter to you?"

His touch, his nearness, made every nerve in her body tingle, and although she wanted very much to tell him the truth, she decided against it. What good would it do? He would never be able to forget who she was or the unfortunate part she had played in his life. He would look at her and remember. The only hope of changing that lay in bringing an end to his hatred, effecting a reconciliation between father and son, a forgiving on both sides. Until that happened, there could be no future for them. "It doesn't," she whispered, but the lie had a bitter taste and deepened the ache in her heart, and when she tried to step away from him, he tightened his grip.

"I don't believe you," he replied softly, turning her in his arms. "Look in my eyes and tell me again. I'll see the truth in yours."

Jennifer could feel tears gathering behind her lids while her mind raced, seeking an answer that would appease him. "Suppose you tell me why," she challenged. If he guessed correctly, maybe he would say something that would encourage her to admit the truth.

A tender smile broke the serious line of his mouth, and the expression in his eyes softened. "All right," he conceded, lifting a golden lock of hair away from her cheek. "I'll tell you what I think." He ran his fingertips

337

up the back of her arm, across her shoulder, and along her neck, finally cradling her chin in his hand. "I think you've spent too much time with me. I think you've let down your guard. I think you've allowed your heart to take over your emotions, and now you're trapped between honor and desire. A frightening place to find one's self when desire is stronger than honor and threatens to shatter one's principles. Don't you agree?"

Jennifer's eyes glowed. "Are you speaking of me, fierce pirate captain, or of yourself?"

Her words rang loudly in his head and made his smile vanish. It was possible. He had never stayed so long with a woman before, and she had made him admit to things he had locked away inside of himself for fifteen years. And the ache in his heart was real. Dear God, had he fallen in love with her? And if he had, was he trapped between honor and desire just as he had claimed she was? He knew the answer to that one. He had learned days ago that he didn't want to take her to England, to hand her over to his father as he had planned to do. He wanted to keep her here with him. He also knew that was impossible.

As many emotions were mirrored in his eyes, Jennifer knew that he was arguing with himself. And as she did, she came to realize that even if she managed to bring peace between him and his father, she and Chad could never share a life together . . . the promise she had made to her father stood between them. A tear glistened in her eye, and she blinked it away. She would marry Chad's half brother as she had pledged she would. But in her heart, she would always love Chad, and tonight she would prove it to him. Slipping her arms around his neck, she drew his mouth to hers and kissed him hungrily.

Chad responded without hesitation or surprise. He had seen the desire burning in her eyes and had felt it stir within him. But her touch, the warmth of her kiss, her willingness sent a raging inferno coursing through his veins. He wanted her . . . more than anything he had ever wanted . . . even the love of his father. Slanting his mouth across hers, he parted her lips with his tongue and ran the tip along the sharp edges of her teeth before pushing inside. He found no resistance there, nor did she fight him when his hands moved to the strings of her blouse and skirt, freeing the garments from her lithe form and allowing them to drop to the floor at their feet. Her chemise quickly followed. But when his fingers began to unfasten the buttons on his shirt, she brushed his hands away to do it herself.

Bathed in the warm glow of the golden sunset, the couple embraced passionately. Their naked bodies clinging, they lived only in the moment. His hands moved downard along her spine to encircle her buttocks and draw her tightly to him, while hers caressed the sinewy ripples across his shoulders, his arms, and his firm jaw before she locked her arms around him and kissed him with more intensity than before. Impatient to have her, he lifted her up, carried her to the bed, and fell with her upon the mattress. He greedily nibbled on the soft flesh beneath her ear, before his lips moved down her neck, across her shoulder, and on to the firm mound of one breast, finally seeking its taut nipple. Meanwhile one hand glided over the silky skin of her thigh and flat belly. Jennifer moaned in ecstasy and dug her nails into the hard muscles of his back, her eyes squeezed tightly shut and her back arched as she welcomed his fervent advances. A molten fire erupted in the pit of her stomach and spread through every inch of her body, setting her aflame with passion. She called out his name in a husky whisper, and he lifted dark eyes, aglow with desire, to look at her. Rising above her, he parted her trembling thighs with his knee and pressed deep within her, and Jennifer responded with breathless urgency. Needing to feel the touch of his naked flesh against her own, she cradled his face in her hands and drew his open mouth to hers. Their kisses became fierce and savage as he moved against her, lifting them both to towering heights. Her nails raked the hard expanse of his shoulders and back while the muscles in his arms flexed beneath his weight. The tiny room they shared became a universe, their bed a cloud of blissful enchantment until passion reached its peak and they glided earthward on the wings of rapture, exhausted and spent, and bathed in the contented glow of their lovemaking.

Jennifer listened to the steady rhythm of his beating heart as she lay curled beside him, her cheek resting on his chest, their legs entwined. The last rays of the dying sunset cast a radiant splendor into the room, and she watched it fade with a mixture of sadness and determination. As soon as Captain Lathrop sent word to her, she would leave this place willingly for that was how it must be. This part of her life had come to an end. But she would recall it fondly and with love, and her final gift to the man who had stolen her heart would be the reunion of father and son. Smiling contentedly, she closed her eyes and drifted off to sleep.

Chapter Fourteen

The thunderous explosion of gunfire jolted the couple out of a sound sleep and sent Chad racing for his clothes while Jennifer came up on her knees with the sheet wrapped around her trembling body. Her eyes were wide for she feared the entire British Navy had attacked the island. Standing silhouetted against the silvery backdrop of moonlight shining on the balcony, Chad donned only his breeches, before he grabbed his boots off the floor and hurried from the room without a word. Afraid and not wanting to be left alone, Jennifer quickly scrambled off the bed and ran out into the hall after him. But by the time her eyes had adjusted to the darkness, he had already disappeared.

"Chad!" she shouted. "Chad, where are you?"

"In here."

His voice came from the direction of his room, and she quickly went to stand in the doorway. She could barely make out his tall shape near the dresser, but when he moved, a pale shaft of moonlight struck the shiny metal of the pistol he held.

"What's happening? Who's doing this?" Her throat had tightened and panic threatened to send her flying into his arms.

341

"My guess would be that it's our visitor," he growled, reaching around in back to jam the gun into his waistband before he bent to tug on his boots.

"V-visitor," she repeated in hardly more than a whisper. "You mean Captain Lathrop? But why?" When she had asked the pirate for his help, she had never imagined he would use force to smuggle her aboard his ship. Someone could get hurt . . . or killed. God, it could be Chad!

"He and I go back a long way, Jennifer. I stole his ship, and I think the time has come for him to try and take it back."

"No," she blurted out when she saw him reach for the knife lying on the dresser. "Please Chad, don't go." She realized it was too late for second thoughts, but she couldn't simply stand by and watch him walk away. Dear Lord, what had she done?

"I have to go, Jennifer. It's my crew and my island he's thinking to take over." He shoved the knife and scabbard through the belt in his breeches and walked toward her. "I want you to stay here where it's safe. Lock yourself in your room and don't let anyone in. If Garth Lathrop knew you were here . . ." He smiled softly at her and touched the back of his fingers to her cheek. "Well, he doesn't treat women much better than I do, I'm afraid. The only difference is that he's willing to pass them on to his crew. Do you understand what I'm saying?"

Jennifer's chin trembled. She knew exactly what he meant. Thinking of the cave filled with treasure, she hit upon an idea. "Chad, wait," she called when he stepped past her and out into the hall. "Maybe you could give him something in exchange for his word—"

"His word?" Chad grunted. "Garth Lathrop would sell his own grandmother if the price was right. He'd take whatever I offered, then come back tomorrow and finish what he's already started. Besides, the only thing I have to give him would be the *Black Falcon,* and by letting him have the ship, we'd all be stranded here."

"What about the treasure?"

Chad was halfway to the stairs when she posed the question, but learning that she knew about his booty stopped him. As he started to turn around to ask her how she had found out about it, another volley of gunfire rent the air and sent him racing to the staircase. Acquiring such knowledge wasn't that important at the moment.

Tears quickly gathered in Jennifer's eyes as she watched his dark figure round the corner and disappear out of sight, for she felt she was to blame for what was happening. Deciding that perhaps she could do something to stop it, she spun around and hurried back to her room to get dressed.

Moonlight dotted the pathway toward the front gate, and once Chad had raced out across the veranda, he decided not to follow the stone trail that wound in and out of the trees in the courtyard. The direct route was shorter. Leaping over one of the granite flower pots lining the porch, he bolted off toward his destination, the place where the stream narrowed enough that he could jump over it rather than use the walk bridge. To his left the waterfall tumbled earthward and collected in the pool below, its roar making it impossible for him to hear anything other than the continuing musket and pistol fire, but the ashen streams of light spilling down between the openings in the palm fronds overhead warned him that he wasn't alone in the courtyard. In its glow he saw a dark figure a few yards further on dart behind one of the trees. Figuring that the intruder wasn't the only one to invade his domain, Chad quickly threw himself to the ground behind the thick cover of

343

ferns, pulling out his pistol as he rolled and came back up on his knees. But before he had the chance to survey the area and, hopefully, spot the location of the man's cohorts, cold, hard metal jabbed him in the neck.

"Get up," the voice coming from behind him ordered, and when Chad did as instructed, his pistol was wrenched from his hand. "Move over there into the light. Captain Lathrop wants to be able to see your face when he pulls the trigger."

He pointed his gun toward the waterfall. Moonlight flooded the pool of sparkling water below it and the ground around it. Chad cautiously followed orders, purposely keeping his back to the man. He still had his knife.

"Cap'n!" the man shouted. "I got 'im. We're over here."

Donald Holman was the first to step out of the shadows, pistol in hand and a satisfied smirk on his face. Chad knew that Holman had waited a long time for this moment. He wanted revenge nearly as badly as his captain. "There was a time, Captain LaShelle," he mocked, "when your ship and crew mattered more to you than a woman ever could. I haven't seen her yet, but she must be one comely wench to make you lose sight of what's important."

"Aye, Donald, she is," Garth agreed, moving into the light. "And it's only fitting that she's allowed to see justice done." He jerked his head toward the house. "Go and fetch her, Donald. I need her as a witness."

Although Chad's attention focused on the man who faced him while he watched Donald from the corner of his eye, Chad silently tried to make sense out of what Garth had said. How could he possibly know that Jennifer existed, much less that she was beautiful? None of his men would have mentioned her. His dark brows came together sharply. None except Marc Bartell. He blinked and raised his chin in the air, inwardly vowing to see that the man paid for his treachery while he considered the reason why Garth needed Jennifer as a witness. Then he remembered his earlier conversation with Lathrop, and the warning Garth had given him about his half brother wanting him dead.

"Charles is behind this, isn't he?" Chad growled.

"Partly," Garth admitted with a smile. "I had always intended to take back my ship. The island was to be retribution for setting Donald and me adrift. Your half brother merely hurried things along. You see, he came to me while I was being delayed in prison, and offered to pay me a substantial amount for proof that I'd killed you. Miss Grey will take care of that problem, especially since she told me that she didn't want to stay here and that she'd pay me to take her back to her betrothed."

Chad's nostrils flared as he sucked in an angry breath. No one had to tell him how Jennifer intended to pay Garth. She planned to use the booty she had found hidden in the cove. Damn her! All the while she'd sweet-talked him, pretended to care about him, she'd known what Garth was about. They had probably planned this whole thing out together, and it wouldn't surprise him to learn that she had made love to him to keep him busy while Garth and his men attacked the village. She had set him up, and he hadn't even seen it coming. God, what a fool he'd been! And to think—he had even fallen in love with her. His eyes darkened all the more as he thought about it, rage glowing like hot coals in their ebony depths. If he somehow managed to live through this, he'd kill her with his own bare hands. He let no one use him as she had.

Seeing that Garth's attention was now drawn toward the house, Chad assumed that Donald was returning with Jennifer. He was convinced of it when a pleased smile spread over Garth's face, and he steeled himself against his own need to look at her. One glance at those beautiful blue-green eyes, that thick mane of golden hair, and he would be lost. Centering his concentration on the man who still held a gun to his throat, Chad slowly, silently, drew his knife when his captor lowered the pistol a mite, obviously enjoying the same vision as his captain. In an instant, he plunged the blade deep into the man's side with one hand and made a grab for the gun with the other. The pirate bellowed in pain, sounding an alarm that brought Garth's eyes upon them as well as the ominous black bore he balanced adroitly in his hand, and before Chad could train his own weapon on his foe, Garth fired.

On her way out of the house, Jennifer had just started across the front room when the double doors to the foyer were thrown open and a man she couldn't recognize stepped through them. Moonlight flooded in around him, placing his face in shadow, but she could tell by his build that he wasn't Chad, and for a second she thought he might possibly be Captain Lathrop. Demanding that he identify himself, she watched him present her with a mocking bow before he told her that he was Captain Lathrop's first mate and that his captain was waiting outside for them. Hesitant, at first, to go with the stranger since she had no way of knowing whether he was telling the truth, she realized she had little say in the matter when he stepped to one side and extended his hand toward the exit. What she witnessed once they had moved out onto the veranda made her curse her uncertainty, for if she hadn't wasted those few precious moments, she might have been able to call out, to distract Captain Lathrop. As it was, she could only watch in horror as the man swung around and fired at Chad.

346

The explosion of black powder echoed through the cove with a deafening roar that seemed to bounce off every vertebra in Jennifer's spine. But that wasn't what caused the scream to lodge in her throat. It was the vision of Chad's body being jerked violently around when the lead ball struck him low in the left shoulder and hurled him backward into the pool. His weight drove him below the murky surface, and Jennifer's hands flew to her mouth, her eyes filling with tears, as she held her breath and waited for him to emerge. With her attention riveted on the spot where he had fallen, she neither saw nor heard Donald move away from her and quickly approach the edge of the pool, his pistol drawn and pointed at the choppy surface of the water, waiting. Seconds ticked by and stretched into minutes, yet Chad failed to appear. Every muscle in Jennifer's body stiffened and her stomach did a flip-flop as she watched the churning water foam and swirl and hold captive the man she had grown to love.

"I'd say he's finished, Cap'n." Donald grinned, shoving his gun back into his belt. "Wouldn't you?"

"Aye, Donald," Garth agreed. "Looks that way." He jerked his head toward Jennifer. "Get the girl. It's time we set sail on the *Black Falcon* again."

Their words did not penetrate Jennifer's terror-stricken mind, but when Donald touched her arm, intending to guide her toward the front gate, she was jolted into awareness. She yanked free of him and raced for the churning pool, blinding tears streaming down her face and Chad's name upon her lips. Then a dark figure stepped in front of her and blocked the way, and Jennifer lost all control when her arm was seized once more.

"Chad!" she screamed, struggling to break the tight grip around her elbow. "God, no! Chad!"

"He's dead, Miss Grey." Garth frowned, positive now

347

that he had been correct in his earlier suspicions about the couple. "There's nothing you can do for him anymore." A strange emotion flooded through him when the golden-haired beauty raised those pain-filled, sea green eyes to him, her dark lashes moist with tears. In his entire life, he had never met a more ravishingly beautiful woman, nor had he felt such unfamiliar stirrings in his heart. They confused him. He had always enjoyed women—in bed or in a flirtation—but this was different. *He* was the reason for her sorrow, and he hated to be. The lines in his brow deepened as he fought to reason it out. She was young enough to be his daughter, yet fatherly instincts weren't impelling him. Could it be he was smitten by her innocence, her charm, her beauty? He gritted his teeth and inhaled deeply. What good would that do? This was a lady standing before him, and he was a pirate. There could never be anything between them!

"Cap'n?"

He was jarred out of his musings by the sound of his first mate's voice, and suddenly, unexplainably annoyed, he roughly shoved the young woman into Donald's arms. "Take her to the *Black Falcon* and lock her in one of the cabins. I'll meet you there just as soon as I'm sure the island is secured."

"Aye, aye." Donald nodded, and a vague frown appearing on his face. He had noticed his captain's peculiar reaction and had wondered at it, but he knew that sooner or later Garth would confide in him. Turning, Jennifer's wrist held tightly in one hand, he stopped abruptly when Garth touched his shoulder.

"No one is to harm her, Donald," Lathrop added a little less sternly. "See to it."

Rather than answer, Donald simply nodded and walked away, half pulling, half carrying Jennifer along with him. A moment later they were swallowed up by

348

the enveloping darkness, and the only clue to their whereabouts was the muffled, woeful sobbing of a young woman.

Garth stared after them for a long while before he finally turned around to check on the crewman who had been stabbed by Chad. Seeing that he was dead, Garth faced the pool and gazed at the showering waterfall that sprinkled a fine mist on the cool night air, and he found himself wishing it hadn't come to this. Years ago, Chad had stolen his ship and had set Garth and his first mate out to sea in a longboat with little chance of survival, but Garth had always liked the wild-spirited young man despite what he had done. Maybe it was simply because Garth had seen a little of himself in Chad—the rebelliousness, the reckless courage, the determination, but never the hatred. Garth didn't truly hate anything . . . except, perhaps, being forced to do what was expected of him. That was the main reason he had left home at such a young age. He had been told that if he planned on inheriting the family estate, he would have to follow in his father's footsteps. That was the last thing Garth wanted to do. He wasn't about to pretend to be someone or something he wasn't just to inherit his father's wealth. It was more appealing and exciting to steal riches. Garth's mouth crimped into a crooked smile. And he met such interesting people this way. His mind returned to Jennifer, and the roguish grin disappeared from his lips. He wouldn't have had this opportunity to meet Miss Grey if he hadn't changed his way of life. But being a pirate meant their relationship could go no further. He had the breeding of a gentleman, but the method he employed to obtain his wealth would bar his acceptance into Miss Grey's circle. Lathrop heaved a disgusted sigh and propped his foot up on one of the rocks lining the pool. Then, leaning forward, he laid his crossed wrists on his knee and stared at the swirling dark waters before him.

"Chad, old friend," he whispered, "your death has caused a problem." He chuckled softly and glanced up at the house. "Or maybe that's what you hoped for." As though really seeing the huge mansion for the first time, Garth straightened and went to stand on the veranda, and a long while passed as he studied every inch of the stone structure. Everything depended on Jennifer's reaction to her betrothed, whether or not she would actually marry the dolt now that she had been with Chad, but if, for once in his life, things went his way and Jennifer decided she wanted nothing to do with Charles Wadsworth, he would offer her the chance to return to this island . . . to live here in Chad's house. Then hopefully, in time, she would grow to care for him. Laughing, he shook his head and started back toward the gate, knowing the chance of that happening was very slim . . . but he'd give it a try. After all, what was there to lose?

A bright orange glow stained the velvety black sky along the shoreline, and a dark cloud of smoke cast an eerie haze around the moon by the time Garth walked along the beach on his way back to the village. He broke into a run once he saw it. One of the buildings was burning. His anger raged as hotly as the fire. He had left strict orders before leaving for Chad's mansion that *nothing* was to be destroyed, but obviously someone had not thought him serious. Every shoppe on this island was necessary. Otherwise, Chad wouldn't have seen to its construction or brought people here to run it. Now it would have to be replaced. Gnashing his teeth as he raced onward, Garth swore that if any of the villagers had died in the fire, the man responsible would pay with his life.

His wrath only deepened when he came within sight

of the village and saw the towering flames that engulfed
Freedom Inn. It was already too late to form a bucket
brigade and try to save it. The roof had collapsed and fire
shot out of every window. All that remained were the
stone walls. Everything inside burned out of control. It
would be only a matter of minutes before there was
nothing left but a charred ruin.

"What the hell went on here?" he bellowed at one of
his crew. "Who did this?"

"It's my doin', Captain Lathrop."

Turning, Garth spotted Marc Bartell. A broad grin on
his face, the man walked toward him through the crowd
of frightened villagers who stood watching the inferno.
When Bartell reached him, Garth stepped back a few
paces to get away from the intense heat of the blaze. He
had to shout over the roar of the fire to be heard.

"Mind telling me how it happened?"

Marc's grin widened as he rubbed his nose with the
back of his hand and glanced over at the burning
building. "I figured LaShelle's first mate would be as
much trouble to you as his captain, so I disposed of him
for ya."

"Disposed?" Garth mocked, noticing the bloody wound
over Marc's left eye.

"Aye. Jason Bingham's in there. Burnt to a crisp by
now." He laughed evilly and looked back at Garth. "He
won't give ya no trouble now."

"You mean you deliberately set fire to the inn?" he
stated more than asked. The muscle in his cheek flexed
when Bartell nodded. "Was anyone else in there at the
time?"

"Just ol' Sullivan. But he was the rebellious sort.
Always was. You're lucky to be rid of them both."
Remembering that Lathrop had gone to Chad's house
in search of LaShelle and the young woman, Marc
straightened and asked, "Did ya find the captain? Is

he dead?"

"Aye," Garth replied, his green eyes narrowing as he fought to control his rage.

"Damn," Bartell grumbled. "I woulda liked to have seen the bastard meet his end. How'd he get it?"

One corner of Garth's mouth kinked into a sarcastic half-smile. "Would you like me to show you?" he asked calmly, pulling his pistol from his belt and pointing it at Bartell before the man had a chance to reply. He laughed at the shocked expression on Marc's face. "I shot him . . . right about here." He leveled the gun at Bartell's heart. "But that's not the best part of it, friend." He sneered. "I didn't even blink when I squeezed the trigger, and I'm not going to blink when I kill you." Enjoying the man's fear, Garth cocked the hammer of the gun quite casually as if what he were about to do was something he did every day.

"Me?" Bartell shrieked. "What the hell did I do? I told ya everything ya needed to know about the village and LaShelle's men. I even helped ya take over the island. Now you're gonna kill me? Why?"

"For several reasons," Garth informed him, the humor gone from his eyes. "For one, I made it very clear that I didn't want any of these buildings destroyed. You admitted that this was no accident—and you killed one of the townsfolk. The building and the man will have to be replaced. But even more important is the fact that I don't trust you. You've served your purpose. I no longer have any need of you." Just as Garth had promised, he didn't blink when he pulled the trigger.

The explosive sound brought everyone's attention to the man who stood over Marc Bartell's body, a pistol still clutched in his hand and pointing at the lifeless shape. Many of the women in the crowd began to cry, certain that they would have to face this callous killer, this pirate who had claimed the island as his own. And the men who stood with them trembled, as they thought much the same thing. Chad LaShelle had never allowed any of them to leave this small piece of land hidden away in the middle of the Atlantic, and they had been forced to abide by very rigid laws, but at least the people living here hadn't feared for their lives. Suddenly, their little piece of heaven, as Hank Sullivan had called it, had turned to hell.

Feeling everyone's eyes on him, Garth shook off the intense feeling of loathing that had built up in him and turned from the dead man, directing his full attention toward the crowd watching him. Seeing the fear in their eyes, he decided that now would be the best time to tell them what it was he expected of them while he was gone, so he crossed to a flatbed wagon, agilely jumped up on it, and motioned for everyone to come closer. Once they had, he shoved his pistol back into his belt, knotted his fists, and stood arms akimbo.

"Captain LaShelle is dead," he stated in a loud voice so that everyone could hear him, then waited until the shock of his news had passed and the islanders had quieted down before he continued. "This island belongs to me now, and you'll obey *my* orders—no one else's—or you'll wind up like him." Raising a thickly muscled, suntanned arm, he pointed a finger at Bartell's motionless body. "There will be no more trials. Just one form of punishment. Death. So I suggest you all listen very carefully. I'm taking Miss Grey with me and sailing to England on the *Black Falcon*. I'll be gone about a month. When I return, I expect to find a new inn built to replace this one. You'll work from sunup to sundown, and no one will be allowed on the streets after dark. All firearms of any kind will be handed over to this man." With a jerk of his head, he indicated the pirate who stood near the wagon. "His name is John Kasper, and he'll be in charge while I'm gone. He and ten of my crewmen will be staying behind to see that my orders are carried out. What's left of Captain LaShelle's men will be coming with me. So don't go thinking that once I'm gone things can be the way they were. They'll never be the same . . . never again. Now return to your homes. You have a lot of work to do in the morning." His green eyes narrowed as he scanned the faces of the people slowly moving away from him, suddenly realizing that since the seizure began, he hadn't seen Willard Anderson. "John, where's the dummy?" he asked, jumping to the ground.

"Anderson?"

"Aye."

"I saw him light out for the hills running like a scared rabbit right after the firing started. He's probably on the other side of the island by now. I don't think he'll be any trouble, if that's what's worrying you, sir."

"Just the same, keep an eye out for him," Garth warned. "He may think like a child, but if he ever gets angry, he could kill a man with one hand." Frowning, he glanced up at the hillside darkly silhouetted against the moonlit sky. "In fact, I'd feel much better if you had a couple of the men run him down. He's no good to us, and if he ever finds out I killed his captain, I'll have to sleep with my back against the wall."

"He'll be cold in his grave before you drop anchor again. Count on it."

"I will." Garth grinned as he reached up and squeezed the man's shoulder. "Do you think the eleven of you can handle things while I'm gone?"

"Shouldn't be any problem, Captain. These people are used to being told what to do and when to do it. I doubt they know how to think for themselves. And with LaShelle and his first mate out of the way, there isn't anyone to lead them. But just in case, I'll keep a guard posted day and night."

"Did you check the supplies like I told you?"

"Aye, Cap'n. Should be more than enough until you return."

"Well, then," Garth sighed, looking the village over one last time, "I guess we'll weigh anchor. See you in about a month."

"Aye, Cap'n," John nodded, then watched Lathrop walk away before calling after him, "Smooth sailing."

Without turning, Garth raised a hand in the air and waved, silently thanking his companion for the good wishes and inwardly praying that the weather would be the only thing he had to worry about.

Standing at the porthole of the small cabin to which she had been taken, Jennifer watched the dark figure in the longboat gliding toward the *Black Falcon*, certain it was Captain Lathrop and that within minutes the ship would be sailing out of the cove on its way to England. Had anyone offered to take her there two weeks ago, she would have been overjoyed. But now it was a different matter. The fire that raged brightly against the dark sky was her fault, and she was to blame for the plight of the village people who were in the hands of Garth Lathrop's crew. Her chin quivered, and before she could blink them away, tears flooded down her cheeks. Worse, Chad was dead because of her.

"Oh, Chad," she sobbed, resting her temple against the glass in the porthole as she stared off in the direction of the mansion, "please forgive me. I didn't think it would come to this I didn't want him to kill you. I just wanted passage to London so that I could talk with your father. I wanted to make peace between the two of you. God, I didn't want you dead!" Overcome with grief, she stumbled to the bunk and fell upon the thin mattress, unaware of the sounds the crew made as they prepared to set sail. Feeling as if the weight of the world lay on her shoulders, she buried her face in the crook of her arm and cried hard and long, until exhaustion claimed her and she tumbled into a fitful sleep.

"It ain't good, Cap'n," Lee Taylor said, holding up the tray of untouched food for Garth to see. "It's been two days, and she hasn't eaten a thing. I know my cookin' ain't the best, but nobody's ever died from it. Maybe you should talk to her."

Garth rubbed the knuckle of his first finger along his jaw and frowned. "I'm not so sure I'm the one who should talk to her. She's acting like this because of me."

"Well, somebody's got to do something. She ain't even come out of that cabin since we set sail. She just stands there staring out the porthole." Taylor's brow furrowed. "She's skinny enough as it is. If she don't eat something pretty soon, she'll waste away to nothing right before our eyes. And you're the one who told us you needed her as proof for that Wadsworth fellow."

Garth's mouth curled disgustedly. "Aye. That Wadsworth fellow." He glanced down the narrow passageway leading to Jennifer's cabin, then back at his cook. "Well, give me the damn tray, and I'll give it my best effort. If bad comes to worse, I'll jam it down her throat."

"That might be easier said than done, Captain Lathrop," Lee advised with a hint of sarcasm. "The look she gave me when I told her to eat chilled me to the bone. She may look like a helpless woman, but I'll wager that wench is capable of stickin' ya with a knife and laughin' while she's doin' it."

Garth chuckled. "I think you're overexaggerating a bit, Taylor, but I'll keep it in mind."

"Aye, you do that, Cap'n." The cook shoved the tray into Garth's hands before he turned and strode away.

Garth watched Taylor round the corner at the end of the passageway and disappear, wondering if, perhaps, he was right about Miss Grey. For a woman who'd offered to pay him to take her to England, she wasn't behaving at all the way she should, and he knew why. She was mourning Chad LaShelle's death. She had fallen in love with the man, and now because of Garth, her lover was dead; she very well might seek revenge. Heaving an exasperated sigh, he started toward her cabin. Since when was he afraid of a woman?

"Miss Grey?" he called out after rapping softly on the door. "It's Captain Lathrop. May I come in?" Tilting his head, he listened for her response or for any sound that might indicate what she was doing. When she neither answered him nor came to the door, he straightened and lifted the latch. Just as Taylor had said, Garth found her standing beside the porthole staring out at the endless, blue-green plain of the sea with its sprinkling of white clouds overhead. He walked further into the cabin and set the tray down on the table in the middle of the room. "My cook tells me you're not eating. I know this isn't the kind of meal someone like you is used to having, but you really should eat. It will be more than a week before we reach England." He smiled over at her, expecting her to grace him with her attention, but she continued to look out at the choppy surface of the sea. While she did, he took advantage of this opportunity to study her beauty; the matchless face, the pale locks of long, yellow hair, the shapely curves, the trim ankles peeking out beneath the hem of her full skirt, and the tiny sandaled feet. She was exquisite and he hoped someday she would be his.

"Why did you have to kill him?"

Her question caught him so off guard that it took him a minute or more to respond. "He gave me no choice,

Miss Grey. He would have killed me."

Blue-green eyes moved to look at him. "But you wanted to kill him. I could see it on your face. You enjoyed it."

Unexplainably, Garth's anger flared. "I did *not* enjoy it. Whether you care to believe me or not, I'm telling you that I regretted his death nearly as much as you. Chad and I weren't exactly friends, Jennifer, but I respected him. I don't know how much he told you about our relationship, but *I'm* the one who helped him escape prison more than ten years ago. I took him on board my ship and taught him the ways of the sea. I thought of him as a rebellious younger brother, and if there had been some other way—" He stopped abruptly when he realized there couldn't have been. He had been hired by this lady's fiancé to murder Chad LaShelle, had agreed to kill him . . . for money. In a burst of rage, he turned on his heel and stormed to the door. "I suggest you eat every bite of food that's on that tray, Miss Grey. Otherwise I'll instruct one of my men to see that you do." Stepping into the corridor, he slammed the door shut behind him and fell back against it, eyes closed and nostrils flaring with each angry breath he took.

Money! Everything in his life was centered around money! It had warped his sense of values, driven him from his home—compelled him to kill the one man in his life he had always longed to call friend. Chad LaShelle had known what he was doing when he'd refused to let himself trust Garth. Garth wasn't worthy of anyone's friendship. Jerking away from the door, he turned and glared at its dark wood graining. And he certainly wasn't worthy of the woman who loved Chad LaShelle. Doubling up his fist, he pulled back, ready to smash it against the door, then froze. Of course! When all else fails, use force. As he stared at his clenched hand, a calm came over him and, with it, a confused frown. Since when had he ever let his conscience bother him? God, what was happening to him? Suddenly in need of some strong drink, he moved away from the door and quickly headed for his cabin. He didn't care whether Miss Grey ate anything or not. She could die in there, for all it mattered to him. He was his own man, and no one—especially no woman—was going to change that.

"Hoist the British colors, Donald," Garth instructed as the *Black Falcon* slowly left the Strait of Dover and sailed toward the Thames.

"Aye, aye, Cap'n," his mate replied, turning away for a moment to pass on the order. Once it had been carried through, he faced Garth again and asked, "Do you think it will be enough, sir? I mean, a man who would hire someone to murder his own brother can't be trusted to pay once the job's done. We might be sailing right into a trap."

"We'll be able to trust him until he's learned his half brother is dead. If he's planning to cheat us, that's when he'll try something." Standing near the helm, Garth folded his arms across his chest and stared straight ahead. "But somehow I don't think he will. Not with his fiancée watching."

"You mean she doesn't know about your deal?" Donald asked, surprised.

Garth shook his head, a faraway look in his eye. He hadn't seen Jennifer since that conversation in her cabin more than a week ago, and if Lee Taylor hadn't told him that she'd started to clean her plate at every meal, Garth wouldn't have known whether she was alive or not. He had decided to stay away from her since her presence seemed to have a strange effect on him, and because sailing right into London was probably the most dangerous maneuver he'd ever executed. Having his mind clouded with thoughts of her could cost him his life.

"No," he finally said aloud. "She thinks I killed Chad in self-defense. And she'll continue to think that until I've been paid."

Donald had known Garth Lathrop for a long, long time. He probably knew him better than anyone else. Sensing his captain was infatuated with Jennifer Grey, Donald feared trouble. Grabbing his friend's arm, he firmly pulled him aside, where the helmsman wouldn't be able to hear them.

"I don't like the sound of that, Garth," he barked in a loud whisper. "What are you up to?"

A lazy smile spread over Lathrop's face. "I think Mr. Wadsworth should pay a little more dearly than he plans on doing. I think his future bride—the woman who fell in love with his half brother—should know the real reason I killed her lover."

"Are you insane?" Donald growled a bit too boisterously. Then, realizing he had drawn the crewmen's attention, he angrily shoved Garth closer to the railing. "Just take the fool's money and run. Every minute we're in port is a minute closer to being caught. And if we're all thrown in prison, there won't be anyone left to break us out. Forget about the damned woman! She isn't meant for you."

"Me?" Garth retorted with a chuckle. "What are you talking about?"

"I've seen the change in you, the look in your eyes whenever you talk about her, the way you behave when she's around. You're taken with her, and I'm here to tell you it'll never work. You're a pirate, a man constantly on the run. It's no life for a woman, not to mention that you're a little outclassed. She'd laugh at you if you even suggested such a thing."

Garth's manner remained cool and casual. "Perhaps,"

he admitted, staring off into the distance again. "But look at it from her standpoint. The man she really loves is dead. The one she was supposed to marry had him murdered, and she doesn't know anyone in England other than Wadsworth, so staying in London isn't important to her."

"And what are you suggesting? That she come to live on the island with you?"

Garth smiled crookedly and shrugged one shoulder.

Venting an angry sigh, Donald turned and walked a few steps to the left, then stopped and spun back around. "You're forgetting one thing, Captain. Maybe her fiancé hired someone to kill LaShelle, but *you're* the one who took his money. If Miss Grey cared as much for him as you think she did, how can you expect her to ever forgive you?"

Garth knew his friend was right, but the old saying "Time heals all wounds" kept coming to his mind. Jennifer Grey probably did hate him at this moment. But with a little luck and some patience on Garth's part, there was always a chance that her feelings toward him would soften—especially after he proved to her that he wasn't as ruthless as he seemed. Inhaling a long, slow breath, he turned away from his friend and, grasping the railing with both hands, watched the magnificent white cliffs of Dover slip past the *Black Falcon*. He had come to a decision while sailing to England, one he hadn't mentioned to his friend and first mate. He had grown tired of his way of life and wanted to settle down in one place . . . with Jennifer. God willing, that was just what he'd do.

It was nearly dark by the time the pirate ship, posing as a British frigate, sailed close enough to London to drop anchor and allow three of its passengers to disembark unnoticed. They hired a rig from a small, secluded livery stable at the edge of town. With Donald acting as the

361

coachman, Garth and Jennifer appeared to be husband and wife. All three had changed into attire befitting the parts they played, their garments having been taken from the trunks full of clothing Garth and his men had seized on their last raid, for they wanted to travel the streets of London without raising suspicion. For Garth, it felt oddly satisfying to be dressed in the fine garments of an English nobleman again. He hadn't worn them in more than twenty years, and for a fleeting moment, he wished his stubbornness and defiance hadn't driven him away from the kind of life he could have had. Suddenly aware of the woman sitting across from him, he closed his eyes and drew in a long, silent breath. There could never be any turning back; he had only the future. If he played it right, this woman would be a part of it.

Light-colored brows crimped with Jennifer's slight frown as she half-heartedly listened to the wooden wheels of the carriage roll across the cobblestone street on its way to the elite part of town where Chad's father lived. When the *Black Falcon* had set sail, she had thought that her last glimpse of the island would mark the end of that part of her life. Then Captain Lathrop had given her the dark blue satin gown she wore, and she'd known that in shedding the white cotton blouse, the short, full skirt, and the leather sandals, she was giving up her last visible link with the tropical isle, its people, and Chad. Now she had to rely on memory. Tears glistened in her eyes, and she blinked them back, steeling herself against the desire to weep. Crying wouldn't change anything. What had happened in her past was over. She had to concentrate on the future. She shivered involuntarily when she thought of marrying a perfect stranger after knowing real love, and she hugged her arms to her, trying to conjure up an image of Chad's half brother.

"Are you cold, Miss Grey?" the deep voice asked, and

she glanced up to see Garth Lathrop's concerned frown.

"No," she answered quietly, shifting her gaze away from him to look outside the carriage at the darkened store fronts illuminated by the glow of the street lamps dotting the way. She had mixed feelings about the man who shared the coach with her. She wanted to hate him for killing Chad, yet she didn't. She should feel gratitude for his willingness to take her to England despite the fact that he was to be paid for doing it, for he was surely risking his life by returning to London where he was, undoubtedly, wanted by the Crown. But she didn't. In truth, she didn't feel anything toward Garth Lathrop. It was as if a part of her were dead and she was incapable of experiencing any kind of emotion whatsoever. Granted, he was rather handsome, and he had dressed tastefully in gold-buckled shoes, silk hose, dark brown breeches, an ivory-colored shirt complemented by a peach ascot, and a snug-fitting coat. His wavy dark hair was now pulled back into a ribbon at the nape of his neck, and had he been a stranger to her, she might once have been tempted to flirt with him. The frown that wrinkled her smooth brow deepened. She doubted that she'd ever again be tempted to flirt . . . with anyone.

The carriage slowed considerably as it prepared to make a turn onto an intersecting street, and Jennifer's stomach churned nervously. She was to have met Sir Charles Wadsworth nearly a month ago when the *Sea Lady* sailed into port. She would have accepted his condolences on the loss of her father, his best friend, and would have been introduced to her fiancé, and then been escorted to the Wadsworth home to be their guest until the wedding. By now, speculation on what had happened to the *Sea Lady* had surely spread through London, and been laid to fact with the passage of time, the ship must have been considered lost. For her to suddenly appear on the Wadsworths' doorstep would be a shock in itself, and telling Sir Charles that his oldest son was dead—no matter how he felt about him—would be a staggering blow to the old man. Jennifer could only hope that her suspicions about his true feelings concerning Chad were correct and that telling him about Chad's confession would ease the pain. What caused the troubled look in her eyes was her indecision as to whether or not she should reveal how Chad had died. Mentally shrugging off the need to make up her mind at this moment, she elected to allow Sir Charles the choice. If he asked, then she would tell him.

Garth had furtively watched as many different expressions crossed his companion's beautiful face, and he wondered what was going through her mind. He was tempted to tell her right then about her fiancé's deceit, but just as quickly decided against it. She might not believe him, and that would only damage his chances of winning her affection. He forced down a sudden urge to laugh, and looked out the window of the carriage. What chances? he asked himself. In a few minutes they would be arriving at the Wadsworths' mansion, and he'd have to escort her up the steps and into the hands of the man she was to marry. There was no time for him to woo her, and very little hope she'd welcome his attentions. His suntanned brow wrinkled. And, of course, that dolt Charles would probably inform the authorities that Garth and his men were in London, have them all arrested, and therefore cheat Garth out of his money. No, it was better that he wait until he had been paid before he let Jennifer in on the truth about her betrothed. A devious smile parted his lips. He'd send her a message informing her of Charles's underhandedness, as well as offer his ship as refuge should she decide to leave the Wadsworth home. Aye, that was what he'd do.

The carriage rounded the final curve on its way to their destination, and Garth realized it was time the two of them discussed what they would say once they met Sir Charles. Wadsworth was a man of high standing in London, and if he suspected who Garth really was, he wouldn't waste a minute in having him arrested. Looking at his solemn companion, Garth leaned forward and braced his elbows on his knees.

"Miss Grey," he said quietly, studying the delicate outline of her jaw, "we're nearly there, and there are a few things we must talk over."

"Such as your being paid?" she asked without looking at him.

For a moment he thought she already knew about his arrangement with Charles, then he remembered her offer to tell him the whereabouts of Chad's treasure in exchange for taking her to England. He sat back in the seat, propped an elbow on the sill of the coach's window, and rested his chin against his thumb and first finger. "That wasn't what I had in mind, but, aye, that is a part of it." His heart seemed to thump in his chest when she turned her head to look at him and the light from the carriage lanterns was reflected in her sea green eyes.

"I can't think of anything else you and I would have to talk about, Captain Lathrop," she said dryly.

Her placid tone of voice disturbed him. He would have preferred anger. "My name for one."

"Your name?" she questioned with a soft laugh. "What's wrong with your name?"

"In London, it's too well known," he admitted, glancing out the window again. "I know I have no right to ask for your discretion in this matter, but I thought, perhaps, we could make a trade." He looked at her again. "My silence for yours."

Jennifer didn't like the sound of that. "What could you possibly know about me that is worth keeping secret?"

"Only the circumstance under which we met. I know

365

you're betrothed to Chad's half brother, and I know how a man would react if he learned his future wife had been—" He paused and cleared his throat. He didn't want this to sound like blackmail, but merely an attempt to protect her reputation. "Well, I thought perhaps we should decide on a story suitable for the old man . . . one that would hide my identity *and* the conditions under which you were forced to live until I came. You agree, don't you?"

Jennifer realized that she hadn't honestly thought about that until Garth mentioned it. Shaming her had been Chad's first intention once he'd learned who she was, and she remembered how horrified she had been when he'd told her. Yet, restoring her honor wasn't the issue. She had promised herself—and Chad—that she would make peace between a father and his wayward son. To do that, she would have to lie about the manner in which the two of them had lived. Besides, what she and Chad had experienced was a private thing, something she never wanted to share with anyone. She looked out the window again, only half seeing the magnificent houses they passed along the way.

"Tell me what it is you think Sir Charles should hear, if it isn't the whole truth," she said calmly.

Garth took a moment to consider exactly how he should word his request. It was important that she be the one to announce Chad's demise, equally important that she not reveal who he was. He blinked nervously when he saw Jennifer looking at him. He knew he was taking too long to answer, and hoped she hadn't become suspicious. "I'll pretend to be Andrew Bennett," he began, "the captain of a merchant ship that was blown off course during a violent storm and subsequently came across an island not charted on any map. We can tell Sir Wadsworth that you had disguised yourself as a young boy in order to save yourself from Chad's men, and that

366

when I arrived, you told me the truth so that I could help you escape. However, when we tried to leave, Chad had other ideas, and one of my men had to kill him."

Jennifer quickly lowered her eyes, hoping that Garth wouldn't see the tears shining in them. It was difficult enough for her to keep from crying without this man reminding her of something she'd rather put behind her. To hear him say that Chad was dead brought to mind an instant picture of the way he'd died, and the awareness that she had been unable to do anything to prevent his death.

"Yes," she whispered, and gulped down the knot in her throat, "that will do . . . all except for the part about how he died."

"But Miss Grey—"

"Don't worry, Captain Lathrop," she cut in, her tone cool and oddly relaxed as she gazed out the window again, "I won't tell him who actually pulled the trigger"—she swallowed hard and fought back stinging tears—"but I won't lie to him and pretend I'm not responsible for Chad's . . . death."

"You?" Garth echoed with a perplexed frown. "What are you talking about?" The troubled look she gave him cut him to the core, and he had to force himself to stay put rather than sit beside her and take her hand comfortingly in his.

"Didn't you tell me that you thought of Chad as a rebellious younger brother?" She didn't give him the chance to answer. "Didn't you say that killing him was very difficult, but that he gave you no alternative?" She cast her attention on the London streets once more. "If I hadn't hired you to bring me to London, Chad would still be alive. Wouldn't he?"

In his entire life, Garth had never felt ashamed of something he had done—until that moment. And it wasn't the ruthless murder of Chad LaShelle that bothered him, but the fact that he had lied to this woman. He had backed himself into a corner, and was now forced to continue the charade for the sake of money. His dark brows came together in a fierce frown. *She* wasn't responsible for Chad's death. *He* wasn't even truly to blame. Aye, he had pointed the gun at the man and fired, but it was Chad's half brother who'd put the pistol in his hand! If only he knew why Charles had wanted his half brother dead after all these years, then maybe he could use that information against the man and ease this woman's grief.

The carriage lurched to a halt, and brought Garth out of his thoughts. Leaning forward, he looked out at the tall, dark mansion belonging to Chad's father, and silently vowed that somehow, someway, he would make Charles Elliott Wadsworth pay for his deceit.

Chapter Fifteen

Frightened blue eyes studied the activity on the shore from a vantage point high above the village, so high that no one could spot the huge bulk of the man to whom they belonged. For two weeks, Willard had spent nearly every daylight hour observing the townsfolk carry off the rubble of what had once been Freedom Inn, then roughly construct the beginnings of a new pub, never once going against the orders of the armed men who guarded them. Whenever a villager didn't move fast enough to suit one of the pirates, he was clubbed across the side of the head or whipped, and at night, Willard could hear the screams of the women who lived in the village. The men Captain Lathrop had left behind were ignoring Cap'n Chad's rules, and if Willard hadn't been alone, he might have tried to stop them. Tears quickly filled his eyes as he thought about his friend.

When the shooting had stopped and Garth Lathrop had boarded Chad's ship, taking her crew with him at gunpoint, then had sailed off, Willard had gone to Chad's house looking for him. He had arrived in time to see two men carrying a body down the steps and had managed to duck into the brush before they'd spotted him. He remembered how hard he had had to bite his lip to keep from screaming out loud when he'd heard them laughing about how easily Lathrop had killed Cap'n Chad. He couldn't understand why the man had wanted to murder someone as kind and gentle as Cap'n Chad, and before the pair reached the place where Willard was hiding, he staggered deeper into the woods. He didn't want to see Cap'n Chad's body hanging limp and lifeless in their arms.

Willard had then gone to the cove where he had taken Jennifer the day before, and he'd sat there for several hours staring down into the swirling waters below him, wondering why she, too, had deserted him. He had seen her board the *Black Falcon* with one of Captain Lathrop's men, and it hadn't been against her will from what he could tell. Even Hank Sullivan and Jason Bingham were gone, for in the two weeks since the takeover of the island, he hadn't seen either man, and neither of them had been imprisoned aboard the *Black Falcon* with the rest of Cap'n Chad's crew. Willard was alone again, and even he had enough sense to know that he could never return to the village. Captain Lathrop and his first mate didn't like him, and from what he could piece together, both men would return to the island. Otherwise, they wouldn't have left their crew behind with guns to make the townspeople do whatever they wanted. If only there was some way for him to win back the island, he'd do it for his friend. But Willard knew that was impossible. He was only one man. He didn't have a pistol, and even if he did, he was certain that he couldn't use it. He didn't like guns because they hurt people. One had hurt Cap'n Chad. Feeling totally useless, he had reluctantly left the secret cove, knowing that he could never return to it. He was a coward, and he didn't deserve to enjoy anything anymore.

He found a small cave nestled high above the village. From it, he could watch everything going on below without the fear of being seen. At night, he sneaked back to his hut and gathered as many of his things as he could carry. After four such trips, he had stripped the hut clean and had fashioned his new home into a suitable place to live. In the early mornings, he'd fish or trap enough lobsters to last the day, and the rest of the time was spent observing the activity of the village. He'd wait until after dark before venturing back to the cave to eat what was left of his morning catch, then crawl into bed and sleep as long as he possibly could. He had always been afraid of being alone at night until Cap'n Chad had told him not to worry, that for as long as he was around, nothing or no one would hurt him. Now his friend was dead, and Willard had to fend for himself again. Maybe it was only his fear of the dark, but twice he'd thought he had heard someone walking outside the mouth of his cave, and he had spent the rest of both nights sitting up huddled in a corner and staring at the darkened entryway. In daylight, when he'd looked around outside for a clue as to how close the intruder had actually come, he'd discovered that a dense growth of ferns and an abundance of large rocks hid the opening from view. Someone would practically have to stumble across it in the dark before realizing it was there. Knowing that made him rest a little easier, but it still worried him that someone had come that close to finding him.

Rumbling noises in his stomach urged Willard to return to his hideout and the sparse meal that awaited him. Everyone else in the village, with the exception of the usual two armed guards, had gone home for the night, and the routine village life had followed for the past fourteen days told him there wouldn't be anything more to watch until morning. If he hurried, he could eat while there was still a little light shining into the cave, then settle himself down on his cot and, hopefully, sleep until dawn. Giving the layout of the small town one last look, he made sure the two men weren't looking his direction, then rose to his feet and turned around.

"Hello, Willard."

A frightened whimper tore itself from Willard's throat at the sound of the unfamiliar voice, and his inability to spot the man added to his terror. But Willard didn't have to see his nemesis to know there was a pistol pointed at him. He had heard it being cocked shortly after the man called out to him.

"W-what do you want?" he whined, feeling his knees tremble. "I ain't hurt nobody. Why don't you leave me alone?"

"I'd like to oblige you, Willard," came the laughing reply, "but the captain gave me strict orders where you're concerned."

He jumped when the stranger moved out from behind a huge palm tree and into view. "What—what kind of orders?" he stammered, his eyes locked on the gun aimed at his midsection.

"Well, Captain Lathrop thinks you might try somethin' while his back is turned, Willard." The man stepped a little closer and motioned with a jerk of his head toward the cave. "This where you been hidin'?"

Willard's chin quivered. "Yes."

"You know, I might never have found you if you hadn't been careless." He chuckled at the puzzled look on Willard's face and pointed at the ground with the muzzle of his weapon. "You didn't cover up your tracks, Willard. Didn't your Captain LaShelle teach you anything?" His mouth twisted into a sarcastic sneer. "I imagine he taught you everything he knew . . . which wasn't much considerin' he got himself killed before he could put up a struggle."

Willard didn't hear the man's last comment. He was thinking back to the time he and Cap'n Chad had gone to a remote stretch of beach so he might learn how to defend himself without having to kill his opponent. They had practiced, for hours, the various ways to disarm a foe, and then had worked on using Willard's bulk to subdue an enemy long enough to tie him up. Willard had never had the opportunity to actually use the knowledge, but Cap'n Chad had assured him that once he was faced with such a challenge, he would do exceptionally well. His pudgy face wrinkled with worry. That time had come, and although he could still hear Cap'n Chad's voice telling him that he could do it, Willard's stomach knotted with uncertainty.

"Now, I never was one for just shootin' a man where he stood," the stranger continued with a half-smile. "And considerin' you ain't really a man makes it even worse. So I'll tell ya what." He waved the gun he held. "Why don't I give ya a sportin' chance and let you run. Course, it won't do ya—" His mocking humor quickly evaporated when he saw Willard burst into tears and fall to his knees. "What the hell—?"

"Oh please, mister," Willard wailed, "don't kill me." Slumping forward on his hands, he dropped his head down, and looking like a huge grizzly bear lumbering back toward his cave to hibernate for the winter, he slowly crawled forward and closed the distance between him and the enemy.

"Get up, ya damn dummy," the man shouted, staggering back a step, "or I'll shoot ya right where ye are!"

"Oh, please . . . please don't kill me," Willard pleaded in a high-pitched voice, his fingers digging into the sandy soil. "I'll do anything ya tell me to do. Just don't shoot me!"

"Then get up!" the stranger raged.

Knowing this would probably be the only chance he'd have, Willard did as the man demanded. However, as he came to his feet, he brought a fistful of the soft earth with

373

him, and before his attacker could guess what he intended to do with it, Willard threw it in his face, temporarily blinding him. In pain, the man bellowed as he clawed and scratched at his eyes, and thinking he might be fortunate enough to hit Willard, he squeezed the trigger. The gunshot echoed through the quiet night air while the bullet lodged itself into the trunk of a tree, and by the time the pirate had wiped the dirt and sand from his eyes so that he could see again, Willard was nowhere around.

"It won't do you any good, Willard," he howled as he awkwardly reloaded the pistol. "I'm gonna find you, and when I do, I'm gonna blow your head off before you have a chance to open that stupid mouth of yours." Rubbing the back of hand across his face once again, he blinked several times, then knelt down and studied the footprints in the soft earth to see which direction Willard had taken. "You can't run fast enough, you big dummy!" he shouted, bolting to his feet to pursue him.

Willard's mammoth size made it easy for the pirate to follow his trail. Ferns were crushed beneath his weight, and any other vegetation that got in his way was broken off or hung limp. A satisfied smile curled the mate's lips as the path took him upward, for he was thinking that Willard's excessive size would soon slow him down, and that in a minute or two he'd spot him up ahead.

"I should have just shot ya when I had the chance," he muttered when the toe of his boot caught a tree root and nearly tripped him. "I could be on my way back to that pretty little seamstress by now, if I had." Stumbling over a rock, he came down hard on one knee, swore violently, and then staggered back onto his feet. But he had barely managed to take another step before he sensed there was someone off to his left. He had no time to spin around, point the gun, and fire. Instead, a crushing blow struck him just behind his ear. An explosion of shining white stars glittered before his eyes, and he tested the hardness of the ground once more, this time with his face.

Willard's heart was pounding so loudly that if a hundred men were chasing him, he wouldn't be able to hear them. His side ached and he had a pain in his chest, but he didn't stop running. He had to get as far away as possible, and he had to do it quickly. The bullet had come awfully close, and Willard knew that the next time he came face to face with the pirate, the man wouldn't miss. His lungs burned, and the muscles in his calves and thighs were beginning to cramp. Indeed, he was near exhaustion and tears filled his eyes when he heard a deep voice call out his name and beg him to stop. But he wasn't going to. He couldn't. That man wanted to kill him, and Willard didn't want to die.

"Damn it, Willard, stop!" the voice shouted, this time sounding a bit winded. "It's me, Jason Bingham, and if I have to chase after you much longer . . . I'm going . . . to . . . collapse."

"Mister Bingham?" Willard cried, stumbling to a halt and turning around just in time to see Jason stagger toward a huge rock and lean against it. "I . . . I thought you were dead."

"If I had to keep that up for another minute, I would be," he panted, wincing as he rubbed his shoulder. "I didn't think a man your size could run that fast or that long."

Cautiously, Willard started toward him, his worried gaze darting from one dark shadow to the next. "That's 'cause I'm younger than you, I guess," he answered distractedly. "'Sides, I always run faster when I'm scared. Is he gone? That man that was chasing me?" He frowned when he looked at Jason again and saw the dried bloodstains on his shirt. Hurrying forward, he fell to his knees beside him. "Are you hurt, Mr. Bingham?"

Puzzled, Jason raised a questioning brow.

"Ya got blood on your clothes," the young man whined as he reached out tentative fingertips to touch the spot.

Jason gave a short, derisive laugh. "This happened the night that bastard Lathrop decided he wanted the village. It's pretty much healed now. Just a little sore. But we haven't got time to talk about that now," he warned, pushing himself to his feet and smiling when Willard offered his shoulder for support.

"Why not?"

"Well, to answer your first question; the man who was chasing you is dead. But the shot he fired—the one that drew my attention—very well could be bringing some of his friends this way. I suggest we get the hell out of here before they come looking for him." Pointing away from the direction in which they had come, Jason hurriedly headed deeper into the dense undergrowth where the fading sunset cast a diffuse orange light. They traveled for nearly twenty minutes before Jason decided to sit down again. "This is the first time I've walked any farther than the mouth of the cave since I got shot," he admitted, his brow dotted with perspiration. "Didn't realize I was this weak."

"You been taking care of yourself all this time, Mr. Bingham? Like me?" Willard asked, perching himself on the rock next to Jason. But before Jason could draw a breath to reply, he rushed on, tears welling in the corners of his soft blue eyes. "Cap'n Chad's dead, Mr. Bingham. I saw two of Captain Lathrop's men carrying him off, and I heard 'em laughin' about how easy it was for Captain Lathrop to kill him. And Jennifer's gone, too. And Hank Sullivan." He was sobbing uncontrollably now. "And they burned Freedom Inn and made everybody a prisoner—"

"Whoa there, Willard." Jason quickly interrupted

him, grabbing one huge shoulder and giving it a rough squeeze. "It's not as bad as you think. If you'll listen to me for a minute, I'll explain."

A tear trickled down Willard's cheek, and he awkwardly brushed it away, his eyes fixed on the man sitting next to him. He wanted to believe things weren't as bad as they seemed, but he didn't know how that could be. Everyone who mattered to him was dead—except for Mr. Bingham. Did the mate have a plan to take back the island? Just the two of them? Willard wasn't sure they could, but he was willing to try. After all, this was Cap'n Chad's island, and as far as he was concerned, it always would be. He frowned as he watched Jason scan the underbrush as though he thought he had heard something or someone.

"I don't think anyone spotted us," he finally said, looking at Willard again, "but let's keep our voices down just in case. All right?"

Reminded of the constant threat of discovery, Willard's eyes widened as he quickly glanced off to his left to make sure Mr. Bingham's assumption was correct. There were no sounds coming from the thick foliage surrounding them. He heard only the gentle rustling of palm fronds high above, for a soft breeze played lightly with them. Feeling a little safer, Willard nodded and anxiously waited for his friend to continue.

"Well"—Jason frowned and sighed heavily—"I guess I should start at the beginning, so you'll understand." He rubbed his shoulder to ease the stiffness in it, then shifted into a more comfortable position on the rock. "Chad suspected Lathrop would try something. He didn't know when, how, or what, only that the man couldn't be trusted. So he asked me, Ralph Murdock, and Andrew Tranel to keep our eyes and ears open for any hint of trouble. Murdock said he'd stay near the pier, Tranel said he'd stand guard up on one of the bluffs so he could watch the village, and I decided to spend the night in the commons at the inn. If anything out of the ordinary happened, we were to send word to Chad at the house."

"Ya should have told me, Mr. Bingham," Willard cut in. "I coulda helped."

Smiling softly, Jason reached out and gently rubbed the young man's shoulder. "I'm glad we didn't, Willard. You'd probably be dead right now if we had. As nearly as I can figure out, Marc Bartell sided with Lathrop, along with a couple of other traitors, and before any of us even had an inkling of what was about to happen, Lathrop's men—and Bartell—got the jump on us. I don't really know what sort of fate Murdock and Tranel met up with—I never saw them again—but Bartell and his spineless friends, Saunders and Jochum, came to the inn with their pistols drawn. Hank Sullivan tried to step between Bartell and me once Bartell made it clear that he was going to shoot me, but Saunders hit him over the head." He unknowingly paused in the telling of his story to reflect on the rage that had consumed him at that moment as well as silently recite a prayer that he and Bartell would meet again someday soon. When they did, *no one* would stop him from killing the bastard.

"What happened then, Mr. Bingham?"

The young man's question penetrated Jason's thoughts, and he quickly cleared his throat while he shifted around on the rock, seeking a more comfortable spot. He didn't want Willard to know what was going through his head. The boy simply didn't understand how anyone could murder another human being in cold blood. But that was what Jason planned to do. He was going to point his gun at Bartell, smile, and pull the trigger—just like that.

"I knelt down to help Hank. He was unconscious and had a deep gash in his forehead. Bartell told me to leave him alone and get up. He said he wanted to look me in the

378

eye when he killed me."

"What did ya do?" Willard gasped, his blue eyes wide.

"There wasn't much I could do. I stood up. When I did, he laughed. He said he had waited a long time for the chance to give me orders. Then he told everyone in the commons to get out, including his cohorts. Once the place was empty, he dared me to go for my pistol. It was still lying on the table beside me."

"Did ya? Did ya go for it, Mr. Bingham? Did ya shoot him?"

Willard's enthusiasm surprised Jason. It sounded almost as if Willard hoped he had killed the man. "I didn't have a choice. I knew that whether I tried to defend myself or not, Bartell was going to fire. And since I knew he was capable of murdering an unarmed man, my only hope lay in the slim prospect of grabbing my gun before he squeezed the trigger." The frown returned to Bingham's brow. "All I remember after that was hearing his pistol go off before I could reach my own, and a pain in my shoulder that seemed to set my entire body on fire."

A disappointed look came over Willard's face. "Ya didn't shoot him?"

"Never got the opportunity, son," Jason admitted with a half-smile. "But I can guarantee you that if the opportunity should arise, I will."

Willard was satisfied with that. "Then what happened?"

"I woke up lying on the floor of a cave with Hank Sullivan bending over me."

"He's alive?" Willard exclaimed. "Where is he? How did he get ya out of the inn before it burned down?"

"Luckily for us, Bartell didn't know about the root cellar. When Hank came to, the place was already in flames. I was unconscious, so I didn't know about the fire. Hank said he figured Bartell would be standing just outside the door in case we tried to leave so he decided to use the cellar. It has two doors." Jason grunted sarcastically. "Or it did have. One in the kitchen and the other out back. There was so much commotion that nobody saw him carry me off into the hills. He took me to a cave he knew about, and doctored me back to health. That's probably where he is right now. That is, if he didn't hear the gunfire and come to investigate," he added as an afterthought.

Willard awkwardly came to his feet. "I wanna see him. Which way do we go?"

"Wait, Willard. There's more I should tell ya," Jason urged, grabbing the boy's arm and pulling him back down on the rock beside him.

"Like what?"

Jason stared at the young man for a moment wondering exactly how he should word it. Willard needed to be prepared, so he wouldn't expect too much, but Jason didn't want to frighten him either. "It's about Captain Chad," he began softly.

"What about him?"

Willard's wrinkled brow told Jason that he had confused the poor lad. Twisting around on the huge piece of granite, he looked him squarely in the eye and demanded, "Promise me you'll listen to every word before you say anything. It's very important that you do. Promise?"

Willard's head bobbed up and down.

"He was wounded, and Lathrop thought he had killed him, just as the men you overheard did. They were convinced of it because the captain didn't surface after he fell into the pool. He knew that if he did, Lathrop would finish him off. I have no idea how he managed to do it in his condition, but somehow he got himself to the opposite side of the pool before he emerged. Then he hid behind the waterfall until everyone was gone."

"But . . . but I saw them carrying his body—"

"Whose body, Willard?" Jason cut in. "Did you truly see who the man was? Or did you just assume it was Captain Chad?" He smiled warmly when Willard shrugged. "He's alive, Willard. I guarantee you that. But you should also know that he's a very sick man. He took a bullet just above his heart, and he was unconscious for the first four days. Hank didn't find him until the following morning."

Willard's joy at learning his best friend had survived suddenly turned to fear. "Is he gonna die?"

"Not if we take good care of him and make sure he doesn't try to get up before he's ready. That will be your job."

Willard's pudgy face brightened with his smile. "You can count on me, Mr. Bingham. I'll make sure he does whatever you want him to do."

"Good." Jason grinned, slapping the young man on the back. "Now suppose we go and see him. But remember. He looks terrible so I don't want you to be frightened when you get your first glimpse of him."

"I won't," Willard vowed, helping his companion to his feet.

As he had done for the past two weeks, Chad had slept most of the day. When he'd awakened, for the first time, Hank Sullivan had allowed him to sit up on the cot he and Jason had made out of broken tree branches and palm leaves they'd shredded and braided into ropes. But even so, his mood was bitter, and Hank found himself praying the first mate would return to the cave soon. Hank had never spent this much time alone with the captain, and although they could no longer be termed master and servant, he was still in awe of the man as well as a little fearful of him. Chad LaShelle had every right to be enraged over what had happened to him and to his island, but Hank suspected there was more to Chad's ugly disposition than that. Picking up a cup filled with cool water, he grabbed the bowl of chicken soup he had made, crossed to the cot, and sat down on the roughly constructed stool beside Captain LaShelle's bed.

"Can you manage on your own this time, Captain, or do you want me to feed you?"

Perspiration glistened in the two weeks' growth of beard covering Chad's jaw, chin, and upper lip; and his eyes were closed as he leaned back against the wall of the cave beside his bed. His pallor was no longer marred by the bright red fever spots on his cheeks, but he was far from being well. Just sitting up had taken quite an effort, yet he was tired of being treated like a baby, of being incapable of caring for himself. He slowly opened his eyes and looked at the bowl of broth Hank held out to him. Mild surprise lightened the darkness of his eyes once he recognized the piece of china as one that had come from his house.

"Where did you find this?" he asked weakly, taking the bowl and resting it on his lap.

"The chicken I stole from the village last night. The bowl, and the other dishes and pots, came from your place. I stole them about a week and a half ago," Hank told him, handing Chad a spoon. "I didn't think you'd mind since they're yours anyway."

One corner of Chad's mouth was lifting in a half-smile when a spasm of pain turned his expression into a grimace. He closed his eyes and waited for the pain to pass, then concentrated on his first bite of broth as he asked quietly, "Is there anyone living there?"

"No, sir," Hank replied, his brow furrowed as he contemplated taking the spoon away from the captain whether the man liked it or not. LaShelle certainly was stubborn. "I overheard two of Lathrop's men talking while I was in the village, and from what I could gather, Lathrop intends to come back. Thinking you're dead, he's laid claim to the island . . . and your house."

And Jennifer, Chad thought rancorously. And that's just what he deserves. She'll play him for a fool the same way she did me.

The spoon fell back into the bowl as he silently wondered whether Garth would have to pay for his mistake the way he had . . . or nearly had.

"Would you like me to do that for you, Captain?"

Brought out of his reverie by Hank's puzzling question, Chad watched Hank nod at the chicken broth he had yet to sample. He declined the offer with a shake of his head. "Did you hear anything else while you were in the village?" he asked, lifting the spoon to his lips. The hot soup tasted good and reminded him of how long it had been since he'd eaten. He took another careful sip before Hank answered.

"No, sir. Didn't want to stick around that long. But I did notice a couple of things."

"Such as?"

"None of the villagers were on the streets, and it's my guess that they're not allowed out after dark." An anguished frown creased his brow as he watched the captain lift the bowl and drink some of his soup. "I didn't want to say anything in front of Jason, sir, but Lathrop's men . . . well, they . . . ah . . ."

Chad's desire for food vanished when his companion hesitated to speak his mind. He dropped the spoon into the bowl and stared at Hank. He already suspected what it was the man had difficulty voicing, especially since Hank had mentioned Jason's name. "Mrs. O'Connor," he observed, his dark brown eyes narrowing.

"Yes, sir," Hank admitted. "And every other woman in the village, young or old, married or not. Every rule you set has been broken, and the townsfolk are paying for it. They're worked like slaves from sunup to sunset. They're locked in their homes at night. The women are raped. The weapons have been confiscated. They can't defend themselves even if they try. Captain"—Hank's voice cracked—"I want to do something for them. I know it may sound foolish, my being an old man and all, but it tears at my insides to know the inhuman acts those men are committing in that village right now." Encouraged by his captain's silence, Hank took the bowl from Chad's lap and set it and the cup of water on the floor next to him; then he slid his stool closer. "I was thinking that maybe Jason and I could sneak down there at night and start smuggling some of the women out."

"No."

Chad's crisp, short response stunned Hank, and he stiffened. "Why not, may I ask?" A mixture of anger and surprise raised the pitch of his voice.

Ignoring the question, Chad glanced toward the cave opening and asked, "Where's Jason?"

Until this very moment, Hank had always thought of Captain LaShelle as a man who stood by his principles. Now he was beginning to wonder. Peeved by the man's callousness, he stood up suddenly and walked back toward the small campfire without bothering to right the stool he had knocked over in his hurry to leave the captain's side. "Went for a walk. Said this place was getting to him. Now I understand what he meant."

Despite the heat of the fire that warmed the interior of the damp cave, Chad sensed the coolness that came from Hank Sullivan's direction. It had nothing to do with the temperature, and at first Chad couldn't comprehend the man's sudden animosity. The innkeeper had asked him a question, and Chad had given him an answer. It wasn't as if he had paid no attention to him. He was about to ask him if he had sat in a patch of nettles when he suddenly realized how indifferent his response must have seemed to the old man. He closed his eyes when his head began to spin, and leaned back against the wall for support until it passed.

"Hank," he said after a while, "I didn't mean that I don't want to help the women in the village. I thought you knew me better than that. It's just that your suggestion gave me an idea that could very well get us back the island, and rescuing the women first isn't a part of it." His shoulder pained him, and he opened his eyes. "You didn't happen to steal a bottle of rum or even some wine during your little escapades, did you? I sure would like to dull this ache I have." He raised a questioning brow at Hank, then silently watched the man turn away from him, cross to the wicker basket sitting on the opposite side of the cave, and lift the requested bottle of wine from inside.

"I ask your forgiveness, sir, for ever doubting you," Hank said humbly as he pulled the cork from the bottle and handed Chad the wine. "You're right. I should know you better than that. My only excuse is that over the past two weeks frustration has clouded my reasoning. It won't happen again."

"There's no need to apologize, Hank." Chad smiled lopsidedly and lifted the bottle to his lips. He took a long drink of the wine, and began to feel a little better once its warming effects spread throughout his tired limbs. "If anyone needs to apologize, it should be me. I got careless with Garth Lathrop, and everyone in the village paid for my mistake." He shifted on the cot, bent a knee, and rested an arm across it. "But now we're going to correct that mistake . . . you, me, and Jason."

"And me!" came the excited voice from the cave's aperture.

Chad didn't have to look in that direction to know who had volunteered to help. He recognized Willard's voice right away. "Well, I'll be damned." He smiled over at

385

him. "I thought you were dead."

"No, sir, Cap'n Chad." Willard beamed as he stepped into the cave, Jason close behind him. The smile vanished instantly when he remembered how Mr. Bingham had found him. He bowed his head and sheepishly admitted, "But I woulda been if Mr. Bingham hadn't come when he did."

"Oh, I don't know that that's entirely true, Willard." Jason chuckled. "You were running so fast I don't think that monster would have caught up with you."

Willard dug his toe into the soft earth floor of the cave and grinned. "Yeah, I was running pretty fast, wasn't I?"

"Too fast for me to keep up," Jason said, winking when he saw Chad's puzzled expression. "I found him tangling with one of Lathrop's crew. The bastard tried to shoot Willard, so I stepped in. Or I should say the rock I picked up took care of the man. He won't be bothering anyone anymore." Weary from the long climb up the hill to the cave, Jason decided to sit down before he asked what Chad and Hank had been talking about when he and Willard had arrived.

Passing on the bottle of wine to his first mate, Chad motioned for Willard to sit down as well, asked if he was hungry, then waited until Hank gave the young man a bowl of soup. "Hank had an idea that might work. I didn't know until just now that he's been sneaking down to the village for whatever supplies we need and he's never had any trouble doing it. Which means that their security isn't very tight. Now, if Hank can steal food, why not a few of the men?"

"You mean smuggle them out and bring them here?" Jason asked with an approving smile.

"We need only enough to even the odds. Then, when the time is right, we'll attack the village and take back what's ours."

"What about weapons?" Jason challenged. "I'm sure

386

Lathrop's men commandeered them all, right down to the sharp-edged hoes."

"I'm counting on that." Chad grinned for the first time since he'd been wounded. "That way they'll simply think the men ran off into the hills rather than be forced to live as they have. As for weapons . . . there are plenty hidden in my house. Hank said no one is living there, and knowing Garth as well as I do, he more than likely gave strict orders that no one was to go inside during his absence." He grimaced suddenly, but there was more hatred than pain in his eyes.

"So when do we start?" Jason quickly asked, hoping to take Chad's mind off the seizure of his house and property.

Hugging his left arm to his chest in an effort to ease the discomfort, Chad took a deep breath and exhaled slowly. "Before we can do anything, we'll have to learn the routine of the guards, and find out what goes on in the village on a day-to-day basis."

Willard practically choked on the soup he was eating. "I can tell ya that, Cap'n Chad. I've been watching them ever since I ran away. There's this many men." He set down the bowl and held up both hands, fingers fanned wide. "At night after everybody goes home, two of them walk up and down the street."

"Does anyone relieve them?"

"Yeah, but I don't know when," Willard told him. "I never watched all night, but the two in the morning ain't the same two from the night before."

"Hank, do you have a watch on you?"

Nodding, Hank hurriedly dug through his pockets while Chad turned back to Willard again.

"Do you think you can find out for us?"

The young man eagerly nodded his head and took the gold pocket watch Hank handed to him.

"This could be very important to us, Willard, so I want

387

you to pay close attention. And I want you to watch until the sun comes up. There's a possibility they change the guard twice during the night, and it's something we need to know. Understand?"

"Yes, sir, Cap'n Chad."

"All you have to do is look at the watch and remember where the hands were pointing when you saw the guards exchange places. That isn't too hard for you, is it?"

"No, sir."

Chad smiled warmly at the young man. "Good. Then why don't you get a few hours sleep. Jason will wake you up when it's time to go, and help you pick a good place to observe the village." The group fell silent as they watched Willard hurriedly finish off the rest of his soup, then hand the empty bowl back to Hank. When the young man stood up and started toward the blanket Hank had spread on the floor of the cave for him, Chad called out his name. "I'm really glad you weren't hurt, my friend. And I'm sorry I broke my promise to you."

"What promise, Cap'n Chad?" Willard frowned.

"The promise I made when I brought you to this island—about keeping you safe."

Willard's face twisted in surprise. "It wasn't your fault, Cap'n Chad. You would have if that mean Captain Lathrop hadn't shot you. I know that." He quickly glanced at the other men who shared the cave. "Everybody knows that."

The corner of Chad's mouth crimped. "Maybe," he answered softly, then closed his eyes as exhaustion flooded through his entire body. "Get some rest."

Willard started to respond, saw Jason shake his head, and decided that it was best he did as he was told. "Yes, sir," he mumbled, then crossed to his bed and lay down. Within a few minutes, he was sound asleep.

"Chad," Jason whispered, wondering if he, too, had succumbed to the blissful escape of slumber. He smiled when Chad opened his eyes. "I didn't want to say anything in front of the boy, but this entire scheme rests on his shoulders and those of an old man." To make sure he hadn't been overheard, he glanced over at Hank who was dishing out two more bowls of soup from the kettle. "You and I are in no condition to pull this off, and you know it."

"By the time Lathrop and his crew return, we will be," Chad guaranteed. Then he grinned at the dubious look his companion gave him. "I'm feeling better every day, and it will be another two and a half or three weeks before Lathrop sails in, maybe even longer."

"Why do you say that, Captain LaShelle?" Hank asked, handing Jason one of the bowls as he sat down on the ground beside the pair.

"It takes that long to sail from here to England and about five to ten days longer to return. If he intended to stay only long enough to drop off his passenger"—his tone remained cool and indifferent as if Jennifer meant nothing to him—"the earliest he'd be back is a little over a month. If he stays on in London for a while, it will be more than that. Of course, we can't count on it. We'll have to have secured the island within the next week and a half."

"Then we should start smuggling the men out right away." There was urgency in Hank's voice. "If we take one a night, we'll have more than enough help by then."

Chad shook his head. "I thought so too, at first. But I've changed my mind."

"Why?" Jason asked, sipping on a spoonful of broth.

"If one or two vanish, and then the next night another pair, the rest of the village might be made to pay, as a warning not to run away. They're suffering enough as it is without our making their situation any worse. And if a whole group of the men disappear at once, we might tip our hand."

"So what do you propose?"

"Of the four of us, I think Hank will stand a better chance of persuading the men we need that the only way any of them can survive this ordeal is to fight, even if it means risking their lives." Chad turned his attention directly on Hank. "I want you to start paying them visits once Willard has given us the information we need on their nightly routine. That's all I want you to do—talk to them. Then once they're convinced and we have enough men to make my plan work, we'll put it into motion."

"And what's your plan?" Jason asked.

For the first time in a long, long while, a devilish grin parted Chad's lips and sparkled in his dark brown eyes. "I don't know yet. I'm still thinking about it."

"Oh, that's encouraging," Jason mocked, not at all amused. "Do you think maybe you'll come up with something before it's too late, or should we consider setting up permanent residence in this cave?" He swung out his arm to indicate the small dwelling, then winced when the effort hurt his shoulder.

Chad chuckled at the man's discomfort which merely brought pain to him, and while the two of them hugged their injured limbs tightly against their sides, Hank sat by shaking his head and wondering if, perhaps, they weren't doomed to this bleak existence after all.

Chapter Sixteen

The Wadsworth residence was everything Jennifer expected it to be. The three-story brick manor house was sequestered from the other less deserving homes along the street by a high, wrought-iron fence which stood rigidly tall and protective of the encompassing row of neatly trimmed hedges. Only a glimpse of the beautifully manicured lawn, the well-tended shrubs and flowerbeds, could be seen through the double front gates. Yard lamps dotted the brick sidewalk leading to the steps and the exquisite entryway, a mammoth front door Jennifer doubted she could open by herself, and long before Donald brought the carriage to a halt by the brass hitching post, she had already decided this house must belong to Chad's father. There was a simple yet stately air about the place that told her Sir Wadsworth was a conservative man who didn't get pleasure out of flaunting his wealth, one who valued privacy. When Captain Lathrop stepped down from the carriage to aid Jennifer in her descent, a chill embraced her as she studied the manor and its grounds. Something about it reminded her of Chad's house, and she half expected to find a noisy waterfall cascading into a pool once Captain Lathrop escorted her through the gates.

"I think, perhaps, Miss Grey, that we shouldn't reveal your identity to whomever opens the door," Garth suggested as he raised the huge, brass knocker and tapped it three times. "Sir Wadsworth isn't a young man, and the shock of learning you're alive could be too much for him. I believe we should ease into it. Don't you agree?"

Jennifer didn't respond but simply nodded her head. It wasn't the effect her sudden appearance would have on him that worried her. It was the story she had to tell.

The latch clicked shortly after Garth's second attempt to summon someone, and the thick, oaken door swung silently open on well-oiled hinges to reveal a neatly groomed man with gray hair. He was dressed in black except for his white shirt, which was a stark contrast to the rest of his attire, and from the manner in which he held himself, Jennifer could only assume he was the Wadsworths' butler. She was sure of it when he gave them a quick once-over, then cocked a questioning brow. The hour was late and the time for paying social calls had long since passed.

"May I help you?" he asked stiffly.

"We have some rather urgent news we wish to discuss with Sir Charles Wadsworth," Garth replied.

"I'm afraid he has retired for the evening," the butler informed them. "If you'd be kind enough to come back in the morning, I'll tell him you were—" White brows came together sharply at the rude way the man on the stoop cut him off by laughing at him. "Did I say something amusing, sir?"

Garth's smile lingered while he shook his head. "No, not at all. I was merely imagining Sir Charles's reaction once he learns you turned us away without consulting him." He presented his arm to Jennifer. "Shall we go?"

Apprehension filled the man who was watching them prepare to depart, and he shot a nervous glance back over his shoulder, perplexed. This wasn't the first time strangers had come to the door seeking permission to speak with his employer, and each time they had come about matters that could have waited until a more sensible hour of the day. Although Sir Wadsworth never seemed to mind being awakened out of a sound sleep to hear someone's petty grievance, this evening before ascending the stairs on the way to his room, he had remarked on how tired he was, and had laughingly asked his servant if he might be able to get one night of undisturbed rest. Frowning at the couple who had started down the stairs, he wished he had the authority to decide whether or not they should be granted an audience with his master. He sucked in a frustrated breath and pulled the door open all the way.

"If you'll wait in the parlor," he called out to them, "I'll inform Sir Charles that you're here."

Glancing at his companion and finding her looking at him, Garth winked triumphantly, which brought an immediate smile to her lips, and his heart beat a little faster. Pausing on the steps, he turned and extended his hand back toward the entryway.

"Who shall I say is calling?" the butler asked once they stood before him in the foyer, his nose raised haughtily in the air.

"Captain Andew Bennett," Garth replied most properly, "of the *Sea Princess*. But my name will not be familiar to Sir Charles as we have never met."

The butler turned his attention on Jennifer. "And the lady's name?"

"Is not of importance at the moment," Garth finished, taking her elbow and nodding toward one of the three closed doors in the hallway. "In here?"

Miffed by Garth's vagueness, the butler didn't respond. Quietly he shut the front door, then crossed to the one Garth had guessed led to the parlor and swung it open. "It will be a few minutes before m'lord is able to receive visitors."

Spotting a wine decanter and goblets on a nearby table, Garth squired Jennifer to one of the chairs situated before the cold hearth, waited for her to sit down, then said, "We'll wait."

"Yes, sir," the man replied. With a slight bow, he made his exit, closing the door behind him.

Garth stared at the sealed aperture while he listened to the butler's footsteps fade into the distance. Certain they were free of eavesdroppers, he turned to his companion. "Would you care for a glass of wine, Miss Grey?"

Jennifer accepted his offer with a soft smile and a nod of her head. She had seldom drunk wine while living at home with her father since the taste of it had not pleased her. But finding herself seated in the parlor of Sir Charles Elliott Wadsworth's home set her nerves on edge. She needed the glass of wine more than she wanted it. Taking a sip from the goblet Garth handed her, she drew in a long breath, slowly let it out, and then leaned back in the chair.

"You handled that man quite well, Captain," she said after a while. "Unless one's used to their temperaments, devoted servants such as he can be difficult. You appeared to have experience."

Chuckling, Garth turned away from the window through which he had been staring out at the starlit night. "William was a lot like him. I always took such pleasure in trying to provoke him."

"William? Who is he?"

Garth hadn't realized he had so easily talked about his past until she'd posed the question. He studied the wine in his glass while he swirled it. "The Lathrops' butler."

394

Jennifer was genuinely surprised and didn't try to hide it. "I didn't know . . . ."

"Few people do," he admitted, shrugging as if embarrassed. "Except my family, of course. But they disowned me a long time ago."

Jennifer recalled his confession concerning his feelings for Chad, and she'd suddenly understood why he'd said he thought of his rival as a rebellious younger brother. The similarity of their lives was unnerving. "Is it something you wish not to talk about? Or might I learn what it is that changes a man who has everything into a criminal?"

Garth smiled brightly, knowing what it was she truly wanted to learn. "Are we talking about me? Or Chad?" he asked, hit suddenly by a wave of jealousy.

A pink hue stained her cheeks, and she dropped her gaze to stare at the fine piece of crystal she held in one hand.

He regretted his biting remark the moment it left his mouth. The last thing he wanted to do was remind her of the man she loved. How could she begin to forget Chad, if he kept bringing up his name? "I apologize, Miss Grey. That was cruel." He crossed to the settee opposite her and settled himself on it. "I chose the kind of life I live out of spite. For as long as I can remember, my father demanded that I follow in his footsteps—dress properly, use proper English, behave the way a gentleman should . . . do what was expected of me." He picked a piece of lint from the knee of his breeches and flicked it away. "I have to admit that I rather miss the feel of rich clothes"—he held up his glass—"the taste of an exquisite wine, and sitting down to dinner at an elegant table covered with white linen on which fine china is arranged. I even miss crystal goblets and sterling silver tableware." He smiled mockingly at her. "Not to mention the company of beautiful young women, instead of the trollops who frequent the sort of places I'm force to patronize." Anger had raised the volume of his voice, and when he realized that, he lifted the wine to his lips, threw back his head, and downed it in one swallow.

"You sound sorry, Captain," Jennifer observed as she watched him leave the settee to refill his glass.

"I never have been until now." He wouldn't face her, afraid she would understand what he meant by the look in his eyes.

"Because you miss the luxuries or your family?"

Laughing, he jammed the stopper back into the bottle and tilted his head back to stare up at the ceiling. "Certainly not my family. My father used to beat me every time I defied him. My mother whored around, even though she was very discreet, and my younger brother preferred his male companions over women. Not the kind of strong bond that would make a man want to go back, is it?" He settled questioning eyes on her and laughed at the horrified look on her face, hoping to change it to a smile. He didn't want her pity. He wanted her love. Turning, he went to the settee again and sat down. "So I guess I miss the luxuries." He took a sip of wine. "And what having them secures for a person."

"Such as?"

"Respect," he answered easily. "People of wealth are held in awe."

"There are different kinds of respect, Garth," she told him, unaware of how her use of his first name affected him. "What you're talking about is truly fear . . . and envy. People without money wish they had it and envy those who do. They fear the wealthy because they know money brings power—something that can destroy them. You don't have to be rich to be respected."

"Well, I'm not rich anymore, and I'm certainly not

respected." He chuckled, making light of her remark though inwardly he wished he were both rich and respected. In that case, they might be sitting in Sir Wadsworth's parlor for a different reason.

Jennifer thought of Chad and of how things might have been between him and his father if stubborn pride hadn't stood in the way. "Isn't it possible that your father did what he thought was necessary for your own good?"

Garth's dark brows slanted downward. "Are you asking me if I think beating a ten-year-old boy is necessary?" he blurted out, more loudly than he would have if he had given himself a moment or two to think about it.

Jennifer silently cursed the part of her nature that always made her want to bring peace between quarreling members of a family. Not everyone could have the kind of relationship she had had with her father. Nonetheless she declared, "I would say that depends on what the child has done to warrant punishment."

Garth unknowingly tensed the muscles across his back as he relived the pain his father had inflicted upon him long ago. "I have a hard time justifying the use of a poker, Miss Grey," he murmured, staring off into the distance.

She knew she had trespassed on his privacy, and she had to agree with him. She couldn't think of a single reason for a grown man to club a child in such a manner. She decided to let the conversation come to an end.

Still caught up in memories of his childhood, however, Garth rose abruptly and went back to stare out of the window. He seldom thought about his past, rarely considered how things might have been if he hadn't run away. Now more than ever he wished he had had the courage to stick it out. Just shaming his father by turning pirate wasn't enough. Having power and wealth would have opened different avenues of revenge.

The latch on the parlor door clicked, prompting Garth to spin around and attracting Jennifer's attention. Both held their breath, waiting, but for very different reasons. Jennifer dreaded telling Sir Wadsworth about his son, and Garth was praying the old man wouldn't recognize him. His worry increased once Wadsworth stepped over the threshold and into the room, for he didn't appear to be the type who was easily fooled. He was exceptionally well built for a man in his fifties, only a slight graying of his dark hair at the temples giving a clue to his age. The clothes he wore fit him perfectly, and were quite subdued. Jennifer reflected that they were like everything else about the Wadsworth home. It seemed only right that he would dress in such a manner. He was very tall and lean, held himself proudly and had a striking resemblance to his eldest son. This last characteristic tore at Jennifer's heart and brought tears to her eyes. She closed them and swallowed the lump in her throat as she listened to Garth explain why they had found it necessary to pay a visit at such an inappropriate hour. He started by telling their host a preposterous story about the numerous misfortunes his ship had had to endure after setting sail for England from the Colonies. Even Jennifer found it difficult to believe, nor did she understand its importance. Frowning, her eyes sought Garth's to silently question his motive in telling the outlandish tale. Instead she discovered that Sir Wadsworth was staring at her. His face was twisted in a pained, yet hopeful, expression, and once Garth revealed her identity, Sir Charles closed his eyes and let out a long, trembling sigh.

"Dear God in heaven," he whispered. "I don't believe it." He laughed suddenly, opened his eyes, and hurried across the room to her. Holding out his hands, he gently pulled her into his embrace and said, "You'll never know how hard I prayed for a miracle, my child." Smiling brightly, he held her at arm's length to study her face. "I should have recognized you right away. You look like your mother."

And Chad looks just like you, she wanted to tell him, but she realized it was too soon. She'd wait until later . . . when they were alone. "I was praying too, Sir Charles," she smiled up at him.

Taking her hand, he gently pushed her down onto the settee so he could sit next to her. "Tell me how my best friend's daughter happens to be sitting in my home when her ship sank somewhere in the Atlantic nearly a month ago?" He shifted his attention to the man who watched them. "Or should I have listened more closely to this young man's rather lengthy account of things?"

Jennifer couldn't refrain from laughing softly at the uncomfortable expression which came over Garth's face. "You'll have to forgive him. The captain didn't want to simply blurt out my name and shock you. And if it weren't for him—" Her smile vanished instantly as she thought, *Your son would be alive.* Forcing back the words, she said instead, "I wouldn't be here."

"Really?" Sir Charles raised an appreciative brow. "Then perhaps I shouldn't have stopped him. Do continue, Captain," he nodded.

Noticing Jennifer's somewhat pleading look, Garth shook his head. "My version isn't truly important, sir. I think you should hear it from Miss Grey."

"Very well," Wadsworth consented, gesturing toward one of the chairs opposite him. "But do make yourself comfortable. Are either of you hungry? I can have Edward bring something."

Both declined, and once Garth had settled himself in the chair, Jennifer began to give Sir Charles a rather sketchy rendition of how she came to be in the captain's

399

company, purposely omitting certain facts—that the island on which she had stayed had belonged to Chad, and that several men had been killed during her rescue, including the man's son.

"Well," Sir Charles sighed once Jennifer had finished, "it seems you and I have a lot to be thankful for, don't we?" He smiled warmly at her when she nodded and dropped her gaze to her lap, not having noticed the curious look she had received from Garth. "As for your help, Captain," he added, turning his attention to Lathrop, "I'd like to repay you for your trouble and for the inconveniences you have encountered along the way. You were under no obligation to escort my future daughter-in-law here, but you did, and I'd like to reward you for your kindness."

"Thank you, sir, but it's not necessary," Garth replied. "It was a pleasure to be of help. Miss Grey is a fine lady, and it was my privilege to be of service."

"And you, sir, are a true gentleman," Sir Charles responded, coming to his feet. "Will you, at least, accept my hospitality for the night?"

"I'd be honored, sir." Garth smiled as he rose.

"Good. Then if the two of you will excuse me for a moment—" Sir Charles headed toward the door—"I'll find Edward and have your rooms readied. We can have a leisurely breakfast in the morning and get to know one another better. Agreed?"

"Agreed," Garth answered, smiling back at Wadsworth until the man had left the room, whereupon he turned to face Jennifer. "I thought you were going to tell him about Chad." He frowned irritably. It was important that she did. He might not get paid, otherwise, and he needed the money if he was going to propose to her.

"I plan to," she snapped, leaving the settee to retrieve her half-empty glass of wine from the table upon which

400

she had set it. "But I didn't think this was the proper time to discuss it. It can wait until after breakfast." Her sharp, quick response not only surprised Garth, but Jennifer as well, and she decided to explain that it was merely her reluctance to tell such dire news in the first place that had made her lose her temper. Yet, as she drew in a breath and lifted her eyes to look at him, she realized that Garth Lathrop didn't deserve an explanation, and drank her wine instead.

Garth sensed her mood and knew its cause. "Aye, 'tis better you wait," he murmured. As his eyes raked over her slender form, he fought down the urge to take her in his arms and kiss away her anger. But to be so bold would only widen the gap that already existed between them. He moved toward the door. "I'd better tell Donald that I'll be spending the night."

"I would think you'd want to leave London as soon as possible," she blurted out, suddenly wanting never to see him again. "I've already told you where you can find the treasure."

He could read the disapproval in her sea green eyes, and it angered him. "I do," he growled, "but I have business to take care of first. Besides, I've already accepted Sir Wadsworth's invitation to stay the night, and if I were to leave now, it might raise suspicion." He lifted the latch and swung the door open. "So I'm afraid, Miss Grey, that you're stuck with me for a little while longer." He gave her a curt, mocking bow and departed.

Giggles erupted from beneath the mound of bedcovers, and were followed by a playful slap to bare skin and a mortified shriek.

"Charles," a woman moaned, "must you really go? Your father always sleeps late in the morning. He'll never

401

know you stayed out all night."

Flipping the covers off his head, Charles glanced at the window and took note of the pale eastern sky. "I've already stayed too long. Look! The sun's coming up." Scrambling from the warmth of the covers, he hurriedly picked up his clothes from the floor, where they'd been tossed in his haste to get Fern Simons into bed. "You have to be patient, love," he told her, yanking on his undergarments, then his hose. "You know that. It shouldn't be much longer before I'm guaranteed my father's entire estate, and then we can be married."

"Shouldn't you wait until you've gotten word about your fiancée?" She pouted, irritably fluffing up the pillows and propping them against the headboard, as she shifted her thin frame around and leaned back in a huff. Then, arms crossed over her naked breasts, she watched her lover dress, eyebrows drawn over opaque blue eyes.

"What are you talking about?" Charles laughed, slipping his arms into the sleeves of his silk shirt. "Her ship sank. What more do you want?"

"How do you know she was on that particular ship?"

Charles's thin lips stretched into a smile. "Because she sent a letter to my father two weeks earlier informing him about her father's death and telling him that she had booked passage on the *Sea Lady*. But even if she didn't board the vessel, her chances of being alive are very slim." He chuckled evilly and tugged on his breeches.

Fern sat up, the sheet clutched beneath her chin, and stared wide-eyed at Charles. "Why? What did you do?"

Plopping down on the edge of the bed beside her, he kissed the tip of her nose, then proceeded to slip on his shoes. "Two months ago—after I found Mama's Bible—I hired a man to go to the Colonies and murder her."

"Charles, you devil!" Fern giggled. "You think of everything."

402

"Mmm." He stood and faced her. How easy it was for him to love this woman who worshiped him. "But what puzzles me is that I've never heard from him. And I should. I only paid him half of what I promised him." He shrugged that off as unimportant, since it meant he'd save a little money if the man never appeared, and reached for his coat.

"So what happens next, lovey?"

"We wait to hear from Captain Lathrop. With Jennifer dead and my half brother disposed of, Father's estate will be mine when he dies."

"Ours," Fern corrected.

"Yes, ours." He laughed, reached out to grab the sides of her face and pull her mouth to his. Then, after he had given her a long, sensuous kiss, he turned, picked up his tricorn, and went to the door. "But only if I don't anger him. Remember what happened to Chad?"

"But he'd never do that to you, Charles," Fern disagreed.

Charles's lip curled. "He would if he knew the truth about me."

"He never will. You destroyed the evidence."

"Yes, I did. Only you and I know the truth." An evil thought struck him and he laughed. "Maybe on his deathbed, I'll tell him. Wouldn't that be fitting? After all these years of living a lie, I'll tell him the truth when it's too late for him to do anything about it. Ah, yes," he guffawed, yanking the door open. "I'll do just that. I'll tell him everything."

Charles didn't bother saying good-bye to Fern. He rarely did since hardly more than a few hours ever passed before they were together again. Leaving by the back door, he went to the stable where he had hidden his carriage, and hurriedly rode off toward home. He had bought the house Fern lived in for the sole purpose of insuring the secrecy of their affair until after his plan had been executed, for he knew his father would strongly disapprove. Charles was already promised to another, but more than that, the eldest Wadsworth disliked Fern Simons. She was a commoner, and Sir Charles had warned his younger son time and time again that those of his station should not mix with those of a different class. Charles had challenged his father's stand on the issue only once, when he had reminded him that Jennifer's father was wanted for murder. It was one of the few times Sir Charles had struck him, and that had made him think twice about going up against his father openly. As Charles raced the carriage down the deserted stretch of road leading back to London, he wondered again just when it was he had started to hate the man he called Father. But was it so hard to figure out? It had begun the day Chad left home. From that point on, he had seen a change in Sir Charles, and he knew that of his two sons, his father loved the one who wasn't legally his the most. At that time Charles's fiendish plot to destroy the Wadsworth family was born. It had taken this long to bring it to fulfillment.

The first streams of morning light shone on Charles as he walked from the stables through the gardens at the back of the house, then through the patio doors and into the dining room. He had decided that if anyone saw him coming in at such an unspeakable hour, he would simply explain that he had been unable to sleep and had gone for an early morning ride in the brisk, cool air. It didn't matter to him that he had used the same excuse countless times and that sooner or later someone would guess what he had actually been doing. The pirate captain he had hired had been gone for over a month, and he was sure the man would be returning any day with proof of Chad's death. Then he could begin the final phase of his odious scheme, and announce to the world that he loved Fern Simons. After about two weeks of adding poison to Sir Charles's food, the old man's health would appear to fail. Then his only living heir could enjoy the dead man's wealth. Spotting the decanter of wine sitting on the buffet, he stopped beside it and reached for one of the matching goblets. It had been a long time since he'd toasted his genius. It was just a shame he couldn't share the plot with his father. For once in Sir Charles's life, he might be proud of his son. Charles filled the glass to the rim, then lifted it in a silent salute. *To the one son who always remained loyal, and to the future King of England.*

"A little early for that, don't you think?"

Charles's hand shook so badly at the sound of his father's voice that he slopped some of the wine out of the glass and onto his breeches. "Yes, Father," he mumbled, exchanging his drink for a napkin before turning around. "But I couldn't sleep and thought perhaps some wine would relax me."

"Try sleeping in your own bed for one night," Sir Charles admonished, casting a cool glance at his bedraggled son. "I would think you'd at least have enough sense to take along a change of clothes, since you're obviously in such a hurry to bed the wench that you can't see to those you're wearing."

Shocked to learn that his father already knew about his all-night rendezvous, he could only stand there and stutter. "The—the—wench?"

Heaving an impatient sigh, Sir Charles turned his back on his son and went to the table on which Audrey, the serving maid, had been instructed to place the tea. Pouring himself a cup, Sir Charles took his usual place at the head of the table, settled himself comfortably and then sampled the brew before lifting his gaze to his son again. "Did you honestly think you could keep it a secret, especially after buying her a house? How many times did I try to warn you? Her kind always love to brag once they've snared a rich one. You'd better just pray your seed hasn't taken." Thinking the conversation was at an end, Sir Charles reached for a cheroot from the box sitting in front of him.

"So what if it has, Father?" his son demanded, haphazardly blotting at the red stain on his clothes. *"I'm* not opposed to marrying her!" Angrily, he threw the napkin back down on the buffet.

Sir Charles casually lit his cigar, exhaled a puff of smoke, and pointed at one of the chairs situated around the long table. "Sit down, son. I have something to tell you."

"You're not listening to me," the younger man raged. "You never listen to me. I said I'd marry her if she's with child!"

Sir Charles stiffened in the chair. "And I said sit down!"

Not wanting to anger his father and spoil his plan Charles cooled his own rage. He'd relent—again—just as he'd always done, but only for a short while longer. Then, as he had promised Fern, he would tell this man the family's darkest secret. He'd tell him on his deathbed. Choosing a place a good distance from his father, Charles jerked out a chair, threw his tricorn on the table, and sat down. Back rigid, knees crossed, fingers entwined and resting on one thigh, he stared straight ahead. He didn't intend to pretend the man frightened him the way he once had.

"It's about your fiancée," his father began.

Charles hated to be lectured. It seemed to him that he had spent his entire life listening to someone's advice— his mother's, his nanny's, Chad's, his father's. Well, in a very short while he wouldn't have to listen anymore.

406

"What about her?" he sneered disdainfully. "Have you changed your mind about how long I should mourn her death?"

The eldest Wadsworth's brows came sharply together. He realized his son hadn't seen Jennifer Grey since she was a little girl and could not possibly love her, but Charles was acting as though a human life didn't matter in the least to him. This was one of the many things about his son that surprised him. Snuffing out his cigar in an ashtray, he leaned forward, cradling his teacup in both hands, and stared down at the brown liquid. When he spoke, his voice sounded tired, something his son failed to notice. "I'm not sure how to say this, yet I don't know why. Since the announcement of Jennifer's death didn't seem to have any effect on you whatsoever, maybe telling you that she's alive won't bother you either. It's a miracle, really, that of all those poor, unfortunate souls aboard that ship, our Jennifer was the only one spared. It's even more puzzling that she was able to float to an island. . . ."

His father's words droned in Charles's ears and grew in volume until the young man thought his head would explode. How could she be alive? It wasn't possible! He had hired a man to kill her. That should have been seen to *before* she boarded the ship. His stomach churned and he sensed a tightening in his chest. All right! So she hadn't been disposed of before the ship sailed, but the damned ship sank. She should have gone down with it! This couldn't be happening. It was a lie—some heinous plot to ruin his life. Fighting off an overpowering desire to let out a gut-wrenching bellow of rage, he gritted his teeth, drew in a breath through flared nostrils, and hissed, "I don't believe it."

"I know, son. I could hardly believe it myself." His father sighed, then collapsed back into his chair. "And I probably wouldn't if I hadn't seen her with my own eyes."

Charles's head snapped around. "Seen her? Where?"

He was already plotting out ways to finish the job he had hired a man to do, and before his father could tell him that Jennifer had arrived at their home last night, his attention was drawn to the dining-room doorway and to the beautiful blonde dressed in blue satin who graced it. Sir Charles rose immediately, a warm, approving smile wrinkling his cheeks. His son could only stare. Jennifer Grey was the most enchanting, ravishing woman he had ever seen.

"I hope I'm not intruding," she apologized in hardly more than a whisper, her dulcet tones like music to the young man's ears.

As if suddenly aware of his rudeness in not having risen upon her entrance into the room, Charles noisily shoved his chair back and awkwardly came to his feet, bumping the table as he did so and rattling the silver tea service in the process. Jennifer's sea green eyes met his almost instantly, and for a scant moment, he reconsidered his decision about her. She was far more breathtaking than Fern could ever hope to be. Her figure was stunningly curved, her eyes were sparkling, her features were perfectly chiseled, and her soft, pink lips . . . He burned to sample them. His blood stirred, and he unmindfully wiped away the fine veil of perspiration that dotted his upper lip.

"Jennifer," his father was saying, "I'd like you to meet your fiancé. Son, this is Jennifer."

She presented him with a most gracious curtsy, one that made his heart flutter, and he smiled weakly back at her, his gaze dropping to the swell of her bosom barely concealed by the satin bodice of her gown before he managed to return her respectful gesture with a slight bow of his own.

"You'll forgive me if I seem a bit in awe," he explained, as his father escorted her to a chair, "but I only just learned about our great good fortune, and still rather find it difficult to believe."

Jennifer hoped her surprise at meeting Chad's brother didn't show on her face. He wasn't anything like the man she'd expected. He was too thin. His features were sharp and bony, and his pale green eyes lacked depth and character. There wasn't a well-defined muscle anywhere on his lean frame. Furthermore, Jennifer sensed something that made her leery of him, as if he shouldn't be trusted. He wasn't at all similar to his half brother. She glanced at Sir Charles, his father, then smiled weakly at him and nodded her head in acknowledgment of his offer of tea.

"There's no need to apologize, Charles," she told the younger man as she watched his father fill a cup and set it down in front of her. "I still have to pinch myself to be sure it's real."

"So tell me every detail," Charles urged, easing himself back onto his chair. "I'd like to know how anyone could survive a shipwreck in the middle of the Atlantic."

Jennifer had wanted to wait until after Sir Charles had had his breakfast before she gave him the news about Chad. But both men had to be told, and she doubted there would be a better opportunity than the present. "I explained most of it to your father last night," she began, then shifted her attention to Sir Charles. "I omitted the worst of it."

The older Wadsworth's dark brows slanted downward in a worried, sympathetic frown, but he remained quiet, waiting for her to tell her story. His son wasn't as sensitive.

"What do you mean, 'the worst of it'?"

Jennifer steeled herself, knowing the impact of what she was about to disclose and wishing one last time that she didn't have to tell it. She let out a slow, trembling breath and lowered her eyes. "The island where I stayed until Captain . . . Bennett came along wasn't deserted as I'm sure I led your father to believe. The truth is, there was a village there." She lifted sad eyes to look at Sir Charles. "And ironically enough, it belonged to your . . . son."

The man's face paled, but before he looked away from her, she saw a glimmer of something akin to joy in his dark eyes. That made it harder for her to go on.

"I spent nearly two weeks there before I was . . . rescued." She hated the word since it was far from accurate, but she had to explain first before she could tell them that it was her idea to leave the island with Captain Lathrop. "I got to know your son quite well, Sir Charles." Tears burned the backs of her lids, and she quickly blinked them away. "And on the day I left, I swore I would tell you what I had learned about him."

"And what would that be?" he asked, a hint of bitterness in his voice. "That he's a pirate wanted by the Crown? The very government which employs me? I'm well aware of that fact, Jennifer. You'd be wasting your breath if you repeated something that is well known."

"Yes, that's the Chad LaShelle everyone knows. But there was a different man inside that tough exterior. He's the one I wish to tell you about."

Pain filled the eyes that met hers. "Different?"

"Yes," she rushed on. "He was a man tormented by his past mistakes, a man who yearned for the love of his father. He told me so."

Sir Charles wanted to believe her, but the same stubborn pride Jennifer had seen in Chad was quite

410

evident in his father. "Then why didn't he tell me himself? Why did he stay away all these years? If he is as tormented by his mistakes as you say, why isn't he sitting here at the table with us? Why didn't *he* bring you back?"

"He couldn't," she blurted out defensively, tears spilling over her lashes and running down her face. "He was killed."

Neither she nor Sir Charles noticed that the man sitting across from her quickly stood up and went to the buffet for a glass of wine.

The anger drained from Sir Charles's face. "Killed? Chad's dead?" Not waiting for an answer, he rose and crossed to the patio door, pausing before them to stare outside, his broad shoulders drooping and his breath coming in ragged heaves. A moment passed before he excused himself from their company and walked out into the gardens.

"What a pity," the dispassionate voice to Jennifer's left proclaimed, and she turned toward it, a frown on her face. "He lived all this time waiting for the day he could ask his bastard son's forgiveness, and now it's too late." Drink in hand, Charles faced her, an evil sneer on his lips. "How did he die, Jennifer? Did you kill him?"

"No!" she cried out, feeling sick and confused. She had just announced the death of this man's half brother, and instead of displaying grief over the news, he seemed pleased. "What's wrong with you? Don't you care that Chad is dead?"

His eyes slowly traveled the length of her. "Chad, is it?" He took a sip from the glass he held and walked closer to the table. "Just how well did you get to know him, Jennifer?"

Outraged, she sprang to her feet. "Well enough to know that he was more of a man than you'll ever hope to

411

be!" She wadded up the napkin she still held and threw it on the table. "It never occurred to me until now why Chad never mentioned you in all the times we talked about his family. He never considered you a part of it. You're not worthy to wipe the mud from his boots."

"Tsk, tsk," Charles mocked, enjoying her fury. He found her even more beautiful when she was angry. "Is that any way for a woman to speak about the man she's go marry?"

Every muscle in her body tightened, and Jennifer wished she had a gun. She'd shoot the cold-hearted milksop right where he stood. "I'm sorry to disappoint you, Charles, but since meeting you, I've decided that I will not honor my father's pledge to Sir Charles. It would be a disgrace to Chad's memory if I did, and I'm sure my father would have agreed."

Charles's milk white complexion darkened to a scarlet hue. How dare she stand there and insinuate that she was too good for him! She was the daughter of a murderer. He would be honoring her if he consented to the union—which he wouldn't. After all, *he* wasn't a pirate . . . or a cowardly murderer. *He* was a man of rank, a man of wealth and power—a respected man! The wineglass shook in his hand. She'd pay for this insult. And she'd pay most dearly.

"I'd be careful about the way I talked, if I were you," he hissed venomously. "As I recall, you're here because your father died and left you without a roof over your head or money in your pocket. Marrying me is your only hope of living in the manner to which you are accustomed. Better, to my way of thinking."

His recital only strengthened Jennifer's conviction. "I'd sleep in an alleyway before I'd sleep in the same house with you, much less your bed."

"Then you'd better start looking," Charles declared,

his eyes narrowing as he raised his glass in a mocking salute.

The advice brought a sarcastic smile to Jennifer's lips. Chuckling derisively, she shook her head and moved toward the patio doors, pausing to look back once she had reached them. "I only knew Chad for a short while, and I've known you but a few minutes, yet even so, I find it very difficult to believe you were both sired by the same man. It's a shame the wrong son died—for Sir Charles's sake." She glared at Charles for a moment, then made a quiet exit. She hadn't told Chad's father everything she wanted him to know, and it was better not to let it go unsaid for a moment longer. Her words might help ease his sorrow over the loss of his son.

A pleased smile lifted the corners of Garth's mouth as he stood in the hallway near the door to the dining room waiting to make his entrance. He had heard nearly all of her conversation with the Wadsworths, and the part he'd enjoyed most was her statement that Charles should have died. He had to agree. The dolt didn't deserve to go on living after all the evil things he had done and said. A devilish twinkle lit up Garth's eyes. Of course, that might be rectified the instant Charles saw him. The shock of finding Garth in his house could very well give him apoplexy. But even if it didn't, Wadsworth had unknowingly helped Garth to take Jennifer away from him. One way or another, the man would pay for his stupidity. Hoping he was correct in guessing that Jennifer had followed Sir Charles into the gardens, since he wanted to catch Charles alone, Garth casually stepped across the threshold and into the dining room, where he paused, watching the man who stood at the buffet with his back to him.

"Good morning, Charlie," he sang out, leisurely folding his arms over his chest and resting his weight on

413

one foot. He laughed openly when Wadsworth spun around, mouth agape, face ashen and a look of panic crimping his brow. "Oh, don't worry about your father," Garth reassured him, with a nod of his head toward the gardens. "He thinks I am Andrew Bennett, captain of the *Sea Princess* and the man who rescued your fiancée from an island inhabited by pirates."

Managing to find his voice, Charles exclaimed in a harsh whisper, "I don't care who he thinks you are, we can't be seen talking to each other. If he were to find out your true identity—" He broke off and shot a nervous glance toward the patio doors. "Well, it could be devastating!"

Garth smiled wryly. "Aye. The two of us might find ourselves sharing a cell in Newgate."

Charles's lanky frame stiffened. "What do you want?"

"Why, to be paid, of course," Garth mocked. "You don't think I came here for a social visit, do you?"

The nobleman's irritation and worry increased. "And you will be. But not here!" He moved past Garth and glanced out into the hall. It wouldn't be the first time he'd caught Edward listening to his conversations. "I'll meet you at your ship. Where is it anchored?"

"Oh, come now, Charlie," Garth rebuffed, crossing to the buffet and helping himself to a glass of wine. "You don't honestly think I'd tell you where to send the authorities, do you? We're two of a kind, you and I, and neither of us trusts the other." Glass in hand, he strolled to the table and sat down in one of the chairs. "How soon can you have the money?"

Wringing his hands as he paced the floor in thought, Charles silently calculated the time it would take for him to acquire such an amount. "By late this afternoon," he blurted out suddenly. "Possibly a little earlier."

Garth took a sip of his wine, then set the glass on the

table and rose. "All right. At five o'clock, I want you to wait at the corner of Dorchester and Byron. Someone will meet you there with a message telling you where to go. You're to be alone. Understand?"

Charles eagerly nodded his head. He would have agreed to almost anything just to get this man out of the house.

"Then I'll see you this evening . . . Charlie." Garth grinned, then headed for the door. Without breaking stride, he called back over his shoulder, "You'll make my excuses to your father, won't you?"

Charles stood as though frozen in place until he heard the front door shut behind his visitor. Everything was happening so fast, and there were so many complications. He swallowed the last of his wine and set the glass on the buffet, his gaze drifting to the patio doors. Just when he'd thought everything was going smoothly, another problem had arisen. Miss Grey *had* to be disposed of now before he could get rid of his father. And both things had to be settled before he heard from Michel Dupree. Sighing irritably, he raised a hand to massage the muscles in the back of his neck, then noticed his wrinkled clothes. But first things first, he mused with a frown. He'd change into fresh garments and visit the bank. Then he'd meet Lathrop in the afternoon and be finished with him. Meanwhile, he'd figure out what to do about Jennifer. Turning abruptly, he headed for his bedchamber.

The gardens on the Wadsworth estate lent it not only an air of beauty, but privacy as well. Tall hedges surrounded the perimeter, and lined the stone walkway that wound in and out of an abundance of trees, flowerbeds and white, wrought-iron settees were artfully arranged along the path. Since Jennifer had no idea of the

415

direction Sir Charles had taken once he'd left the dining room, and because there were three rock trails from which she might choose, she decided to follow the one to the right for no particular reason other than it was closest to her, and set off at a brisk pace. She had walked for only a minute or two before she found Sir Charles sitting alone on one of the settees, and she paused a moment to contemplate whether or not she should disturb him. Her decision was made for her when he sensed her presence and looked up, his tired and drawn face brightening in a vague smile as he came to his feet.

"I beg your forgiveness, my dear," he apologized, holding out a hand to her. "I was rude to leave you. But I needed to be alone for a while."

"I understand," she assured him, accepting his offer to sit beside him. "And I apologize for intruding. But what I have to say shouldn't wait. You must know the whole truth about your son's"—the word stuck in her throat—"death. And maybe once you have, you'll understand why I can't marry Charles."

The lines in his brow deepened, but he didn't respond.

"After I learned who the pirate captain was," she began, her voice low and filled with sorrow, "and after I discovered that everyone on the island was loyal to him, I realized how difficult it would be for me to leave, especially if he learned who I was. Papa didn't tell me much about the fight you and Chad had just before he ran away. In fact, Papa hardly told me anything at all. Because of it, I was afraid of Chad. I honestly thought he would kill me." A sad, half-smile turned up one corner of her mouth. "And there was a time when I was certain of it—when he'd figured out who I was by reading the ship's log. It had washed ashore with other debris from the *Sea Lady*. He was furious. But it didn't take long for me to realize that he wasn't truly angry with me; his rage was

416

caused by something that had happened long ago." She paused in her recital of events when Sir Charles rose from the settee and walked a few steps away.

"Yes. He was angry with me."

She could hear the pain in his voice. "At first, I thought so too. But I soon learned otherwise. He was angry over what had happened between him and you, and upset because he had never tried to correct the situation. He loved you, Sir Charles, but he never had the courage to come back and tell you. He was afraid his love wouldn't be returned. He was afraid you still blamed him for his stepmother's death."

"Oh, God," Sir Charles moaned, dropping his face into his hands. "I said those things to him in my grief. I never meant them. I struck at him in a blind rage when he hit upon the truth. *I* was the reason my wife left that day. But I wasn't enough of a man to admit it—to take the responsibility for her death. I blamed my son, and now he's gone, and I can never beg his forgiveness for all the pain I've caused him."

Jennifer quickly rose and rushed to his side, gently touching his arm as she fought with her own tears. "I told him for you, Sir Charles."

He lifted pain-filled eyes to look at her. "What?"

"Chad and I talked at great length about what happened. I told him that my father wouldn't have acted any differently than you had, and that because you and my father were such good friends, which meant you thought alike, I felt that I could speak for you when I told him that you were sorry for what you had done."

Tears glistened in Sir Charles's eyes. "And did he believe you?"

Chad might not have said so, but Jennifer was sure he had. "Yes," she told him without hesitation.

"And did he forgive me?" Wadsworth sounded like a

small child begging for reassurance.

"Yes. He did." She smiled, then took his elbow and led him back to the settee. "Sit down and rest a moment. I'll bring you a glass of sherry."

But when she turned to leave him, he caught her wrist. "And you won't marry Charles because you love Chad."

Jennifer wanted to tell him what had provoked her decision, but she felt he had suffered enough without having to learn of his surviving son's bitterness. "Yes."

A soft smile parted his lips. "George and I were right the first time. We should have left well enough alone."

"You couldn't have known."

"I suppose." He shrugged. "But at least I've done one thing right by you."

"And what's that?"

"The plantation you and your father took care of for me will be yours when I die. It's in my will. You'll always have a place to live, Jennifer." He dropped his gaze away from her and added almost as an afterthought, "It was to have been Chad's. But I was afraid something like this might happen to him—he lived such a reckless life—so I decided that if his death preceded mine, the property in Virginia would be yours."

Jennifer's tears started anew, and rather than try to speak, she bent, kissed him on the brow, and turned for the house.

The knock on the front door stopped Charles midway down the stairs, and the last button on his waistcoat went unfastened as he stared at the thick oak portal, fearing Garth Lathrop had come back.

"No, Edward," he called out to the butler who suddenly appeared in answer to the summons. "I'll see who it is. You go about your business."

"Very good, sir." Edward nodded, then did a turnabout and headed toward the back of the house.

Charles waited until he was certain Edward couldn't overhear what Lathrop had to say before he descended the remainder of the steps, hurried to the door, and swung it wide.

"Michel," he exclaimed the instant he recognized his friend and co-conspirator. "I—I wasn't expecting you so soon. Is there a problem?"

Taking his hat from his head, the tiny, fine-boned Frenchman shot a worried glance past Charles and into the hallway. "No," he whispered, shaking his dark head. "But we need to talk. Ze parlor, perhaps?"

"Yes, yes, of course," Charles quickly replied, moving out of the way to allow his visitor to enter. Swinging the door shut, he extended a directive hand toward the suggested room and followed Michel Dupree into the parlor.

"Ees your father home?" Michel asked quietly as he watched Charles secure their privacy by closing the door behind them before crossing to the portals dividing the parlor from the dining room and bringing them tightly together.

"Yes, but he's in the gardens right now." He motioned for Dupree to sit down on one of the chairs near the hearth while he took his visitor's hat and placed it on a nearby table. "He just received some rather distressing news, and I imagine he'll go for a carriage ride shortly. That's what he usually does when he's upset. It's perfectly safe to talk here." Anxious to hear what his companion had to say, Charles settled himself on the chair next to Dupree and leaned forward, his elbows braced on his knees. "So . . . tell me why you're here. Has Monsieur Bourget acquired the men we need?"

"*Oui*," Dupree nodded. "Everything ees set. They will

419

start arriving on your Hampshire estate within ze week. How soon will ze duke be returning home?"

A displeased expression wrinkled Charles's face. "Not for more than a month at the earliest. But even so, it doesn't give me much time." Rising, he aimlessly paced the floor and then paused near the closed double doors. "If this is to work, Sir Reardon must be named successor to my father's seat in Parliament before he can be disposed of. And *I* must be named to succeed him before we can even consider the rest." Cradling his elbow in one hand, Charles tapped his chin with one fingertip, deep in thought. "I guess I'll simply have to abandon my original plan. Poisoning Father will simply take too long." The shattering of crystal in the adjoining room instantly told him that someone had listened in on their entire conversation. Spinning about, he seized the doorknobs and shoved the sliding panels aside in time to see a flash of blue satin disappear through the patio doors. Enraged by the thought that Jennifer Grey was about to ruin everything he had worked so hard to achieve, Charles raced into the dining room, yanked open the silver drawer of the buffet, and grabbed the first sharp knife he saw. "Michel," he called, running toward the exit, "you must leave, immediately. You mustn't be a party to this. There'd be too many questions."

"Oui, monsieur," the Frenchman agreed, picking up his hat as he dashed off toward the front door.

Most of what Jennifer had heard made no sense to her, but she was aware that she had become an unwilling witness to some demonic plot to kill two innocent men— one of them being Charles's own father! Had the shock of hearing such evil plans not made her hand tremble, she wouldn't have dropped the glass of sherry she had poured for Sir Charles, *and* she wouldn't be running for her life at this moment with a madman chasing after her. And he was chasing after her. She could hear the heels of his shoes pounding against the stone walkway behind her. Or was it the frantic beating of her heart? Without giving much thought to the consequences, she glanced back over her shoulder to make sure, inwardly praying the whole affair had been a nightmare and that at any second she would wake up. But that wasn't so. She knew it the instant she saw the knife in Charles's hand. Panic filled her, and she let out an ear-piercing scream that not only frightened the birds from their lofty perches in the trees overhead, but caught Sir Charles's immediate attention. He bolted from the settee on which he'd been waiting, and raced off in Jennifer's direction, shouting her name as he ran.

"Sir Charles," she screamed, tears streaming down her face. "Oh, please! Help me!" Blinded by emotion and short of breath, she suddenly doubted that she had taken the path that would lead her back to her ally and frantically decided to cut through the tall hedge. But it was too thick for her to penetrate, and by the time she ralized that, Charles was upon her. Grabbing her by the arm, he threw her to the ground.

"You bitch," he hissed, lashing at her with the knife.

Instinctively, Jennifer raised her arm to ward off the attack. The blade cut into her flesh, and sent a burning fire through every nerve in her body. She cried out in pain, but her cry was nothing more than a whimper that sounded faint and distant even to her own ears. In a daze, she saw the towering figure above her raise the knife a second time, but she was too weak, too frightened to defend herself, and merely shrank away. Then, as if the voice came from heaven, she heard Sir Charles calling out to her.

421

"Here!" she screamed. "Hurry!"

Suddenly her attacker was gone, but even though her head was spinning and her arm throbbed furiously, Jennifer sensed he hadn't truly fled. No! He was hiding! He was waiting somewhere close by, ready to strike out at the man who was racing down the pathway to save her. She staggered to her feet. She wouldn't let this happen. She was responsible for Chad's death. She wouldn't be to blame for his father's.

"Go back!" she wailed.

But it was too late. She could see Sir Charles now, and he hadn't understood her warning.

The instant he saw her—saw the bright crimson stain on her blue gown, the way she clutched her bloody arm against her tiny frame, and the horror reflected in her eyes—Sir Charles stumbled to a halt. Who had done this vicious thing? Who was it Jennifer had warned him about? Why would anyone want to kill a beautiful, young woman like her? A thousand questions whirled about in his head, but before he had the time to consider any of them or take a step toward her, something moved in the hedge to his right. Whirling about, he was barely able to recognize the crazed man who leaped out at him or to see the knife gripped in his hand before the impact of their collision knocked them both to the ground. After they'd rolled over several times, it was his misfortune to find himself beneath the wild man, and in a desperate struggle to fend off the attack, Sir Charles grabbed his son's throat with one hand, his wrist with the other, praying that he might keep the threatening steel blade at bay.

Jennifer's first reaction was to go to Sir Charles—help him in any way she could. But when she took a step forward, her knees buckled and she tumbled to the stone path.

"Charles, no! Oh, please! Someone stop him!"

The flash of shiny metal gleamed brightly as the

younger man repeatedly plunged the knife into the body of his victim, mercilessly, relentlessly. Bile rose in her throat, gagging her, and whether it was Sir Charles telling her to run or her own instinct, she didn't know. But she somehow managed to get to her feet.

Run, the voice called again. *Save yourself*.

Blinded by tears, pain, and the grotesque vision of a brutal murder, Jennifer staggered away from the house.

Chapter Seventeen

Jennifer came awake with a start. Yet, when she tried
to rise, the pain in her arm forced her back down on the
soft bed of straw beneath her. Darkness entombed the
tiny space where she lay, and it took a full minute or two
for her to remember where she was and how she'd got
there—and the reason it had been imperative that she
find a place to hide. The knife wound, the loss of blood,
and the shock of that terrifying ordeal had so sapped her
strength that she had only been able to go as far as the
Wadsworth stables before she'd unwillingly given up
trying to go any further. Fortunately, it had been too
early in the morning for anyone to be about the place,
and thus, unnoticed, she'd made her way into a stall near
the back of the building, one that had appeared to be
infrequently used. After looking at the deep gash in her
arm, she'd known that it would have to be tightly bound
in order to stop the bleeding. It had taken some effort on
her part to tear a strip from her petticoat and then wrap it
securely around the wound, but she'd managed. Then,
feeling faint, she had lain back on the mound of straw and
closed her eyes, too exhausted to even think about what
she should do next. She hadn't intended to fall asleep,
and now that she was awake and realized the entire day

had elapsed, fear set in, of what had transpired since the morning. It was useless to hope Sir Charles had survived his son's rampage. He had been stabbed too many times. Nonetheless, she had to find the constable and report the cruel and heartless act before Charles found her and finished what he had set out to do.

Awkwardly sitting up, Jennifer was surprised to discover that the hours of sleep she had involuntarily taken had helped to renew her energy. She was no longer light-headed, and even though her arm throbbed, she was reasonably certain she could stand. However, she quickly abandoned that idea when she heard the agitated conversation of the two men who were entering the stable. Instead, she slithered to the back of the stall, where she would be masked by shadows.

"All I'm sayin' is that I don't believe a young woman 'alf Sir Wadsworth's size could 'ave stabbed 'im that many times without 'is 'oldin' 'er off."

"Are ye callin' 'is son a liar?" the other challenged.

"No. I'm thinkin' maybe 'e's mistaken, is all," the first replied.

"Mistaken?" his companion echoed. "'E was standin' right there!"

"Then why didn't 'e try to 'elp?"

"'E did! 'Ow else would 'e 'ave gotten 'urt 'imself?"

Having no answer, the first man silently headed toward the tack room at the back of the stable, lighting the way with the lantern he held high in front of him. Its yellow glow flooded into each stall he passed, and when he came to the last, he stopped suddenly, a curious frown on his face.

"What 'ave we 'ere?" he asked, studying the straw-covered floor at his feet and the red stains dotting a trail. Stooping, he tested the substance with his fingers. "Was one of 'is Lordship's stallions injured? This 'ere is dried blood."

426

"Let me see," his companion excitedly demanded, rushing to his side. "It surely is." His gaze followed the spotty path into the stall beside them. "Look! There's more in 'ere." He pointed a finger at the crimson specks in the straw.

"And 'ere." The first man bolted off to follow the trail leading to the back door of the stable. "It ain't no animal what did this. Ain't none of 'em little enough to squeeze through 'ere."

"I'll wager it was the woman!"

"The one who killed Sir Wadsworth?"

"Aye. And we better be tellin' 'is son." Without waiting for his friend to agree, he spun around on his heels and raced off.

Jennifer was thankful for the cover of darkness that aided her in her flight away from the stable. But she ran only a short while before she staggered to stop and collapsed beneath the billowing branches of a tall, flowering bush at the side of the alleyway. She was crying too hard to see where she was going. How could any of this be real? Why had she been thrown into the middle of some horrible, satanical scheme to end the life of a man who, to her way of thinking, was guilty only of being human? Whatever had driven his son to attack him? Had Charles lost his mind? Or was she the one who was crazy? Her arm ached so badly she clutched it against her chest and rocked to and fro, sobbing softly. She wanted to go home. She wanted to return to Virginia, to the plantation where she had lived with her father. She knew that Charles would probably go to court to take it away from her, but she wanted to be someplace where the people around her would protect her, love her, care for her. She thought of Chad, and the memory of their turbulent relationship deepened her sorrow. Her first experience with love had ended in tragedy, and she doubted she would ever again be strong enough to give free rein to her emotions. She had been hurt so badly in the past three months that it hardly seemed worth the risk. Brushing at her tears with the back of one hand, she glanced down the alleyway. Maybe she should just turn herself over to the constable and have done with it. She had no relatives in London, no friends. She wasn't even familiar with the layout of the city. How could she possibly survive on her own? Sir Charles Wadsworth had been a member of Parliament, and his son had accused her of murdering him! If she told the truth about what had happened, no one would believe it—especially after her identity was uncovered. Nearly twenty years might have passed since her father had been accused of the same crime, but he'd never been pardoned, and she would be looked upon as the same sort of person as he. She would be hanged with only the briefest of trials. And that was precisely what Charles wanted. Some of her spirit returned. Her chin came up, and she straightened her shoulders. Well, she wouldn't oblige him. She'd simply disappear and leave him to worry about when she would reappear and expose him for the vile creature he was.

The warm, delicious aromas coming at her from all directions suddenly reminded Jennifer that it was dinnertime and that there would be very few people traveling the streets at this hour. Her chances of being seen would be lessened. Yet, once she had left her retreat, she simply stood in the middle of the alley, uncertain about which direction to take. She had no money, no place to stay. She didn't know a single person in London, *and* she couldn't risk seeking employment to support herself. Charles had most assuredly given a full description of her to the authorities. No, it was best that she leave this city. A bit discouraged, she started off with no specific destination in mind, trying very hard not to notice the smells that filled the air. After all that had happened to her, it was hard for her to believe that she could possibly be hungry. But she was. And the rich aromas that surrounded her made her mouth water.

Don't think about it, she scolded herself. Pretend the smell of frying fish makes you sick. Yes, that will do it. Fish makes me sick. I hate fish.

A half-smile broke the determined line of her mouth. *I like catching them, though. I'll bet if a fisherman saw the unorthodox way I—* Suddenly, she thought of the island and of why she was no longer there. But more than that, she realized how wrong she had been. Her face brightening in a hopeful expression, she paused only long enough to figure out in which direction she should head to get to the river. She did know someone in London, after all. She must get to Garth Lathrop before he ordered his crew to weigh anchor.

Terrified blue-green eyes watched a pair of red-coated horsemen dismount and approach a group of fishermen who had just returned with their day's catch. The fishermen were only a few yards away from Jennifer, who was hiding behind a rain barrel alongside a warehouse, so it was very easy for her to hear everything that was said. The soldiers were looking for a blond-haired, young woman dressed in a blue gown which more than likely was covered with blood. She was wanted for the killing of Sir Charles Wadsworth, and whoever brought her in would receive a sizable reward for helping to catch a murderer. Although the fishermen admitted they hadn't seen such a woman, they assured the soldiers that they would keep an eye out for her. Fishing hadn't gone well for them, and they could certainly use some coin to help feed their families.

Shrinking back behind the wooden barrel, Jennifer

squeezed her eyes shut and bit her lower lip. She had to remain perfectly quiet in order to escape the soldiers— and now a band of fishermen. It had taken her more than an hour of walking and hiding to come this far, and since she hadn't truly paid much attention to her surroundings when she'd ridden into London in the carriage, she wasn't exactly sure how much farther she had to go. However, she realized that the longer it took her, the more danger she was in. This wasn't the first time she had seen the royal soldiers questioning people along the way. By now nearly all of London had probably heard about Sir Charles's death and the reward offered for capturing the woman his son claimed was responsible. The frown which married her brow deepened when it suddenly occurred to her that Captain Lathrop wasn't the sort to be trusted. After all, he was a pirate, a man who lived off the misfortunes of others. If he heard there was easy money to be made by simply handing her over to the authorities, mightn't he do just that? A new concern tore at her insides. Now she wasn't sure whether her decision to ask for his help was a wise one. Yet, the alternatives were not at all encouraging.

The clop-clop of horses's hooves against the brick street jerked her attention back to the soldiers, and waiting for a chance to move on, she cautiously peered out around the edge of the barrel, then watched the men rein their mounts in the opposite direction. The fishermen, too, were leaving, and for a very brief moment she contemplated stealing the tiny rowboat she saw tied to the wharf. It would provide a more comfortable and faster method of leaving London, but at the same time, it would put her in a very vulnerable situation. Anyone with a good eye could easily aim a musket at her and— She cringed at the thought, and stood up. If her predicament weren't so scary, it would almost make her laugh. She was a young woman who, not more than three months ago, had donned silk and satin ball gowns and had attended the most elegant affairs held in Jamestown, but now she was alone in a strange city—a strange country!—and she was wanted for the murder of her father's best friend. It was bizarre!

Well, you can't afford to just stand here trying to make sense out of your position, she thought. You've got to decide what to do and you'd better do it quickly.

Jennifer's arm ached, she wanted to sit down for a while, and she was desperately hungry. She also knew she couldn't delay leaving London. By morning, her dilemma would only worsen. Garth Lathrop had shown a softer side while she was in his care, but that had been done in light of the promise of money. Lathrop wasn't the answer. She'd have to do this on her own. Guardedly, she moved to the other side of the alley where she'd have a better view of the street and the soldiers who were riding back toward the heart of London, and an idea came to her when she saw a stack of crates at the end of the pier, the word "tea" painted on them. It wouldn't be easy to hide out on board a merchant ship for very long, but if God would grant her this one small favor, maybe she wouldn't be found until after the vessel was at sea. Having made up her mind, she set her full attention on the gangplank resting on the wooden dock, then stepped out from between the buildings. She realized her carelessness the moment her wrist was seized, and she was yanked off balance and into the strong arms of her assailant.

The angry, vengeful scowl on Garth's face warned even his first mate to leave the captain alone rather than try to talk him out of his black mood. Charles Wadsworth had held up his part of the deal and had paid Garth the money he'd offered him to kill Chad LaShelle. But it was Wadsworth's new proposal Garth hadn't appreciated, even though he hadn't let on to the man. It seemed that after Garth had left the Wadsworth residence that morning, Jennifer Grey had suddenly, unexpectedly changed from a gentle-natured, polite young woman into a knife-wielding vixen and had brutally murdered Charles's father. Charles had barely escaped with his life, and according to him, the knife wound across the back of his hand proved it. When asked, Charles had been unable to explain what had provoked Jennifer to want to kill the old gentleman, so Garth had silently decided that it was because the whole story was a lie. Oh, Sir Charles was dead. That part he believed. But who had done the stabbing? A man with his son's devious mind—a man who had ordered the death of his own half brother— wouldn't think twice about killing his father. Yet to lay the blame on someone like Jennifer was inexcusable. Enraged at the thought, Garth jerked himself up from the chair on which he sat and stalked about his cabin, arms clutched behind his back and a murderous look in his eye. And to top things off, the fop had wanted to pay Garth to find her—to end her life in any way he chose. Garth wouldn't have been half as upset if Wadsworth had come only to him with that request, but he had already sent word to the King and he had offered a substantial reward to anyone who captured Jennifer. If Garth's men didn't find her first, she'd be dead by morning! God! How could he have been so stupid as to leave her alone in that man's house when he'd known what Charles was capable of doing?

"Sweet God in heaven," he roared. "If it's the last thing—the *only* thing—I do of value in my miserable life, I'll see that Wadsworth dies in a most fitting and painful manner!"

Furious, he went back to his desk and, seizing the half-empty bottle of rum he had left upon it, raised it to his lips for a long swallow. It burned all the way down, but he

432

didn't mind. It felt good. It relaxed him. It dulled some of his anger. He threw himself into the chair, slouching down so that he could rest his head on the back of it. The bottle gripped in one hand, he stared off blankly into space, contemplating various ways of making Charlie regret the day he was born. A quick death was the last thing the man could hope for. Maybe Garth would tie him to the bow of the *Black Falcon* and then set a course for shark-infested waters. If Wadsworth didn't drown, he'd be ripped apart piece by piece—a little at a time. A half-smile curled Garth's lips. Maybe he should just put that creature into a rowboat in the middle of the Atlantic as Chad had done to him. Only Charlie would be dumped onto the old, splintery boards of a longboat without a stitch of clothing to protect his bony, worthless, lily-white hide from the sun and the salt spray.

Chad, Garth thought. Chad, my friend. I've done a lot of stupid things in my life, but killing you was the worst. I regretted it even before I pulled the trigger. I regret it even more now. You and I should have been the brothers. We should have been on the same side. We always did like the same things. Maybe even in love. Did you love Jennifer, Chad? Half as much as she loves you? A fourth as much as I—?

He lifted the bottle to his lips, again. For as long as he could remember, he had envied Chad. Was it possible the feeling he had for Jennifer was born out of that envy? He took another drink and closed his eyes. It didn't matter. He only knew he would put his own life in jeopardy to save hers. If that wasn't love, he didn't know what was.

A commotion in the passageway outside his cabin instantly brought Garth to his feet. Awkwardly setting down the bottle of rum, he hurried to the door and swung it wide. The second he saw Donald and the tiny form the man held cradled against him, a mixture of emotions flooded through him, the strongest being rage.

433

"That bastard," he hissed, taking Jennifer's unconscious body into his arms. No one had to tell him who was responsible for the bloody clothes she wore or the wound concealed by the dirty, scarlet-stained rag wrapped tightly around her arm. "Where'd you find her?"

"Not far from here," Donald told him, a displeased look on his face as he watched his captain and friend carry the young woman to the bunk and gently place her upon it. After Wadsworth had left the *Black Falcon* earlier, Donald and Garth had gotten into a very heated argument when Garth had announced that they wouldn't be setting sail until Jennifer was safe on board. The girl, Donald had protested, could be anywhere in London and finding her could take days, even weeks. The longer they stayed in port, the higher their risk, and Donald didn't cherish the idea of winding up hanging from the gallows or rotting in prison just because of his friend's obsession with a woman. The rest of the crew had agreed even though they'd never actually said so, and when Garth had ordered the men to start searching for Jennifer, Donald had reminded him that if the crew had to choose between loyalty and a bag of coins, the majority would take the latter, which meant that Garth would most definitely never see Miss Grey again. The alternative, he'd declared, was for Garth to offer a higher reward for her than the Wadsworth fellow, and he'd jokingly added that if it was high enough, even he would be tempted to search for Jennifer. The sum Garth had named was staggering, and at that moment Donald had realized his captain would do just about anything for Jennifer Grey. It had been difficult to convince Lathrop to take his turn looking for the girl after the sun went down, when there was less of a chance of someone recognizing him, but Donald had finally won the argument.

"Was she like this when you found her?" Garth asked, as he took a rag and dipped it into the water bowl.

"No," Donald said. He helped himself to a drink of the captain's rum. "She fainted when I grabbed her. I'm not sure whether she recognized me or simply thought I was one of Wadsworth's men." He took a second swallow and asked, "Now can we weigh anchor? There's too many redcoats roamin' the docks to suit me."

"Aye." Garth waved a hand at the man. "Assemble the crew and set sail as quickly as possible. We've got to get Miss Grey out of London."

Lathrop placed this woman's safety before his own. Surprise deepened the lines around Donald's eyes, then faded. What had he expected? "On any particular course?"

"To the island, naturally," came the harsh reply. Sitting down on the edge of his bunk, Garth laid the damp cloth on Jennifer's brow, then looked up at his first mate, a dark scowl on his face. "Unless you have some objection."

Donald shook his head, disgruntled. "Makes no difference to me where we sail. But I would like to get paid before we shove off. Maybe you don't mind risking your life for this woman, but I do."

Garth started to say something but changed his mind. "Top left drawer," he growled instead, turning back to his ward. "But don't take any more than is due you or I'll have you keelhauled."

Donald had only demanded the reward in an effort to make his friend see how foolhardy he was. Obviously, his ploy hadn't succeeded. Sitting down at the desk, he opened the top drawer to his left and helped himself to his reward; then he settled back to watch Lathrop tend to Miss Grey's injured arm. Several moments passed before the mate decided to try again. "Garth," he began, becoming mildly irritated when his companion blatantly ignored him. "Garth, I don't think you realize what's happening to you."

"Let it lie, Donald," Garth warned, and Holman quickly came to his feet.

"No. I can't." He crossed the small cabin to stand beside Garth. "We've been friends for too long, gone through too much for me to just close my eyes and say nothing. I know what's going through your head, and it's stupid! Miss Grey can never love someone like you—"

"Someone like me?" Garth rallied, bolting to his feet to stand nose to nose. "Right now she's just like me. She's wanted by the Crown. There isn't a safe place for her to live. And I'm not asking her to love me. I'm only asking her to let me take care of her."

"And you'll be content with that for the rest of your life?" Donald challenged.

"If I have to, aye."

"Then you're a fool!" Donald turned away and went to the door. "Or a liar." Yanking the portal open, he cast one last look at his friend and made an angry exit.

Maybe I am, Garth thought as he stared at the closed door. Or maybe I'm just foolishly hopeful.

Turning his attention to the woman who had caused him to fight with his old friend, Garth's breath caught in his throat when he discovered a pair of soft, sea green eyes staring at him. Wondering just how much she had heard, he smiled feebly and hoped the warmth flooding his face hadn't darkened his cheeks.

"You're safe now, Miss Grey," he said. "We're setting a course for the island where no one will find you." Too embarrassed to look at her any longer, he went to the wash bowl and pulled down the towel that hung on a hook above it. He was praying that Donald's rowdy departure had awakened her, but he thought otherwise when he turned back to the bunk, bowl and towel in hand, and saw the look on her face. Hoping to distract her, he shook his head when she struggled to sit up. "Lie still," he said.

436

"You need your rest. I'll tend to that wound, then have something brought in for you to eat." Placing the bowl on the seat of the chair, he sat down on the edge of the bunk and reached out to finish taking the blood-stained rag off her arm. Jennifer pulled away and disregarded his suggestion to stay put.

"I think I should apologize to you, Captain Lathrop," she said.

"Me?" He laughed nervously. "What for?"

"Several things," she answered with a sigh as she leaned her head back against the wall. "One of them is for misjudging you. I assumed you'd turn me in for the reward. I was wrong, and I'm sorry."

Garth smiled and started to answer, but Jennifer raised a hand to silence him.

"Please. Hear me out," she warned. "Your first mate is right about me, and you should hear the reasons why." She paused a moment to gather her strength as well as her courage before confessing all the emotions she had kept inside herself. "I never loved a man before until I met Chad. I doubt I'll ever feel like that again. Maybe it's foolish to waste one's life mourning a lost love, but I'm sure that's what I'll do. And that, sooner or later, the gratitude I feel toward you will turn to hatred. I'll start remembering why Chad and I never had a chance, and you'll always come to mind—I'll remember that you were the one who pulled the trigger." She closed her eyes and swallowed the knot in her throat. "But even if there was a chance I might not feel that way, it wouldn't be long before you would become dissatisfied with the unadventurous life living on an island would provide. Then you'd start hating me." She opened her eyes and smiled softly. "So you see, there's no hope for us."

Garth knew she spoke the truth. He had gone over the same arguments in his head time and time again, always

437

coming up with the same answer. Though it pained him, he had to agree. "Then maybe we can settle on a compromise."

She raised a questioning brow.

"You'll live on the island for as long as you wish, and I'll come to visit whenever I get the chance."

"I'll agree to that." She smiled tenderly.

Jennifer hadn't realized how painful it would be for her to return to the place where she had met Chad until the island came into full view. The only change she could see from the bow of the *Black Falcon* was the new tavern that had been built where Freedom Inn had once stood. But it wasn't this physical change that brought tears to her eyes. It was a more subtle difference, something she couldn't touch, but only feel inside her. Suddenly, she wondered if returning hadn't been a mistake. It would merely take her that much longer to get over losing Chad.

The crew hurried about their work, hoisting sails, dropping anchor, and preparing the longboat for those going ashore. Jennifer wasn't even aware that they were dead still in the water until she sensed someone standing next to her. Lifting her gaze, she smiled weakly back at Captain Lathrop.

"I would imagine you're ready to stand on solid ground again"—he grinned—"and have something a little more tasty to eat than what you've had for the past three weeks." He nodded at the arm she had cradled in a sling. "How are you feeling today?"

She shrugged one tiny shoulder. "Thanks to you, much better," she admitted. "I guess I really don't need this anymore."

He caught her hand when she started to pull her arm free of the sling. "Don't rush it. Maybe once you're settled in, you can go without it for a while."

438

Her attention was drawn away from him when a group of pirates on shore, upon recognizing their comrades, fired off several rounds in greeting, and Garth gladly took the opportunity to study her beautiful profile. They had spent a great deal of the time at sea on deck or in his cabin with Donald as their chaperone. He was pleased it had turned out that way, for without his first mate there, Garth knew his will would have crumbled and if he had forced Jennifer, that would have ruined their already somewhat questionable friendship. Donald's presence had also prevented him from telling her the truth about Chad's death. He wanted to be perfectly honest with her, but deep in his heart he realized that doing so would probably be a terrible mistake.

"Jennifer," he said quietly, turning to lean forward against the rail and absently watch the water foam and swirl about the hull of the ship. "I want to offer you something, and if you refuse, I'll understand."

Curiosity created a wrinkle between her brows, but she didn't say anything. Instead, she faced him, giving him her full attention. This was important. She could hear it in the tone of his voice.

"Before—when I thought— Well, I want you to have Chad's house." Unable to look at her, he lifted his gaze and stared out across the water toward the sandy beach. "A lady such as you should have a place like that to live in, and I'd feel better knowing that you do. It's safe there. No one can get to you while I'm away." Uneasy, he cleared his throat, stood erect, and absently straightened his attire.

Despite the fact that this man was a pirate, and that he was responsible for Chad's death, there was something about him that wouldn't let Jennifer hate him. If anything, she felt sorry for him. She honestly thought that circumstances had made him what he was, and that if he were given the chance to start over again, he would choose a different way of life. Smiling softly, she murmured, "I'd be honored, Garth. Thank you."

He looked as though the weight of the universe had been lifted from his shoulders when he grinned back at her. "Good," he answered excitedly, taking her elbow and guiding her toward the ladder and the longboat. "Of course, you'll have to have some servants to help take care of the place. It's too big for just one person to handle. I can talk to some of the people in the village and see who would want the job. I think you'll need a butler and a maid to start out with. Maybe even a gardener."

"One person will be enough, Garth," she said determinedly. "Taking care of the house will keep me busy. I'd go crazy if I didn't have something to do."

"All right," he conceded. "Whatever you wish. It's yours."

"Do you really mean that?" she asked, stopping midway across the deck. "Whatever I wish is mine?"

Garth answered without hesitation or thought. "Aye. Anything."

"Then I want you to promise me something."

His dark brows slanted downward, suspiciously. "Such as?"

"I want the people of this village to have their freedom."

"What?" he exploded. "Why, they'd—"

"I want them to be given the choice neither of us have. I want this island to be their home only if they wish to stay, and I want those who remain to live without fear."

"Jennifer, you don't know what you're saying. Those people would revolt within the week and there'd be total mayhem."

"Not if they were given the authority to punish themselves." Excited now, she stepped closer to him and rested her hand on his arm. "What I'm proposing is that this village be like any town in England, with its own mayor, sheriff, public officials, judge, and jury. These people aren't truly criminals. They're victims of injustice . . . just like me. They're good, honest people, and I'm sure they can prove it if given the opportunity."

"And what happens to you, if they all decide to leave?"

A confident smile parted her lips. "I don't think they will. They're more or less trapped here the same way I am. But at least they'd be happy knowing they have a say in what goes on around them."

Garth stared at her for a long while, fighting down the urge to laugh. "You should be the Queen of England, Jennifer Grey. If you couldn't talk someone into doing what you wanted, you'd simply have to flash those big, green eyes at a man and he'd agree to anything." He shook his head as he took her arm and started again. "We'll give it a try. But I'm not the least bit sure it will work."

"It will," she answered, without the slightest doubt.

Golden streams of sunset played on Jennifer and Donald as they walked the stretch of beach toward Chad's house. Neither spoke, as both were caught up in thought. Donald worried that the change in his captain's nature might soften his judgment where his band of buccaneers was concerned, while Jennifer wondered at the eerie difference she had sensed in the village when she and Garth had met his men at the pier. It wasn't anything she could put a finger on, only that the situation seemed tense. It was possible that the villagers had simply chosen to finish their evening meal rather than meet the ship, but it seemed rather strange to her that they had done so.

"Captain said I was to make sure you were safely inside before I left," Donald told her when they reached the long stairway which led to the iron gate at the top. "And I was to tell you that he'd join you later with something to eat."

Jennifer politely nodded her head, turned for the

steps, and climbed several of them ahead of Donald before she said, "You don't like me very much, do you, Mr. Holman?"

Donald's blue eyes widened in surprise. "I-I don't . . . it doesn't really matter much one way or the other, Miss Grey. But I can't say that I really dislike you. It's just that women and the sea don't mix. Cap'n Lathrop nearly forgot that."

"How much do you know about him, Mr. Holman? About his roots, I mean."

Following one step behind her, Donald unconsciously reached up and took her elbow when the way steepened and there was a chance she might fall. "I know he came from a wealthy family, if that's what you mean."

"Then perhaps you can understand why his meeting a woman with the same sort of background affected him the way it did. I reminded him of what he could have had if he had stayed at home, and that made him doubt his choice. We talked about it, and I think he realizes now that he can't really be happy unless he is the captain of a ship." She paused at the gate and faced Holman. "I just wanted you to know that. A captain needs his first mate, a man he can trust. And his first mate must not doubt him." She smiled crookedly and glanced back over her shoulder at the mansion, adding, "I'll be all right now, Mr. Holman. Thank you for walking with me." Without looking back, she pushed the wrought-iron gate open and went inside.

The huge house and its gardens were still just as beautiful as she'd remembered. A new patch of flowers bloomed alongside the path she followed, and she stopped long enough to pick a couple. But as she stepped onto the walk bridge and saw the sparkling water running under it, the painful memory of how Chad had died flared up in her mind, and she turned tearful eyes on the place where it had happened. Lost in the shadows of evening, the waterfall and its pool were barely visible, and she was honestly glad she couldn't really see them. It was bad enough just thinking about what had happened without having to see that spot as well. She squared her shoulders and hurried on.

Once she'd entered the house, Jennifer realized how tired she was. Garth had told her that he wanted to talk with his men awhile, so she decided that she would have time to take a nap before he arrived with her supper. Crossing the spacious front room to the staircase, she quickly ascended it. Forcing herself not to stop in the doorway to Chad's bedroom, she hurried into her own. It was just the way she had left it, although someone had seen fit to make the bed and pick up her night clothes, for they lay neatly draped over the arm of the rocker. The French doors stood open, allowing the warm rays of sunset to flood in and grace the room with a golden glow. It felt good to be here, and at the same time, it saddened her. Lifting her arm out of the sling, she pulled the white piece of cloth from around her neck and tossed it onto the bed as she headed toward the balcony.

A warm breeze played with her hair as she stood there staring out at the sea, and although the evening was peaceful and quiet, the reality that this island would be her home for the rest of her life caused a knot to form in her throat. She had been exiled here for something she hadn't done. Feeling a little sorry for herself, she turned away from the beautiful scene and, going to the bed, sat down and kicked off her shoes. Maybe she'd feel better after her nap.

She was rudely awakened sometime later when four huge, yellow paws were placed solidly in her stomach and an intrusive wet nose nudged her face, and although she was frightened at first, once she recognized the feel of her one and only true friend, Kinsey, she grasped him tightly in her arms, laughing.

"Where did you come from?" she giggled, burying her face in his fuzzy neck as she sat up. "Were you hiding in here all this time, just waiting to pounce on me once I fell asleep? Huh?"

The tomcat purred all the louder as if admitting that that was what he had done.

"Well, I missed you, too," she laughed, scratching him behind the ears. "Has someone been taking care of you while I was away, or did you have to resort to catching mice? I must say, you don't seem any the worse for wear. Still just as fat as always."

A sound from somewhere in the house startled the feline and before she could catch him, Kinsey sprang off her lap and across the bed onto the floor to disappear into the shadows. Jennifer had heard the noise, but had simply considered it due to the creaking of a house. Now she noticed that the fading sunlight no longer shone into her room. Garth had left her with the impression that he would come to the house within the hour, but judging by the direction in which the silvery streams of moonlight fell into the room, she guessed three times that amount had elapsed. Was she simply overreacting because of the strain she'd been under, or did she truly have cause to worry? Either way, she decided to investigate, and slid off the bed.

At first, all she could hear was her heart pounding in her ears, but she crossed the room and stood to the side of the door, listening. Then she spotted the darkened shape of the tom as he casually pranced out into the hall as if he hadn't a care in the world, and she relaxed, thinking that if she could catch the furry little beast, she'd wring his neck. Well, maybe not, she relented. But he most certainly would spend the rest of the night outside. Straightening, she stepped through the doorway and headed down the hall after him. The moonlight shining into the house from the windows on the main level created strips of shadow when it hit the banister, but it revealed the path Kinsey took as he darted from darkness to light. Calling out his name, she hurried after him. But when he reached the end of the hall where the passage turned to the left and the flight of stairs began, she watched the tom come to an abrupt halt and then sit down as though he were waiting to be picked up. A confused frown barely had time to draw her brows together before a tall figure, standing in the dark near the cat, moved forward a step, reached down, and lifted Kinsey into his arms. She opened her mouth to scream, but nothing came out.

"Who—who are you?" she demanded in a trembling voice.

Rather than answer, the man moved toward her and into the ashen glow of moonlight, giving Jennifer a clear view of his face, and the instant she saw his dark hair, the lean, square jaw with its stubble of two-day-old beard, the gold earring he wore, and the unmistakable scar in his lower lip, everything around her began to swirl. She staggered back a step or two, positive her mind had played some sort of evil trick on her. It couldn't be Chad. He was dead! She had seen Garth shoot him. Tears burned her eyes, and when she blinked, they streamed down her face. He wasn't really standing here. Her mind had conjured up this image of him because her heart longed for him.

"Go away," she heard herself beg. But the image remained. "Please. Go away!"

The figure slowly bent and lazily deposited the cat on the floor, then started toward her.

"No!" she screamed, spinning on her heels and racing back to her room. Once inside, she slammed the door shut behind her and twisted the key in the lock, her heart thundering so wildly that she could hardly make out the sounds his boot heels made when they struck the wood floor in the hallway. Then the doorknob rattled in her hand, and she jumped back as if it had burned her fingers, her tear-filled eyes affixed to the thick oak barrier separating her from her nightmare. In the next instant, the door was kicked open with a deafening roar and a shower of splinters, and a man's huge frame filled the archway. In a panic, she stumbled back across the room when he advanced, afraid that if he touched her the fires of hell would ignite everything around her and send her to a blazing death. When he shot out a huge hand and seized her wrist, she screamed. Yet, at that moment when flesh met flesh, she knew he was real.

"Chad?" His name caught in her throat and sounded like a strangled cry for help.

Seeing her, touching her, hearing her speak was almost more than Chad could bear. For weeks, he and his men and the people of the village had plotted to regain control of the island once Garth and his crew returned. It had worked, exactly as he had guaranteed his misfit warriors that it would. What he hadn't expected was that Garth would be bringing Jennifer back with him.

His plan had succeeded because his victims had been caught off guard. None of them had expected to be confronted by a town full of armed people when the villagers' weapons had been confiscated weeks before. Nor had Lathrop and his men suspected that the men who would lead the revolt were those they had thought dead. The pirates and their captain had walked boldly into a trap, their eyes wide open and their guns put away. For as long as he lived, Chad would never forget the look on Garth's face when he'd appeared. Nor would he forget the feelings that had stirred so violently inside him as he'd spotted Jennifer walking down the pier beside his foe. For an instant, he'd wanted to aim his musket at her and fire. But the turbulent emotions that tore at his heart hadn't allowed him to reach for his weapon, and he had remained hidden on the hillside, watching.

Once the enemy had been secured, Chad had started for the house, to which he had seen Jennifer head. A million thoughts had raced through his mind. Why had she come back? If all she had ever truly wanted was to leave the island, to escape him, what had made her change her mind? He'd wondered if he should just shoot her before she had a chance to explain, before she could lie to him? Or should he torture her, make her watch while Garth and his men were executed one by one, knowing she would be left for last? Aye. He was angry enough to do either of those things. And he had the right. For the first time in his life, he'd allowed himself to give way to his emotions. He had fallen in love with her and she had betrayed him. He could pull out his pistol and kill her right where she stood and *no one* would blame him. He wanted to. More than anything in the world he wanted to end her life just as surely as she had ended his, for he knew that even if he turned from her right now and cast her from him forever, he would spend the rest of his days in misery. She had killed something inside him, and he would never be the same.

The soft fragrance of her hair and skin assailed his senses, and fire erupted in the pit of his belly. When he placed his hand on her arm a burning sensation seared his every nerve, and before he could stop himself, he yanked her forward, grasped the back of her head with his other hand and crushed his lips against hers. She responded instantly, clinging to him as though she were clinging to life. In that moment he didn't care what she had done. He wanted to make love to her, forget the pain, forget the lies, pretend none of it ever happened. He wanted to believe she was here in his arms because she loved him, that love had brought her back to the island, to his house, to him.

Impatient fingers tore at the fastenings of her gown

and quickly slid the garment from her shoulders, yet he found no resistance and that puzzled him. If she hated him so, she would help plan his death, how could she willingly give herself to him? Was this, too, a lie? His lips moved down her throat to a bare shoulder while he untied the strings of her camisole and let it drop to the floor. Then his open hands cradled her breasts, thumbs stroking their taut peaks. Still, she did not fight him. Encouraged by her eagerness, he stepped back, pulled his pistol from his belt, and clumsily laid it on the dresser before he reached for the buttons on his shirt.

Jennifer couldn't begin to explain what it truly was she had seen at the pool that morning so many weeks ago, only that her perception of it had been wrong. God had taken care of the man she loved when her foolishness had nearly cost him his life. Well, it would never happen again. He was here with her, safe in her arms, and she would fight off the world to protect him. Brushing away his hands, she unfastened the buttons on his shirt as tears of joy streamed down her face and into the corners of her mouth, their taste salty. When his garment glided breathlessly to the floor, neither of them noticed, for she had already wrapped her arms around his neck to pull his mouth to hers. They kissed savagely, furiously, their bodies molded in a passionate embrace, and all the happenings in the world outside that room ceased to exist.

Lifting her in his arms, he carried her to the bed and gently placed her upon it. Then, after shedding the rest of his clothing, he set a bent knee upon the mattress and paused. Moonlight from the balcony flooded in to bathe Jennifer's silky flesh in an ashen glow and to cast shadows over her luscious curves. His blood warmed at the sight of her, pink lips slightly parted, and at the passion he saw burning in her eyes. She was the most beautiful creature God had made, and for this moment, she belonged to him. Dropping down, he placed his hands on either side of her shoulders, and resting his weight on them, he parted her trembling thighs with one knee, then slowly lowered himself onto her, capturing her lips with his while he pressed his manly boldness full within her. His strokes were long and sure as he tasted the sweetness of her mouth, her firm, round breasts and hardened nipples brushing against his chest with each move he made. As lust consumed him, in a fierce need to sate his passion, he caught her up in his arms and forgot all else but the ecstasy of their union.

For a time, Jennifer had thought she would never be happy again. Now that she knew differently, she reckoned that pain as punishment for her part in what had nearly ended in tragedy. But now she had gone full circle, and she was back in Chad's arms, whispering his name, giving freely of herself, body and soul, and pledging never to leave his side again. Tears of happiness stole from her lowered lashes as she clung frantically to him, moving with him, sharing the spiraling heights of their desires until the forging heat of their ardor exploded in a fiery blaze and all that remained were glowing embers of their passion.

A playful, disappointed pout curled Jennifer's lip when Chad pulled away from her and sat up against the headboard, unwilling to lie cuddled in her arms. Shamefully immodest, she rolled onto her side, propped her head up on one hand, and ran her fingertips up the long, lean, muscular length of his thigh. But this only seemed to enrage him, something Jennifer couldn't understand. When he left the bed and began to dress, she sat up and pulled the coverlet over her, the hurt she felt bringing tears to her eyes. She couldn't imagine what she had done.

"Chad!" she whispered, rising to her knees, the quilt wrapped around her. "What's—" She started violently

449

when he spun around suddenly and glared back at her, more fury in his dark eyes than she had seen in any man's, and although she wanted to know what it was that enraged him, fear of his wrath stilled that desire. Instead, she cowered back against the headboard and watched him stoop, pick up the clothes she had discarded in the heat of passion, and angrily hurl them at her.

"Get dressed," he growled, grabbing his pistol off the dresser and shoving it into his belt. "I've got something I want you to see." He glared at her a moment longer before he turned and crossed to the bedroom door to wait. Standing in the archway, he leaned forward, his weight resting on the hand he pressed against the jamb, and stared down the hall as if the very sight of her infuriated him.

A tiny inner voice told Jennifer not to press the issue. If Chad wanted her to know what was wrong, he'd tell her. For now, she'd have to be satisfied trying to figure it out for herself, and while she pulled on her clothes and fumbled around in the seimidarkness for her shoes, she frantically and silently went over the possibilities, praying for a clue. During their last few hours together— before that awful experience at the waterfall—she had tried to convince Chad that he mustn't blame himself for his stepmother's death. She had said that it had been an accident—nothing more, nothing less, that his father's reaction had been natural, only a result of his grief. It had seemed that Chad had understood. With a perplexed frown, she stood and slowly approached him. It made no sense for him to be angry over that. It had to be something else. But what? She winced when he roughly took her arm and shoved her out into the hall ahead of him. It confused her that his mood had changed so. He had been tender and gentle, passionate in his lovemaking, and now he was behaving as though he wished to kill her. It was frightening.

His pace was hurried, his grip unkind, as they descended the stairs, crossed the large front room, and went out onto the veranda. Jennifer practically had to run to keep up to him, but she knew he would simply drag her along if she faltered. She tried to ignore his treatment of her as they started down the long flight of stone steps toward the beach, to concentrate on what had provoked it. Their talk that night, weeks ago, had been passionate, sweet until the explosion of gunfire had made them bolt from bed. She had been so frightened that she couldn't remember what they had said to each other before Chad had raced out of the house to help his men. She wished she could. His anger with her must be due to something she had said to him.

The usual ten-minute stroll along the beach to the village was cut in half by Chad's quickened pace, and Jennifer noticed that the closer they came to the buildings the angrier he seemed to become. He had claimed he had something he wanted her to see, though she couldn't imagine what it was. Then she remembered Garth, and a new fear arose within her. Was it already too late for her to explain how Garth had saved her life? The muscles in her throat constricted as she fought off that horrible thought. Even if it wasn't, Chad probably wouldn't listen . . . or care. Garth had tried to kill Chad, and furious as Chad was, it wouldn't matter to him what Garth had done for someone else—especially her.

The bright, flickering orange light ahead of them immediately drew Jennifer's attention, and for a second, she thought the entire town was aflame. But as they drew closer, she realized it was nothing more than the glow of torches held by the members of the village. Kneeling before them, hands bound behind their backs, were Garth and his crew, their clothing torn and their faces bruised and bloody. It was a fierce sight, for in her heart, Jennifer realized those standing around the bound men were simply waiting for Chad's order to execute them all.

"Chad, please," she begged, trying to break his tight grip on her arm, her tears threatening to choke her. "You can't do this!"

His steps never wavered nor did his hold on her ease. He closed the distance between them and the crowd, then brutally shoved her down near Garth, his dark, penetrating scowl cutting through her like a double-edged knife.

"I can, and I will," he hissed. "This is *my* island, *my* village, and *I* decide the punishment."

Knowing he wouldn't listen to her, Jennifer quickly scanned the sea of hostile faces staring back at her, looking for one with a spark of compassion. "Willard!" she sobbed when she saw the young man standing next to Jason Bingham, his head lowered and his massive frame trembling. She rose awkwardly to her feet. "Willard, make Captain Chad listen to me. Please don't let him do this! Captain Lathrop saved my life, Willard. Willard!" The last was torn from her throat as the young man turned and walked away. Frantic, she faced Chad. "His whole crew risked their lives to save mine. Your half brother framed me for murder and put a price on my head. The entire city of London was searching for me, and these men disregarded their own safety to find me." When she realized her words had no effect on Chad—his expression remained unchanged—she swallowed her tears and decided on a different approach. "If you want to punish someone, punish me. What happened here"— she indicated the village with a sweep of her hand— "wouldn't have come about if it weren't for me. I offered to pay Garth to take me to London. I wanted to talk to your father. I wanted to make peace between the two of—"

"Enough," Chad snarled, but Jennifer couldn't stop.

452

"He didn't mean to shoot you. You left him no choice!"

"Enough!" he bellowed again. "I won't listen to your lies. Not anymore."

"Lies?" she echoed, her lower lip quivering. "I'm not lying to you. Why would I—?" She was nearly knocked to the ground when Chad angrily brushed past her, his shoulder bumping hers. Her own temper flaring, she spun around and grabbed his arm, jerking him to a stop. "He didn't want to kill you. He told me so!"

Chad's dark brows came together sharply as he glared back at her, his nostrils flaring in tethered rage. "And did he also tell you what brought him to this island in the first place? Did he tell you that my half brother *paid* him to kill me?"

Jennifer felt as though her breath had been knocked from her. "What?" she managed to ask.

Chad laughed derisively. "Oh, I suppose you're going to stand there and tell me this is the first you've heard of it."

"It is, Chad," a voice put in, and all eyes turned to the man kneeling closest to the couple. "Every word she told you is the truth. I'm the one who lied," Garth admitted with a heavy sigh. "I let her go on thinking that she was to blame for what happened here that day. I did it because I wanted her to fall in love with me." A sarcastic smile played on his lips. "A bit pompous on my part, wouldn't you say? She watched me kill the man she loved, and I expected her to find it in her heart to love me."

"Garth, don't!" Donald Holman warned.

"And why not?" Lathrop asked, as he looked at the man kneeling beside him. "What difference does it make now? I'm as good as dead. I might as well try to leave this life with some dignity."

A shriek of outrage abruptly ended their conversation,

and both men gaped in wide-eyed surprise when they saw Chad trying to wrestle his gun from Jennifer's hands.

"Let go of me," she screamed, struggling to hang onto the weapon. The crowd nervously backed away when her thumb found the hammer and cocked it, then gave a collective sigh when Chad yanked the gun from her fingers. "The bastard deserves to die!" Jennifer shouted, tears streaming down her face. "He lied to me! He told me he didn't mean to kill you, and he let me blame myself for your death. You were going to kill him anyway. Why did you stop me?" Suddenly exhausted, she slumped to the ground and gave way to her despair. For the past two months, starting with the unexpected death of her father, she had suffered one tragedy after another, more than anyone should have to face. Yet, she had survived. And she had done it all alone. Well, she was tired of being strong, of fighting to survive, of having to prove herself every time someone doubted her. Covering her face with her hands, she sobbed uncontrollably, not caring who watched, who sympathized, or who understood.

The pistol dangled from Chad's fingers as he stared down at her, his thoughts of revenge clouded by his love for her. He wanted to believe Jennifer, but the bitterness that had built in him over the years wouldn't let him. He had not trusted anyone since he'd run away from home, and it was difficult for him to begin now. There were just too many unanswered questions.

"What's the matter, Chad?" Garth smiled mockingly. "Is all of this a little too much for you to swallow?"

Brown eyes shifted to look angrily at him, but Garth wasn't intimidated.

"Well, maybe you should hear the whole story, then decide for yourself." He nodded toward the weeping young woman. "I don't think she cares anymore whether or not you do, but I owe her that much. I owe it to both of you." He settled back on his heels and glanced around at the villagers who remained quiet and observant. "When my crew and I sailed here six weeks ago, it was with the sole purpose of taking over the island and all the people living on it. I had been paid to kill you, and that was what I intended to do. I hadn't expected to find Jennifer, a beautiful, young woman who had fallen hopelessly in love wiht a callous, ruthless pirate. As always, I envied you, and I decided I wanted her as well as everything else that belonged to you." He snorted and shook his head. "Of course, it didn't work out that way."

"Garth," his first mate pleaded, "don't waste your breath. He isn't going to believe a word you say."

"Maybe not." Garth smiled, appreciating his friend's concern. "But I have to say it. Jennifer's suffered enough, and I want this hard-headed half-wit to understand that." He looked back at Chad. "I ran into her on the beach near your house. She told me that she wanted to leave the island and that she would pay me if I helped her to do so. At first, I figured you had treated her like the other women you'd come across, and since part of my deal with your half brother was to bring proof that I had killed you, I decided Jennifer would willingly oblige. That's why I waited until she could watch. I knew differently the instant I pulled the trigger.

"When we arrived in London, I took her to your father's house, and since she was blaming herself for your death and because she felt I helped her escape, she graciously agreed to keep my identity a secret from the old man. I could have just dropped her off at the door, but I needed to know your half brother heard about your death from Jennifer, the witness I needed." Remembering what had occurred drew Garth's brows together, and he couldn't look at Chad anymore. He gazed off toward the shoreline "I left the house after talking with your half brother, and went back to my ship to wait for him to bring the money he owed me. When he showed up, his hand was bandaged and he proceeded to relate an outlandish tale, declaring that his fiancée had suddenly gone mad, killed his father, and tried to stab him,"

Chad had stood by quietly, listening to every word and wondering how much of what Garth said was true. But the shocking announcement of his father's death sent a cold chill throughout his entire body. His dark eyes shifted, glared at Jennifer. *My father's dead, and she didn't think it important enough to tell me?*

Garth misread the accusing look on Chad's face and frowned angrily at him. "And if you believe that milksop's story, you're a bigger fool than I thought. Jennifer didn't kill him. Your half brother did. What motive would she have? And she certainly isn't crazy." His upper lip curled disgustedly. "Except for falling in love with the likes of you."

Now it was Jason Bingham's turn to defend the young woman. "I have to agree, Chad," he said, moving out of the crowd to confront his captain. "If she had managed to get the gun away from you a moment ago, I sincerely doubt she would have shot Garth, though she certainly had just cause. Murdering someone isn't in her nature."

Chad honestly didn't believe she had killed his father, but the pain he felt made it appear that he did. Unable to explain, he turned away from those watching him and walked a few steps toward the beach.

Realizing this was something that shouldn't be shared with so many, Jason ordered his men to take their prisoners—except for Garth—to the blacksmith shop and put in irons. As for the villagers, he told them to return to their homes. For that night, the excitement was over. Once the crowd had dispersed, Jason motioned for Hank Sullivan to help Jennifer to her feet. Then he instructed him to take her to the inn for a cup of hot coffee. He, Chad, and Garth would be along in a minute, he said.

"Chad," Bingham said softly, having come to stand beside him once everyone was gone and where Garth couldn't hear him, "I'm sorry about your father. I've known all along how much he really meant to you, and I suspected the day would come when you'd swallow that stubborn pride of yours and make amends with the man." He sighed heavily and kicked at the sand beneath his feet. "You can still do that. You can avenge his death. But in order for you to be at peace with yourself, you're going to have to talk with Jennifer. You're going to have to understand why she did what she did, and then forgive her." He glanced up at the brooding man. "When you're ready, we'll be waiting at the inn." Filled with compassion for his friend, Jason reached up and squeezed Chad's shoulder before turning around and walking away.

Chapter Eighteen

Morning was just beginning to stain the eastern sky when the click of the doorlatch caught Jennifer's attention. Somberly and halfheartedly she wondered who it was. Chad had not come to the inn as his first mate had said he would, and after a short search of the town and his house, Jason had suggested everyone go to bed, for he knew that Chad had gone off by himself to think. But Jennifer hadn't been able to sleep. Too much had happened for her to just close her eyes and forget. She would have liked to board one of the ships anchored in the bay and sail off toward Virginia. She didn't belong here. More than that, she didn't want to stay. She wanted to go home, and even Hank Sullivan's plea that she change her mind and stay with him at Freedom Inn wouldn't sway her. Watching the door swing slowly open, she gave a breathless, trembling sigh, certain that Hank had returned to try his arguments one more time. Leaning her head back against the window frame, she sat perched on the sill from which she had looked out across the sea for the past hour, and her placid expression changed to interested curiosity when Hank failed to step into view. But then, Hank wouldn't have opened her door without knocking first. He never had before. It wasn't in

459

his character. Rising, she crossed to the aperture, seized the knob and swung the door wide open. There in the hallway, his head turned away from her, stood Chad.

Although he looked as if he, too, hadn't slept all night—there were deep lines around his eyes—he had taken the time to change his clothes. But that wasn't the only difference Jennifer noticed in him. He had shaved all the stubble from his face and chin, had washed, trimmed, and cut his hair, and he had taken the gold earring from his lobe. Tears flooded her eyes, and Jennifer unknowingly pressed the knuckles of one hand to her mouth. She didn't want to cry and spoil everything. It had taken a lot for him to come this far. Finally, after several long, silent minutes, he faced her.

"I don't think I've ever told anyone that I was sorry," he began, his voice low, the words hard for him. "But then, I guess I never felt the need until now." He took a deep breath and exhaled slowly. "I'm sorry, Jennifer. For doubting you, for hurting you, for being the cause of all your suffering. I know I don't deserve it, but I'm asking for your forgiveness. Can you find it in your heart to forgive me?"

Suddenly, Jennifer didn't care if she drowned them both in her tears. "Oh, yes! Yes, I forgive you," she sobbed, throwing herself into his arms and kissing him passionately.

It had taken all of his courage to come to her room and speak his piece, for he'd had only a slim hope that she would let him recite it. He'd meant it when he'd said he didn't deserve her forgiveness. He was convinced he didn't deserve her love either, nor would he have blamed her if she had confessed that he had destroyed it. But the instant her lips touched his, he knew it wasn't so. His arms came around her, crushing her to him, and he returned her ardent embrace with all the passion of a man in love.

"Oh, Chad," she wept, clinging to him so fiercely that he doubted anything or anyone could tear them apart. "I thought I had lost you."

Chuckling, he leaned back to look in her eyes. "Given a week of my miserable moods, you just might wish you had."

"Never," she assured him, her loving gaze drinking in the sight of him. "You look like an English gentleman, Chad. It becomes you."

"On the outside, maybe," he confessed. "But there's still an awful lot of rogue hidden underneath." Reaching up, he tenderly brushed away her tears with his thumb as the smile disappeared from his lips. "We need to talk about what happened. I have to have some answers."

"I know," she whispered, nodding over her shoulder toward her room. "It will be more private in here."

A silly half-smile kinked his mouth. "No, love." He shook his dark head. "Since I look like a gentleman, it's time I acted like one." He bowed slightly at the waist and held out his hand toward the stairs. "Will you join me for breakfast in the commons?"

Overwhelmed by the change in him, Jennifer smiled, though bright tears glistened in her eyes. Returning his polite gesture with a curtsy of acceptance, she slipped her hand into the crook of his arm and walked with him to the staircase.

"Chad," she said as they descended the steps. "After we've talked, I'd like to find Willard. I want him to know why I left the island the way I did."

"I think he has a fairly good idea." Chad grinned as he patted the hand resting on his arm. "He's truly the reason I'm dressed the way I am."

"What do you mean?"

He helped her into a seat at one of the tables, motioned for Hank to bring them some coffee, and sat down in a chair opposite her before explaining "I went for a long walk last night to try to sort things out on my own. Willard came looking for me." He chuckled softly. "I think that young man's in love with you," he admitted with a smile. "It's easy to understand. Anyway, he told me that I was a fool—"

"Willard said that?" she cut in, her question laced with laughter.

"Surprised me, too. I guess you could say he was a little upset with me, like everyone else on the island. He told me that if I wasn't so blind, I would realize how much you loved me, and that if I cared at all for you, I'd crawl to you on hands and knees, begging your forgiveness." He smiled to himself as he recalled the courageous way Willard had stood up to him; then he asked in all seriousness, "If I had told you how I felt, would you have stayed?"

Jennifer started to answer, but she spotted Hank walking toward them with a pot of coffee and two mugs, and elected to wait until they were alone again. "It wasn't as simple as that, Chad." She sighed and looked away from him. "I was engaged to Charles. I was bound by a pledge to go to him. But that wasn't the real reason I left." A sadness shone in her eyes when she raised them to look at him again. "I left because I loved you." Chad started to interrupt and tell her that didn't make any sense, but Jennifer quickly cut in to explain. "I had to honor my father's wishes and marry Charles, but that wouldn't have changed how I felt about you. I thought, since there couldn't be a future for us even if you had said you cared about me, that I could at least make peace between you and your father by telling him what you had told me." She could see the anguish in Chad's dark eyes before he turned his head and stared across the room, and she quickly reached out and touched his hand. "Chad, your father told me all the things he said to you that day were said out of grief, that he honestly didn't mean any of

462

them. He never blamed you for your stepmother's death. He blamed himself. He said *he* was the reason she left that day, and that he wasn't man enough to accept the responsibility. Instead, he'd shoved it off on his innocent son. He loved you, Chad, and one of the last things he said to me—we thought you were dead—was that he would never be able to beg your forgiveness."

"And because of Charles, I'll never be able to ask for his," Chad growled.

"Maybe you won't be able to stand before him and actually say the words, Chad," she said comfortingly, "but he knew it was what you wanted. I told him everything you had admitted to me."

Rising from his chair, Chad went to the front door of the inn and gazed absently at the early markings of dawn in the sky. A long while passed before Jennifer noticed that he seemed to have accepted her guarantee that his father had forgiven him by the way he raised his chin and slowly exhaled. And when he spoke, his voice no longer sounded strained. "Tell me how he died," he said calmly, continuing his vigil at the door, "and how Charles managed to accuse you."

Jennifer's stomach knotted as she unwillingly brought Charles to mind. Tears burned her eyes, and she blinked them back, knowing it wouldn't do any good to cry. "Your father and I had gone out into the gardens to talk. He was taking the news of your death quite hard, so I left him to go back into the house and fetch him a glass of sherry. While I was in the dining room, I overheard your half brother and another man talking in the adjoining room. Most of what I heard didn't make any sense. But Charles did say that he would have to abandon his original plan to poison your father, that it would take too long." Jennifer closed her eyes, willing herself to be strong. She swallowed hard and took in a deep breath, and when she opened her eyes again, Chad was standing

463

near the table waiting for her to continue. She sensed the rage burning within him. "All I could think of was to get to your father and warn him." Her memory failed her and she shook her head. "I'm not sure exactly how Charles knew I was in the dining room or how he figured out that I had heard what he'd said, but the next thing I knew, he was chasing me through the gardens with a knife in his hand. He knocked me to the ground and tried to stab me." Unconsciously, she touched her arm, drawing Chad's attention to the bandaged limb. "I screamed for your father to help me." Reliving the nightmare was almost too much for her, and she choked back a sob. "Charles attacked his own father, Chad. He stabbed him again and again and—" Suddenly, she was drawn up from her chair by a pair of firm and gentle hands, and pulled comfortingly into Chad's strong embrace.

"Don't think about that part of it," he coaxed, kissing the top of her head as she laid her cheek against his chest and wept softly. He waited a moment or two until she seemed to have calmed a bit, then asked, "What happened then?"

"I ran away. I knew your father was dead, and that I couldn't help him, so I ran." She slipped her arms around him and hung on. "I was bleeding a great deal from the stab wound, so I managed to go no farther than the stables. I must have passed out in one of the stalls because I remember being startled into wakefulness by the sound of men's voices. They were discussing Sir Charles's brutal murder, and one of them said that everyone in London was looking for the blond-haired woman accused of the slaying." She lifted her head and looked up at Chad. "I knew I had to leave the city, and the only person who would help me was Garth. I didn't know Charles had hired him to murder you or I wouldn't have gone looking for him. You must believe that."

"I do," he quickly assured her, gently pushing her

back down onto the chair. Perching a hip on the edge of the table, he poured her a cup of hot coffee and handed it to her before calling out Hank's name.

"Yes, Captain?" the old man responded as he stepped out of the back room.

"If Jason isn't up yet, wake him and have him fetch Captain Lathrop," he instructed. "I want them both here as soon as possible."

"Yes, sir." Hank nodded and started for the stairs.

"Chad," Jennifer said, pulling his attention back to her, "why would Charles plot out the murder of his own father, such a sweet, gentle man?"

Chad's brows came together in an angry frown as he thought of several possibilities, none of which he cared to share with her at the moment. "I think the answer might lie in what you overheard him saying, and the identity of the man with him. Did Charles call him by name?"

Jennifer shook her head. "I don't think so. But he was French. I knew that by his accent."

"What were they talking about?"

The smooth line of her brow wrinkled as she fought to remember every word. "The Frenchman was telling Charles that 'they' would start arriving on his Hampshire estate within the week. I don't know who he meant by 'they,' but I got the impression that there were a lot of them . . . whoever 'they' are." She thought for a moment, then said, "He also wanted to know how soon the duke would be returning home. Do you know a man named Reardon?"

"Alexander Reardon?"

Jennifer shrugged her shoulders. "They never said his first name, but Charles said something about it working only if Reardon was named successor to your father's seat in Parliament before he was disposed of, and that Charles had to be named successor to Reardon before the rest could even be considered." She looked frantically at

465

him. "Does any of that make any sense to you?"

"A little," he frowned, rubbing the back of his hand along his jaw. "My father has property in Hampshire, and Sir Alexander Reardon owns land adjoining ours. I've known him since I was a child. He'd always come to visit whenever our family spent time on the Hampshire estate. He and Father were very good friends unless something happened to change that, since I left home." He looked at her again. "And did Charles know when Reardon would be returning?"

The faint line between her brows deepened. "He said not for more than a month. He wasn't sure. Why? Do you know what this means?"

"Not exactly. But there's a chance Alexander Reardon would."

He was starting to say more when the sound of footsteps on the stairs interrupted and drew his attention that direction. He watched Hank, Jason, and Garth descend, Garth's wrists still tightly bound. Obviously, Jason had decided it was his responsibility to make sure their prisoner didn't escape, and to do that, he had more than likely tied Lathrop to a chair in Jason's room for the night. From the looks of him, Chad figured Garth hadn't had much sleep, and one brow lifted approvingly. Maybe he'd be willing to talk in exchange for a bed and something to eat. Every condemned man is allowed his last meal.

"Hank," Chad called when the eldest of the three started back toward the kitchen. "You have a right to hear this." When Hank nodded and rerouted his steps, he stood up, grabbed an empty chair, and set it away from the table. Motioning for Jason to deposit his companion on it, Chad took his place near Jennifer, then crossed his arms over his chest while he watched his first mate roughly shove Garth down upon the seat. A long while passed as the two pirate captains stared silently at each

466

other, and although those who witnessed the exchange felt Chad had the right to order Lathrop's death, there was something about the way he looked at the man that hinted at the possibility Garth might be spared. They were sure of it when Chad said, "There's only one reason why I haven't hung you from the yardarm, and that's because, at this moment, I need you. But it wouldn't take much to change my mind." Twisting around, he casually reached for the coffee pot and filled his cup. He took a sip, then returned his attention to Garth. "Suppose you relate the conversation you had with my half brother concerning the deal the two of you made. And don't leave out a single word." He took another sip of coffee, but his eyes never left Garth.

The second Garth had left Jennifer in Donald Holman's care, he'd stepped off the pier and headed to Freedom Inn, there to be met by a roomful of armed villagers. He hadn't expected to see another sunrise. Nor did he honestly think he deserved to. Now, the man he had tried to murder was giving him the opportunity to enjoy life a little longer. Yet, he wasn't sure that was what he preferred. A quick death was much better than a slow, agonizing one, and if anyone knew how to deal the latter out, it was Chad LaShelle. His gaze drifted to the beautiful woman sitting beside Chad, and his heart ached at the hatred he saw shining in her sea green eyes. She would probably never forgive him for what he had done nor would she believe it if he said he wanted to help. He chose to keep his thoughts to himself.

"Charlie paid me a visit while I was in Newgate," he began, shifting his concentration back to Chad. "Only at first, I didn't know who he was. I had been sentenced to hang, and this dandy told me he had made arrangements to smuggle me out of prison and he said he would pay me a healthy sum if I agreed to dispose of someone. It wasn't until he mentioned your name that I figured out why he

467

seemed familiar to me." Uncomfortable, Garth winced and asked, "Do you think you could untie me? My hands are numb."

"You don't need your hands free to tell me what I want to know," Chad answered coldly. "Keep talking."

Some of Garth's humor surfaced, and he smiled lopsidedly. "No, but I can remember things much more clearly when I'm not distracted."

A flicker of amusement flashed in Chad's dark eyes and then disappeared. Glancing at his first mate, he said, "Maybe his memory would sharpen a bit if we tied him to the end of the pier and waited for high tide."

Knowing Chad meant it, Garth challenged sportively, "And how do I know I won't end up there anyway even if I tell you everything Charlie said?"

A faint smile lifted the corners of Chad's mouth. "You don't," he answered quietly, simply.

In all the years he had known Chad LaShelle, Garth had never been able to outsmart him. Not even that day at the waterfall. Grinning, he nodded in surrender. "There really wasn't much more than that, but he left with the impression that no one else knew about his scheme."

"Why do you say that?" Jason asked.

"Because once I figured out who he was and called him by name, he told me to keep my voice down. And when I asked him why he wanted his own half brother dead, he said his reasons were his own . . . as if it were solely his own idea. My guess is he was doing it for money." He looked at Chad. "An inheritance, maybe?"

Chad started to shake his head, thinking it wasn't possible. His father had disowned him.

"He might be right, Chad," Jennifer declared. "Your father told me that he had willed the property in Virginia to you, and that if you preceded him in death, the plantation would be mine. Everything else your father owned would more than likely go to your half brother."

"And by marrying Jennifer, he'd have it all." Jason nodded. "Makes sense. But I don't understand why he killed Sir Charles and put the blame on her *before* they were married? He'll never own the property in Virginia now."

"He had no choice," Chad quickly explained. "Jennifer overheard him discussing his plan to assassinate a close friend of my father's, the man who would be successor to my father's seat in Parliament." His expression turned hard. "Of course, my father had to be dead first."

"Good Lord," Jason groaned. "The man's a demon."

"Are you saying Charlie plotted to kill his own father so that this other man could take his place?" Garth cut in. "What would he gain by that?"

Chad chose to use Garth's name for his half brother. "Charlie would be next in line," he said. "But only if he had all of my father's property."

"All right," Jason concurred. "That explains why he wanted you dead. But what was the hurry? All he had to do was sit back and wait."

"Because something bigger was about to happen," Chad told him. "Jennifer also heard Charlie and his cohort talking about a group that was planning to go to our Hampshire estate. It's in southern England. She said the man was French, and everyone knows that England and France are at odds."

"You're saying he's a traitor, Chad," Jason admonished.

"Doesn't surprise me," Garth replied with a chuckle. "If he has no loyalty to his family, he certainly wouldn't give a damn about his country."

The squeal of Jennifer's chair drew everyone's attention, as she pushed it away from the table, and those looking at her knew that something very disturbing had brought her to her feet. A look of terror was on her beautiful face, and her slender body was trembling so that Chad thought she might fall. He hurriedly went to her.

"What's wrong, Jennifer?" he asked, catching her in his arms.

"It's what Garth said—about Charles not having any loyalty to his family." Tears glistened in her eyes when she lifted them to look at Chad. "It made me realize how unimportant I was to him—that if things hadn't turned out the way they had, he probably would have had me killed sooner or later. I don't know why, exactly, but that thought made me remember the man who murdered Megan and Modesty, the one who killed Mr. Stuart when he tried to help."

"The man you said you recognized as a deck hand from the *Sea Lady?*"

"Yes!" she exclaimed. "I never told you this because at the time it wasn't important, and I'd forgotten all about it. He said something to me there in the warehouse that night that didn't make sense then, but it does now. He said I was a very hard person to catch alone, that he'd been trying to do it for some time." She could tell by Chad's expression that he didn't understand what she was getting at. "Chad, I think Charles hired him to kill me."

"Sweet mother of God!" Jason roared. "He's not a demon. He's the Devil, himself."

Garth's chair crashed to the floor when he hurled himself from it. "Chad, damn it, untie me right now. If you're not going after him, I am!"

"You?" Jason cut in before his captain had a chance to reply. "Why would you want to go? And what makes you think we'd trust you? You'd probably sail around to the other side of the island and then wait for a chance to finish what you started weeks ago." He pulled the pistol

470

from his belt. "Why, I ought to shoot you right where you stand for what you tried to do to Chad."

"Jason, wait," Chad intervened, pushing Jennifer behind him. "I think there's something you should know about Garth and me. Something that happened a long time ago. Something that makes us sort of even."

"Even?" Jason echoed angrily. "He tried to kill you."

A wry smile twisted Chad's handsome features as he stared at his longtime foe. "I never told you how the *Black Falcon* came to be mine, and you never asked. I think it's time you learned. It used to belong to Garth. I took it from him, it and the crew; and I set Garth and his first mate out to sea in a longboat with very little chance of surviving. I never did find out how he managed it." He raised dark brows as he turned to Lathrop. "You'll have to tell me about it someday."

Garth smiled brightly. "I don't think so, Chad. I might have to do it again, if you have your way."

Chuckling, Chad nodded at his first mate. "Untie him, Jason. If we're going to try to stop Charles, we'll need all the help we can get."

A gray mist hugged the earth and masked the approach of a huge frigate. Her mainsail was furled, and her crew was rushing about in an attempt to maneuver the vessel closer to the steep rocky coastline. Morning light struggled to penetrate the gloom, increasing the urgency of the moment for those standing at the bow, because its appearance meant they had little time left to drop anchor, lower the longboat, disembark, then get out of the cove without being spotted.

A crisp breeze whipped Jennifer's skirts and tugged at the bonnet she wore, but she paid it no mind. What she, Jason, and the crewman, John Banks, were about to do took precedence over anything as insignificant as foul weather. For nearly the duration of the voyage from the island to this cove—to the left of it lay Sir Charles's estate, to the right Reardon's, and between them the town of Fareham—Chad, Garth, Jason, and Donald Holman had closeted themselves in the captain's quarters making plans. If what Jennifer had overheard that morning in the Wadsworth home had come true, it might already be too late to save Sir Alexander Reardon. Nearly six weeks had passed since that day, and Charles had stated that the duke would be returning home before this. Though no one voiced such thoughts, Jennifer was sure they all hoped something had delayed the man's arrival, and that their scheme to trap Charles in his own web of deceit would succeed.

Jennifer had been surprised by the way Chad and Garth had put aside their mistrust to join forces. At first, she hadn't understood why Garth wanted to help. A man such as he—a pirate, a murderer—didn't seem likely to want to do something honorable. Chad had given her the answer. He knew Garth was doing it for several reasons. First of all, Garth loved adventure. Second, he wanted to prove to Chad that he regretted having nearly killed him. He honestly didn't want their strange sort of competition to end; he had known that the instant he'd pulled the trigger. Third, he owed Sir Reardon. The duke and Garth's father had at one time been friends years ago. Garth wasn't sure the friendship had lasted, but because of it, a while back Reardon had used his influence to change Garth's sentence from hanging to life imprisonment. At the time it hadn't seemed like much of an exchange since death would have been preferable to Garth, but it had given his crew the chance to break him out of Newgate. Of course, it hadn't altered Garth's way of life. He'd been in prison many times since then and had always escaped. But he'd never forgotten what Sir Alexander Reardon had done. Now he felt he could pay him back. However, foremost in Garth's mind was the need to clear Jennifer's name. He had confessed to Chad that he felt his greed had caused the trouble she was in, and since he realized his love for her would never be returned, he at least wanted her to be happy. Given her freedom and Chad she would be.

As Jennifer stood a few feet behind the two men, watching the easy manner in which they talked, she found herself stunned by the way she had gone from liking Garth Lathrop, to hating him, and now, oddly enough, to respecting him. She didn't trust him anymore than Chad did, and should their situation become one of self-survival, she knew he would save his own hide first. Still, she had to admit that their plan stood a better chance of succeeding because of him. It had been his suggestion that they take his ship, the *Challenger,* rather than the *Black Falcon* for the simple reason that the former was a swifter sailing vessel and would cut several days off their sailing time. It had also been his idea that they leave half of their combined crews behind on the island to protect it while Chad was away. Since Jennifer hadn't sat in on the discussions which had taken place in Chad's cabin, she had no way of knowing how much of the plan had been Garth's, but she was fairly certain Chad had listened to everything the man had said.

She was brought out of her thoughts when Chad turned to confirm his order that the longboat be made ready, and his movement caught her eye. They had spent every night of the voyage in his cabin, cradled in each other's arms. They didn't always make love. Sometimes they didn't even talk. They didn't have to. She knew what he was thinking by the look in his eyes, the way he held her, kissed her brow. And as the ship neared their destination, they seldom left each other's side, for they knew deep down inside that there was a chance this could be the end for one of them. What they were about to do was very dangerous. Willing herself not to think about it, Jennifer took a deep breath and exhaled slowly as she watched Chad walk toward her.

"Have you got my note for Sir Alexander Reardon?"

The deep resonance of his voice warmed Jennifer to her very soul. Nodding, she touched her fingertips to the bodice of her gown, underneath which was the sealed piece of parchment he had given her.

"And you understand that you must be the one to hand it to him, that no one else must do it for you?"

"Yes."

He stared at her a moment before a soft smile curled his lips, and he reached out to gently pull her into his arms. Holding her tightly to him, he kissed the top of her head, wishing he didn't have to let her go. If there had been some other way to prove her innocence, another method of getting his note to Sir Reardon, he would have made her stay behind with Hank Sullivan and Willard. The thought of that young man brought a frown to Chad's brow.

"Jennifer," he whispered, "if this should go badly for us and I'm not able to return to the island, I want you to promise me something."

Every muscle in her body stiffened at the thought of spending the rest of her life without him. She wanted to tell him that God would watch over him, yet she knew in her heart that the Lord could only do so much. "What is it?" she asked instead.

"If I'm wrong about Reardon and he chooses to believe Charles rather than fact, I want to know now that you'll return to the island where you'll be safe. I've asked Garth to escort you there, and he said he would. I know it's hard for you to understand why I would put my trust in him after all that's happened between us, but I do. Say you will."

Tears burned her eyes and choked off her response. All she could do was nod.

"And there's something else," he went on, resting his chin on the top of her head and breathing in the soft scent of her hair. "I have to know that Willard will be cared for. He's a little boy in a man's body, and he's too innocent to survive on his own. I made him a promise the day I brought him to the island, one I might not be able to keep. I told him that I'd take care of him. Will you do that for me should something—"

Twisting in his arms, she lifted her tear-streaked face to look at him. "We'll do it together, Chad," she whispered. "You and I. We'll come out of this together, and we'll spend the rest of our lives taking care of Willard."

Her confidence brought a smile to his lips, and he kissed the tip of her nose. "I wish I had found you sooner, Jennifer. I wouldn't have wasted all these years hating." The muscle in his cheek flexed, and he turned his head to stare absently off into the distance. "My father might be alive if—"

"Don't!" she scolded. "There's only one person to blame for what's happened, and that's Charles."

"Excuse me, Captain," a voice interrupted, and they turned to find Jason standing behind them. "It's time we left, sir. It will be light soon."

Nodding, Chad waited until Jason had left them alone again before cupping Jennifer's face in his huge hands and raising her mouth to his. He kissed her long and passionately, and their embrace confirmed all the emotions only she could arouse in him. Then, without a word, he turned and, with an arm about her, walked toward the ladder and the longboat. His gaze never left her as he watched the small craft glide effortlessly toward a break in the sheer rock wall. There the passengers could

475

disembark and begin their ascent upward through a crevasse toward the top. It wasn't until nearly ten minutes later, after he had lost sight of her, that he turned and ordered his crew to sail for deeper waters.

"Jennifer," Jason said as the trio stood in the cover of trees several hundred feet away from Reardon's home watching for any sign of movement. "Chad told me to remind you that if something goes wrong and you're put in any danger, you're not to wait for me or John. You're to climb back down to the beach and wait for him. He'll be sending the longboat at dusk when it's safe for the ship to sail back into the cove. You understand?"

She smiled softly. "Yes, Jason. I understand."

"Good," he grinned, turning to study the yard and the buildings surrounding the duke's mansion. "God, I pray he's there and nothing's happened to him. He's the only chance any of us have."

"We're all praying for that, Jason," she argued. "I just hope he'll give me time to explain." Squaring her shoulders, she exhaled a long sigh. "Well, I guess I won't know whether he will or not until I try." Smiling encouragingly at Bingham, she patted his hand and said, "Wish me luck."

Jason snorted. "All I can give. And be careful." His brow furrowed as he watched the brave young woman step out into the open and head toward the lane winding its way to Reardon's front door.

This was the riskiest part of Chad's plan—and the most important. It had been decided that a woman, alone, stood more of a chance of being granted an audience with the duke than a group of men, and that Sir Reardon would more likely believe the woman's story if it came from the one person who had witnessed Sir Wadsworth's murder rather than from someone who was simply retelling it. Thus, Jennifer was the only candidate.

476

Everyone else believed if Jennifer's part in their scheme failed, or if Sir Reardon was already dead, there would be no hope of trapping Charles—except Chad. He still had one more possibility to explore before he would resort to shooting his half brother, and that would be to find Maida Tanner, his father's mistress and the Wadsworths' housekeeper.

A thin spiral of smoke coming from one of the chimneys permeated the thick fog which clung to the house and everything around it, and Jennifer's stomach churned. Someone was inside the mansion. Focusing her attention on the front door, she forced herself to remember why she was there and to ignore the fear that seemed to close in around her like the heavy mist. The rock drive circled around a small pond as it cut through the spacious front lawn. Jennifer followed it to the entrance, a single, dark oak door recessed beneath a stone archway. Stepping up to the brass knocker, she whispered a brief prayer for luck and then rapped three times. It seemed to her that an eternity passed before she heard footsteps, and she jumped when the doorknob rattled.

"May I help you?" the white-haired butler asked, one eyebrow raised in disapproval over such an early morning visit.

"I beg your forgiveness for not waiting until later," Jennifer apologized, realizing this man stood between her and success, "but I have urgent news for Sir Reardon. Is he at home?" She held her breath, praying his answer was the one she wanted to hear.

"And may I tell him who's calling at this"—the butler cleared his throat—"this hour?"

"My name, sir, is not important at the moment," Jennifer rushed on, fighting back the urge to run past the man and scream out to Reardon, no matter what the

477

consequences. "What is, is that he be told I carry a message from Sir Charles Wadsworth's son."

The man's brow wrinkled. "Sir Charles Wadsworth?" he questioned. "But the duke only just left—" Remembering that it was not his place to determine his employer's associates, the butler straightened, slightly embarrassed, and invited Jennifer to wait in the parlor. "I shall inform Sir Reardon that you're here," he stiffly told her once she had followed him into the room and had taken a seat on the bright red, upholstered settee. "It shall be a few minutes, miss, since he is still in his chambers."

"Thank you." Jennifer smiled, then let out a sigh once he had gone. Now she need only convince the duke of the truth. Remembering Chad's note, she unfastened the bottom two buttons at the neckline of her dress, withdrew the message, and fixed her attire once more. Her hand trembled as she stared at the yellow parchment, for she realized that she had no idea what was written on it.

Nearly ten minutes passed while Jennifer sat nervously listening to the ticking of the mantel clock, and she bolted to her feet when the door to the parlor swung open and a very tall, very handsome man—Jennifer guessed him to be in his early sixties—filled the framework. Even though his gaze swept her from head to toe, a mixture of curiosity and surprise reflected in his gray-green eyes, she instantly sensed why Chad had felt comfortable in seeking out Sir Reardon's help. The man was dressed in expensive clothes, and even wore a diamond ring in one hand, but the easy manner in which he carried his broad-shouldered physique and the casual way he asked her to sit down again, belied the arrogant façade presented by most men of noble birth. Jennifer felt she could trust him, nonetheless, his mere presence

478

in the room set her nerves on edge. She swallowed the lump in her throat as she watched Reardon take a chair opposite her, aware that he was closely eying her as if he already knew what had brought this stranger to his house.

"Sir," she began, the silence surrounding them seeming to hammer at her ears, "I must apologize if I led your butler to believe—"

"Jennifer, isn't it?" Reardon cut in, as if he hadn't heard a word she had said.

"Sir?"

He smiled softly, rested his elbows on the arms of his chair and toyed with the ring on his left hand, his eyes studying every detail of her face. "I believe that's what George and Katherine named their daughter. You are Katherine Grey's daughter, aren't you?" He laughed at the baffled expression which married her smooth brow, then went on to explain. "The likeness between mother and daughter is unmistakable. I knew who you were the moment I opened the door and saw you. What puzzles me is why you're here. I didn't think your father would ever tell you about me." His face paled instantly once he saw the confused look she gave him and knew he had been right in the first place. George Grey hadn't told her. Embarrassed and horribly uncomfortable, he left his chair and went to the window to stare at the grounds, praying she wouldn't press him for an explanation. It was better, perhaps, that she didn't know.

Jennifer's mind raced back to all the conversations she and her father had had about his life in England. Surely, she would have remembered if he'd mentioned Sir Reardon's name. Obviously, he had known him well. So why wouldn't her father— Suddenly she made a connection. There had been a time when her father, struck with melancholy, had tried to drown it in wine.

During this period he had confessed to doubting how much his wife had really loved him. It seemed there had been another man in Katherine's life before he had come along, a man she had wanted to marry. She hadn't; Jennifer had never been told why, and she hadn't asked, since she truly loved her father. But now, judging by the way this man was behaving, she wondered if . . .

"He did, sort of," she replied. "He just never told me your name. Did you love my mother?"

The man by the window didn't move, but Jennifer assumed by his silence that she had drawn the right conclusion. Finally he sighed. "At the time I didn't think so." He faced her again, a vague smile wrinkling one corner of his mouth. "That's why I let her go. I knew differently when she married George, and I was devastated when I heard she had died. You were only a little girl then, weren't you?"

Jennifer nodded.

He laughed then, as he moved away from the window and sat down in the chair near her. "If anyone other than you heard me say this, I'd be thought to have lost my mind. But I just couldn't believe Katherine's daughter cold-heartedly murdered one of my closest friends. Please, Jennifer, tell me what truly happened."

Jennifer quickly masked her anxiety, thinking his confession the answer to all of her prayers. How odd that her mother, a woman she had never gotten to know, one who had been dead for nearly twenty years, was helping her out of trouble.

"I'm not sure exactly where to begin," she admitted with a frown. "So much has happened, and there isn't time to go into too much detail." She shifted to the edge of the chair seat and took a deep breath as she looked him straight in the eye. "I'm here, sir, because of a conversation I overheard. It cost Sir Charles his life, and s the reason the blame for his death was placed on me. I don't know how he's planning to do it or why, but Sir Charles's son wants you dead."

Reardon stiffened in his chair, but said nothing.

"It has something to do with his gaining power and influence in Parliament. I heard him telling a Frenchman that he was going to poison his own father, then dispose of you to secure it. And that's not all. This man told Charles that a group of men would be arriving on his Hampshire property within the week. That was more than a month ago. And both of them were very interested in when you'd be returning home. That's why we thought the attempt on your life would happen here. Has there been such an attempt?"

The lines around Sir Reardon's eyes deepened as he digested everything she had told him, and before he answered, he left his chair again to pace the floor. "I only just returned late last night," he absently replied. He stopped suddenly and faced her. "You said Charles's cohort was French?"

"Yes. Does that make a difference?"

"It would certainly explain a lot of things." His aimless trek resumed. "Ever since his father's death, Charles has argued that Parliament should place an embargo on French goods. England's relationship with France is strained enough without doing something as foolish as that, and I couldn't understand why he was so adamant . . . until now. The mayor of Fareham paid me a visit last night to complain about the new warehouse being built on the edge of town—on Wadsworth property—and to say that none of the townsfolk had been hired to do the work. He also told me that a lot of strangers had shown up over the past seven to eight weeks, and that he thought they were living on Charles's estate." He paused near the fireplace to think for a

481

moment, his arm resting on the mantel and his fingertip tapping his chin.

"And you think that has some bearing on Charles's plan to murder you?"

"It does if what I suspect is true."

"Which is?"

He faced her. "I have the last say in Parliament. With me out of the way, it goes to Charles. Now, if Charles placed an embargo on French trade, the price of such goods would soar. A man could become very wealthy smuggling in French merchandise, couldn't he?"

"The warehouse!" Jennifer exclaimed when it all seemed to fall into place.

"That's what I'm thinking." Reardon frowned again, considering other possibilities, and suddenly remembered something she had said earlier. "Jennifer, moments ago you said 'we.' Are you here with someone else?"

Having forgotten all about Chad's letter, she jumped to her feet and held it out to him. "It would take days to explain, Sir Reardon, so I'm going to have to ask you to just trust me. Chad LaShelle brought me here, and he's the one who's figured out what we know. He wants to help you. He wants to avenge his father's death, for you see, Sir Reardon, it was actually his half brother who stabbed Sir Charles to death."

"Dear God." Reardon moaned and staggered back onto the chair, the parchment quivering in his hand. "How could he be so heartless?"

Spotting a decanter of wine sitting on a table near the door, she hurried to it, intending to pour him a glass. But when she turned back to him again, the wine held out in front of her, she found he was already absorbed in Chad's note. She set aside the wine, and stood perfectly still while he finished reading the message, although her curiosity was aroused when a surprised expression came over Sir Reardon's face.

"Have you read this?" he asked, indicating the note.

"No, sir. No one has."

He was thoughtfully quiet for a moment before he abruptly rose to his feet and headed for the door. Upon reaching it, he hurriedly pulled it open and motioned for her to go with him. Together, they crossed the front hall and went into his study. "Where's Chad now?" he asked without looking at her as he rounded his desk and sat down in the chair behind it.

"He, his crew, Garth Lathrop and some of his men are waiting on the *Challenger*. It's anchored off shore where it can't be spotted."

Reardon's head came up at the mention of Garth's name, and Jennifer misunderstood the look on the man's face.

"Sir, I know every one of those men are wanted by the Crown, and that your first instinct is that they shouldn't be trusted, but I give you my word—"

"Say no more, Jennifer," Reardon cut in, his hand raised in front of him. "Garth's father and I go way back. I've always hoped someday that young man would do the right thing." He smiled. "And I'd say that day has come. It just surprised me is all." Opening a top drawer, he took out a piece of paper and reached for the quill resting in its peg atop the desk. After hurriedly scribbling something down, he dropped the feather-tipped pen back in the well and grabbed his seal and wax. "Does Chad have a plan?" he asked, rising from the desk and crossing toward her, the sealed parchment held in one hand.

"It depended on whether or not we arrived in time to stop the assassination attempt on your life," she told him as they left the study and went into the front hall again. She waited to explain their options until after Sir

Reardon had summoned his butler, handed the message to him, and instructed him to see that it was delivered with God's speed. Then, as she was drawing a breath before continuing, the roar of cannon fire in the distance caused the earth to tremble, and sent Jennifer racing for the door.

It was nearly midnight before the Wadsworth carriage pulled up in front of the house and Charles descended from it. He had just come from Fern Simons's bed, where he had spent the evening celebrating the success of his year-long scheme to become the richest man in all of England. By now, the mercenaries his French collaborator had hired were probably toasting the completion of their part in his plan—the death of Sir Reardon. He had sent word to Michel Dupree the moment the duke left London for his estate on the southern coast, informing the man not to waste a second in disposing of his last obstacle. Closing the gate behind him, Charles headed for the front door, snickering to himself. That had been the part of his ploy he loved best—murdering Sir Reardon and placing the blame on a band of pirates, buccaneers led by one Garth Lathrop. The fool had believed him that day in prison when he'd said that someone else would be buried under his name. That had been a lie. Charles needed Lathrop alive—to be found guilty of Alexander Reardon's brutal death and to be executed for it. Elated by his brilliance, Charles threw back his head and roared with laughter as he reached for the doorlatch and swung the portal wide.

"Good evening, Edward." He chuckled when he met the startled butler in the hallway. "I told you that you didn't have to wait up for me. Why haven't you gone to bed?"

484

The man glanced nervously toward the open parlor door and whispered, "There's someone here to see you, sir. They've been waiting since late this afternoon."

Charles's humor vanished. "They?" he questioned. Unless something had gone wrong, Michel wouldn't come to his house. And Edward had said 'they.' Who could it possibly be? Without waiting for the man to reveal the identities of his visitors, Charles stepped to the threshold of the parlor and froze, for seated in one of the wing chairs near the fireplace was none other than Sir Alexander Reardon, the man whose death Charles had been celebrating. What was he doing here? What did it mean? Was it possible Michel hadn't received his message?

"Good evening, Charles," Reardon acknowledged, coming to his feet and extending his hand to the lady sitting opposite him. "You remember Maida Tanner, don't you?"

Charles's attention absently moved to the shapely woman who accepted Sir Reardon's hand and rose graciously from her chair.

"And then perhaps you don't. As I understand it, she left your father's employ shortly after Mary Elizabeth's untimely accident. Charles, Miss Tanner was your housekeeper for a while."

Charles remembered her name . . . clearly. She was the woman his father had been with the night he'd argued with Mary Elizabeth. She was the reason Mary Elizabeth left the house the following morning. She was actually to blame for Chad's running away. But what in God's name was she doing here? Managing to get a grip on his surprise, he straightened his attire, tugged on his wig, and came further into the room. He'd play along until he could make some sense of it all.

"Yes, of course, I remember. It's just been a long time

485

since—" Failing to understand any of this, he turned his attention back to Sir Reardon. "Excuse me, Alexander but I thought you went home yesterday. I must admit that I'm completely confused by your visit."

"You won't be in a minute." Reardon smiled as he left his place beside Maida to slowly cross the room. Walking past Charles, he paused near the door that had been left open, seized the knob, and gave it a shove, unaware of the hand that came up to stop it from closing all the way, but concentrating on the fact that he had revealed yet another visitor hidden in the shadows behind the door. Sir Reardon's smile widened as he watched many expressions flash across Charles's face before the youngest among them recognized the man he had called half brother all his life. The likeness between father and son was undeniable. "Ah," Reardon proclaimed, "I see you've figured out who this is. It's understandable why you wouldn't have at first. After all, it's been—what?— fifteen years since the last time you saw each other."

Charles's mind reeled. His breath came in ragged heaves and a thin veil of perspiration dampened his clothes. "No," he gasped, stumbling back a step. "It can't be! He's . . . he's . . ."

"Supposed to be dead?" Reardon finished. "Just as I'm supposed to be dead?" He laughed sarcastically when Charles shook his head, frantically denying the accusation. "Don't waste your breath trying to make me believe that you have no idea what I'm talking about, Charles. I know every detail of your little scheme, right down to the fact that *you* were the one who killed Sir Charles. Your friend, Michel Dupree told us everything. He certainly was surprised to find Chad and a shipful of men waiting for him when he and the others decided to cross the cove and attack my home." Reardon's mocking humor turned to rage. "You are the lowest of vermin! How could you

486

kill the man who raised you, gave you his name, a place to live—"

"I didn't!" Charles shrieked. "Jennifer Grey murdered him. Why would I kill my own father?" He turned a damning glare on the man who stood by silently listening. "You'd believe him over me? He's the bastard son of Sir Charles! A pirate. A rogue! I'm the legal heir, not him. I'm a lord, a member of Parliament—"

"You're nothing, Charles," Chad hissed. "You're the son of a fisherman . . . and my father's mistress."

Charles's mouth fell open, and he jerked his head around to stare at Maida Tanner.

"I've known all along," Chad continued. "I found Mary Elizabeth's Bible with her confession in it on the day she died. I should have destroyed it then, but I didn't. I don't know why. If I had, none of this would have happened. Mary Elizabeth loved her husband so much that when her baby was stillborn, she couldn't bear the thought of telling him she was unable to give him a son, a legitimate son. So she swore her maid to secrecy and took the newborn child of a fifteen-year-old girl. You were the child, and I guessed that Maida Tanner was the girl. You found the Bible, too, didn't you, Charles?"

"Yes!" he exploded, his eyes blazing with hatred as he faced Chad once more. "And I burned it! Then I set out to get rid of everyone who stood in my way. I knew I had no right to any of this if the truth were ever learned, so I planned to have them all killed." His gaze shifted back to the woman standing near the fireplace. "All of them except my real mother . . . *because I didn't know who she was!*"

"No one did, Charles," Maida confessed, her voice cold and steady. "I never told anyone. Only Mary Elizabeth and her maid knew. Your real father didn't. In fact, he didn't even know I was pregnant." She laughed and sat back down in the chair. "Not that he would have cared," she admitted. "Nearly five years passed before I suddenly began wondering what you looked like, how tall you had become, if you favored me or your father, and I decided to find out. I came to this house pretending to be looking for work. Mary Elizabeth didn't recognize me—she'd only seen me a few times—and she hired me as housekeeper. Then I met Charles, and I fell madly in love with him." She smiled and glanced over at Chad. "But there was one person I could never fool, Charles's only real son." Tears came to her eyes, and she lowered her head. "When Mary Elizabeth died, Charles threw me out of the house and told me never to come back. But I never stopped loving him." She glared up at her son. "And the day he died, I swore I'd see his murderer pay. I was only too happy to cooperate when I received Sir Reardon's note this afternoon telling me that Chad LaShelle had guessed my lifelong secret."

Charles could almost hear the swish of steel as the executioner's ax swung earthward, and something inside of him snapped. Pivoting on one heel, he rushed to the small three-drawer chest where Sir Charles always kept his dueling pistols, and before either Chad or Sir Reardon could guess his intent, he withdrew one from its box and spun back around, leveling the weapon on Chad. The crack of gunpowder rent the air. Blood splattered against the wall. And Charles was knocked off his feet by the lead ball that cut into his chest and punctured his heart, plummeting him to the floor. His body convulsed only once before he made a strangled choking sound and withered into a lifeless heap upon the richly colored oriental rug beneath him.

In that split second between the time Chad realized his life was in danger and the moment his hand moved to the butt of the pistol stuck in his waistband, he saw the puff of smoke and heard the explosion of gunfire to his right.

In the next instant, he realized Charles was dead, and he turned his attention on the door, watching it slowly swing inward as Garth stepped into the room.

"Ya owe me one, Chad, ol' friend." Lathrop grinned, nodding toward the body lying on the floor. "Or shall we just call it even?"

Epilogue

Dark ocean waters tipped golden by the last rays of the setting sun held within their grasp a lone frigate, her sails unfurled and billowing full against the breeze. Near the helm stood her captain, feet braced against the rhythm of the sea, arms folded over his chest while he issued the order to set a west, southwesterly course for the Bahamas. High atop the ship's mainmast flew the flag of England, a symbol that this pirate vessel now sailed the Atlantic under the protection of King George.

"Do you think he'll ever come back?" Jennifer asked, hugging her husband tighter to her as they stood on the shore of Grey's Island watching the *Black Falcon* sail into deeper waters.

"Garth?" Chad chuckled. "Every chance he gets. And it won't be because he misses me." He gave her a playful squeeze, then kissed the tip of her nose. "What I doubt is the length of time he'll sail under a British flag. He's been a pirate too long."

"And what about you?" she smiled lovingly, reaching up to trace a fingertip along the scar in his lower lip.

"How long will you take advantage of the pardon King George gave the two of you and your crews?"

Capturing her hand in his, he placed a light kiss upon her knuckles, and said, "I don't see where I have much of a choice. A man who holds property in England can't very well be a pirate, too," he teased. Wrapping both arms around her, he settled his attention on the ship he had insisted Garth command.

A moment of silence passed between the couple as they stood watching the *Black Falcon*. Chad was thinking how great it felt to be free, free of the worry over being caught and sentenced to hang for acts of piracy, free to make choices in his life, but more so, free of the guilt he had carried for so many years. Jennifer was thanking God that Garth had blatantly ignored Chad's order that he stay with her the day Chad, Sir Alexander Reardon, and Maida Tanner had confronted Charles in his home. If Garth hadn't, Chad might have been killed. A smile parted her lips as she studied the tall figure near the helm of the ship, for she was still amazed at how Garth had tried to kill Chad, then had saved his life.

"What are you thinking?" Chad asked when he saw her smile.

Snuggling closer, she laughed. "About what I heard someone say one time—that there's honor among thieves. Is that what you and Garth have?"

Chad chuckled. "I suppose. But I never will fully trust him. Not where you're concerned." Without warning, he bent and swooped her up into his arms. "The man doesn't care if a woman's married or not."

"Do you care, Chad?" she asked in all seriousness. "Will there come a day when you regret marrying me?"

His dark eyes warmed with love for her. "My only regret will be that I didn't find you sooner, Jennifer. But I will never . . . never curse the day I took you for my wife."

Tears of joy filled her eyes, and when she blinked, they spilled over her lashes and raced down her cheeks. Slipping her arms up around his neck, she kissed him feverishly and silently pledged that he would never find cause to change his mind.

CHILLING GOTHICS
From Zebra Books

MIDNIGHT HEIRESS (1933, $2.95)
by Kate Frederick

Aunt Martha's will held one stipulation: Barbara must marry the bastard son that Martha never acknowledged. But her new husband was tormented by secrets of the past. How long could Barbara hope to survive as the . . . *Midnight Heiress.*

HEATH HALLOWS (1901, $2.95)
by Michele Y. Thomas

Caroline knew it was wrong to go in her cousin's place to Heath Hallows Abbey; but the wealthy Hawkesworths would never know the difference. But tragedies of the past cast a dark and deadly shadow over Heath Hallows, leaving Caroline to fear the evil lurking in the shadows.

SAPPHIRE LEGACY (1979, $2.95)
by Beverly C. Warren

Forced into a loveless marriage with the aging Lord Charles Cambourne, Catherine was grateful for his undemanding kindness and the heirloom sapphires he draped around her neck. But Charles could not live forever, and someone wanted to make sure the young bride would never escape the deadly *Sapphire Legacy.*

SHADOWTIDE (1695, $2.95)
by Dianne Price

Jenna had no choice but to accept Brennan Savage's mysterious marriage proposal. And as flickering candlelight lured her up the spiral staircase of Savage Lighthouse, Jenna could only pray her fate did not lie upon the jagged rocks and thundering ocean far below.

THE HOUSE AT STONEHAVEN (1239, $2.50)
by Ellouise Rife

Though she'd heard rumors about how her employer's first wife had died, Jo couldn't resist the magnetism of Elliot Stone. But soon she had to wonder if she was destined to become the next victim.